The Least Amount Of Awful

Jennifer Millikin

ISBN: 979-8-9868099-5-3
www.jennifermillikinwrites.com
Cover by Okay Creations
Editing by Emerald Edits
Proofreading by Sisters Get Lit.erary Author Services

For Tary, the original Buttercup.
Supporter, role model, mother figure, aunt, friend.

Prologue

C olbie
Seven years old

"That man is a child."

My mom hurries into the kitchen, wearing a look on her face like she's forgotten something.

It's me. I've slipped her mind. That's what happens when she fights with my dad.

An hour seems like a long time to forget your own daughter. An hour seems like a long time for grown-ups to fight, too, but that's what my mom and dad were doing. I know, because they yelled so much it made my tummy hurt, and I started looking at the time on the microwave clock. Keeping track of how long they'd been fighting made me forget about being forgotten.

Sort of.

Today Mom's wearing her fancy-lady lawyer clothes, and the black high heels I sneak into her closet and try on.

1

She stomps across the tile floor, and the clicking of her heels hurts my ears. She wrenches open the cupboard door, knocking aside the coffee can, the packets of sugar, the flavored syrup. She's angrier than usual, but I know what's coming, and there's comfort in that.

I stay quiet, seated at the small table in the kitchen, and wait.

"Your father," she starts, placing emphasis on the word *your* in a way that always makes me feel like it's my fault, "never takes anything seriously. Thinks life is a game, a party." She turns her fierce gaze on me. "Well, it's not. Life is hard, and sometimes we have to make difficult choices." Her fingers drum the countertop. *Ba-da-dum. Ba-da-dum.* "That man is not a good partner. He quit his job, and for what? Because it's not fun. He doesn't like it."

My dad quit his job? Will there be enough money? Yesterday Angela came to school wearing new sneakers that lit up when she walked. I was going to ask for them, but now I won't.

Mom keeps going, lowering her voice so she sounds like Dad. "All those small towns up north are about to boom. I could start my own business." I can tell she's making fun of him, and that makes me sad. And mad. She makes a face, and now she sounds like herself again. "Ok, sure. It's just that easy." She snaps her fingers and says, "Bam. Done. I wished it, and it appeared." Now she's shaking her head. "He's a dreamer, and dreams get crushed. I should've known better. That man was a mistake from the beginning."

My belly feels really yucky now. I love my dad. He has smiles that stretch across his face, and freckles on his earlobes. He tells jokes and he swings me around and he calls me Sugar Bear. He's not a mistake.

I take a bite of my toast with strawberry jelly, hoping my stomach will stop hurting.

Mom didn't approve when Dad taught me how to use the toaster, but he did it anyway. I'd asked him what happens if you touch the red coils where the bread goes. He said it would burn me. I told him it didn't look like fire. He put his big hand on the top of my head and said, "If you're hankering to see if it's hot, I'm not going to stop you. It'll burn you, not kill you. Life is short, Sugar Bear. Take chances." Then he winked.

I didn't touch the red coils.

Mom bends down so she can look me in the eyes. She's so pretty. I have her dark brown hair and eyes, and, as she likes to say, her 'can-do attitude'. I don't know what that means, but I like it because her voice sounds proud when she says it.

Mom's eyebrows pinch together with determination. "You're my responsibility, Colbie. When you were born, I made a promise to myself to keep you safe, and protected."

I don't like her words. I don't like them at all.

"Where's Daddy?"

She thumbs a smear of jelly from the corner of my mouth. "He left."

"When is he coming back?"

"He's not."

I don't understand. Daddy loves me. I'm his sugar bear. "Never?"

"We're going to work something out. He'll see you, but he will not live here anymore."

I start to cry. Mom firmly tells me to toughen up. I wish she'd cry for once, because this seems like a good time to cry, but she doesn't. She never cries.

"You're going to be ok." She pulls me into a hug, and the

silkiness of her blouse and the familiar smell of her hairspray makes me feel a tiny bit better. "I'm here, and I love you, and I'll be everything you need." She pulls away, forcing my gaze to meet hers with a soft touch on my jaw. "Chin up."

I swallow her words, and my broken heart. I have to do what she says.

I can't lose her, too.

* * *

Jake
Ten years ago

A suitcase is flung open on the bed. A backpack lies beside it. Erin's in our closet, yanking clothes off hangers that smack against the closet wall in her haste.

I hover next to the closet door, watching, as waves of shock roll through me.

"Where are you going?" I hiss angrily, doing my best to keep my voice down. Tension stiffens my limbs, my jaw tightens, but our two-month-old son continues to sleep peacefully in my arms.

"I'm done." Erin avoids eye contact, but her voice wobbles.

"Done?" I'm dumbfounded. People use that word to describe when they're done eating. Not done with their child. With their boyfriend.

I don't know why I'm shocked. Wasn't the writing on the wall? Last weekend she didn't come home. I took a screaming baby to the drugstore in the middle of the night because we didn't have formula, and Erin wasn't answering her phone. The middle-aged woman working cashier told me Robbie might reject the bottle, and I think I held my breath until we got into the car and I mixed the water with the powder.

Robbie was so hungry he gobbled every ounce, then burped three times and passed out.

I'm itching to raise my voice now, but I can't. Robbie knows he's safe in my arms, and I won't trade that for the momentary satisfaction it would bring me to yell at Erin for what she's about to do.

Erin pushes past me, still no eye contact and her arms loaded with clothing. She dumps everything into the suitcase and turns to me. Her arms are crossed. There's something wild in her eyes, like an animal cornered.

Or caged.

"Yes, Jake. I'm done. Done playing house with you"— she gestures angrily at the one-bedroom apartment we live in—"or whatever this is. I'm twenty-one, and I don't want"— her gesturing hand drops to Robbie—"this."

She's talking about Robbie. Robbie is *this* to her.

To me, Robbie is everything.

"He needs you," I choke out.

Erin gives me a look so filled with loathing it makes me tighten my grip around our son. "He needs my tits. And I'm sick of being a cow." She closes the suitcase. The tinny sound of the zipper bounces off the walls, magnified.

I'm doing everything I can not to come out of my skin right now. My mind is a mess of emotions, words I want to scream, but can't. "How long are you going to be gone?" It's a struggle to keep my voice low, but I manage it. For Robbie.

Erin shoulders her backpack. She grabs the handle of her suitcase, yanking, and it hits the ground beside our bed with a thud.

"Forever." She says the word without fanfare, its depth hidden by anger layered over suffering. Erin is a good person, and I know the only way she'll get through this is if she holds tightly to her anger, letting it carry her through.

5

"Don't act sad," she adds, glaring at me. She looks down to Robbie.

There's a glimmer of something in her eyes, something that isn't terrible, but it's gone in a flash. Her gaze lifts. "Neither of you like me anyway."

"He's a baby." I shift so he's more visible, and it's not until I do that that I realize I've been angling him away from her. "He's programmed to love you."

She huffs with disbelief. "Is that why he cries every time I hold him?"

"He feels your fear. He knows you're nervous." That's what I read on the internet after I saw how Robbie reacted to Erin. Once was one thing, but over and over he cried when she held him. If he wasn't nursing, he was crying. Until she handed him back to me, that is.

"It's too bad you don't have tits. Then Robbie wouldn't need me at all." Erin says this with hatred, but her emotions might as well be made of sheer fabric. I see right through them, to the anguish and fear she holds down deep.

"Maybe talk to Dr. Tatum? He told us to look out for postpartum depression—"

"That's not what this is." Erin takes a step toward me, a lone finger shaking in my face. I hollow out my chest and tuck Robbie as far into me as he can go, protecting him. From his mother. How messed up is that?

Erin takes whatever she was about to say or do, and pushes it down. Her lower lip trembles, and her chin lifts. "What about you, Jake? Do you love me?"

I take a deep breath, preparing myself to lie. I'll do it. I'll lie to keep Robbie with his mother. We'll get her help, figure out how she can bond with Robbie. It'll be ok.

"Don't." Erin's voice and face are hard. "I already know the answer." She walks from our room. Through the small living room. Out the front door. The door closes with a soft click. An ending that deserved a crash, received only a whisper.

I sink back onto the bed, feeling like Robbie's twelve pounds is now twelve thousand.

How am I going to do this alone? I'm twenty-one. Barely old enough to legally buy beer.

Robbie finishes his nap on my chest, and a few tears sneak out and run down my cheeks. I'm spent, but I need to think. Make a plan. So that's what I do.

It takes three days for Erin's parents to call me and tell me they're planning to sue for custody of Robbie.

It takes three seconds for me to tell the Brinkmans to bring it on. I have plenty of hubris, but no money. And Erin's parents know it.

The only reason I'm here in Tucson, and not at home in the small town of Green Haven, is because I'm on scholarship.

The Brinkmans think because of my age, and the fact I'm still enrolled at the University of Arizona, I'll roll over and let them do what they want. A twenty-one-year old wants only to party and go to class, right? Wrong. They believe they'll wear me down.

They won't.

I know what I have to do, and it starts with leaving college, and ends with going home. I have only one hope when it comes to getting a good lawyer and keeping my parental rights.

It doesn't take me long to pack up our things. One of my friends agreed to take over my lease, and he moves in tomorrow.

Green Haven is a four hour drive, and it's my first time driving that far away with Robbie. When he was born, my mom and little sister made the drive to Tucson to meet him.

Car packed, I double-check the car seat, the latch, the five-point harness over his tiny chest. All is good. A half-mile into our long drive, I pull over and perform a third check.

When I arrive in Green Haven, I don't stop at my mom's house even when I pass it. Or, my house, I guess. We're moving in with her and my sister until I get a job and get on my feet.

I'm headed somewhere else right now. Somewhere where I can get the help I need.

At the far edge of town is the neighborhood where Emmett Jones lives. He's well-known around town, both for his successful construction business and his jolly nature.

He was my dad's boss, until my dad went downhill. I spent summers working for him starting at fifteen, and he's the only person I know who can help me now.

I pull into his driveway and cut the engine. A deep breath fills my lungs, and I pinch the bridge of my nose. Robbie wakes up when I lift his seat from the car, and when he looks me in the eyes, I get the feeling he's asking me to please be a good dad, because I'm all he has left.

Car seat in one hand and diaper bag in the other, I make my way up the front walk.

Emmett's wife, Victoria, answers my knock. Her hands go to her cheeks, eyes wide. "Oh my word," she breathes, looking down at Robbie. "Come in, come in." She ushers me inside.

Emmett appears from the hallway. He takes one look at me, clutching the handle of the car seat, then says, "Let's have a talk in my office."

Chapter 1

Colbie

Bad things happen in threes.

At least, that's what I've heard. But, what about when two bad things happen simultaneously? Do they count as one? Or one, and two?

Bad Thing One bumps my table with his gyrating hip. He doesn't spare me a look, not even an apologetic glance. He's too focused on making sure he's in time with the other fifty people who are now performing a complicated dance in the middle of the public square.

Step ball change. Pas de bourree.

They're very good. Crisp lines, and clean transitions.

I shift in the cheap plastic chair, leaning away from the flash mob participant. When I first sat down, this large open area between stores was full of people, but mostly they were sitting around reading or scrolling their phones. I thought it would be a quiet place to FaceTime Brad. As soon as he answered, all the strangers around me jumped from their seats and began to dance.

9

Turns out, this wasn't a good place to sit down and call Brad. For more reasons than one.

"It's loud there," Brad complains, stress tugging at the edges of his voice. "Maybe this isn't the best time to talk."

As of twenty seconds ago, Brad is Bad Thing Two.

My attention moves back to my phone. On the screen, Brad tightens his tie. People around me who aren't dancing hold their phones aloft, recording. I wonder if the person behind me is also capturing me, in the foreground of their video, as I discover another woman in my boyfriend's hotel room.

"It's certainly a bad time for you," I point out, my volume increased so he can hear me. I'm so calm, I might as well be answering a question about what toppings I prefer on pizza. *Extra pepperoni, please.* But not on the inside. In there, in that space deep in my chest where I keep my emotions, I'm wailing. This betrayal hurts.

Brad freezes, one hand on his tie and the other gripping the knotted fabric at his neck. The woman, standing in the hotel bathroom with the door half-open, stills.

It's amazing, really. This is all happening because Brad placed his phone in just the right position where I could see the mirror on the hotel room wall. If not for that, I wouldn't have seen the reflection of the woman standing in a pencil skirt and lacy black bra, running a hairbrush through her silky blonde tresses.

Brad doesn't look ashamed. He looks like he's preparing his reason. "Colbie, it's just that you—"

The music grows louder. Brad's lips are moving, but I can't hear what he's saying. That's probably for the best.

"Brad," I yell, anger overtaking shock, "I hope you get an STD."

My shout coincides with the exact moment the music shuts off abruptly.

Oh, shit.

The silence becomes the sound, the quietude bouncing off the surrounding structures.

My gaze lifts from the screen. Hundreds (millions?) of horrified expressions pile on me. The worst comes from the two people in the center of the crowd, the man on one knee and the woman standing before him. They both look like they would enjoy punching me in the throat.

I gulp. "Congratulations?"

Then I grab my phone, tuck my purse into my chest, and flee.

⁙

"Some second-rate internet news site wrote an article about it. They made you sound like a scorned woman who ruined the proposal on purpose," Christina, my best friend and business partner, informs me with her lips around her straw. The mid-afternoon sunlight filters through the window of the bar, illuminating her golden hair.

You'd think after spending all our time together managing a four-location exercise business, we'd be ready for a little space. But, no. She's the first person I called when I wanted to get a drink.

"Don't sugarcoat it," I say dryly, stirring the tiny red straw in my drink and watching the ice cubes knock into each other.

She takes a sip of her paloma, looks at me with a softened gaze, and says, "Wouldn't dream of it. Everyone needs someone who will tell them the truth."

"Yeah, yeah." I frown, but she knows I don't mean it. It's

important to have people in your life who aren't afraid to say things you don't want to hear.

Christina has always been, and will always be, my biggest cheerleader. She's the first person to tell me when I'm right, and the first person to tell me when I'm wrong. It doesn't always feel good, but I can't remember a time when I wished she would have kept her mouth shut.

Everyone should have a Christina.

"So," she drums her fingers on the bar. "Do you want to talk about Brad?"

My lips roll together, rubbing in the lip balm I applied a few minutes ago. This vodka soda is beginning to do its job, loosening the tension in my neck that's been locked in since I caught Brad cheating two days ago. Drinking during the day doesn't usually bode well for me, but it felt right given the occasion. We should probably order fries. Fries feel right, also.

I look down at my hands in my lap, shaking my head back and forth ever so slightly. "I keep going over it in my head, and I can't figure where exactly I went wrong with Brad." I tried harder with him, knowing what my prior relationships had said about me. In the end, it didn't matter.

Christina's stiff pointer finger extends until it's in my downcast vision. "Absolutely not." She kicks me lightly under the bar in an effort to draw my gaze to her. Her face is stern. It's almost laughable, because she's petite and has a round, borderline cherubic face. You take one look at her and you're instantly certain she rescues bunnies, or baby animals of some sort. In truth, she's a honey badger. "Brad cheating on you is not your fault."

I tuck my legs under my stool to protect from further assault. "They are all my fault."

"Don't even think of bringing up the Buffoon Squad."

The Buffoon Squad is Christina's nickname for the men I've dated.

Jack, the dentist. We broke up, and he married the next woman he dated.

Quint, the restaurant manager. We broke up, and he married the next woman he dated.

Miller, the pilot. We broke up, and he married the next woman he dated.

I always thought the lineup sounded like a joke that didn't have a punchline, but *lucky me!*, there is now a punchline. It's me. I'm the punchline.

Now I can add Brad, the money manager. We were still dating when he decided to poke someone else in the whiskers.

I look knowingly at Christina. "You have to admit, a pattern has emerged."

She blows from one side of her mouth to push away a section of curtain bangs that has drifted into her eye. "I'm the one before The One," she pantomimes all the instances I've made this statement.

I nod once, matter-of-fact. "Correct. Ten bucks says Brad marries hotel woman."

Christina ignores my woeful bet. "And how do you feel about that?"

Christina has been in therapy for the past year. What she learns in her therapist's office seeps through into her everyday language, which means it has become a part of our conversations.

I don't go to therapy. Not because I don't need it. It's more that I don't want to need it. But, even I can admit some sort of outside viewpoint might be helpful. Especially given where I've landed, once again.

There's a pinch in the center of my chest as I admit the

fear that holds me bound so tightly. "Maybe they are all onto something." I knock back the remainder of my drink. "Maybe the writing is on the wall, and I'm refusing to read it."

She's shaking her head before I can finish my sentence. "No way. Don't do that."

"Don't do what?"

"Don't internalize their choices."

"Choices they made in reaction to me?"

"Brad should not have cheated. That's not on you."

"He said what they all say about me, just using different words. Practically the same exact reason." In my mind I see their reasons, floating by like ticker tape at the bottom of the TV financial channel.

You are emotionally unavailable.

You don't seem like you care.

I fell in love with someone else, because you weren't emotionally present.

Who knew men are so gung-ho for emotional women? I guess it's time to peel my Men Love Bitches sticker off my stainless steel water bottle. I don't actually have that sticker, but I saw it in a bookstore, and was drawn to it because of its irreverence. I didn't buy it, but I wanted to.

Christina finishes her drink. "What was it Brad said, specifically?"

That same tiny pinch assaults my chest once more. Yesterday he'd dropped off a few items I'd left at his place, and attempted an apology. *It was the first time, I didn't plan it, yada yada.* Maybe it was the vague tone of voice, but it seemed like he was sorrier to have been caught than to have committed the infraction. The more I think about it, the more I think he was relieved. "He said he looked into my eyes one day and realized I was never going to love him."

"Ouch." She blinks twice, hard. "Was he right?"

"My immediate answer is no. But if I take more time to think about it," I shrug, trying not to let on how much this bothers me. I'm not only disappointed in Brad. I'm frustrated with myself. Am I broken? "He might have a point."

I had plans to give him my heart, but when it came down to it, would I have?

The bartender stops by, and I place an order for a basket of fries and a chicken sandwich. Christina shakes her head when I order a second round. "Not for me," she says to the bartender. He turns around to his computer. "I'm teaching in a couple hours," she reminds me. Christina teaches a handful of classes each week, while I stay firmly on the management side of the business.

"Ahh right. The after-work crowd." I lift invisible weights and chant, "We must, we must, we must increase our bust."

Christina laughs and presses her boobs together. "If only it were that easy." She pushes away her empty glass. "Do you want to take tonight's class? Might be good for you to ballet barre it out. Embrace the burn."

'Embrace the burn' is Christina's favorite thing to say when a class full of people are shooting daggers at her while their thigh muscles melt with sheer exhaustion.

"Can't." I take the second drink the bartender places in front of me. "I have to sit here and feel sorry for myself."

Her intrusive gaze pins me. "Can I speak bluntly?"

I eye her warily. "Do you know any other way?"

Her lips quirk in a smile. She takes the drink from me and sets it on the fresh napkin that accompanied my second drink. Then she grabs my now-empty hand and squeezes it gently. "I say this with all the love I have in my heart. You have daddy issues. And you need to figure them out."

"Ouch. There's probably a nicer way to say that."

"I know. I'm sorry." She grins in a not-actually-happy way. "But not really."

I don't mind when Christina's right, but this time is the exception. I blow out a heavy breath, lips vibrating, and give voice to thoughts that don't feel like they belong to me. "Maybe I should go see him." I sip my liquid courage, enjoying the sting.

"He's invited you to Green Haven, like, a dozen times. At least you know you're welcome."

Somewhere deep inside, hidden in a shadowed corner, my seven-year-old self steps forward. She wants to see the man she loved with all her heart. She wants to know him again.

Dammit. Thirty-year-old me doesn't want to see him, right? My dad is a lovable guy, and I don't want to love him. If I can keep feeling hurt, I can keep punishing him for leaving me and eventually tapering off his presence in my life.

Only, I kind of don't want to anymore. I'm so tired of it all. It takes more energy to nurture the resentment and pain than it does to let it go. And look what it's doing, how it's affecting me now, how far the pain of yesteryear can reach.

I sigh, rubbing under my eyes with my fingertips. I'm making the decision, right here and now. I need to do something different, because what I've been doing for years clearly isn't working for me. "I'm going to visit my dad." I take a deep breath, letting those words sink in. Then I repeat them, for good measure, with a shred of thrill ribboning through. "I'm going to visit my dad."

Christina's plump, lip-gloss slicked lips press together. Her hands steeple, and she slips them between her knees.

I laugh at her. "You don't have to physically restrain yourself to keep from clapping. You can be happy for me."

She releases her hands and claps twice. "I'm proud of you. Look at you, growing and shit."

"Yes, that's me. Growing and shit." My tone is dry, but inside I'm quaking with fear.

She laughs loudly. The bartender drops off my food, and Christina stands. "Those fries are my cue to leave. I'm wearing white leggings for class today, and they show every little everything." She smacks the bottom swell of her rear end.

I lift a fry and point it at her. "Including your camel toe."

"What?" she whisper-shrieks.

I nod and pop the fry in my mouth. "True story."

"I have worn those stupid pants"—she holds up three fingers—"thrice. How are you just now telling me this?"

"I forgot. Besides, shouldn't your husband tell you this stuff, too?" Christina and Daniel have been together since we were in college, and they got married a few years ago.

"He probably likes it." She reaches over and takes an entire handful of my fries, wielding them at me like swords. "Dead to me, that's what you are."

"As long as I don't have to embrace the burn."

She laughs again, and swats at my behind. "Here," she says as she rummages through her purse. She locates what she's after and presses it into my hand.

I turn it over. A business card?

Avery Woodruff. Licensed Marriage and Family Therapist.

"Thanks," I say dryly, "but I'm not married, and there's a negative chance of me getting on a couch with my mom or dad."

"Those are her specialties, but she'll still see you. I promise, you'd love her." Christina backs away with a wave, then turns for the door. "Thanks for the drink," she calls over her shoulder.

I'm still laughing when she's gone, and it hits me what a good friend Christina is. An hour with her, and somehow I feel better. Lighter. Brad cheating is not my fault. Rationally, I understand that.

But the heart is not a rational creature. Later tonight, when I'm alone at home, this brightness will fade.

May as well enjoy it while it lasts.

I signal the bartender for a third drink. Why not?

Chapter 2

Colbie

This precise moment is why not.

I'm dialing my dad's work number after a call to his cell phone went unanswered. It's now imperative that he know I'm coming to see him. It is the Most Important Thing. We have lost time to make up for. Twenty or so years of fractured relationship, in fact.

"Jones Construction," answers Blake, my dad's administrative assistant.

"Hi Blake, is—"

"Not Blake," the guy on the other end says, in a way I'd say is not necessarily a bark, but also isn't very welcoming.

I frown. "Hi Not Blake, is—"

He *growls*. It's the only word I can come up with to describe the sound.

I shift on my stool and nearly fall off. "Excuse me, Not Blake, but I believe there may be a mountain lion or oversized rodent of some sort near you. Better take cover."

He answers with a sigh, thick, heavy, like interacting with me is akin to having his underarm skin caught in a vise.

"Listen, I don't usually answer the phones and—"

Courage of the liquid variety pulses through my veins. "I'm the boss's daughter." Even I can hear how haughty I sound.

"Greer?"

That name steals the wind from my sails. My chutzpah dissipates. "Colbie," I correct, all attitude and irritation. The *other* daughter.

Then this guy, whoever he is, laughs. He chortles like Santa and a hyena are being simultaneously tickled.

"I'll go get your daddy, Princess."

Now I'm the one growling. I despise being called Princess. Or babe. Or darlin'. Or really anything cutesy. Maybe because, if I close my eyes, I can still hear my dad call me Sugar Bear.

I seem to have recovered my sass, along with a healthy dose of indignation. "You—"

"Relax, Princess." His deep voice is practically purring now. "Calm down."

When, in the history of ever, has telling someone to relax and calm down actually worked? In my experience, it serves only to escalate the situation, and is really just a device men use to mindfuck women.

"Whoa, whoa. I'm not over here mindfucking anybody."

Oh. I hadn't meant to say all that out loud. I glance outside my little bubble at the bar and see two guys seated nearby, staring at me. So I didn't just say all that out loud, but also *loudly*.

"Listen," I say, my voice returning to normal volume. "This is Emmett's daughter, Colbie, and I need to speak with my dad. He didn't answer his cell."

The guy is quiet for a few seconds, like he's deciding if

he's going to do what I've asked. He made it clear he doesn't usually answer the phones, which probably means it's not his job to find my dad, either.

I clear my throat. I need water, stat.

The alcohol and chicken sandwich are performing an unpleasant tango in my stomach. But not the fries. They're above such behavior.

"He walked out of the trailer about twenty minutes ago, and I'm headed out to meet him now. I'll tell him you called." His voice has cooled a little, and I'm encouraged enough to take a stab at kindness. This conversation aside, I usually prefer it over all else.

"It was nice sparring with you," I say, aiming for cheerful. "I didn't catch your name, though."

"Blake?"

I shake my head, annoyance creeping in. Is this guy serious? "I thought we established you're not Blake?"

"I'm not talking to you," he growls again. There's a desperate edge to his voice. "Blake just walked in."

"Let me talk to him." I push away my plate so the food isn't directly beneath my nose anymore. I'm really not feeling so good. I toss the therapist's business card on top of the half-eaten sandwich, too. "You shouldn't be allowed to answer the phone, by the way. You need training on how to speak to people."

No response. There's a pause, and a few seconds pass. "Colbie," an out of breath voice says my name. "This is Blake. I was running back to the trailer to call you. Victoria and Greer, too."

The sick feeling in my stomach pauses to make way for that feeling you get when you know something is wrong. "Why?"

"Your dad collapsed. An ambulance is on the way."

21

Here it is. Bad Thing Three. Panic races through my body. My breath bottoms out, and I grip the edge of the bar with my free hand. "What?" I finally manage to ask. "What happened?"

"I don't know." Someone else speaks in the background, Not Blake probably, and Blake says, "Colbie, I'm going to call you as soon as I know something, ok?"

"Please," I respond, but Blake has already hung up. I grab cash from my wallet and lay it on the bar, forgoing the water I desperately need.

I slip into the bathroom, then turn on the water and make a cup with my hands. After four handfuls, I hurry into a stall and vomit.

My stomach, emptied of its contents, doesn't feel better. This sick feeling doesn't come from food or drink, but rather a lifetime thinking *someday*.

Someday I'll face my demons.

Someday I'll work on myself.

Someday I'll let my dad repair our relationship.

What if someday never comes?

Chapter 3

Colbie

"You could come with me." I drag my roller suitcase from the closet floor of my bedroom and hoist it onto the bed where my mom sits. She raises her meticulously arched eyebrows, silently asking *Are you serious?*

"I shouldn't be gone more than a few days. I'm just going to visit him. Make sure I've shown my face." I'm careful to keep my tone in such a way that it sounds like I'm doing an unpleasant chore. I learned a long time ago not to say anything positive about my dad in front of my mom. It only leads to what she believes are well-meaning reminders that he will always let me down.

I turn back to the dresser, digging through an open drawer. I'm trying not to pay attention to the way my stomach tosses at the idea of what I'm about to do. Three days in Green Haven, most of which will probably be spent at the hospital. It isn't what I had envisioned as a reunion with my dad, but at this point I'm grateful to be getting this chance at all.

It could've easily been a funeral. He'd had a seizure on

the jobsite, hit his head on the corner of a sawhorse on the way down, and then again on the hard ground when he landed.

Blake had called to update me on my dad's condition, as promised, about four hours after he told me my dad collapsed. Here I am, twelve hours later, getting packed. I have the feeling all the clothes in the world won't prepare me for what I'm about to do.

My mom hasn't said a word, so I look at her. She leans back on the pale pink bedspread, her eyes tipped to the ceiling. "You know Victoria." She says my dad's wife's name as if that's all the explanation needed. "She'd blow a gasket if I showed up at the hospital. She's always hated me." She says it with this exhausted tone, as if she hasn't detested Victoria since the first time I came home from the weekend visit where my dad introduced the realtor who sold him his new house as his girlfriend.

There's no way in hell my mom will say yes to coming with me to Green Haven, so it's safe to press the issue. "Who cares about Victoria? You're my mom, you have every right to be with me." I know how this game is played. We've been playing it for more than two decades. My mom needs to hear she's wanted, so when she says 'no' she feels she's the one in control. "Don't let her keep you away if you want to see him." I extract a handful of underwear and toss it in my suitcase. "I'm sure he would like to see you."

She sends me a disbelieving look.

"It was a long time ago," I say carefully, pulling a few shirts from the closet and laying them on the bed. The subject of my dad has always been a land mine around my mom. She used to tell me everything that was wrong with him until I could tell the entire woeful tale myself. All by the age of ten. "Do you think maybe you're over it now?"

She reaches over and begins folding my shirts. "There are some experiences in life that you can't come back from. The very best thing you can do for yourself is design a life where you feel the least amount of awful."

I was eleven the first time I remember her saying those words to me. Girls who'd been my friends the week before had turned on me suddenly, telling me there was blood soaking through the seat of my jeans. I'd crept down the aisle of the full math class, a notebook pressed against my behind, my ears filled with their cruel giggling. I went to the bathroom, terrified of what I would see. There wasn't any blood.

I understood exactly what my mother meant when she'd said those words. Design a life where you set yourself up for the best outcomes. Sounded like a good idea to me. But how do you do that when you can't see the mistakes you're about to make? Or when people dressed as sheep turn out to be wolves? Or become wolves along the way? What if you've avoided what you thought were traps and pitfalls, but they would've been the best thing for you?

The older I get, the less I believe that particular line of wisdom from her. Exhibit A: My string of failed relationships. Exhibit B: The possibility that a second chance with my dad may never come. I can't get a man to stay with me, and I refuse love from the only man who would step in front of traffic to save me.

What has the least amount of awful done for me so far?

I look at her, sitting on the bed. She's been a good mom, but right now I feel disappointed in her. It would be nice if she would encourage me to mend fences with my dad. But, no. I'm over here feeling like anything I do for my dad is also somehow a slap to her, like the two events are mutually inclusive. That's how it's always felt.

25

And, just like always, the lead heaviness of guilt pushes at me, because I'm leaving her behind to see my dad. It's like being a kid all over again, knowing I was leaving her for the weekend because it was my dad's turn to have me.

I poke at the clothes in my suitcase. "I feel like I should see him."

My mom places my folded shirt inside and reaches for the next. "I'm not telling you not to go."

Ah, the double negative. There's always more behind it.

"But you aren't telling me I should go."

"Your father is a charming man. He's charismatic, and full of ideas. He likes shiny things, but eventually all things lose their shine." She says it loftily, like a shaman doling out sage advice.

An uncharacteristic desire to object to her claims darts through me. I don't challenge her often, because she's far more skilled at arguing and it exhausts me to try. Right now, though, I'm feeling brave. "Then how is it he's been married to Victoria for so long? And raised Greer?"

I force the name through my teeth. It feels cruel that he went on to have another daughter, one he stuck around for. A son would've been easier on my heart.

"That's a very good question, and I do not have an answer." She shrugs her shoulders in a *sorry about your luck* way. It's not an argument, but it is a dismissal.

My dad's twenty-year marriage to Victoria is a piece that doesn't fit into the puzzle, but I don't want to press my mom. Nor do I have the time. It's almost midday, and I need to get on the interstate before it becomes a parkway of desert-dwelling Phoenicians seeking cooler temps and pine trees.

I finish my packing, and Mom walks out with me. I toss

my small suitcase and even smaller toiletry bag in the trunk.

"Call me," she says, wrapping me in a vanilla-scented hug.

"I will."

I kiss her cheek, then slide in my car. With a final wave, I'm off. She pulls out after me, going the opposite direction.

Nerves tumble around my stomach. I stop for coffee, then join the early birds racing up the I-17.

I have no idea what I'm getting into, but I'm certain I need to be caffeinated.

⁘

If I don't eat something soon, I'm going to faint.

Plus, the rise in elevation has my ears in desperate need of popping, and the cover to my sunroof is stuck open so the sun blazed its way through my scalp for the last two hours.

Gingerly I press two fingertips to the part in my hair and wince. I think I might actually have a little bit of a sunburn.

I've turned off the I-17, but it's still twenty more miles to the Green Haven town line. It, among so many other small towns throughout this area, is situated adjacent to the Verde River. What sets Green Haven apart from the surrounding towns is its bustling antique scene. People travel from all over to go antiquing on the main street. So many, in fact, that the townspeople voted to build a second main street, two streets over from the original. It boasts multiple restaurants, a drugstore, hardware store, market, and arcade. Nary an antique shop in sight.

I have memories of coming to Green Haven with my dad when I was young. He'd been right about the construction industry booming in this area of Arizona. After he left our house, he moved here. I went with him on his first mission to find a home, and we'd stopped at the Verde River before we hit Green Haven town limits. Dad rolled up his jeans and together we stepped into the calm water. High from the sugar in my Slurpee, I kicked and splashed and got us both wet. Dad only laughed, and when we got back to his truck he pulled an unused flannel from the back seat and gave it to me to dry off. That night we stayed at the Green Haven Inn, which wasn't all that nice but the price was right. More than anything about that trip, I remember eating buffalo chicken wings for dinner and being too stubborn to admit my mouth was on fire. My dad ordered a glass of milk for himself, then pushed it over to me, claiming he was too full to drink it.

We went house hunting the next day, and I was thoroughly unimpressed. Coming from the sprawling metropolis of Phoenix, the town of Green Haven left a lot to be desired, at least in my childish opinion. Where was the McDonald's with its PlayPlace? The roller skating rink? The indoor trampoline park?

Dad decided that the third house of the day was the right one for him. It was sixteen hundred square feet with a tidy backyard. Just enough room for him, he declared, bopping the end of my nose and adding, "and my little sugar bear when she comes up to visit." I didn't notice the sparks between my dad and our realtor, but looking back on that day with an adult's view, I see the attraction.

As soon as he was settled in the house, he poured a small concrete pad to extend the back patio, and I pressed my hands into the wet concrete. Using the pointed end of a nail, he scraped 'Sugar Bear' below my prints.

I visited often. He was busy getting his concrete business off the ground, and once it had legs, it took off. Too busy to lose hours driving back-and-forth to pick me up from Phoenix and take me home, he asked if my mom could make the drive. I think they heard her say no all the way in Nevada.

"You left us, then you move two hours away and expect me to drive her to see you?" My mom yelled into the phone. "Do I sound like I'm interested in making your life easier?"

It was the first time I felt less like a person, and more like a problem.

He made the drive.

For a while.

Eventually his relationship with Victoria progressed. He sold the house with my handprints and moved into the house they still live in today. Then they had Greer. The time between visits grew longer. I turned into a preteen, and then a teen. The visits became less enjoyable. After the banal updates were out of the way, there was nothing to talk about. People can only take long stretches of awkward silence for so long before they throw in the towel. One day I woke up and realized it had been a year since I'd seen him.

Fine, I'd thought. I was thriving as a high school sophomore, on the school newspaper, and in three advanced classes. I was popular enough that I wasn't bullied, but not so popular every girl secretly hated me. *Fine.*

Now I'm an adult. I'm partial owner and operator of a thriving multi-location business. I'm thirty years old, I pay a mortgage, I'm asleep by ten on Saturday nights, and I've developed a dairy intolerance. How much more of an adult can I be?

Despite all that, being here, on the edge of Green Haven, is making my heart beat faster.

I ease my car off the road and into the gas station. I'm

not looking forward to eating gas station food. My stomach is already rolling at the prospect of seeing my dad.

Beggars can't be choosers, and I need to keep my blood sugar steady. This is difficult enough without adding fainting to the mix.

I slide my car into a space, then make my way into the store. There's nobody around, not even an employee at the cash register. I head for the hot food.

Hot dogs rotate under a heat lamp. Foil-wrapped burritos crowd a warming tray.

I try not to wrinkle my nose as I consider just exactly how long this stuff has been sitting here. Packaged food is probably safer right now.

I'm reading the labels of two different items when the little bell above the door tinkles with the notification of a new arrival. I peer around the end of the aisle and watch the new person step inside.

He makes quite a show of stepping in, ducking his head because he's so tall. He's maneuvering through the door because his shoulders are broad, and he's only opened one door instead of the two that are available.

"Afternoon, Mr. Whittier," a woman says, coming from a door marked 'Employees Only'.

"Hello, Ms. Martha," the guy says, tipping his chin down in acknowledgment. He has a strong jawline, a straight nose, and a voice that is deep and rumbly with just the right amount of gravel.

She frowns playfully at him. "You don't have to call me Ms. Martha anymore. It's been twenty-five years since I was your teacher."

"As long as you call me Mr. Whittier, I'll call you Ms. Martha."

She strides behind the counter, moving her hip to avoid

the corner. She's surprisingly spry for a woman who I'd guess is at least seventy. "Are you here for a hot dog?"

The guy stalks to the hot dogs, which are also closer to me. "You know it," he says, and for a short second I think I've heard his voice somewhere. It's probably Christina's fault, always making me watch those Hallmark movies with the sexy lumberjack with the kind of voice that reaches all the way down into a woman's nether regions.

Not that this guy is sexy.

Or has a voice that reaches down into my nether regions.

But if a girl had to be objective, this large man is none too shabby. Expansive chest, arms that dip and rise in all the right places, and now that he has passed the aisle I'm awkwardly gawking from, I also see that his tapered waist gives way to a fine backside.

"Are you getting a hot dog, too?"

I startle and turn toward the woman. She's smirking.

Busted.

"Oh, I um..." I brave a quick peek at the man. Sidenote: he is beyond sexy.

Briefly I consider sauntering over and making hot dogs my new favorite food. But then the smell and sight of the brownish pink hot dogs breaks through my daydream in a way that can only be achieved by a phallic-shaped stick of not-really-meat.

"Just grabbing a snack." I hold up the pistachios.

"That coffee is freshly brewed," Martha says, pointing at the little coffee station in the corner.

It also happens to be right next to where the hot lumberjack is standing. Is Martha playing matchmaker?

Smiling at Martha, I say, "I'm not going to turn down coffee."

She watches me walk over and set my things down. I busy myself with removing a cup from the sleeve on the counter. The guy moves to walk by me. He's bigger up close, and I feel dwarfed by him as he passes.

By the time I pour myself a travel cup, he's handing over cash to pay for his food and a Gatorade.

"Everything all right, honey?" Martha calls.

I set down the creamer. It has a total of two ingredients: milk and cream. I can tolerate dairy if I have my digestive enzymes. But guess what I forgot to pack?

I'd rather attempt to outrun a bear than announce my dairy intolerance right now. I look at Martha and finally have full-on eye contact from the sexy Paul Bunyan holding an open wallet in his palm.

He has hair the color of mesquite before a rain, and eyes that are an unfair mixture of moss and emerald. If I saw them up close, would they have flecks of gold? Maybe little brown dots? Right now those eyes are fixed on me, eyebrows lifting slightly as both he and Martha wait for my response.

My response? Was there a question asked of me?

Oh, right. Creamer.

"Do you happen to have a non-dairy creamer?" I smile apologetically, as if my dairy intolerance is something I checked off on a list of human afflictions that sounded like they could be fun. "Maybe almond or cashew milk?"

The guy makes a disbelieving grunting sound. "Never heard of milking an almond or cashew before."

I frown and mentally take back every good thought I've had about this man in the last ninety seconds. "Milk doesn't only come from udders," I inform him.

"It doesn't come from udders at all." He looks at me with pity, like my level of stupidity bodes poorly for all of humanity. "It comes from teats."

"Right," I mutter. The back of my neck warms. "Anyway. Martha, do you have something that didn't come from a teat?"

"Sorry, honey, we're a half-and-half kinda joint." She lifts a finger in the air and says, "Wait a minute, I might have something for you."

She hands the guy his change and he stomps out, but not without first sending me a look of befuddled astonishment, like he can't believe I exist.

I have the sudden urge to stick out my tongue. I don't, because I'm not ten years old, but I really want to.

Martha comes over and reaches under the counter where I'm standing, arm disappearing, then reappearing with a small woven basket. "Aha!" Triumph tugs her voice up an octave. She thrusts the basket at my chest and goes back to her perch at the register.

I look down at the tiny plastic cups of creamer. A thick layer of dust coats the surface of them. And while they're most definitely non-dairy, it's probably not safe to ingest them.

I take two and drop them into my purse, then put a lid on the coffee and tuck the basket back onto the shelf.

"Just what I was looking for," I say to Martha. "Thank you very much."

"You're welcome." She rings me up, and I hand her cash.

"You passing through?" She places my change in my outstretched palm.

"Green Haven is my destination. I'm Colbie Jones."

Martha's gaze flies outside, to Mr. Whittier removing the gas nozzle from his truck. "Is that right?" she says slowly, like she finds something amusing. "You're Emmett's niece?"

"Daughter." *Other* daughter. I refuse to say it out loud.

"How's he doing? Heard he took a nasty fall on that new job on the other side of town."

"He's hanging in there. I'm headed to the hospital to see him now."

The old woman's eyes sparkle. "Welcome to Green Haven."

I step out into the sunshine, pistachios and coffee in hand. I pause on the sidewalk to sip my bitter black coffee. The sun is warm, but not too hot. It's September, a month I typically don't enjoy because the rest of the country is going on about pumpkin spice flavored everything and it's still hot in Phoenix. But here, it's actually nice. Tall trees provide shade, and the Verde River is somewhere nearby. I haven't hit the actual town yet, but I can already tell the pace is slower, like it's a flavor in the air that can be tasted.

A truck roars to life and I startle, a mouthful of coffee dribbling down my front. I'm wearing white. *Great.*

Mentally I sift through what shirt in my suitcase is easiest to reach without lugging the whole thing from my car and opening it on the sidewalk.

The truck rumbles up to me, but instead of continuing on, it slows down. The brakes whine as it comes to a stop.

Mr. Whittier has the window rolled down, and a smirk on his face. The forearm he has propped on the door is covered in a light dusting of hair, and corded muscle.

I give him my best *fuck-off* look. "I'm not in the mood to be told how stupid I am because I'm not well-versed on the names and functions of a cow's body parts."

If he hears my words or my tone, he doesn't act like it. Not at all. Instead, he takes a leisurely perusal of the front of my shirt. "You got yourself quite a stain," he says, that amused grin plastered to his face.

My thighs clench involuntarily, and I shove off the feeling of heat in my center. "Take your eyes off my chest." My biological clock punches my inner feminist right in the tit.

His gaze lifts slowly, defiance seeping from him. "Interstate is that way," he points. "You better get a move on. This whole town is full of dairy, Princess."

My jaw drops, and I'm left with nothing but shock and the smell of fumes as he drives away.

Chapter 4

Colbie

"Hi."

My dad's eyes open at the sound of my voice. He blinks twice, then a grateful smile blossoms on his face. Despite the setting, and the situation, he looks thrilled to see me.

I'm over here doing everything I can to keep my gasp in my throat.

I'd been so busy thinking about seeing him again that I didn't focus on what he would look like.

Bruises.

Stitches.

A large bump on his forehead.

My heart lurches.

The beeping of his heart rate monitor keeps a tally of the bloated seconds we spend staring at each other. He lifts his arms for a hug, IV tube dangling. "Hey, Sugar Bear."

My heart twists at the nickname, and the tone of his voice. Normally he speaks like he's in the midst of a party. Loud, boisterous, joyful. Right now he sounds like a part of his inherent jubilation has been snuffed out.

36

I step all the way into his room, and up to his bedside, folding myself carefully into his outstretched arms. He smells like I remember, like earthy dirt even when he's clean, and soft cotton. A smell I forgot I loved. The continuity of it kicks me between the ribs. He squeezes me a little tighter. "Be careful," I warn. "I don't want you to disrupt your IV."

"It's taped on," he replies, holding me for an extra second. "No need to worry."

The hug ends, and I step back. I take in his face, freckled like a constellation, and his rumpled reddish-brown hair. He's a large man, and it's comical to see him in this small bed, as if someone is playing a joke.

This is all very surreal. The white walls, the metal railings of the hospital bed, the fake flowers in the center of the small table in the corner. *Him.* He, too, is surreal.

It's been a year since I last saw him. He'd needed to buy a specialty tool for his business, and he called me on his way to Phoenix and asked me to get lunch. I'd had plans with a friend that day, but I cancelled them and refused to let myself consider why I'd been willing to clear my schedule for him.

Christina is right. I really do have daddy issues.

I look at him, and my entire body fills with emotion. Some feelings I can identify, some I don't even have a name for. I'm *flooded.* Suddenly, I have the intense desire to run. Hop in my car, and go back to Phoenix. But I don't. I square my shoulders, and muster a smile. "How are you feeling?"

"Been better," he says, nodding. "Been worse, though, so I guess it evens out."

"Are you in pain?"

"They have me on something. I didn't ask what it was."

I breathe a laugh. He grins. I forgot how much he loves

making people happy. Well, I guess I didn't forget. More like I tried to forget, because when someone hurts you, you tend to block out their best attributes.

"You didn't have to drive up here," he says, his tone making it clear he thinks all this has been blown out of proportion. "It was just a fall."

My eyes narrow at his 'tough guy dumbing down an injury' routine. "It was a lot more than a fall."

He grumbles, something incoherent except for the word 'damn'. "I'm getting up there in age. Shit happens." The tough guy façade breaks just enough for me to peek in and see his fear. His worry. "You here for long?" he asks, hope lifting his tone. His eyes are bright as he asks the question.

"I thought I'd stay for a few days."

He beams. "You can stay with Victoria and Greer at the house. We have plenty of room, and they'd love to see you."

Would they?

I don't say it. There's no need in dredging up the past, especially right now.

"I already have a room at the Rose Hotel, but thank you."

His smile droops, but he recovers quickly. "That's great, Sugar Bear. The Rose Hotel is a nice place."

I'm not sure what to say, but, true to form, my dad is ready with question. That's another one of his positive attributes. He can create and carry a conversation, no matter who it's with. "Dance studio treating you well?"

I nod, settling into the topic. "The studios are success-ful. Packed classes. We put displays and clothing racks in the front of all the locations and we sell a rotating selection of local goods, along with some higher-end exercise cloth-ing. It was a good move, business-wise." I love my job. It brings me real joy, and it's not just the endorphins pumping through the stores throughout the day.

"That's great. Do you get a chance to work out?"

"A few times a week."

"Good, good."

"How is"—I falter—"*was* work going for you?"

He frowns. Probably not at my question, but at the word I had to change to past tense. "You should see this custom home we're starting. Like something out of a movie." My dad lets out a disbelieving chuckle. "You'd think the guy and his wife are being hunted. The guy asked for false walls and a safe room."

I smile at the consternation in my dad's tone, but my amusement is followed by an immediate twinge of annoyance. It took all of ten minutes for me to feel fond toward my dad, but I should know better. On the heels of every good moment with him, is a painful memory. Shaking it off, I ask, "Are you at all concerned about why the homeowners asked for those things?"

"Nah. It's not my job to ask questions."

I nod, and quiet descends. My dad studies my face, and I look down at the floor, pretending not to see him. It's like he's memorizing it. A soft, reverent look sinks into his eyes, and it's unsettling. The man who abandoned me shouldn't be trying to know me. He should stay in his role as abandoner. When he's there, I'm aware of what I'm dealing with. It's safer for the heart to dance with the devil it knows.

My dad's phone rings. I retrieve it from the table and hand it over. He glances at the screen and grimaces. "Insurance. Victoria called our insurance guy this morning. I better take this."

"I have to run out and make a phone call, too." That's

not true. I don't have a call to make, but I do need to get my bearings. I back out of the room. "I'll come back in a little while."

Chapter 5

Jake

I'm running a towel over my wet hair when the text message from Victoria comes through.

> Can you come to the hospital? Emmett would like to see you.

I push the phone away and finish drying myself off from my shower. I was dirty and hot after work, like I always am. I try to get my after-work shower out of the way before Robbie arrives home from school, but that was derailed today by a stop at the convenience store. Without Emmett, I'm the de facto boss on the job, and I worked through lunch. I walked into Martha's feeling bad-tempered and hungry. Not a great combination in general, and especially not great for running into Emmett's daughter.

I didn't know it was Colbie right away. Emmett keeps a photo of her on his desk, right beside Greer's, but it's an old photo. Maybe ten years or so?

The fancy little car parked in front of the convenience store was the only one in the lot, aside from my own truck, so I knew the car belonged to the other customer in the store.

I also knew that customer did not belong to the town of Green Haven, not just because I've lived here most of my life, but because nobody in this town drives a two-door shiny black Mercedes.

I felt her eyes on me as I'd walked past the aisle she stood in, but I didn't bother to look up. I was dirty, and sweaty, and covered in desert dust. More than likely all I would've seen if I'd looked at a woman who drives a car like that was a lip curled in disgust.

Doesn't mean I didn't take notice of her, though.

She smelled like vanilla and oranges, reminding me of an orange creamsicle. Her toenails were painted bright red, and her slender ankles led to defined calves. That's as far as I got in my downturned, two-second survey of her.

I realized it was Colbie when she made that ridiculous request for milk made from nuts. It was the first time I looked at her full-on, and I saw Emmett in her face. She has his nose.

Also, she's heart-stoppingly gorgeous. Glossy brown hair, eyes the color of caramel, fringed with sooty lashes. She was kind to Martha, which I liked, but then I remembered I don't want to like Colbie.

Blake called her yesterday and updated her on her dad's condition, and she'd told him she'd drive up. Honestly, I didn't believe she'd show. I've been by Emmett's side for years, listening to his half of the conversations when he asks her to come for a visit. Then, after he hangs up following one of her bullshit excuses, I've watched him cry. Not every time, but many of them, and it tore me up to watch Emmett, my mentor, a man who has become a father to me in the last decade, shed tears over his little girl. Maybe because I know what it's like to have a child, to love them with a force that feels superhuman. I asked him once why he doesn't drive down to visit her, and he told me she doesn't ask him to come.

My guess is that Colbie will only be here a short time, just long enough to have notched a few points for coming around when Emmett was hospitalized, and then she'll hop in that fancy car and return to the valley. Hopefully I can avoid her for the duration of her time in Green Haven. That would probably be best.

I need to get going to see Emmett, so I call my mom and ask her if she can watch Robbie. Emmett probably wants to talk to me about the custom home we've been working on. It'll be boring for Robbie, plus I don't want him to see the way Emmett looks right now. I was at the hospital last night, and it isn't pretty.

I don't know when he'll be able to come back to work, so he'll need someone to take over while he's out. As the foreman, that responsibility naturally falls to me.

My mom agrees to let Robbie hang out at her place. She's never said no to spending time with Robbie. I think she likes being a grandma even more than she liked being a mom, and that's saying a lot because she was the kind of mom other people wished they had.

I get dressed, then find Robbie in the kitchen with his hand at the bottom of a chip bag. I reach out and muss his hair. "You're going to Mimi's this afternoon."

"Da-ad," Robbie whines. "I was at Mimi's last night while you were at the hospital. I just got home from school. I don't wanna go anywhere."

"I know buddy, but sometimes we have to do things we don't want to do." I walk from the kitchen into the living room, and Robbie follows.

43

"But I'm not an adult yet." He lightly kicks his backpack where it lies on the floor.

I try not to smile. "What's that supposed to mean?"

"Adults are the people who do things they don't wanna do. Not kids."

I nod my head. "Ahh. Kids should never have to do things they don't want to do. Understood." I move fast, encircling his small waist and turning him upside down.

Robbie smacks at my thighs, laughing. "Put me down."

I lower him carefully. Robbie extends his arms and tucks his chin, somersaulting. It's a sequence we've perfected over the years.

He stands upright and tries to act mad, but he can't keep a straight face. A smile tugs at one corner of his mouth when he says, "I have homework, Dad. I can't go to Mimi's."

"Mimi will do your homework with you." I poke him in his side. "She knows the answer to 2+2."

He sends me an exasperated look only a ten-year-old is capable of. They still have the baby fat from early childhood, mixed with what is the beginning of an onslaught of teenage attitude.

"I'm doing long division with decimal points. Does Mimi know that?"

I point at his backpack. "Do you have your math book in there?"

He nods.

"If Mimi doesn't know it yet, she'll use that math book to teach herself." I'm not being facetious. My mother is smart as a whip. She never went to college, but she can teach herself anything and everything she sets her mind to. I motion out front, where my truck is parked. "C'mon. Hustle up."

"Alright," Robbie groans reluctantly.

I shoulder his backpack as Robbie walks out ahead of me, and lock up my house.

"Why do you have to take me to Mimi's house anyway?" Robbie asks as he climbs into the back seat of my truck. "Aren't you done with work for the day?"

"I am," I confirm, "but I need to visit Mr. Emmett again."

"What?" Robbie says, instantly upset just like he was yesterday when I told him what happened. "I want to see Mr. Emmett." Robbie and Emmett have a special bond, and I can think of more than one reason why.

I wait for the click of the seatbelt before closing the door. I get in the driver's seat and say to Robbie, "Mr. Emmett doesn't look like himself right now. I bet he would rather you see him when he looks a little bit better."

"How does he look?" Robbie's eyebrows pull together in worry.

I take a moment to consider my answer. Yesterday Emmett was hooked up to machines and his head was wrapped in gauze. I didn't stay long, because Victoria and Greer were there and I felt like I was intruding. I'm not sure how he'll look today, but it might not be that different.

"He looks scary, buddy. He has a big bandage on his head."

Robbie crosses his arms. "I'm not afraid of bandages, Dad."

If only that were the extent of it. Emmett's sudden seizure on the jobsite didn't send him gracefully to the ground. He smacked his forehead on the corner of a sawhorse on his way down, leaving him concussed. The face first landing on the hard earth left him with abrasions and cuts. Robbie doesn't need to see that.

"Soon, Robbie, when he's back home and up for visitors. But not today."

Robbie pouts for most of the drive over to my mom's. She meets us in the driveway, opening up Robbie's door and stepping back so he can hop out. He slings his backpack over one shoulder, grumbling "Bye, Dad" on his way into the house.

My mom leans against my truck. "Is he in a mood?"

"Something like that."

She tips her head, intrusive gaze digging into me. "Are you in a mood?"

I've been in a mood ever since I saw Colbie Jones, to be perfectly honest. And if I'm being even more honest, with myself of all people, what really has me in a mood is the fact I felt both physically and mentally attracted to her. I'd sat in my truck, devouring that hot dog and watching her step out onto the sunny sidewalk. Her shapely calves and thigh muscles that scream *I work out* stole my attention, and a few of my brain cells also.

My mom waits for an answer, so I say, "I'm upset over Emmett." It's kind of true.

My mom does not detect the partial untruth. She rubs my arm, one side of her mouth upturned in a sad smile. "He's going to be ok, that's the important part."

"Yeah." I nod my head toward the house. "Robbie has long division with decimal points."

My mom lifts her head up and down one time, matter-of-factly. "Sounds like a good day to remember how to do long division with decimal points."

"Better you than me," I quip. My job requires plenty of calculations, just not that kind. I spend a lot more time on the square footage side of math. "I'll see you in a couple hours. Thanks, Mom." I place a swift kiss on her cheek. Without my mom, I'd be pretty damn lost.

"You're welcome." She goes inside and I drive to the hospital.

My hands shove into my pockets as I ride the elevator to the third floor. I don't like hospitals. I've never been inside one and had a good experience.

When my dad went into the hospital, he never came out. That was his own fault. To this day, I can't find a shred of sympathy for that man. Everything that happened, he brought on himself.

The elevator dings, and the doors open. I didn't think to ask if Emmett had been moved to a room different than the one he was in yesterday, but I don't have to. Emmett's voice filters out into the hallway, and I follow it. He's like a watered down version of Santa Claus. That's the reason he dresses up as Santa for the Green Haven Christmas parade. Who better to transform into jolly old St. Nick than an equally jolly man?

I stride into the room, assuming he's talking to Victoria. Mid-step, I realize my mistaken assumption. Two long, lean legs stretch out, crossed at the ankles. Red-painted toenails. The owner of those legs shifts to see who's entered the room. There may as well be a billboard behind Colbie's warm brown eyes, communicating that she likes me about as much as I like her.

If Emmett hadn't spotted me I'd be backing out of the room right about now. Ingrained propriety and all-around kindness have me feeling a little bit bad for the way I acted

47

on the phone, and in the gas station. It really doesn't matter if I like this woman, she is my boss's daughter.

"Jake," Emmett says, sending his bright smile my way. The color of the bruise on his cheek has deepened since yesterday evening, a purple-blue the shade of an angry summer thunderstorm.

I duck my head at him and walk all the way into the room. "Emmett, hello. You already look better than yesterday."

"Pfft." Emmett waves his hand. "Lie. I look like shit."

He offers a handshake, and it's a relief. The guy loves a good handshake. I've known him for years, and I see him at least five days a week, sometimes more, and he always shakes my hand.

I cross in front of Colbie, the burn of her eyes on my back.

Emmett's hand is callused, like my own. "I want to hear about how work went today, but first—" He gestures behind me. "Meet my daughter, Colbie."

I drop Emmett's hand and step back so I can see her. "Nice to meet you, Colbie. I'm Jake."

Colbie's mouth drops open, but she closes it quickly. The muscles in her jaw tighten like she's physically straining to keep something inside.

Emmett doesn't seem to notice the death rays shooting from his daughter's eyes. "Jake's my foreman. He's been with me for more than ten years."

Colbie plants her feet on the ground and pushes to stand. Even at full height, the top of her head only reaches the middle of my chest. I'm used to being taller than nearly everyone else in the room.

To me, Emmett says, "Jake, you probably recognize

Colbie from her picture." To Colbie, he says, "I keep a photo of you on my desk."

Colbie looks at her dad as if this surprises her. She recovers, offering her hand up to me, and I lower mine down to her.

"Nice to meet you, Jake," Colbie's voice is sweet, but the look on her face is deadly. She squeezes my hand tightly, though she's a long way from inflicting any pain. Because of the way we're standing, Emmett can't see his daughter's expression. He can only see mine, so I school my features into something open and friendly.

"It's a pleasure to meet you, Colbie. Please let me know if you need anything while you're in town. I'd be happy to recommend some restaurants. The Joint makes its own burger seasoning, and their *cheeseburgers* and *milkshakes* are so good you might cry."

She drops my hand, looks me dead in the eyes, and mouths *You're an asshole*.

It's everything I can do to keep from bursting out laughing. It's possible this woman is a little bit of bold, wrapped up in a very attractive package. Lethal combination.

"Jake and Colbie, take a seat." Emmett points to the place Colbie had been sitting. There's a second chair, and a small round table. Colbie leads the way. She sits up straight, as if there is a thread connecting the top of her head to the ceiling. This irritates me, mostly because it calls to attention my poor posture. I keep my eyes on Emmett and surreptitiously straighten my spine.

"Ok you two, listen up." Emmett looks at each of us in turn. I'm getting the sense he's about to drop a bomb on us.

I lean forward.

"I'm not able to work for the foreseeable future."

He says it casually, as if he's asking me to run to the

store for an item forgotten from his grocery list. As if he didn't put his entire savings into starting the company, and twenty years of sweat equity. The custom home job is Emmett's baby. This isn't slabs of concrete or retaining walls, this is the kind of job Emmett can point to later, when he's bidding on bigger jobs. It's a bullet point on a resume, the beginning of a custom home builder business.

"Oh-kay?" Colbie sounds as confused as I feel. "I'm sorry to hear that."

"Why?" The left side of my face scrunches as I try to understand what he's not saying.

Emmett's happy-go-lucky disposition falters. "I've been through a lot of testing today, and the doctors think my seizure happened because I was dehydrated, overheated, and my blood sugar was very low." He looks at the ceiling, choosing his words carefully. "There's no way for them to tell if it will happen again, and that knock I took on the way down really did me in. There isn't anywhere safe to fall on a construction site, and now I have to start dealing with insurance, and that's just another headache I don't need."

I grimace, trying not to remember the wound and the blood that gushed from it. Bright red at the site, deep red on his clothing.

I slump in my chair. Screw having a good posture. "The job, boss?"

"That's why I asked you here," he says, addressing me only. "We need to talk about the Russell house. We need to make sure we have all our ducks in a row going forward. The Russells need to know Jones Construction is still able to deliver."

"You know we can," I say confidently.

"I know," he nods. He turns his full attention on Colbie. "I was thinking we should put another Jones at the helm."

Um...what?

Colbie, the person who knows nothing about construction and custom homes? At the helm?

Emmett can't hear Colbie's intake of breath because he's not close enough, but I'm a mere eighteen inches from her, and it makes its way over to me loud and clear.

An Emmy.

An Oscar.

Whatever award it is for outstanding actor, I should receive it. I do not scowl, I do not frown. I do not show dismay or shock, or any of the negative emotions tumbling around inside of me.

"Dad." Shock winds its way through Colbie's tone. She should definitely not be an actress. Or play poker. Ever. "I have a job in Phoenix. A business. I have...I have..."

"I know, I know. You have Brad. You have a life."

The indignation I'm feeling makes way for the tiniest bit of relief at knowing she has *Brad*. It's good for my brain, and my second brain in my pants, to know she's off-limits. Not like she wasn't anyway, but still.

Colbie shakes her head, eyes wide with astonishment. "Why me?"

"You're smart. You have a good head for business. You used to come with me to jobsites." He smiles wistfully, as if watching a memory play like a home video in his mind. He looks down at his hands, folded on the stark white hospital sheet, and then he says, "I fully expect you to pass." Suddenly this man who has been so influential in my life, who has literally shown up for me when my own father couldn't, looks like he is at a loss for words. He lifts his gaze, and I see in his eyes how desperately he loves his daughter, how much he wants to be near her.

And Colbie? She holds Emmett's stare as the seconds

tick by. His gaze softens, the corners of his eyes coming to pleading points. Colbie's expression remains unchanged. I'm over here about to capitulate to whatever Emmett could possibly ask of me, and his own daughter is wearing her ice queen crown.

What the hell is she waiting for? Why doesn't she just tell him no and let him ask me? Why is she dragging him through each painful second? Every person in this room knows what her answer will be.

"I'll do it."

Her response reverberates off the walls.

My neck heats as I gape at her. Award rescinded. I have blown my cover.

Emmett's relief, and the jubilation that follows, billows out of him like smoke from a chimney. "That's great," he booms. He smiles so big it looks like the corners of his lips might actually touch his ears. "Jake, I know you've already met Colbie, but let's try this again. Jake," he directs a stiff palm at me. His chest puffs with pride as his flattened palm shifts to my left. "Meet my daughter, Colbie. Your new boss."

•••

The cool evening air is welcome after the frigid temperature of the hospital.

I can't get away from the arctic air entirely. An ice queen walks beside me.

Either that, or she's in shock. Colbie agreed before she knew the requirements of the job. Once Emmett told her it could take as little as ten months, or up to two years because of the complexity of this type of job, she looked like she was going to faint. If she hadn't been sitting, she probably would have hit the deck.

I'd like to know how it is that Colbie can walk away from Phoenix and make a temporary move to Green Haven. According to Emmett, she has a life, and a job. A Brad. *Ugh, what a name.* I picture a Lacoste polo, collar popped. Boat shoes, even though he's in a landlocked state. I came across plenty of Brads in college.

Colbie pauses a few feet from the entrance, digging in her purse. She spares me the most fleeting of glances as she tucks her keys into the palm of her hand and presses a button on a key fob. A few rows away, her car beeps, lights flashing.

A flush of embarrassment steals over the back of my neck. My truck has a blanket across the back seat because the seat is ripped up from years of tossing tools back there. I do my best to keep it clean, but I can't keep it from looking used.

I stop at the curb. Colbie stops, too. I'm not sure what to say.

"Well," I tuck my hands into my jeans. My shoulders hover up near my earlobes. "See you around the jobsite, Princess."

Her eyes narrow. "See you there, Not Blake."

I do my best to keep from smiling. In a twisted way, I like verbally sparring with her. She's perpetually ready with a return barb. I spend a majority of my time around the crew of guys I work with, and a ten-year-old. Both are great, but neither are an intelligent, attractive woman.

I can admit she possesses both those qualities and still generally dislike her.

I'm walking away when she says, "Is the jobsite operational on Fridays?"

I whip around. "Huh?"

"Friday? The day after Thursday, but before Saturday?"

The remark is snarky, but there's this look on her face, this vulnerability. It calls to me on a biological level, something like *man protect woman from all that could harm her.*

Fucking cavemen.

She's waiting for me to answer, her eyes brown and warm like buttered toffee, head tilted. It's the kind of look that could make a man forget his own name.

"No," I grunt. It's a lie. A lie, lie, lie, and now I can't correct it because I'll look like an idiot who really doesn't understand the order of days of the week.

"Ok," she says brightly, pulling her shoulders back. "I'll see you there on Monday."

"Right," I nod. "Bye." Then I hightail it out of there in my loud, rumbling, taped seat truck.

I call my mom and ask her to keep Robbie for another hour, then I send a text to my best friend Rhodes telling him I'm grabbing a beer if he wants to join me.

By the time I pull into the parking lot at the bar I'm already feeling bad about lying to Colbie, even when I didn't really mean to. I'm also slightly annoyed at myself that I can't even tell a little lie and not feel like I should do thirty-to-life.

Shit. I'll have to make this right.

I send a text to Victoria requesting Colbie's phone number.

I can't keep her off the jobsite, even if I want to.

Chapter 6

Colbie

"I swear I've never seen anybody look at me with such open hatred." I balance my phone in the center of my steering wheel so I can see Christina better. I called her the second I got in my car after Jake drove off in that big, loud truck of his. I'm still sitting here, the large tan hospital building looming in front of me. I suddenly have a lot to do, but calling Christina was first on that list. Mostly because she is my business partner and I'm going to have to figure out how to do my regular job, plus manage the construction of a custom home.

I'm good. It's fine. Everything is fine.

Christina sucks an unidentified liquid through a metal straw. "You're going to do both jobs? How?" Her eyebrows pinch together. Of course she's focusing on the most diffi-cult part of all this. I'd rather stick to lighter topics, like how Jake wishes I'd take my broom and fly home.

My hair swirls in my face from a breeze pushing through my open car windows. I push it back and assure her it will all work out. "We'll need to hire that third person we talked about. Until then, I'll do the business stuff at night.

And construction during the day." It's not like I plan on having any type of personal life while I'm in Green Haven.

Christina rests her straw on her lower lip as she decides how to answer. "You didn't have to say yes to your dad." It's her way of telling me I've brought all this on myself.

I prop my elbow on the top of my door and lean my cheek on a closed fist. "I didn't feel like I could say no."

"Seriously? You've made a whole pastime out of telling that man no. You're like a no Olympian."

"That's exactly why I had to say yes." As an added bonus, me saying yes made Jake's eyeballs bulge and the vein in his neck throb. "I was looking at him in that hospital bed, and it really hit me that we have no idea how much time we have left. Any of us could be gone in an instant." The backs of my eyes sting. "I keep picturing him having a seizure and hitting his head, then falling on the dirt." The events play over and over in my mind, and the picture always shifts right after, to me as a little girl on his shoulders. I haven't thought of him in this capacity in years, but now the memory has been dragged to the surface in stark relief. "What if he'd died? I would feel so guilty. Then I'd be saddled with that guilt for the rest of my life." And I'd be robbed of the chance to make things right. To love him. To let him love me. That feels like too great a price to pay just because I'm afraid of getting hurt.

"Ahh," Christina nods her head. "So you're actually doing something selfish by staying there and seeing this job through for him. You're taking care of future you."

I nod, accepting her convoluted reasoning. "Thank you for understanding." I perform a half-bow in the confines of my car.

Christina adopts a serious expression. I know what's

coming. "Why did you really say yes to your dad?" Her eyebrows lift with her question.

I make a face, forming a microphone with my fist and tapping my furled hand with two fingers from my opposite hand. "Is this thing on?"

Christina ignores my joke. She's like a dog who has located a buried bone. "I know you were put in an awkward place with the way he asked you, but you could've said no." She points at the screen. "And you didn't. Why?"

"I already said—"

She's shaking her head. "That's the easy, most obvious answer. Try answering honestly. You don't even have to say it to me. At some point, you might want to try saying it to yourself."

"Someone went to therapy today." I sigh, and look outside my car. At the trees, leaves dancing in the light from the parking lot lamps. The bright, crescent moon. The colored lights of a row of fast food restaurants adjacent to the hospital. Anywhere but at my best friend.

"Another defensive answer," she shoots back.

"I'll think about it when I'm alone later tonight, all nestled in my questionably clean sheets at the hotel."

Her nose wrinkles. "I saw a documentary once—"

I hold up a hand. "I'm going to have to stop you right there. Because, unless a pillow top mattress with high thread count sheets suddenly appears out of thin air, I'm sleeping on that hotel mattress."

Christina pulls two fingers across her lips, zipping them. "Tell me about Jake. The man who hates you more than I hate beets."

This, I can do.

I touch my cheeks with my hands and widen my eyes,

Home Alone style without all the shouting. "The guy is massive, Christina. Like...like some kind of Norse god."

"Thor." She says it like *duh.*

"If Thor had brown hair, obnoxiously long eyelashes, and a dimple in his left cheek, then yes."

She snorts. "You just described your type."

I roll my eyes. "Hardly. You know I go for the clean-cut, good boy type."

She snorts a second time. In the background, Daniel asks if she's ok. "Fine, babe," she calls, grinning. "How are those good boys working out for you?" she asks me.

"Clean-cut men aside, pleasant disposition is my non-negotiable." I think back to how he spoke to Martha in the gas station. "He might actually be an ok person. I over-heard him being kind to an old lady." He also looked upset when my dad asked me to take over the job. Did he feel slighted? He's the foreman, so it's safe to assume the job would've gone to him. Maybe he knew my dad was going to ask me, so when he saw me at Martha's he was primed for general unpleasantness aimed in my direction. That still doesn't explain the way he spoke to me on the phone yesterday.

"So far it's just you he's been less than pleasant toward?"

"My sample size is tiny, but yes. I'm telling you, the guy wishes I'd never come here." I blow out a heavy breath that vibrates my lips. "He probably wishes bad things on me. I bet he's already fashioned a doll and he's poking it with needles."

Christina's laughter tumbles into my car and out into the cool night air. "What do you suppose he used to make the doll?"

"Probably gnawed on a tree limb."

She laughs harder. "This guy really brings something out in you."

"I know." I don't like it. It feels a little raw, this desire to bite back at him, to say how I feel. Three interactions with Jake and I feel a loss of control in his presence. "My dormant inner snark has been waiting for him my whole life."

"Or maybe he's exactly what you need."

I groan. "Don't even go there."

"What?" Christina's hands lift like she's innocent. "I'm just saying, he's nothing like anybody you've dated before. Look at you, getting all riled up just talking about him."

I roll my eyes. "It's not any of that, I assure you. I'm angry with the entire male population at the moment."

She looks at me disbelievingly. "Ohh so you're still upset about Brad, and you're taking it out on him?"

"Who?"

"Brad."

"Who?"

"STOP IT."

I snicker. "I'm sure I'm not still upset about Brad. I am, however, feeling...verklempt."

Christina sighs. "You're supposed to give me a warning when I need my dictionary."

"It means I'm overcome by emotion and I have no words."

"Why not just say that?"

"Why say with many words what I can say in one?"

"Ok, smarty pants. You're verklempt. Got it. What are you going to do about Jake?"

"There's nothing to *do* about him."

"You could *do* him."

I give her my 'come on' face, but in my mind all I see are

59

Jake's forearms, the muscles ropy and flexing when his hands fist. "He's my employee now. And I'm taking a break from dating. From men. From anything romantic in general."

"When did you decide that?"

"Two seconds ago."

Christina nods. "Not the worst idea you've had. Once bitten, twice shy."

"If that's our equation, I'm quadruple bitten, eight shy."

She smiles at me like the sad, pitiful creature I am. "What can I do for you?"

"Support me as I embark on what is possibly a foolish endeavor. And pick up the pieces when I inevitably implode because I have no idea how to even start learning about custom homes." What am I doing? Why am I doing this?

Christina gives me a look like the answer is obvious. "Uhhh try the World Wide Web?"

"Yes, of course. I have a non-romantic date with the internet. And probably a bookstore for manuals on construction sites that I'll have to keep handy and hidden." I stifle a yawn. Physically I didn't do much today, but emotionally I'm drained.

"When do you start?" Christina asks. "You're going to stay in a hotel for months?"

I rub my face. There is a lot to think through, and it all starts with lodging. "Tomorrow is Friday, which seems like a weird day to start. My dad didn't give me much to go on. He was kind of out of it at the end. Maybe a painkiller was kicking in." I sneak a glance at my watch. It's only eight, but my body thinks it's midnight. "As soon as I hang up with you I'm going to look for a place to rent. Grab some dinner. Maybe tip some cows." That last one was a joke. I don't know if tipping cows is a real thing. Also, it sounds mean.

"There are cows?"

"Not that I've seen." I look around as if cows will magically appear out of thin air. In front of a hospital. Off one of the busiest roads in Green Haven.

"When are you telling your mom?"

I groan. "Never."

She laughs.

"Soon. By Saturday, at the latest, because that's when I was supposed to go home."

Daniel appears behind Christina. He rests his head on her shoulder, and she smiles like her whole night just got better. "Hey, Colbie," Daniel says, "do you mind if I steal my wife away? I just finished the marinara but I think it's missing something. Christina is the marinara whisperer."

I wave a hand. "Steal away."

Daniel places a light kiss on Christina's cheek and retreats.

"Sugar," Christina whispers at me.

"Huh?"

"Sugar is the secret ingredient in the marinara sauce. He thinks I have some kind of magic touch, but it is literally just a pinch of sugar."

I cover my laughter with my hand. "Has he not seen you add the sugar to the sauce?"

"He leaves the kitchen. He says he likes the mystery."

"You guys are weird." And amazing. And so damn lucky.

Christina hears everything I don't say, and responds with, "I know."

We say goodbye and I slip my phone in my purse. I spend a few seconds looking up at the third floor of the hospital. If I'm thinking of the layout correctly, my dad is in the fourth room to the left of the end of the building. Even if I have it wrong, the point is that he is there, physically close for the first time in so long. The reality of that overwhelms me.

I was hardly able to hug him when I saw him. I was being careful with him, but I was also being careful with me. My heart. This man used to give me piggyback rides and now I can barely accept a simple hug from him.

Not because I don't want to, but because I have the hardest time allowing him to love me. And I hate how much I still want him to, despite all feelings and actions to the contrary. Why is that? How can a person be an adult, and still have so much of a child left inside them?

This is exactly what Christina meant when she said I needed to be honest with myself about why I decided to stay and help my dad. Working on my relationship with him is one thing. Staying where he lives and taking over his business is quite another.

Chapter 7

Jake

"Dude. Stop."

"I'm not kidding."

"Emmett would never—"

"He did."

Rhodes, my best friend since forever, whistles disbelievingly. "What was Emmett thinking?"

"Probably that he wants to keep her in town, and this is how to do it."

"Do you think there'll be problems having a female on the construction site?" Rhodes' eyebrows lift. He works in a male-dominated industry also, and his mind has likely gone to a place where mine hasn't ventured until now.

"You mean, there are too many lions and only one lioness?"

Rhodes laughs, shaking his head. "You and Robbie watch too many nature shows."

"I don't think it'll be a problem. She has a boyfriend." I rub at my eyes with the heels of my hands. "I can already tell it's going to be one hell of a ride from here on out."

"Are you going to have trouble taking orders from her?"

"I have a lifetime of experience taking orders from women." Usually my mom and sister are at least smiling or don't look like they want to kill me when they're telling me what to do. Unlike Colbie, who I believe would enjoy watching me choke on one of these chicken wings I'm eating.

I guess she *really* hated being called princess.

Rhodes shakes his head. "I meant because she doesn't know what she's doing on a construction site, and you do." His gaze flickers over my shoulder. His mouth purses, lips quivering like he's suppressing a laugh.

I turn around on my stool and see what has Rhodes laughing. Kiersten Stanley, and her crew of moms, have just walked in. I whip around before they spot me. They mean well, but they're like a pack of hyenas egging each other on. Kiersten has made it known time after time that she would jump my bones—her words—if I'd be down.

I am not down. I do not want my bones jumped by Kiersten. There's nothing wrong with her, per se. She's attractive. Her son is in Robbie's class, but he's not all that nice to Robbie. Also, her voice is like nails on a chalkboard. And she loves talking shit about people, which I hate.

Unless I'm with Rhodes, eating spicy wings and drinking a cold beer, and the person I'm shit-talking about is none other than Colbie Jones.

The only reason I'm here is Colbie, because she has burrowed under my skin in almost no time. If Kiersten makes her way over here and starts giving me that look she's always sending my way, I'm going to blame that on Colbie also.

I still can't believe Emmett is handing Colbie this job. My ego is wounded, and underneath it all, my feelings are hurt. I've been working for him for Robbie's whole life. He's the reason I have Robbie. Why would he ask Colbie to take over? She's going to run Jones Construction straight into the ground. Is that what he wants?

I lean back on my stool and glance around Short Stack, the little dive bar we've been coming to since we turned twenty-one. It's the kind of place where the bar top is perpetually greasy even if it's recently been wiped down. There's an oversized corkboard on the back wall with a large sign above it that says 'Wanted'. It's covered in hand written signs declaring various things people are seeking.

Wanted: person to mow my lawn weekly.
Wanted: three-drawer dresser, gently used.
Wanted: a woman who doesn't
bitch or nag.
Wanted: a man who does shit without needing to
be bitched at or nagged.

Those last two are related. Who doesn't like to watch a marital spat play out on paper for anybody to see?

Rhodes crunches through a mouthful of pretzels and wipes the crumbs off on his jeans. "How's the Russell house coming along?"

"Good so far, but it's only just begun. I'm sure something bad will happen. Too many moving parts for there not to be a problem." I wonder what Colbie will do when one of the inevitable problems arises? Jones Construction has never done a job of this size. The Russells came to Green Haven talking about building a second home, and Emmett entered a bid without much confidence of being chosen. There had been other bids, most notably one from the same contractor who built The Orchard in Sierra Grande. I was certain he'd win, not only because The Orchard has become locally famous, but because it's run by a member of the Hayden family, and everyone knows the Haydens are Arizona royalty.

Then the Russells shocked us by choosing Jones Construction.

We've never done a job of this size, let alone a job that required so much collaboration with other people. There's more that goes into building a house than I could've ever guessed. I'm learning a lot, and I'm tucking away every nugget of information for the future. One day, I'm going to work for myself. Maybe I would've worked for Emmett for the rest of my life, but Emmett's injury lit a fire under my ass. I have to look forward, especially if Emmett's giving this job to Colbie, instead of me.

Rhodes shifts in his seat. "I still can't believe that rich couple blew into town and decided to build a massive house. What asshole even approved the building of the place?"

"Assholes," I correct. "You need all kinds of permits and inspections for a place like that."

The place is a compound. All the way to the east a few miles outside of town, where there aren't any other homes. Why they chose that area, I can't begin to imagine. Nor do I think they'll be on their own out there for long. Not with the way this town is beginning to sprawl. We're constantly fielding calls about new work. Emmett has been so busy he's had to turn down jobs, something he swore he'd never thought would happen. He calls his business's early days 'sparse', and damn do I know what he means. Things are good for me and Robbie now, but once upon a time, they weren't. I was a single dad juggling diapers, formula, and doctor's visits without insurance.

'Didn't have two dimes to rub together' wasn't just a saying; it was my reality.

I finish my beer and ask for a water. Rhodes isn't much of a drinker himself, and always keeps it to one. He gets up for work before the sun rises, and goes wherever he's sent. He's a lineman, and there's always a lot of work to be done. Climbing those big electrical poles is a dangerous job, but it pays well. He must have a lot of money in savings because the guy never buys himself anything. He's been wearing the same ball cap for as long as I can remember, though he promises he washes it.

I sip my water and tell Rhodes, "The Russell wife said she wanted to live in the woods."

Rhodes's expression says *come on* mixed with *what the fuck*. "Did anybody tell her she should've gone further north? There aren't woods around here."

I grin. "There are some pine and cottonwoods around the place. But not many, and not for long. If she went south five hundred feet she'd be in the desert."

Rhodes smacks his leg and laughs. "I'd like to be there the moment she realizes she essentially lives in the desert." He rattles the ice in his water and tips the cup to his mouth. "What's Emmett's daughter like?" he asks, crunching through a piece of ice.

"Don't even think about it," I reply, sharper than I intended. Rhodes is a good guy, and there isn't any reason why he shouldn't be interested in Colbie, but just... No. Plus, she has Brad.

Rhodes raises his eyebrows, and I try to explain. "She's a piece of work. You should've heard her hassling Martha about coffee creamer." Colbie was actually perfectly polite, and almost apologetic about the creamer, but I feel desperate to dislike her.

I flick my middle finger on the bar in exasperation. "And now she's taking over Jones Construction's biggest job like it's nothing. She doesn't know shit about the business, and now she's my boss? Come the fuck on."

Rhodes blinks in surprise, slowly sipping his water. "I don't think I've ever heard you say that many words consecutively."

I slide my water glass through the sweaty moisture it left on the bar top. "This woman isn't difficult to be mad at."

Rhodes eyes me knowingly, and it only manages to piss me off more. "You sure it's her you're mad at?"

"What is that supposed to mean?"

"You've known her for one day." He shrugs. "Sounds to me like you're mad at the wrong person." Rhodes stands and throws down a twenty. "That should cover yours, too. Go home and meditate or something. You're snare drum tight."

I flip him the bird behind his back.

He points left as he walks away, directly to the mirror that runs the length of the bar, and returns my gesture.

Then, as if the universe really just wants to fuck me tonight, I catch Kiersten's gaze in the mirror. She waves and offers a tentative smile. I return her greeting with a head nod and quickly avert my gaze. I don't want to be rude, but I don't want to encourage her either.

By some stroke of luck Kiersten does not approach me, and I'm feeling grateful about that. I would be gracious and kind because that's how I was raised to behave. Unless I'm in the presence of my new boss, apparently. That woman already seems capable of taking my ingrained manners and tossing them in a blender. Maybe Rhodes is right. I should start meditating.

I finish my water, retrieve Robbie from my mom's house,

and we go home together. We run through the nighttime routine, watch a thirty minute show on national parks because Robbie loves anything having to do with nature, and I carry Robbie to his bed when he nods off on the couch.

I tuck him in just the way he likes, with the comforter around his shoulders. I pause in the doorway, glancing at his face bathed in a swathe of light from the hall.

Everyone says he looks just like me, but that's because they don't know his mother. If they did, they'd see her in the shape of his eyes and his cheekbones.

Before I go to bed, I pack Robbie's lunch for the next day. I want him to get in the habit of doing it himself, but sometimes I like to do it for him. I think about Colbie while I'm assembling the lunchmeat sandwich. I'd better tell her the jobsite is operational tomorrow. If she finds out I didn't, she's going to think I'm keeping her from the job, and that's only going to look bad for me. It'll show how sore this loser really is.

I finish up Robbie's lunch, tidy up the kitchen, and shoot Colbie a text.

> This is Jake. We're working tomorrow. There isn't an address yet, but it's a few miles off the 287. We start when the sun's up.

I don't start that early, because I have to get Robbie to school, but the rest of the crew will be there. Normally Emmett would be there with them.

I stay up for a half hour, reading a book and waiting for her response.

None arrives, and finally, I go to bed.

Chapter 8

Colbie

The check-in area at the hotel is neat and tidy. The couch is an ivory and cream damask, flanked by walnut side tables with ornate legs and shiny gold hardware. Behind the check-in counter, the walls are papered with a rose print, and the rest of the walls are painted a delicate baby pink. I can't tell if the front desk is an antique, or just made to look like one.

Keli, the same woman who checked me in last night, sits at the front desk again today. She grins widely as I approach, her light brown chin-length hair swishing along her delicate jawbone.

"Hello, Miss Jones," she greets. "What can I do for you this morning?"

"Two things, please. The first, do you know where I can get a phone charger? I know I packed one, but I can't find it anywhere, and my phone is dead."

"There's a Walgreens on Fifth and Elm." With a flattened palm she gestures in what I assume is the direction of the Walgreens.

"Thanks. Now, the second request is a little odd."

She crosses her arms and makes a sound like nothing I say can possibly surprise her. "Try me."

"It turns out I'm going to be staying in town longer than expected. Do you happen to know of anybody who is renting out their house? Or has a room available I can rent?" That second one makes me cringe, but I can't imagine there's a large market for VRBO's or Airbnb's in Green Haven. Becoming somebody's roommate might be the best I can get.

Her head tips sideways and her mouth opens, but she gets caught on a thought and closes her lips. Her head shakes back-and-forth the tiniest amount, as if she is denying herself.

"Just say it," I singsong.

"I...," she hesitates, and continues after I nod at her encouragingly. "I know Emmett Jones is your dad. And I know he has a big house with a lot of rooms. So if you're looking for a place to stay..." her voice trails off and she lets her statement hang in the air between us.

"Both those things are true," I start slowly, weighing my words. For all I know, this woman is related to Victoria. Which would also make her related to Greer. It's a small town, increasing the probability that a person might run into Victoria's relatives. Or friends. Or anybody Victoria adjacent.

I snap on my most earnest smile. "I want to be certain I give my dad and Victoria their space while he is convalescing. Sometimes situations like that can be stressful, and I don't want to add to the stress." I shrug as if my point is a forgone conclusion. "So, is there any chance you know of anybody who would like to let me rent their home?"

I really hope she says yes. I cannot stay with my dad and Victoria. I can't go from rarely seeing my dad, to living with him. As for Victoria...I don't even know what to think about her. Greer, too. There's too much history for me to suddenly become the fourth member of their household.

"You know," Keli pulls her purse from under her desk and riffles through it. "My parents are snowbirds. Normally they'd be leaving Minnesota and coming here by the end of next month, but they are staying there this winter because my sister's having a baby." She taps her cheek as she considers. "They might not mind making a little money off the place while they're not using it."

Would you look at that? Maybe the universe wants me here. Surly foreman and no real knowledge of custom home construction be damned. "I'd really appreciate if you could ask them. I'm supposed to check out tomorrow."

"I'm sending my mom a text," Keli explains, fingers flying over her phone. "I'll let you know what she says."

"Thank you, thank you so much. You have no idea how helpful this is."

"In all honesty, this would be helping my parents out, too. My dad has been complaining about the increase in property taxes this year. He'd be pretty happy to offset that cost." She pokes at her phone screen and smiles over the desk at me. "Sent. Now we wait for a response."

"That's gre—" A loud rumbling in my stomach breaks through the word. "Good Lord," I press a hand to my stomach, embarrassed. "I guess that sandwich I had for dinner last night wasn't enough."

Keli points out the front door of the hotel. "Go grab some breakfast at Honeybee. You'll love it there. Everyone does."

I thank her and exit the front doors, pausing on the sidewalk to grab my sunglasses from my purse. The sun here is as relentless as it is in Phoenix, even if it's not as hot. I slip them on and look left to right, searching out signage or a marker for something called Honeybee.

Half a block down, a large, gold letter H grabs my attention. It's on a white background on a sign that swings from a chain. Bingo.

I peek in the store windows as I make my way down the street. Green Haven is actually very cute, and not nearly as backwards as I thought it was when I was younger. I'd wanted to vilify it because it felt like this place stole my dad from me. The same goes for Victoria and Greer, probably, and that's a pretty tough pill to swallow.

The hard truth is that nobody stole my dad from me. He left of his own volition. Now, in a twist of events so unlikely I could've never in my wildest dreams guess they would occur, he is asking something of me. Something big. The angry adult inside me wanted to refuse last night. The little girl inside me wants so badly to deliver.

I want to do a good job. I want to show him how capable I am. How amazing and wonderful.

I can step into alien situations and make them work for me.

I can learn how to build a home. How to pour concrete, and deal with contractors, plumbers, electricians, architects, and anybody else.

I want to show him I am the best person, and he never should've left me.

⁛

A bell tinkles when I enter Honeybee.

"Hey there, darlin'," an older gentleman says. He waves from his place near a soda fountain.

"Hello," I wave back, my head on a swivel as I take in

the gorgeous space. An entire wall is covered in matte black honeycomb shaped tile, and the wood floors are the prettiest rustic brown, with shades of black running through it like veins.

"Take a seat wherever you like," the older man says, coming to the front of the restaurant. "Though, if you don't mind, I'd like to make a request that you sit at the counter." He motions to the side, where a low-slung white quartz counter takes up most of the area. Beyond it is the kitchen, with a rectangular cut-out window. Through it I spy a man with a red bandana standing over a grill. "You're the only person in here," the sweet old man says, "and I'm in the mood to chat."

"What if I'm not in the mood?" I ask with an impish grin. I'm already making my way to where he's directed me.

"Unless it involves tape, I've got a hell of a time keeping my trap shut." The old man steps behind the counter. His steps are slow and purposeful, with a little bit of an old man shuffle. He doesn't have much hair, and what he does have falls over his ears in white wisps.

I settle on a round black leather seat, taking a menu from the metal clip affixed to the edge. "Should I be concerned that I'm the only person in here?"

"Not at all," he says, leaning an age-spotted forearm on the counter. "You wandered in after the breakfast rush, but before lunch." He points back at himself. "Jiminy."

"That's your name?"

"Ever since I can remember."

"Jiminy," I try it out. "Like the cricket?"

"I suppose so," he answers. He turns toward the coffee maker. "Would it also be all right if I suppose you would like some coffee today?"

"Please," I say, louder and more forcefully than I mean to. "Please," I repeat, using my indoor voice.

"You're in luck," he says over his shoulder. "I've just brewed a fresh pot."

"Bless you, dear man." I take the steaming mug of caffeine from his outstretched hands. I'm dying to hear details about this place, and Jiminy himself, but I don't want to be impolite by asking outright.

"Need some half-and-half?" Jiminy holds up a carton.

"Black coffee is fine." I don't dare ask for a form of milk that was not taken from a cow. What if that's a touchy subject in Green Haven? I can't make an enemy out of Jiminy, not when I have the budding feeling he might become an ally to me in this new territory I'm finding myself in.

"May I recommend the omelet? We fill it with veggies from the garden behind the restaurant."

"Say no more," I answer, tucking the menu back where I found it.

"You must be Emmett's other daughter," Jiminy says after he hands the slip of paper with my order on it back to the cook.

My initial reaction is irritation and discomfort, but it's not the old man's fault, so I very carefully tuck my real feelings behind a polite mask.

I take a big glug from my coffee and set it down. Maybe by the time I get to the bottom of this cup, I'll begin to feel halfway human. "Do people in this town have magic abilities?"

Using two fingers he scratches at his head just above his ear. "Not that I know of."

"You're the second person this morning to know who I am without me telling them."

He looks apologetic. "Sorry about that. I guess you're a bit famous right now."

"Why is that?"

"You've just taken over one of the biggest businesses in Green Haven."

My jaw drops. "How could you possibly know that?" I point back at myself. "*I* barely know that."

"Bartender over at Short Stack overheard Jake and his buddy Rhodes discussing it last night."

Great. I upset the guy so much I drove him to drink.

I wrap my hands around my warm mug. "Do you all get awards for fastest time it takes you to spread gossip around here?"

He grins. "I like you, little lady. You've got spunk." He tops off my coffee. Jiminy pours one for himself.

I lift the cup, both in cheers and in thanks.

"Nice to have you in here right now," he says, motioning out at the rest of the place. "This time of day is always boring. I like to be on the move." He moves his arms like the wheels of a locomotive. "Most people have made their way to work by now, 'specially that new crew of yours. Those guys are on the jobsite by the time the sun comes up. We're not even open at that time, but as soon as we're open one of the crew members shows up with a breakfast order for everybody."

I sputter on the hot liquid in my mouth as Jiminy's words register in my brain. "It's a Friday."

"All day until midnight."

"So, it's a workday?"

"I'd say so, but"—he shrugs—"what do I know? This place is open seven days a week."

"For my dad's crew, I mean. Has someone from the

Jones construction crew already been in here this morning?"

"Order up," the cook hollers. Jiminy retrieves my breakfast from the little window and slides it in front of me.

"Not yet." He sets down an extra napkin. "They're running late, but that's to be expected, I guess. Emmett being gone means their ship is without a captain." He surveys me. "Though, I guess their captain is sitting right here, letting her breakfast get cold."

My fingers vibrate with anger as I unwrap the paper napkin ring from around my napkin and utensils. "I didn't realize I had to captain the ship starting today." I spread my napkin on my lap, pulling in a deep breath. I don't want to look like some slouch who didn't show up for her first day of work, but I also don't want to give away that Jake lied to me. The natural follow-up question to that revelation would be *why?*

I should've asked more questions of my dad yesterday afternoon in that hospital room, but I'd been overwhelmed. All those machines, the *beep beep beep*, and the sight of my dad, it all came together like a multi-car accident. Not to mention Jake, sitting a mere two feet from me, hostility rolling off him in waves. It was like my brain short-circuited, and I said yes without spending much time considering the details. Most notably, when am I expected to start?

I wish I'd thought to ask Jake for his phone number. If I had it, and if my phone battery weren't dead, I'd be calling him now and ripping into him for keeping me off the jobsite on purpose.

Dick move.

The crew might already know about me taking over this job, and if they do, now they think I can't be bothered to show up.

"Eat," Jiminy gently reminds me.

I smile gratefully, picking up my fork and taking a bite of my omelet. "Oh my gosh." I cup my hand around my full mouth. Jiminy grins proudly. He knows how good it is.

At the front of the restaurant, the bell chimes. In my peripheral vision I see a person walk in, but I don't bother to look who it is because I'm too busy eating.

"Well well, there you are." I can hear the smile in Jiminy's tone. "I've been waiting for you to come in."

Loud footsteps, to the point of nearly stomping, make their way through the place. If I didn't know any better I'd think we were being approached by a stray elephant.

Jiminy stretches out his hand over the counter. "Give me the order," he says to whoever is behind me, "and the cook will get started."

I take another bite of my omelet, looking down at my plate as the clomp of boots gets louder and louder behind me. Suddenly a large body takes up my left field of vision.

I know who it is, and my whole body warms with irritation.

Jake leans on the counter, inches from me. He wears a gray t-shirt and jeans, and smells like someone doused him in sawdust and sandalwood and whatever else makes a man smell so damn delicious.

The fact that I'm thinking this way about my saboteur makes me angrier than I was five seconds ago.

Jake clears his throat in an obvious way.

I glance over and roll my eyes.

"Trying to see the back of your head, Princess?" Jake sits back, smirking as he folds his long legs under the average-sized counter. One stool separates us.

"I bet those long legs of yours would fit better at a booth.

There's one free all the way over there," I point to the furthest corner of the place.

He doesn't act like he's heard me. Instead, he props an elbow on the counter and leans forward, taking up half the space between us. "The crew and I waited around for our new boss, but when she didn't show we decided to get some food." His chin tips up and his tongue slips out to moisten his lower lip. "Lo and behold, here she is, enjoying herself a leisurely breakfast. Though I believe this would be called 'brunch'. I guess I can tell the crew I found our boss."

I take a deep breath and stow my sharp desire to toss my coffee in his lap. As much as I detest the idea, Jake might be the person who ends up helping me the most on the job, and I'd rather not have to mend many fences when it comes to him. "Last night you told me you didn't work today." My voice is tight, my annoyance clear. I don't mind him knowing I'm pissed at him.

"And then I texted you around ten-thirty last night telling you I was wrong. I sent the address and what time you should be there." He lightly smacks the counter with a flat palm. "I called you this morning, too. Straight to voicemail."

"My phone is dead. And how did you get my number?"

"Victoria."

I flinch. "Did you tell her I didn't show up?"

He shakes his head. "Would it be a problem if I did?"

"Yeah. I don't want her or my dad thinking I can't handle this."

His eyebrows draw together like he's trying to figure something out. "But you can't handle this." He doesn't say it meanly, but he does say it like it's a fact. Which is plain wrong. That is not a fact.

I steel myself and stare directly into his eyes. "You haven't seen me try."

The corner of his mouth twitches. "Alright, Princess. Prove me wrong."

"I hate being called Princess."

"I'm aware." He leans closer, his gaze so intense it's hypnotizing. His irises are ringed in brown, and gold flecks scatter throughout the green. It's entirely unfair that a man should be given eyes that beautiful. I drop my gaze, because if I don't...I don't know.

There are many possible endings to that thought, and most of them aren't a good idea.

Jiminy arrives with three bags of food and four large coffees in a carrying tray.

Jake sits up and moves back-and-forth a few degrees on his stool, working his wallet from the back pocket of his worn jeans. My eyes roam over his clothing as he pays his bill.

Technically, his clothes are clean. The fibers are stained with grease and sweat and concrete, but laundered. Over and over and over, probably. I bet that fabric is silky soft by now. His work boots are a lighter shade of brown around the toe, likely from wear, and speckled with dried concrete.

"See anything you like?"

My face reddens at having been caught. I lift my gaze slowly, deliberately, like I'm not mortified, and look him in his eyes. "No."

Jiminy cackles. "I don't think I'm ever going to let you leave Green Haven, Colbie. I'm going to keep you."

Jake pushes to standing and gathers the food and coffee. "If you're going to keep her, you better invest in some fancy non-dairy creamer. That's what you prefer, right?"

I give him a dirty look, noting how he did not call me

princess this time, even though it would have fit well at the end of his sentence.

"That true?" Jiminy demands, his bushy eyebrows pulling together.

"Plain coffee is just fine. I promise," I add, attempting to quell the disbelief in his expression.

I turn my attention from Jake, making it blatantly obvious I'm ignoring him, and take another bite of my breakfast.

A stream of air blows hot against the side of my head, and even without looking I feel him, the way his broad chest hovers an inch from my upper back. "Maybe I'll see you around the jobsite sometime." His words vibrate over the shell of my ear. "Boss," he adds, but it sounds like both a chide, and a challenge. *You were late for your first day, and you don't know what you're doing.*

If what he said was true and it really was just a miscommunication, it still doesn't matter. Either way, both of those things are true.

I chew and swallow, but I do not give him the satisfaction of a response.

He walks away, cool air settling over my body as the heat from his chest dissipates.

I count to three and then, as sneaky as I can manage, peek over my right shoulder. He's nearly to the entrance, arms loaded down so he uses a hip to push open the front door.

I can see why he had to coax his wallet out of his jeans. They are so damn tight.

Why, oh why, does somebody that maddening get to have an ass like that?

Jiminy's low whistle drags my attention from Jake's retreating form.

He's standing behind the counter, hands tucked in his khakis. His eyes twinkle.

"What?" I ask.

"That boy never talks to anybody as much as he just talked to you."

"When you say talk, do you mean harass?"

"Hah," Jiminy barks. He clears away my empty plate and mug. "Keepin' ya, Miss Colbie Jones. I'm keepin' ya."

I pay the bill, then leave Jiminy with a smile and a promise to be back soon. I have a construction site to get to.

Chapter 9

Jake

I'm handing out a late breakfast to the crew when I spot her Mercedes in the distance. The damn car sticks out like a sore thumb in this town.

"Is that one of the Russells?" Javi looks like he hopes he's wrong. Javi worked custom homes in Phoenix, and he swears the homeowners are notorious for showing up unannounced and acting like they know what's going on. Thankfully the Russells live in northern California, so it won't be easy for them to drop in on us. Not often, anyway.

"That"—I push a burrito against Javi's chest—"is Emmett's daughter."

"I thought his daughter is a school teacher?"

The fancy car gets closer. "This is his other daughter."

"I didn't know he had another daughter."

I cringe internally. "Do me a favor and don't say that to her." I get the sense there are hurt feelings. Interesting, considering I always thought it was Colbie doing the hurting.

"No prob."

Colbie creeps the last one hundred yards, probably

trying not to kick up dust. It's considerate of her, but also pointless. Unless we're actively hosing down the ground, dust is inevitable.

She pulls up and puts the car in park, but it takes her a full minute to get out. Maybe she's taking deep breaths or something. I probably would be.

I'm walking over to check on her when her door opens. The first thing I see is the extension of one long leg, and some shoes that are not going to cut it on a jobsite. Had she been wearing those at Honeybee?

I come to a stop and cross my arms. "You're a walking insurance liability. They make footwear and clothing better suited to a jobsite." What is wrong with me? Every time I open my mouth to say something to this woman, it's like an angry version of me speaks instead.

Colbie extricates herself from her vehicle. With those heels on—wedges, I think my sister calls them?—the bottom of my chin almost meets the top of her head.

Colbie shoots me a look that says the day has only just begun and she's already had it with me. "Are you about done with all your remarks? Because I have a job to do, and I can't have an employee constantly trying to get in the way of that." She crosses her arms, one eyebrow lifting up on her forehead. I've always been jealous of people who are able to do that. It adds emphasis to whatever they're saying.

I lift my hands in surrender.

"Lovely," Colbie says, uncrossing her arms. She looks around.

"There isn't much to see now," I explain. "But give this place a few months, and you'll be amazed at what we've accomplished."

Colbie surveys the site of the future home. "It really is

just getting started." She works the side of her lower lip with her teeth.

"What were you expecting?"

"You heard what my dad said to me at the hospital. That's all I know."

It's odd that Emmett would ask this much of Colbie, yet give her little to go on.

I pull off my hat and scratch my head. "We were working through getting the lot graded when your dad collapsed. Compaction testing was scheduled for yesterday afternoon, but it was moved to Monday for obvious reasons."

She nods, and I think we both know she's pretending to understand what I'm talking about. "So you're here today because...?"

"Because we're supposed to be. Because nobody said to take the day off. Because those guys"—I point a stiff finger in the crew's direction—"want to know if Emmett's ok."

"They showed up here because they want to know how Emmett is doing?"

"Your dad is good to them. They care about him. We've all been together for a long time, and they're worried about him. They saw it happen."

Her head tips sideways. "But you didn't."

"Nope. I was on the phone with you."

"But you saw him after." Everything about her softens. Her face muscles, her voice, the look in her eyes.

The vulnerability I saw last night in front of the hospital is seeping through again. I allow myself two seconds to think about what it would be like to hold her in my arms, and then I smack that thought directly in its foolish face and send it packing. There is no way Colbie would ever want me to comfort her.

85

"Yeah," I answer, confirming I saw Emmett right after the injury. I refrain from supplying details. I don't think she wants them.

Her shoulders pull back suddenly, as if she's come to some kind of conclusion. "Is Blake in the trailer?"

"Yes." My eyes flick over to the place where Blake stays all day. I know he does a lot for Emmett in terms of keeping all the subcontractors organized, and keeping Emmett organized too, but I can't imagine it takes eight hours a day. A few times I've walked in on him typing furiously on his personal laptop. He closed it quickly each time, and wouldn't tell me what he was doing. I bet he writes erotica under a fake name.

"I'll be back soon." Colbie waves at me and makes her way to the trailer. I watch her go, navigating the dirt and small rocks in those shoes. As long as she stays in the trailer it's not a safety issue, unless you count one of the crew members staring at her and tripping and falling into her as creating an unsafe environment.

As it is, it's difficult for me to tear my eyes off her.

"That's the new boss?" Javi speaks from beside me, making me flinch. I hadn't noticed him walk up.

"Yep."

"Hmm."

"What's that supposed to mean?"

Javi shrugs. "I thought this was just gonna be your typical custom build, but I'm getting a feeling this job is going to be more interesting than I thought."

Between Colbie's feistiness, charm, and stubborn determination, I'm inclined to agree with Javi.

I pat him on the back, steering him away from Colbie's retreating form. "Buckle up, mi amigo."

Thirty minutes later, Colbie exits the trailer.

She asks everybody to gather around, then she introduces herself. "I'm sure you're all wondering why the hell Emmett Jones asked me to oversee this job, instead of his foreman." She gestures in my direction. "The answer is...I have no idea. I have not set foot on a construction site in almost twenty years. I know how to work a trowel, and put my handprint in concrete before it hardens. That's about it."

The guys struggle not to show it, but I can tell they're all concerned about the future of this job, and, consequently, their livelihoods.

She continues. "What I can tell you, is that I'm qualified to run a business. I am currently the co-owner and operator of a four-location exercise business in Phoenix."

How is this the first I'm hearing of this? I feel like an ass for the loads of judgment and negative comments I've been sending her way about not being capable.

She holds her hands aloft as if she's admitting something. "I am not saying that it's the same thing. There are many hands involved in a project of this scale." She pauses to look at each man in turn. "A few of you look worried, and the ones who don't are probably better at hiding it."

Some chuckling rumbles around the group.

"Just because I don't know much, doesn't mean I won't learn. I'll ask you questions, I might ask you to show me how to do things. You're the experts here"—she pats her chest—"not me."

Is that...? Yep. It is. That's respect sweeping over the crew's faces, all because Colbie is showing them the very same thing. Respect.

"I understand what happened to my dad was scary for you. You're concerned for him, and I appreciate that. He's doing well, and is expected to be released from the hospital tomorrow. He swears more than half of the tests the doctors are running are just so they can bill his insurance."

The guys all laugh again.

I don't laugh. It would mean I'd have to stop being astonished. Does Colbie have any idea how similar she is to her father? I've seen him stand and speak to his crew a hundred times, just like Colbie is doing now. She commands the floor—or dirt—just like Emmett. She's easy-going and natural, and the guys soak it up like the desert in a drought.

And I do, too.

"So..." Colbie clasps her hands in front of her chest. A mischievous smile curves her lips upward. "My first question for all of you is: do you like snow cones?"

She points behind our heads. We all turn to see what looks like an ice cream truck bumping over the unpaved road.

Chapter 10

Colbie

The snow cones are a hit.

Chapter 11

Jake

I love snow cones. Dammit.

Chapter 12

Colbie

Keli is refilling the silver tray of complimentary cookies when I walk into the reception area of the hotel late that afternoon.

"Hi," she says, her eyes lighting up. "I talked to my parents." She holds out the tray. "Want a cookie?"

"No thanks, I had something sweet a little bit ago. I'm sugared out." I purse my lips, waiting for Keli to tell me what her parents said. This morning I was feeling mostly trepidation at the idea of staying in Green Haven, but after spending time with the crew, I'm feeling... well, let's just say I'm feeling less apprehensive. I heard stories about their families, and learned one guy's wife had their second daughter three weeks ago. Javi had a blue raspberry snow cone, and the rest of the guys teased him relentlessly about his blue-stained lips. One guy said something crude involving an alien, and Jake came down on him about watching his mouth.

I'm not sure how I feel about that. I don't want the guys' behavior to change just because I'm there now. I'm a grown woman. My ears aren't that delicate.

But I liked the way Jake stepped in.

"So," Keli beams as she slides behind the front desk. "My parents said they would love to rent to you."

Relief slides through me. I'm one step closer to making this all possible.

"You can move in as soon as you want. You can even go tonight, and I'll change your hotel reservation." Keli grabs a single key off her desk and holds it out. "It's in a nice neighborhood down the street from the elementary school. The school crossing guard and her husband live next door. Alma and Arthur. Sweet old couple." Keli drops the key in my outstretched palm. "The husband doesn't get around well anymore. She'll want to have you over for dinner. She's a terrible cook, so plan to eat before or after you go."

I breathe a laugh. "Thanks for the info. And the advice. And the place to stay."

"You bet. My mom asked you to mail her your rent checks because she says she doesn't trust those 'money transfer apps'." Keli rolls her eyes. "I'll write down her address for you. She also said the sheets on the guest room bed are fresh, and asked that you refrain from opening her nightstand drawer." Red blooms over Keli's cheeks.

I smile as I take my keys from my purse and thread the new addition onto my key ring. "I think it's a universally agreed-upon rule that you never open a woman's nightstand. It's sacred."

"Well, I'm glad I know about that ahead of time. When the day comes that the good Lord calls her home, I'm going to drag that nightstand to the backyard and set fire to it."

I laugh. "Good plan. I'm going to get my things packed up. Thanks again for everything."

Keli waves a hand. "Stop thanking me. You've done that enough. How's your dad?"

"Doing ok, as of last night."

Keli nods her head and looks as if she's trying not to say something. She's probably thinking 'why don't you know how your dad is doing *today?*'.

Excellent question. She doesn't ask it though, so I'm not forced to answer. A small arrow of guilt stabs at me.

Keli pulls a phone charger from her purse. "Did you still need this? I grabbed this one when I went home for lunch."

"I stopped and bought one, but thank you." I tap two knuckles on the top of her desk. "I'll go get packed up. Is it a problem if I check out early?"

Keli shrugs. "Fine by me."

I go to my room, then plug my phone into my new charger. Notifications pop up, but I ignore them. The guilt at not knowing how my dad's doing today has gotten to me.

I bring up my contacts and type in the name of the one person who will know the most recent updates on my dad.

Victoria.

∴∴∴

My dad answers.

My fists unclench. A breath of relief slips from between my lips.

"Dad, hi."

"Hey, Colbie. Didn't expect your old man to answer, did you?"

I use one hand to arrange the pillows on the bed, then sit back. "I called Victoria's phone, so..."

"She ran down to the hospital cafeteria to get a cup of coffee. She left her phone here and I saw your name when it was ringing, so I answered."

"I was calling to get an update on you."

93

"I'd rather have an update from you."

"About what?"

"Did you go to the jobsite today?"

I almost didn't, thanks to your foreman.

"Sure did." I keep my tone sunny. "I met the crew. They all seem like nice guys."

"Yeah, well, I really know how to pick them. Jake helping you out? Getting you acclimated?"

"Uh," I falter. I don't want to tattle, or add propellant to the fire. "He told me about the compaction testing." And then I, immediately after stepping into the trailer and meeting Blake face-to-face for the first time, searched the Internet for what compaction testing meant.

"Good, good," my dad answers. He sounds tired.

"I called the inspector and confirmed that he'll be out on Monday at nine."

"That's Blake's job."

"I wanted to speak with him. This way he knows to expect me on Monday, and not a man."

"Jake helping you out?"

I pull the phone from my face, looking down at it in confusion. My dad asked that same question two minutes ago. Has he already forgotten? I bring the phone back to my ear and answer the question a second time.

"He's been helpful."

"Glad to hear it. He's a good guy. Knows a lot about the business. He'll be a good resource for you as the job continues."

Maybe my dad's exhausted. Medication? It's probably the painkillers, whatever cocktail he's on. That's why he asked me the same question twice in fewer than five minutes.

"How are you?" I ask.

94

"Aww, I'm fine." There's a trace of irritation in his tone. "They're keeping me here another night. It's all a bit unnecessary, but what do I know? I pour concrete for a living."

I don't like how he dumbs down his work. In fact, now that he has said that, I'm remembering other times he has made similar comments. "I bet most of those doctors and nurses don't know how to pour concrete."

"Then I guess it's a good thing they have me."

His upbeat attitude makes me smile. "I have to get going. I found a place to stay and I need to get moved in." Not that I have much to move. I packed for three days, which means I'll be making a trip down to Phoenix as soon as possible to get more of my things.

"Call if you need anything. And come by tomorrow. Have dinner with us."

"Victoria might want to get you settled before you have a guest."

"You're my daughter, not a guest." He sounds irritated again. It's atypical for him, but then again, he's probably fed up with being in a hospital bed.

To appease him, I say, "I'll call Victoria tomorrow and set up a time."

Satisfied with my answer, he wishes me a good night and hangs up.

I throw all my stuff in my bag and exit the room.

I'm pushing out the hotel's front door, suitcase rolling along behind me, when Keli calls out, "I forgot to tell you, my parents like lawn ornaments."

I look back at her. "Lawn ornaments? Like, decorations for your lawn?"

"Yeah. The house number is difficult to see from the street, but all you really need to know is to look for the flamingo."

Well.

Well, well, well.

There's no need to use an address to locate Keli's parent's place. She wasn't kidding about the lawn ornaments.

I'd pictured a lone flamingo, standing sentinel on a single leg.

Nope.

This flamingo has friends.

A flock of them.

I navigate into the driveway and put my car in park. I don't get out. I simply turn to my left and admire the pink birds dotting the grass yard. Without counting, I'd say there are twenty.

Oh my. What eccentricities does the inside have in store for me?

Answer: not many.

For people who like a multitude of the exact same lawn ornament, the interior of the home is surprisingly plain. A plaid couch with a comfy looking throw blanket folded over the back. A newer model TV, and an armchair that looks like it deserves to be slept in.

I peek at the kitchen. Updated sometime in the last decade, probably. A dining room table that seats six, with a pretty rug underneath and a cool chandelier made from old-looking bottles. The guest bedroom has an old-fashioned roll top desk with gold hardware, a simple bed with white bedding, a dresser and a nightstand.

I open the nightstand. It's empty, thank God.

I unpack, eat the takeout I picked up on the way here, and learn the master bathroom has a steam shower and jets coming out of the wall. I'll definitely be showering in there. It puts the second bathroom closer to the guest bedroom to shame.

It isn't until I'm sliding under the sheets that I remember the ignored notifications on my phone. Pulling it off the nightstand where it's being charged, I see the same report of one voicemail and three texts.

I hit the voicemail play button and turn it on speaker. Christina's voice fills the air, and automatically I miss her. I guess I'd better get used to that.

"Hey lady," she says, and there's chatter in the background of wherever she is. I check the time the voicemail was left, and deduce she was just about to teach a class. "I'm checking in. There was a small issue with payroll today. Leila says her raise didn't go through. Would you mind checking on that? Love you, bye."

I swipe to delete the voicemail, add the payroll task to the app I use for my to-do list, and open the messages. Unsurprisingly, Christina followed up her voicemail with a text an hour later.

> Forgot to ask you how your first full day as a temporary resident in Green Haven went.
> :)

The next text message is my mom, wanting to know why I haven't called her yet. I respond, telling her I'll call her tomorrow. The thought of having to tell her my plan makes me cringe, and puts an uncomfortable, sick feeling in my stomach. She's going to be furious. Maybe that shouldn't matter, considering I'm an adult. Family is an odd concept though, and it's difficult to break patterns and halt habits.

Though I think saying yes to my dad counts as disrupting the status quo. Calling it a *disruption* is probably downplaying it. My mom will view it as seismic activity shaking foundation.

And maybe it is.

And maybe that's not so terrible.

The last message is a number I don't recognize. I bring up the message and find there are several, including one from last night.

> Good call on the snow cones today. You're a regular hero.

Jake. I smile at the screen, a flutter of excitement waking up in my belly.

> Heroine.

Thirty minutes later, his reply comes in.

> My bad. I forgot who I'm talking to.

> And who would that be? A princess??

> A businesswoman.

> I was braggy, wasn't I?

> No. You were a boss.

A boss? I know text messages forgo a lot in terms of tone, but I think Jake sounds proud of me. I'm considering how to respond when the three little dots appear, so I wait.

> The guys already like you.

Just the guys? I don't dare ask that, even though I'd like

to. Besides, I'm sure what Jake is doing now is merely tolerating me.

> Well, yes. Snow cones.

It's more than that.

> Oh yeah?

The dots appear, disappear, then reappear. Twice. What is it he's struggling to say? The message comes through.

You remind them of your dad.

I stare at the screen, breathing through the sting of being verbally slapped.

A funny feeling starts in my stomach. A turbulent mixture of yearning and horror.

I place my phone facedown on the nightstand and turn out the light. That's enough texting for tonight.

Chapter 13

Jake

I try not to look at my phone first thing in the morning, but today I can't help it. I'm too curious to know if Colbie ended up responding after I went to sleep.

There's a text, but it's not from her.

I think I went a step too far.

Everything was finally going well between us. Maybe it was the foul comment from Jeff at work yesterday, igniting in me this desire to erect a modicum of propriety. When I'd told Jeff to act like he knows how to behave, I took notice of the smile that tugged at one corner of Colbie's mouth. That small inroad prompted me to text her last night.

But then I went and stuck my foot in my mouth.

Colbie obviously doesn't want to hear she reminds people of her dad. Why? What are her reasons?

When she wasn't in Green Haven, it was easy to assume it was she who pushed Emmett away. And even if that remains true, I'm starting to realize I was only seeing one side of things. Now Colbie's here, going from one-dimensional to three, and I'm picking up on things.

How would I feel if people who knew my dad didn't know I was his son? The answer is easy. I'd feel terrible.

A few weeks ago I never thought I'd say this, but I'm starting to see things from Colbie's point of view. Or, at least I'm starting to see that there's another viewpoint on it all.

To me, Emmett is the greatest person on earth who isn't blood related to me. To Colbie, he's something else, and I'm beginning to feel curious about what that might be. Maybe it's because I have a son, and I find the complications and intricacies of a child-parent relationship interesting.

I look at the other text on my phone, willing myself not to swipe it away. I pinch the bridge of my nose and roll back over.

I can't deal with Robbie's mom right now. Truth be told, I didn't think I'd have to deal with Robbie's mom *ever*.

I manage to avoid the notification of an unread message all through my morning routine. I drink coffee. Water the houseplants. Wipe down the inside of the fridge and throw out expired food. Robbie wakes up. I kiss his sleepy, messy hair and make him pancakes with mini chocolate chips. I let him watch his iPad while he eats, something I only do when he's sick. Maybe I feel bad for Robbie this morning.

Erin's text message has thrown me, even if I haven't read it. Just seeing her number, ten digits I don't have stored in my phone because I want zero communication with her, throws off my mood.

This is her second attempt at communication since I was awarded full custody of Robbie. The first was the day Emmett was injured.

Robbie's voice breaks through the tightness in my chest. "Dad, can I ride my bike?" He hops down from his stool.

"Stay on our block." I toss a napkin at him, and point to

my cheek. He mirrors me, wiping the chocolate smear from his skin. "Don't forget your helmet."

He skips out of the room to go change out of his pajamas, and I eat his remaining food, then store the rest in the fridge for tomorrow's breakfast. I grab a few tools and the new bathroom fan I picked up from the hardware store yesterday. I'd rather be riding bikes with Robbie, but the screeching sound the fan makes is so off-putting that it has the priority this morning.

Before I get started, I glance at my phone again, just to see if Colbie responded yet. I don't want to see Erin's number, but it's worth it if I get to see Colbie's.

Still no.

My thumb hovers over Erin's text. Better to get it over with and see what she has to say. At least Robbie's not in the house and I can curse without him hearing me.

Jake, please. He's my son, too.

My grip tightens on the phone. I could block her, but I'm afraid that would only fuel her. She knows the town I'm from. I'm not on social media, but it wouldn't be hard to find me. She'd probably show up in town and ask the first person she saw if they know me.

I hate that she's doing this. Why can't she stay gone? We're fine without her. Robbie is a happy kid. I've bent over backward to make sure he wants for nothing. Even when it was next to impossible, even when I had to go without and wear my old work boots when I desperately needed new ones, Robbie's shoes always fit. The only thing I've ever asked my mom for are her babysitting services, and I'm damn proud of that. There's nothing wrong with having help, and between my mom and Emmett, I had plenty, but none of it was a monetary handout. Nobody thought a twenty-one-year old college kid could win sole custody and successfully become a single-dad, but I did.

Erin ran away, but Robbie and I were fine. To this day, we're still fine.

One swipe of my finger, and the message disappears.

As if it were never there to begin with.

Chapter 14

Colbie

I'm told the crew doesn't work on Saturdays, but I'm tempted to drive out there and double-check.

In the end, I decide not to. Without the soil compaction test, there isn't anything for them to do.

I brew coffee and take it to the front porch. The air is still cool in the mornings. If yesterday's heat is any indication, the sun will burn out the cool air by midday.

Two wicker chairs sit side-by-side on the porch, and I choose the one with fewer protruding dried-out pieces. Maybe I'll replace these chairs for Keli's parents as a thank you gift for opening their home to me.

Thinking about Keli's parents reminds me I need to call my mom. She didn't respond to me last night when I told her I'd call her today, and I know what that means. My mom is intelligent, and she can sniff out a change in my atmosphere with uncanny accuracy. Not calling her when I arrived in Green Haven was a message in itself, and I bet she's steeling herself for my call.

But not yet. I'll call later, after I've enjoyed this slow, beautiful morning.

The neighborhood is quiet. One person walks their dog down the road, opposite the elementary school. All the houses are on the small side, and the yards are well-kept. I wonder what everyone thinks of the flamingoes? I've yet to meet my neighbors, Alma and Arthur, but I bet they'll have an opinion. How could they not? Hot pink doesn't exactly blend in with the landscape.

I get a second cup of coffee and watch the neighborhood come to life. More people walking dogs, a handful of runners. The runners wave as they pass, the dog walkers stop and chat. I introduce myself to the first couple walking a Golden Retriever, and when they hear my last name they ask if I'm related to Emmett. Jones is arguably one of the most common last names in the United States, but to the residents of Green Haven it immediately draws a connection to one of its most well-known residents. I tell her yes, Emmett is my father, then she tells me I resemble him. I smile politely, nod, and they continue their walk.

You remind them of your dad.

That's what Jake had said, and his words prompted me to shut down our text conversation.

The comparison to my dad is meant as a compliment, but it's an odd thing being compared to someone for whom you have complicated feelings. I think I would hate it if I looked nothing like him, but that doesn't necessarily mean I love that I do. Like I said, complicated.

A young boy rides up on his bike. His brown mop of hair flops around his forehead. He wears camouflage print shorts, a gray sweatshirt, and navy blue Chucks on his feet. He looks over at me, and I wave at him. He lifts a hand to return the gesture at the same time his front tire hits a rock in the middle of the sidewalk. The bike stutters and wobbles, and the forward momentum is enough that he goes tumbling off his bike.

I rush forward, spilling coffee on my sweatshirt in my haste. The boy lies in a heap, half of his body on the lawn and the other half on the concrete. Before I get there he's rolling over and sitting back on his knees. He looks at his hands, palms flipped up, and examines them.

I drop down beside him. "Hey there," I say softly. "Are you ok?"

He gulps and nods, a lone tear snaking its way down his face.

"May I see your hands?" I ask, one of my own outstretched. I don't have any medical supplies, so I can't actually help this kid, but I want to see what we're dealing with.

He holds out his palms. Scratches bracket the skin, the lines bright red and speckled with dirt and whatever else.

"Does it hurt anywhere else?"

He nods. "My knees."

I look to his legs. Red blossoms from both knees, more than what is on his hands.

"Can I walk you home? Are your parents there?"

"My dad," the boy says, climbing to his feet. "I live two houses down. You don't have to walk me." He reaches for his fallen bike, but I get there first. Righting the bike, I grab the handles.

I'm not letting this kid walk home alone, even if it's only two houses away. "You focus on walking, and I'll push your bike."

"Thank you," he says, starting off back the way he was riding from. "I'm sorry to put you out. I'm sure you were busy."

Did this kid just apologize for getting hurt in front of my house? I stare in wonder at the cowlick on the crown of the kid's head.

"No worries, dude. What's your name?"

"Robbie." He looks up at me. His eyes hold a smattering of gold amongst the green. He looks familiar, but I don't spend more than a few seconds trying to place him before I give up. "What's your name?" he asks.

"Colbie."

He nods, slipping his hands in his pockets. He winces, and removes them. "Ouch," he says. "I already forgot they hurt."

Robbie stops in front of the house and says, "This is where I live."

The screen door opens and a man in a backwards ball cap and eyeglasses hurries out of the house, something dangling from an outstretched arm.

"Robbie, you forgot—" the man skids to a stop so abruptly, there should be smoke at his bare feet.

For fuck's sake. What is it with the universe throwing me together with this guy?

"Hi, Jake." I wave half-heartedly.

He starts for us again, and he's scowling. Did I imagine those friendly text messages last night? "What are you doing with my kid?"

I'm stunned. Jake is a dad? He doesn't wear a wedding ring. Not that a person has to be married to have a kid. But, where is Robbie's mom? When I'd asked Robbie if his parents were at home, he'd said his dad was there. Does that mean a mom isn't present?

Also, Jake wears glasses? So I guess he wears contacts at the jobsite? And why do the glasses look unfairly good on him? They're round, rimmed in copper-colored wire. Like the sweats he's wearing, they look made for his body. When I wear sweats, I look like I'm wrapped in burlap.

"Hello?" Jake barks, waving his arms. "I asked you a question."

I cross my arms. I don't appreciate being spoken to like that. "I accosted him on the sidewalk and demanded he join me in forming a two-person band." I turn to Robbie. "Do you know how to play the tambourine?"

Robbie grins. He's missing a molar on the upper left, and bottom right.

"Very funny," Jake responds, tone clipped. He bends down so he's at eye-level with Robbie. "Are you ok, bud?"

I, very begrudgingly, admire this defensive dad side of Jake. I like the papa bear protecting his cub vibe. It's...sexy. There, I said it.

Robbie holds out his hands, then flips them over and points to his knees. "I fell off my bike in front of Colbie's house. She helped me."

Jake stands, his eyes searching my face. He looks confused, and I think I spot some wary fear amongst the many shades of green. "You have a house here?" Every word is saturated with his extreme displeasure at the concept. Honestly, it almost sounds like he's in pain.

What happened to the guy texting me last night, calling me a "hero"? I'd like him back, please. "I'm renting a house here. In case you don't know, renting is when a person gives money to a homeowner in exchange for—"

"Colbie."

Jake growls my name, and though my brain interprets this menacing sound as a threat, my libido supersedes evolution and sends the sound to my lady parts instead.

Which is inconvenient, not to mention useless.

He's hostile. Cantankerous. Sour, and downright rude to you. Also, an employee. And, apparently, a dad.

Jake bends again, so he can look Robbie in the eyes when he speaks. I bet it makes Robbie feel important and respected. It's sweet, the way he does this, and—

Absolutely not. I shove the warm fuzzies right into the trash where they belong.

"Go get in the shower," Jake says to Robbie, his tone gentle. "Make sure you wash your hands and your knees with soapy water. You need to get the bacteria out of the cuts, and then I'll get you bandaged up." He pulls himself upright and ruffles the top of Robbie's head. "I'll be in in a minute to help you out."

Robbie starts to walk away, but Jake clears his throat. Robbie turns around and looks at Jake. Jake inclines his head to me.

"Thank you for walking me home." Robbie grins, eyes mischievous. "I don't know how to play the tambourine, but I'm sure I can learn."

I burst out laughing. Robbie continues on into his house.

Jake is staring at me with a look that holds far less exasperation than a few moments ago. My laughter dissolves. "What?" I ask.

He holds the look for a bit longer, then says, "Nothing." His hands tuck into his pockets.

I nod curtly and start to turn around. "I'll see you on Monday."

"Wait," he says, his tone reluctant.

It's his hand on my arm that stops me. It's the rough, callused touch on the sensitive skin of my wrist that freezes me in place.

I look down. His large hand wraps around me, fingers

intertwining, as pulses of electricity shoot up my arm. My entire body is at attention.

My gaze meets his. He feels it, too. I see it in the movement of his Adam's apple as he gulps, the frenzy that has overtaken his eyes, and the heavy breath that parts his lips.

He finds his voice, and says, "I'm sorry I was rude. I didn't mean to be. Thank you for walking Robbie home."

"It was just two houses," I answer, attempting to decrease the amount of good in my deed. I need to put space between us. Whatever this is between us is intense, and not at all what I expected or wanted. I gently tug on my wrist, and he releases me. The loss of that simple touch hits me immediately, and I feel inexplicably bereft. Clearing my throat, I say, "I didn't know you have a son."

He nods as he scratches his thumb along his jaw. He looks slightly dazed, and I like that. "It's just me and Robbie."

There is so much more to unpack in those five little words, but it doesn't feel like my place. Nor should I want it to be. But it does feel like he wants me to know it.

I'm not sure how to follow up his admission, so I say, "I'll see you around, neighbor. Don't come to me if you need sugar, because I haven't been to the grocery store yet." I'd stopped at a little corner store on my way here last night after grabbing my takeout, and all I got was enough to get me through this morning.

"Noted." Jake offers a mock two-finger salute. After a moment of awkward silence, he asks, "What are you up to today?"

Small talk? It's not what I expected from him.

"Errands. Shopping, mostly. I've been told I'm not allowed on the jobsite without the proper footwear." I throw him a look.

He frowns. "You're not. It's—"

"A hazard." I barely keep from rolling my eyes. "Thanks, Safety Steve, but we've already had this conversation."

"You're cute when you're feisty."

Excuse me? My nose wrinkles. "That was so patronizing."

"Guess it comes with being a dad."

Questions bounce through my mind, but I keep them locked away.

Where's Robbie's mom?

Is she in the picture?

Jake nods at the front of my shirt. "You spilled something on your shirt." He smirks. "Again."

I'd forgotten all about my coffee spill when I rushed to help Robbie. I look down at the brown splash directly over my chest. At least I'm wearing a darker color this time.

"I have a hole in my mouth," I joke, brushing uselessly at the stained fabric.

Jake's eyes widen.

"What?"

He shakes his head, lips pursed.

"Just say it."

"You're not going to like it."

I gesture with my hand, like I'm saying *out with it.*

He stares at me, reluctant. "Fine," he mutters. "Your dad says that every time he spills something on himself when he's drinking. *There's a hole in my mouth.*"

Now I'm the one pursing my lips. I nod slowly. "Gotcha."

Awkwardness descends. He's probably wondering what my problem is. I'm starting to wonder what it is, too, which is really a quandary because I thought I already knew.

Jake nods. "Enjoy your errands."

"Thanks." I walk away, but a tingly feeling tumbles down my spine, and I know without a doubt he's watching me.

I'm halfway home when I allow myself a peek back.

I was right.

His eyes are on me.

He startles when he realizes I've looked back at him. He dips his chin at me, then walks to his front door. I'm sure Robbie is ready for his help.

I go through the motions of getting myself ready to run errands. I feel off-kilter, like a shaken snow globe.

Jake being less than awful?

That throws a wrench in things.

❧

Green Haven's biggest non-chain grocery store, Bensons Market, is my last stop of the day. The back seat of my car is loaded down with my new boots, clothing appropriate for the construction site, more clothing to get me through another week before I can go back to Phoenix and take from my closet, and two books. I'd had to drive an hour to a bigger town with a bigger bookstore, but they had what I was after. *How To Run A Construction Business*, and *Custom Home Building A-Z*.

I'd stopped at Honeybee for lunch, and Jiminy introduced me to as many people as he could. He told everyone I'm Emmett's daughter, and I watched them quickly replace their initial confusion with a warm welcome.

Is there a part of me that would have liked it if my dad had made sure everyone on God's green earth knows he has two daughters? Yes. Is that realistic? I suppose not. But, the heart is funny like that. It doesn't require reality to feel.

My cart is half-full of produce, peanut butter, and bread, when I round the freezer aisle and hear the words, "Fucking shit," howled from the end of the aisle.

One eye-full of the cursing person has me turning around and heading back the other direction. I'm not ready for this. I need a little more time to make a plan. Maybe grab a lemon bundt cake and coffee. Or shots of tequila.

I stop next to an end cap of greeting cards, drawing in a deep breath. I can do this, even if it's not at all how I planned to approach my sister.

Half-sister.

Does it matter?

I creep back around the aisle. Greer's still there, ten feet away, holding tightly to the pointer finger on her left hand. She makes a pained face and stares down at her hand.

Here goes nothing.

I push my cart closer. "Need a ride to urgent care?"

Her head snaps up. She drops her injured hand and glares at me. "I was wondering when I was going to see you."

I hold one arm out to the side of my body. "Ta-da!"

Greer has dark hair like her mother, the same olive skin and full, expressive eyebrows. She's stunning, to put it mildly.

She looks me up and down. "You exercise a lot." She doesn't say it like she has an opinion on whether that is bad, or good. She's simply making an observation.

"Thanks?" I edge closer. I need to get to the frozen sliced chicken, and Greer happens to be standing in front of it.

She doesn't move. "You've been here for two days." Hurt clings to the accusation in her tone.

I soften. She's not at fault for anything that happened between me and our dad, and yet I still place blame on her. "I'm sorry. Things have been insane the last forty-eight hours. I had to find a place to live, and I needed new clothes, and food."

"I heard." Greer steps away from the freezer case. "My mother won't shut up about it."

I'm sure she's just thrilled I'm taking over the job. I grab the bag of frozen chicken and toss it in my cart. "If it makes you feel any better, I haven't seen her yet either."

Greer makes a face. "Why would that make me feel better? You're not exactly her biggest fan."

"Nor is she mine."

Greer's eyes squint as she sways in a half circle, her hand basket bumping each thigh. I'm not sure what to say next, but it's me who needs to speak. The problem is, I have no idea what to say. Our relationship is complicated. She's blood, and although I love her, she'll forever be the daughter my dad stuck around to raise. That kind of pain is perpetual, a constant poke from a knife that never dulls.

In the beginning, we tried. I was excited to have a little sister. My dad drove down to Phoenix to get me and then drove me back here to Green Haven to meet Greer after she was born. I stared down at the tiny bundled baby, a thrill running through me. I remember thinking that I had a family now, even if my mom wasn't a part of it. And then I felt guilty for thinking that, like I'd done a bad thing by envisioning a happiness that didn't include my mom.

I'd wanted to fit into my dad's new family, but I was a puzzle piece that never had the right shape. I'd arrive for a visit and find that I was the odd man out, simply because I wasn't there often enough to understand what was going on when I was there. Greer was a colicky baby, and one day she cried so loud I couldn't hear the TV. I turned up the volume, Greer turned up her own internal volume, and Victoria yelled at me. My dad had been out checking on a jobsite, and when he got home I'd been too afraid to tell him what happened. We saw each other so little, I couldn't bear to have him angry with me. It was safer to be silent, to keep the water calm. I pushed away everything I felt so I could keep my dad. Looking back now with an adult's eyes, I see how everything came together to form the beginning of the end.

None of that is Greer's fault. She is an innocent bystander, present only because of circumstance.

For a moment I'm swept up in a feeling of familial tenderness, and I almost hug her. Almost. I refrain, because I literally have no idea how to go from the way I feel, to showing her my feelings.

"I better get going," I say, at the same time Greer says, "Dad got out of the hospital today. He says you're coming over for dinner."

I blink in surprise. Great. I'm sure Victoria is thrilled.

"I can tell by the look on your face you don't want to." Greer grabs something from the freezer case and throws it in her hand basket with more force than is necessary. "Fine. Just go hide out in whatever place you've rented and steer clear of us the entire time you're working on this job. I'm sure that's what you'd prefer."

As much as Greer is trying to hide her hurt with anger, she cannot. It's too tall an order. If there's anything I understand, it's what we use to hide our hurt. My personal choice is evasion.

Until now, that is. I think there comes a point in a

person's life when they simply cannot continue running from what hurts. They must stop, turn around, and step into the pain, if only for the purpose of emerging on the other side.

Not to mention how much more difficult it is to push people away when you're standing in front of them. "I'll be there," I tell Greer.

She stares at me, her brown eyes deepening in color. Her raised shoulders lower, inch by inch. Her jaw muscles relax. "Ok." A look of hope sneaks onto her face. She was always quick to forgive, and sensitive.

I smile at her. "Just tell me what time, and what I can bring."

Greer waves a hand. "Six. Just bring yourself."

"Will do."

"I'll see you tonight, then." Her tone is warmer than it was a minute ago. She passes me, and at the last second she reaches out, squeezing my forearm lightly.

The backs of my eyes burn.

I go home, put away my groceries, and spend the next hour reading from my new book. I learn about digging footings, and rebar, and how concrete sets in different climates. It's fascinating, how the work of many can create a home for few.

When I leave for dinner, Jake is in his front yard with Robbie. They wear mitts, and play catch with a baseball. Robbie waves as I drive by, and I wave back. Jake dips his chin in acknowledgment. I nearly roll down my window and tell him where I'm going, but decide against it. It's obvious he has an opinion on me, and my relationship with my dad. I don't understand why, and I'm not going to go out of my way to change it.

My only stop is at the florist who is minutes away from

closing for the day. She hands me a large, brightly colored arrangement.

Greer said not to bring anything, but I can't show up empty-handed. No need to add yet another arrow to Victoria's quiver.

Chapter 15

Jake

"Where do you think Colbie was going, Dad?" Robbie stares after her car. He looks back at me and tosses the ball.

I catch it and shrug. "I don't know, bud."

Robbie's lips twist. "She looked pretty." He ponders this for a moment. "Probably a date. It's a Saturday night."

I frown. How does this kid know about dates? Not from me. And it's unlikely she was going on a date, unless her boyfriend came to town. Maybe he did.

I feel a flicker of annoyance thinking of Colbie seeing Brad, and then two things happen at once.

First, I realize I'm jealous of Brad.

Second, I realize I'm annoyed with myself for being jealous. Maybe it's time I start seeing someone. I can't run around with a little green monster on my shoulder for the next however many months I'm working with Colbie.

Robbie cuts into my thoughts when he says, "Don't you think she looked pretty, Dad?"

The very thing I was trying not to notice is the very

thing my son wants to talk about. "Colbie looked nice." I rub my fingers over the ball. "Eyes on me, Robbie."

His gaze snaps to me, and I underhand the ball. He catches it easily and huffs. "Overhand, Dad."

We've only started playing catch with a real baseball in the past few weeks. I was hit in the face when I was thirteen, and I haven't forgotten how much it hurt. I'd like to keep Robbie from knowing that pain. "Overhand has more force," I explain, hoping he'll give in and let me be overprotective. "Underhand gives you more time to react and judge the distance and timing of the catch."

Robbie releases a long, loud groan. "I can do it, Dad."

I stare at him, and he stares back at me. "Fine," I grumble.

Robbie doesn't cheer at his victory. He widens his stance, bends at the knees, and lifts his glove to hover in front of his left shoulder.

I throw the ball, and it lands limply three feet in front of him.

"Dad," Robbie shouts, frustrated. He walks to the ball and kicks it. It rolls over the grass to my feet. "Throw it for real."

"Fine." I pick up the ball. "Keep your eyes on the ball," I remind him.

His eyes lock on my hand and he says, "I know, Dad."

I throw it with more speed this time, enough to actually reach him. He sticks his arm out, glove open, and misses the catch. The ball sails past his glove, and directly into his right shoulder.

He makes a pained face, grabbing at his shoulder with his gloved hand.

I mutter an expletive and jog over to him. "Let's get

some ice on that shoulder." I try to guide him toward the house, but Robbie stubbornly stays rooted in place.

I say, "We'll try again tomorrow," but my offer isn't enough for him. He's still holding his shoulder when he responds, "Overhanded." He gives me a serious look, attempting to lock me into an agreement.

A long steady breath streams from my nose. Despite my fear of hurting him, I'm proud of his resilience. "Overhanded," I agree.

A smile breaks on his face, and he strides into the house ahead of me.

I get Robbie situated on the couch with an ice pack on his shoulder, then start dinner. The sounds of a nature show filter into the kitchen while I get to work making spaghetti sauce.

My mind wanders while I cook. Robbie was right. Just in the handful of seconds it took Colbie to pass by our house, I saw how gorgeous she looked. To be honest, she's always stunning. Even when she's angry. And irritated. I watched her smile at Honeybee yesterday morning, and found myself thinking it would be nice if I was on the receiving end of that smile. And then I mentally kicked my own ass, because how stupid is that? Not only is she my current boss, but she's a royal pain in my backside, and—the icing on the fan-fucking-tastic cake—she's Emmett's daughter, the same woman who has made the greatest man I know, cry.

And now she's my neighbor? I spent half of yesterday watching her at the jobsite, partially because I was terrified she was going to hurt herself in those nonsense shoes, and partially because it's hard not to stare at her. She has this... this...quality about her, and it's driving me insane. It would be one thing if all I did was find her physically attractive, but that's not it. Something in my chest feels weird when I look at her, and I don't like it.

I don't know what it is. I remember being attracted to Robbie's mom, but it didn't feel like this. With Erin, it was infatuation, pure and simple. I was twenty and awkward. I felt like a jackass, and she was a worldly city girl. Her parents were well-off, and I worked weekends as a barback for spending money. She was in a sorority and pre-med. She smiled all the time and had a belly button ring. I don't find that attractive now, but at the time it was the sexiest thing this small-town kid had ever seen.

When it comes to Colbie? It must be intense dislike that's making my chest feel this way.

Except for that whole *I wish she would smile at me* bull-shit. What the hell is that? The next time I take out the trash, that thought better be buried at the bottom of the bin.

I pile noodles into two separate bowls, then use a measuring cup to ladle meat sauce on the top. I pluck the entire roll of paper towels off the counter and wedge it in between my arm and my body.

"Dinner's ready," I announce, walking into the living room.

Robbie discards his ice pack and reaches for a bowl. He gets himself situated and points at the TV screen. "A new male hippo showed up and challenged the male hippo that was already there. He won, and now he's the dominant male hippo and he's killing a calf who belonged to the first male."

Robbie sniffs, and I put an arm around him. "You can turn the channel if it upsets you."

He shakes his head. "No. It's just a part of the animal

kingdom." He twirls his fork in his pasta and loads up a gigantic bite. "Why doesn't the mother fight for the baby?"

A knife, a sword, a goddamn bayonet slices into my heart. Robbie first asked about his mom when he was seven. He wanted to know why he didn't have a mom like other people. I told him his mom couldn't be a parent, and waited with my heart in my throat for a follow-up question. None came.

The question he's asking now seems innocuous, but it has teeth. There's more going on in his mind than he's letting on.

"I think," I say slowly, praying to God my response is what he needs to hear, "in this case, the female hippo has to allow nature to take its course. If she interferes with the male hippo, he might kill her."

Robbie considers this. "Maybe the other older hippos are hers, too. She needs to stay alive for them, even though they aren't babies anymore."

I have no idea if this is correct, but it seems to mollify Robbie, so I agree with him.

We keep eating, and the program moves on to something less violent. Robbie nudges my elbow. I look at him and he smiles at me, the corners of his mouth stained crimson with pasta sauce.

"Good thing we're humans, not hippos." His heel bumps the couch as he kicks his leg. "We're just a couple of bachelors, right, Dad?"

For fuck's sake, the kid knows what it means to go on a date, and be a bachelor? I want to ask him where he's learning stuff, but I'm afraid if I call attention to it, it'll make it a thing. I don't want it to be a thing. So I say, "Bachelor," and pound my chest with one fist, while I make sounds like a gorilla. The other hand still holds my spaghetti.

Robbie mimics me, and the attempt to turn his high-pitched child's voice into a lower register is the cutest thing I've ever heard.

Damn do I love this kid.

Chapter 16

Colbie

My mother begins blowing up my phone right as I'm pulling into my dad's driveway.

I spaced calling her today, and when I say spaced I really mean I forgot on purpose.

She calls twice in a row, and follows that up with three text messages. I guess she's decided she's done waiting for me.

Pausing in my open car door, I send her a response telling her I was busy today and I'll call her tomorrow.

I tuck my phone in my purse, glancing up at my dad's house. It's four times the size of the little house he bought when he first moved here. He made updates to it along the way, keeping it modern and on-trend. I prefer the small house he lived in when he first came to Green Haven, where my handprint sits in hardened concrete.

That house was back when I felt close to him, a time when I could close my eyes at night and imagine myself in his arms, his chest shaking with laughter and causing my whole body to quake. He'd been separated from my mom for a year by then, and yet I still look back at that time with a fondness I haven't felt in so long.

Nothing is what it used to be. Nothing. Not even me.

I knock on the front door. Victoria answers quickly, as if she'd been nearby when I knocked.

"Colbie, hello," she smiles warmly as she places her hands on my shoulders and squeezes.

This affectionate welcome isn't what I'm expecting, and I'm knocked off guard. Where is the reserved woman who has held me at arms' length for years?

"For you," I announce awkwardly, thrusting the flowers at her. Not *hi*. Not *hello*. Not *why are you being nice to me?*

"Thank you," she says graciously, taking them from my arms. "These are lovely. Please come in." She steps back into the house, her dark hair in stark contrast to the white walls.

I step inside. I've only been here a handful of times since I stopped seeing my dad on a regular basis, but it smells exactly as I remember it. The spicy scent of the cigars my dad enjoys periodically clings to the walls.

Victoria stands back, waiting for me to clear the door before she closes it. Tension permeates the air between us as we linger in the cavernous foyer with nothing to say. Or maybe there is everything to say, and neither of us know how or where to start.

"The house is still beautiful," I remark, not just to have something to fill the quiet, but because it's true.

"Thank you." Victoria pivots and walks, flowers in hand. She keeps talking, and I have to catch up to her. "I redecorated last year. It was time to freshen things up a bit."

"Oh? Where did you go for all the décor? Probably not any of Green Haven's antique stores." I can't help it. I'm

125

baiting her. I know she went down to the valley to go shopping. What Green Haven has in charm, Phoenix has in interior design stores.

Why do I care that she went to Phoenix and didn't call me? Why does it hurt to think she's written me off, when I have done the same to her?

Victoria walks into the kitchen and sets the flowers on the counter. Everything in the kitchen is new, too. White cabinets, fresh countertops, and a marble backsplash.

Victoria does not answer my question. She rummages around in a bottom cabinet until she finds a large vase. She fills it with water, arranges the flowers inside, and looks at me. I'm trying to remember the last time I saw her, but it's been so long that I'm coming up empty. Two years ago, perhaps, when she and my dad were on their way to the airport in Phoenix? They'd driven down early so we could get lunch together. Even then, we'd had my dad doing what he does best, supplying topics for conversation. Now we're on our own.

Victoria fidgets with the flowers, rearranging them unnecessarily. I can tell she wants to say something, so I remain silent, waiting.

Her mouth opens. "Colbie, I—"

"Colbie!"

Greer flies into the room. Her greeting at the market must've been some kind of armor she wore just for me, because right now my little sister is enveloping me in a warm hug. I'm taken aback, but determined not to show it.

I return her hug, even though it doesn't feel natural. I'm leaning into this experience, from here on out. Starting with my little sister. "Hi, there."

She pulls away, her dark waves bouncing against her

shoulders. "That's how I should've acted earlier when I saw you. I'm sorry. I was thrown off."

I smile ruefully. "And hurt."

She nods, taking another step back so we aren't talking in one another's faces. "And hurt."

Victoria stands behind the island like the point to our triangle, arms crossed as she watches us. "Colbie, your dad's been looking forward to seeing you today. Just wanted to give you a heads up, he's still a little...loopy." She drifts over to the refrigerator, coming away with a bottle of white wine. She tips it toward me, silently asking if I would like a glass.

"Yes, please."

Greer raises her hand. "Me, too."

Victoria unscrews the top, and fills three glasses. She tosses the empty bottle in the recycling and hands a glass to each of us. Like earlier, I can tell there is more she wants to say, so I stay quiet and watch her take a long drink of her wine.

She looks exhausted. Wrinkles pile at the corners of her eyes, her mouth droops. It's not just the work of gravity; it's distress.

She lowers her glass. "I need to wake your dad up from a nap, but before I do, I want to tell you something."

My grip tightens on my wineglass. I glance at Greer. She looks at me with concern, instead of at her mother with interest. She must already know what her mom is going to say.

Victoria begins. "Between your dad hitting his head on the sawhorse, and also on the ground, he experienced a mild TBI. The doctors have no way of knowing if it's temporary, or if it will continue."

"TBI," I repeat, my whisper weaving its way through my memories of my past couple interactions with my dad.

"Traumatic brain injury," Greer explains, thinking I may not know what TBI stands for.

I can't do more than nod at her. I can't use my words right now. There's too much emotion tumbling through me. Namely, regret. Followed by guilt. What was I doing punishing him for so long? What was the point of it? It didn't fix anything. It didn't make me feel any better. All it did was prolong the pain, and add to it.

"Does he know?" I ask.

Victoria nods. "The doctors were straight with us, but I'm not sure how much really took hold for your dad. He's a very optimistic man. To a fault, sometimes."

Greer dips her chin encouragingly at her mom. "Tell Colbie what Dad said when he got home from the hospital today."

Victoria pushes her hair back from her face. "He said he's not sure he believes the doctors, because he hasn't seen any evidence of a brain injury." Her voice is strained. "He says if it weren't for the physical injuries, nobody would know something was wrong with him."

A weight settles on my chest. "He asked me the same question two times in a row yesterday on the phone. I blamed it on his painkillers."

"He has lost his temper a couple times, and that's a symptom, too." Victoria takes another long drink, and I get it. If I weren't driving, I'd chug this glass of wine, and a second one while I was at it.

"What happens now?" For the first time in my life, I don't feel like Victoria and I are on opposing sides. Her forthrightness about my dad's TBI makes me feel like she's brought me into the fold of their three-person family.

"We try and go on with life, I suppose." Victoria shrugs resolutely. "I don't know what Emmett's going to do all day when we all go to work." She shakes her head like she's at a loss. "He can't be on the jobsite, and pretty soon that's going to turn him into a bear." She places her wine on the counter. "Anyway, I'll go wake him. He wants to be in charge of the grill, and I'm getting hungry."

Victoria leaves the room. Greer pulls a plastic-wrapped tray of sliced vegetables from the fridge. "For the grill," she explains as I look them over. "Eggplant, zucchini, and yellow squash."

"Sounds amazing. Anything I can do to help?" I want to be put to use, but I don't know this kitchen well enough to jump in without instruction. I remember enough about this house to get myself to the guest bathroom, but that's about it.

Greer gets me set up brushing all the vegetables with oil and seasoning them. While I do that, she assembles ingredients for a cold pasta salad. I'm trying desperately not to think about my dad, and his TBI. Mild or not, it's a life-altering diagnosis.

Greer has had longer to process everything, so she's ready for small talk. "How have your first days in Green Haven been?"

I nod slowly. "Interesting. So far, my favorite person is Jiminy."

She pretends to huff. "I'm offended."

"My favorite new person," I amend.

"Not Jake?" Greer grins. "He's gorgeous. And the man can rock a pair of Levi's."

We share a knowing look, and I nod in agreement. "I can't tell if he's nice, or rude, or if he saves all his venom for me because I'm so special." I drizzle the olive oil on the sliced veggies and begin to brush like I'm painting on canvas.

129

Greer pulls a knife from the wood block next to the stove. "It must be you. Jake is fantastic."

"Thanks," I say dryly.

"His little sister is a few years older than me, but she has been my friend since we were young. And I'm his son's teacher." She pauses her chopping of salami. "Do you even know he has a son?"

I picture Robbie, with his mop of brown hair and green eyes he likely inherited from his father. "I met Robbie this morning when he fell off his bike in front of my house."

"You live by the school?"

I nod. "I forgot you are a teacher." I make a face like *oops*.

"It's my first year," she explains, letting me off the hook. "I love it, though the moms can be a little much."

"Not the dads?"

"Moms are typically more involved in the day-to-day stuff. Jake's the only single dad, and there are a couple single moms hanging around waiting for their chance to pounce." She selects a wooden spoon from the utensil holder on the counter and points it at me. "If you're plan-ning on falling in love with one of the best bachelors Green Haven has to offer, I'd recommend doing it quickly. One of the moms in particular has been circling like she means business."

I shake my head quickly. "Sounds great for a romance novel, but not real life. I'm telling you, Jake struggles to be civil around me." Except for when he's gripping my wrist and swallowing hard and his eyes burn with intensity.

Greer frowns. "I've never seen him be rude. He's either done a good job of hiding it, or you bring it out in him."

"That's what my best friend Christina said."

"That you bring it out in him?"

"That he brings it out in me." I grab a pepper mill and grind pepper over the oiled vegetables. "He called me Princess until I told him I hate it."

Greer snorts.

With the pepper mill suspended in mid-air, I look over at Greer's bemused expression. "What?" I ask, though I'm positive I know the answer. I try not to let it make me too pleased, but it doesn't work.

"I think he likes you. I've never heard him give a nickname to anyone except Robbie." Greer throws all the ingredients into the cold pasta just as my dad walks into the room. His hair is neatly combed, and he's traded in the light blue hospital gown for jeans and a soft-looking flannel.

He grins broadly, glancing from me to Greer and back again. "Look at my girls."

A lump parks itself in my throat.

"Hey, Dad," Greer says, the words easily rolling off her tongue.

"Hi," I say, forcing cheer. Being here, assembling dinner with Greer and greeting our father, feels like something that could only happen in a dream.

He walks over to the fridge and pulls out a jug of iced tea. "Colbie, I heard through the grapevine that the guys already like you."

"Grapevine?" My eyebrows lift.

"Jake," he explains. "I texted him this afternoon asking for an update. Good call on the snow cones."

"It was nothing. They all came to work, even though there wasn't any work to do. I felt bad, and I thought it would make a good impression." Grabbing a kitchen towel, I wipe my hands and shrug.

"It did," he says, pouring a glass of tea. "I didn't even know a snow cone truck is a thing in Green Haven."

"I drove by it on my way to the jobsite. The owner of the truck said he lives in Sierra Grande, but he travels to all the small towns in Central Arizona. It was pure luck that I saw him and he had just finished up a kid's birthday party."

I glance up at my dad, my gaze roving over his freckled face. I used to run my fingers over his freckles, connecting them like constellations. He'd hold still, hardly blinking, as I'd announce *This is Orion's Belt. That's Big Bear.*

Dad leans his lower back against the lip of the counter. "Jake said it wasn't just the snow cones. He told me how good you were when you spoke to the guys."

He's looking at me with unfettered pride, like he knew I could do it, and nothing could make him happier.

The way only a parent can look at a child. With reverence.

Even though it feels good, like a big bite into a warm cinnamon roll or the first sip of a fancy cup of tea, it's painful. His reverence and pride only feels good because it has been absent. I want to be like Greer.

Hi, Dad. Like it's nothing. Old hat. Second nature.

That won't be happening though, now or ever, so I decide to take what's available and say, "I'm happy to hear Jake had nice things to say. Certainly better than the alternative."

Greer thumbs behind herself. "My phone's ringing." She turns, and I watch her back as she hurries out.

My dad continues. "I know the job is just beginning, and there's a long road ahead, but it means a lot to me. You doing this, it's..." his voice tightens. "I know it's not easy for you to be here. In Green Haven, or in my house."

We never talk this way. We dance around hurt feelings, but we never acknowledge them. Maybe his recent health scare has made him ready to face uncomfortable topics.

I stare down at the colorful slices of vegetables, but I don't see them. Not really. "I'm trying."

"I appreciate you trying, Sugar Bear."

This time I don't hate the nickname, just the ache it releases.

"Brad going to come up and visit you?" he changes the subject, for which I'm grateful, but it's hardly an improvement.

I shake my head. "Brad and I broke up." It isn't until now that I realize I haven't thought of Brad once since arriving in Green Haven. I didn't even think about picking up the phone to tell him I'm staying here. Or that I was coming here at all. Or about my dad's injury.

Shouldn't I have at least thought to call him, even if I caught myself one second later and remembered there was no longer a boyfriend to call?

My dad picks a small cube of cheese from the pasta salad and pops it in his mouth. "He's a fool."

It's so unexpected that it puts a smile on my face. "You don't even know what happened."

He shrugs. "I don't need to know."

"He cheated on me." I say it carefully, trying not to sound too disparaging. Once, in high school, my mother had too much mulled wine on Christmas Eve and told me my father had cheated on her when they were married. I'd been planning to visit him for the New Year, but I'd canceled my trip after that, as a show of solidarity to my mom.

Looking at him now, it's hard to believe he could ever be that guy. Maybe one day, Brad will have kids and grandkids, and they will all refuse to believe he was ever capable of such a choice.

"Like I said, he's a fool." Dad goes back to the fridge, but this time he comes away with two large zip-top plastic bags.

One carries steak, the second holds chicken, both covered in marinade.

He sets the bags on the counter, pressing his hands on the surface beside them. For a moment I fear something is wrong and he needs help. But then he looks at me across the island, and I see in his eyes a mountain of sorrow.

"I'm sorry to hear you experienced that level of betrayal." His voice is clear and thick, emotion softening the corners, as if he wants to be certain I hear the apology. Feel it, even. Immediately I think of my mom on that festive night, lips stained purple with wine. Is he acknowledging what he did all those years ago?

I nod. "Good to know sooner rather than later, right?" It's awkward after that, and it's obvious neither one of us knows what to say next. When Victoria floats into the room, I'm actually grateful to see her.

She looks expectantly at my dad. "Ready to grill, hon?" Then she glances at me, and smiles, and it feels genuine. I'm grappling with this new version of Victoria, trying to reconcile her with the person my childhood self knew her to be.

Maybe all this time, I wasn't the only person growing up.

Maybe she was, too.

⁂

Dinner is more than good.

It's enjoyable.

My dad is the center of attention, and it puts me at ease because it's normal for him. He is good at making conversation, and finding common ground.

When I go to leave, Victoria tells me to call her if I need anything.

Greer tells me she's going to text me during the week so we can set something up for next weekend.

My dad walks me out to my car. He whistles when he sees it, and says it's a fine piece of machinery.

Then he tells me he loves me.

I try. I try so hard to move those words up out of my chest, ascending through my throat and between my lips.

But that's the odd thing about emotions. A person can feel them, but that doesn't mean they can verbalize them. Sometimes, they can't even identify them.

My eyes fill with tears. I want to be a person who can say "I love you, Dad" and not have it feel monumental. Like Greer.

Dad wraps me in a hug. "You don't have to say it back. Hell, you don't even have to feel it." He releases me and looks me in the eyes. "You just have to know that I do."

I get in my car. He stands in front of his house, waving, until I can no longer see him in my rearview mirror.

And me?

I sob the whole way back to my flamingoes.

Chapter 17

Colbie

"I think I've heard you wrong." My mother's voice is hard, disapproval snaking through.

The muscles in my upper back tighten as I push away my immediate feeling of wanting to backtrack so I don't upset her. It's unbelievable, but I want to stay in Green Haven and work on my relationship with my dad more than I care about my mom's feelings right now. "I know it sounds crazy, but—"

"He got to you." She says it simply, like it's a forgone conclusion. "I knew he would."

"Mom, it's not like that. He needs help."

"From someone who doesn't know anything about the business?" Contempt colors her tone.

Anger rises in me. It's an old anger, as familiar as a beloved song, but now I'm letting that anger surface. Something I've never done before. Gathering my courage, I say firmly, "I need this."

"You need this?" Her tone is cutting, derisive. "You need to let him hurt you *again*? I raised you better than this, Colbie."

Again.

I hate the way she says that word. It's not only a reminder of past occurrences, it's an opinion delivered on a silver platter of disappointment.

I want none of it.

What I want is the chance to try with my dad. Maybe that will lead to heartache, but maybe not. It's been years since I've given myself the permission to even try. This is a rare opportunity, and I'm beginning to see that.

Bolstered by the miles between us, I say, "I think you're making a big deal out of nothing."

She laughs in a mean way. "We'll see about that."

I think maybe she wants to see me fail, and it makes me sad alongside that latent anger. What kind of mother wants to see her daughter hurt, just so she can be right?

I'm done. With this conversation, and with her. "I have to go, Mom."

I'm talking to nobody. She has already hung up.

Chapter 18

Jake

I'm dropping off Robbie at school on Monday morning when my phone rings.

"Emmett," I answer, "How are you?"

Craning my neck, I search for Robbie's brown hair in a sea of other children walking to the playground. I'm waiting here on the sidewalk in case he wants to turn around and give me one last wave. He used to do it without fail, but now he only does it about fifty percent of the time. Still, I make sure I'm ready for it one hundred percent of the time.

"Good, good," Emmett answers. "Do you have a few minutes?"

I locate Robbie and his bright red backpack.

"You bet. What's going on?" Just as Robbie is about to enter the school gate, he turns around and searches for me. I'm careful to keep my smile casual so he doesn't see what a big deal that is for me. I lift my hand for one final wave.

"Colbie was over here on Saturday evening."

"Oh, yeah? How'd it go?" A weird feeling of relief washes over me as I learn she was headed to her dad's on

Saturday night instead of on a date. I'm also happy for Emmett. I can't imagine how happy he was having Colbie in his home.

I'm just about to start walking toward my truck when someone taps my shoulder.

I turn around and stifle my automatic groan.

"Hi, Jake," Kiersten says, adding a little extra femininity to her lilt. "I was just wondering if you are—"

Emmett is talking too, and I can't focus on either person. I point at the phone I have pressed to my ear.

Her hands fly to her mouth and her eyes widen. "I'm so sorry," she whispers.

Emmett's still talking, and I'm starting to feel frustrated. "Emmett hang on, I'm sorry. Give me a minute."

I raise my eyebrows at Kiersten. She's wearing dark lipstick, and there's a smudge of it just beyond the corner of her mouth.

"I was wondering if you were coming to the parent happy hour at Caruso's this Friday night?" Her expression is hopeful. "I need to make a reservation, so I'm trying to get a headcount."

"Parent happy hour?" This is the first I'm hearing of this.

"Yes," Kiersten says, smiling at me like she finds my cluelessness endearing. "A flyer went home in Robbie's backpack last Friday."

"Must have missed it," I answer.

"So, can I count on you to attend?"

There are plenty of things I would rather do than attend a parent happy hour, but I understand it's importance. It keeps me connected to the parents of Robbie's classmates, and aware of what's going on socially and in the classroom.

"Sure," I answer. "I'll be there."

Kiersten claps her hands together. "Perfect. Don't worry, it won't just be you and a bunch of moms. Cash's mom is bringing a date." She winks mischievously. "Your friend, Rhodes."

"Great. See you then," I respond, not letting on that I'm shocked to hear Rhodes is going on a date with someone from Kiersten's mom brigade.

I back away and restart my conversation with Emmett. "Sorry about that."

"Sounds like you were accosted," he laughs. "Someone trying to sell you something?"

I picture Kiersten's smeared lipstick. "Something like that."

I climb into my truck and close the door quickly, before any other vultures descend. "I'm all ears now."

"Colbie seemed a little stressed when she was here. She mentioned she's still doing the job she has in Phoenix. Remotely. She's trying to hire someone to help out, but said she plans to work evenings, and be at the jobsite during the day."

"Uh-huh," I say, pulling out onto the road. What did Emmett think would happen when he asked Colbie to take over? He knew she had a job in Phoenix. A life. A boyfriend.

Interesting that the boyfriend didn't come to Green Haven with Colbie, especially when she thought she'd only be here for a few days. How does he feel about her deciding to stay?

Does he feel electricity when he brushes the inside of her arm, like I did?

Emmett's talking again. "I was hoping you could help her out? With the Russell project? I know you might be wondering why I didn't ask you to be the lead on the job. It's just—"

"You don't owe me an explanation." Emmett has been trying to bond with Colbie for years, and her taking over his job is an opportunity. I'd never ask him to pass that up.

"I—"

"Emmett, I know," I assure him. He sounds like he feels bad, and he doesn't need to. "There will be other jobs. Other opportunities."

"You'll help her?" he asks. He's probably rubbing his upper arm with his opposite hand. He always does that when he's feeling hopeful.

"I'll help her." I'll also have to do my best not to stare at her, or feel jealous of her boyfriend, or like when she smiles, or all those other ridiculous things I've been feeling since she walked into a gas station asking for nut milk.

If she was successful in her shopping on Saturday, she'll be wearing the right shoes today. That means she probably won't be in the trailer all day. Which means she'll probably be out walking around and getting in the way and inviting harm to herself and others.

Yeah, she's going to need to be watched. Closely.

"I appreciate it, Jake. Really. You know what it means to me to have her here in Green Haven. I wish it were under different circumstances, but I'm not the one calling the shots."

I've always appreciated Emmett's unswerving faith in God. "You helped me keep my kid once upon a time," I remind him, not like he needs it though. "I'm returning the favor."

"It was nothing," he says gruffly. He gets choked up when he thinks about that time, and about Robbie. So do I.

"It was something," I insist. "By the way, I put money in your account this morning."

"Don't you think it's just about time you stop doing that?"

"Not until my debt is paid."

"The debt's been paid."

I send a half eye-roll up to my truck's ceiling. There's no use arguing about it.

"One more thing," Emmett says. "I don't know if Victoria or Colbie has told you, but there's some stuff going on with my brain from the injury. Mild TBI, the doctor's are calling it. Might go away, might not."

I stay quiet, waiting for more, but that's all I get. He doesn't sound upset by it, more like he accepts it.

"I'm sorry to hear that," I tell him.

"Ah, don't be sorry. Such is life, Jake. Shit happens."

I pull into a spot down the road from Honeybee. "I better get going. I'm stopping to grab breakfast for the crew." It's not my turn, but my stomach is grumbling and I can feel the hangry coming on. Seems like a good idea to be well-fed to start off my week with Colbie.

"Tell Jiminy I'll be in soon."

"Will do."

"And take care of my girl."

I'm positive Colbie would hate knowing I've been asked to look after her.

"Will do," I repeat.

I hang up and walk into Honeybee. Jiminy's bent over a newspaper I know damn well is open to a crossword puzzle. He takes one look at me and says, "Colbie was in here two hours ago picking up breakfast and coffee for everyone."

I close my eyes and shake my head. I don't know why I'm surprised after all the shit I gave her for eating a late breakfast in here last week. She probably did it to prove a point.

Point proved. Her alarm clock works.

I order a fresh cup of coffee and pass along Emmett's message.

Colbie has figured out exactly what to wear to work. The problem is I don't like it any more than what she wore on her first day.

Deep down, I know the problem really is that I like it more than I should. Tight jeans that mold to the curve of her ass. She has them rolled up at the bottom where they sit on top of her laced boots. She wears a white tank top underneath a light brown corduroy button up. Buttons undone.

We are on day four of this outfit. Like the rest of us, she wears the same thing every day, trading out the shirts for different colors. Yesterday, it was maroon. The day before, it was hunter green. Not that I'm keeping track. Because I'm not.

Right now Colbie has everyone gathered around for a morning meeting. Morning meetings are one of Colbie's new additions, along with a water bottle refill station in the trailer and a selection of electrolyte powders.

I've learned quickly that when Colbie cares, she shows it. She endeavors to provide for people, to meet needs, to help where she can.

Who meets Colbie's needs?

I don't think it's Brad. I don't have a solid reason to assume this, and yet I do.

The guys are pretty happy about the water and the

electrolytes, but I thought for certain they would mutiny about morning meetings.

Nope.

At first I thought the crew was placating her, but that was wishful thinking. They genuinely like and respect her. It's not only that she commands a space like Emmett. Two days ago, when the guy who runs the hydraulic digger didn't show, she grabbed a shovel and was out here digging footings with the rest of us. Yesterday, she tied off rebar. She wears a hot pink tool belt. I have no idea where she got it, and I don't want to ask because I fear it may come off sounding like I appreciate it a little too much.

Spoiler alert: I'm having all kinds of indecent and obscene daydreams involving that tool belt.

Colbie stands at the twelve o'clock position, the rest of us situated around her like numbers on a clock. She smiles at the group of men. Instead of keeping my gaze on her, I look around at the men's faces, especially Jeff. That fucker can't keep his eyes off the front of her tank top. I clear my throat loudly and draw his gaze, along with several others. I give him a long, hard stare and he immediately nods his head. Message received.

"Alright, guys," Colbie claps her hands together once, loudly. "Foundation is being poured today, as you already know. The readymix company didn't have enough concrete for us locally, so they are bringing up another truck from Phoenix. The first truck should be here in about"—she checks her watch—"thirty minutes. We'll do the first pour, and hopefully it won't take too long for that other truck to make it up the I-17." She smiles again to let them know her meeting is adjourned. The guys break away, and Colbie heads straight for me.

"Jake?"

"Hmm?" I ask, trying not to be like Jeff. It takes Herculean effort, considering her white tank top has dipped down and her breasts bounce and sway with every step she takes in my direction. *Emmett's daughter. Emmett's daughter.* The reminder is all I need to halt the tightening in the front of my jeans. The word boyfriend wasn't working, so I found an alternative that did.

"I have a meeting with the architect today," Colbie says. "I know it's not great timing, with the foundation being poured and everything, but I've been studying his drawings and I had a couple questions for him."

"You can understand the drawings?" I'm floored. I look at those drawings, and all I see are hieroglyphics. I'm learning, but it's not easy. Until now I've been strictly a concrete guy. I started as a finisher, and over time worked my way to foreman. Still, reading blueprints that detailed is light-years from where I am now.

Colbie's eyes narrow. "Why do you insist on insulting me?"

"What?" I shake my head. How is it that I always manage to upset this woman? It all started because I answered that stupid fucking phone on a day I shouldn't have been allowed anywhere near people. I walked into the trailer to ask Blake a question, but he wasn't there. I decided to wait for him, and while I waited I checked the voicemail left on my phone from an unidentified number earlier that day. It was the first time I'd heard Erin's voice since the day I walked out of the court room with full custody of Robbie.

I know I don't have a right, but I...I was just wondering if I could see Robbie.

I punched out a text message to the number she called from even though I had no idea if she could receive messages at that number.

145

NO.

There wasn't a response from her.

Then the phone in the trailer rang. I shouldn't have answered it. My blood was pumping and I was geared up for a fight. People talk about mama bears being protective, and I know that's because the moms are the ones who stick around and raise the cubs, but what about when the dad sticks around to be the single parent? Does he get to be papa bear? Because I sure as hell feel like all the qualities ascribed to a mama bear could describe me on any given day. Especially on that day, when Erin's pleading and hesitant voice trickled through my phone.

I answered the trailer phone, and Colbie's tone reminded me of way back when, when Erin would come into class five minutes before it started, sling her backpack on the table, and tell me about her day. Now, with the clarity of hindsight, I know the two women don't sound alike. But in that moment, when I learned the caller was Colbie, all I could see was Erin.

It did far more than anger me. It reached down deep, to a place in my heart where fear sits like a perpetually stoking fire.

I took it out on Colbie. Callous and insensitive, I called her princess. My tone made it clear the word wasn't meant nicely.

And then at Martha's gas station, I'd given her shit for asking for non-dairy creamer. I was worried and upset about Emmett, and Erin's voicemail still clung to me like a burr beneath my skin.

With all that as context, do I deserve Colbie's automatic assumptions that whatever I say is likely to be an insult or negative?

Yep.

I run my tongue along the inside of my mouth, searching for a way to explain myself. The truth is probably best, but it would require me to tell her things only my mom, sister, Rhodes, and Emmett know.

Colbie stares at me, waiting. Beyond her shoulder I catch sight of a truck approaching. Knowing we're running out of time, I say, "I can't read those blueprints for shit, and I've been trying for more than two months. Didn't mean that you shouldn't be able to. I only felt surprised because I can't, and that makes me feel stupid."

Colbie glances at the truck. "You're not stupid. My dad taught me how to read blueprints when I was a kid, before..." her voice trails off. "Anyway, these blueprints are about one hundred times more difficult to read than the ones back then. Those were just concrete pours, even the ones with steps and ramps and retaining walls were child's play compared to what I tried to read yesterday."

She brushes her hair aside as she speaks, and I like watching her. It sounds like she's frustrated with herself, so I say, "These blueprints also include the building of a house complete with fake walls and secret rooms. I doubt even Emmett would be very good at reading them."

She offers me a grateful smile, and a single firework detonates in my chest. Maybe I've made up for meanly calling her princess. A little, at least.

She bites her lower lip as the architect pulls his truck beside all the others and turns off his engine. "What that really tells me is that we're probably going to need him to spend more time here."

I'm nodding my agreement when the architect climbs from his truck. Somewhere in the back of my mind I've been assuming the architect was a middle-aged man with a receding hairline and a paunch. He's young, tall, and blond, and even I, with my sexual orientation firmly in the straight category, can see that he is a handsome dude.

Colbie leaves me without a backwards glance. She waves as she walks toward the guy, and even though I can only see the back of her head I'm certain she is smiling. He rounds the bed of his truck, hand extended. They shake, and he places his other hand on top of the handshake, sandwiching her in.

Am I jealous? Fuck yes, I am, though I have no good reason for it. Colbie isn't even single.

She steps away and points to the trailer. The architect reaches into the back seat of his truck and comes away with two long rolls of paper, presumably the physical blueprints.

They make their way to the trailer, and he opens the door for Colbie.

I walk over to where the rest of the guys are standing around the back of someone's truck, their forearms propped along the sides.

"Who was that, Jake?" Jeff points at the trailer with his chin.

"The architect. Colbie had some questions about the blueprints."

Jeff nods. "Why do you look pissed?"

I grimace. "I'm not pissed."

"Uh, ok. You look pretty fucking pissed."

I glance at the trailer. I can't help it.

"Ohhhh."

I don't have to look at Jeff to know he's smiling. I hear it in his voice.

Every guy who had been standing around is listening to us now. Javi smirks.

"Don't get any wrong ideas," I bark.

Jeff squints at me. After a moment, he says, "If it's her

safety you're worried about, you don't have to be. Blake is in there."

"Right," I agree, smacking the side of the truck. In the distance, I see the mixer traveling the same road the architect took. "Alrighty boys," I holler to the crew. "Get ready. Here comes the concrete."

The first truck lumbers down the road, and we start grabbing our tools.

Chapter 19

Colbie

I 'm forcing myself to pay attention to Landon, the architect. It's hard when I keep thinking about Jake, and the way he admitted he had trouble reading the blueprints.

It's certainly not because he's lacking in any way. Most people would have trouble reading them. Blueprints are something you have to learn.

"So," Landon says, bending over the humongous sheet of thick paper. He points at one of the angles. "This is the false wall. If it's pressed here"—he taps the upper right hand corner in that space of the drawing—"the door will swing open. There'll be a small button built into the wall that will activate the mechanism."

"Gotcha." I nod. "All of that is currently being built by the specialty company?"

"Yes." Landon turns to face me, arms crossed in front of his chest. "Emmett should have the details in his email. I've worked with this company on prior projects, they do good work."

"Would you mind sending those details to me as well?"

"No problem." Landon removes his phone from his back pocket and looks at me, waiting.

I recite my email address, then he taps one finger on the phone a few times.

"Should be in there," he says after a moment, sliding the phone into his back pocket. "How is your dad doing?"

"Good. Recovering."

"It's nice you're able to help him on this job." Landon offers a smile. He has nice teeth, but they're not so perfect that it's obvious he went through orthodontia.

I shift my weight, resting my hip against the desk. "Would've been nicer if it had only been a patio pour. I would've even taken a warehouse with loading docks." Compared to this custom build, those would've been over in a blink. Then again, had the job been over in a blink, I wouldn't have had the chance to settle in here and get to know my family.

Did I just think of them as family? I mean, yes, technically, they are. My dad and Greer, because we share DNA, but Victoria, too? I'm going to have to wrestle with that thought later, when it's just me and the stars and a glass of wine.

Landon's head tips to the side. "You sound like you know what you're talking about. Are you in the business?"

"I have memories of listening to my dad talk about jobs, and I went with him to some, but beyond that, no." I walk to my desk and reach into my purse, hand stilling. "I'll show you my secret weapon if you promise not to tell anybody."

Landon holds up three fingers. "Scout's honor."

I lift the books in the air. Blake smirks from behind his laptop. He knows all about my instructional books.

"Seriously?" Landon crosses the small trailer in two strides. He takes the book from my hand and flips the pages.

"You've made highlights," he says, astonished. "And notations in the margins."

"My studying skills have always been stellar," I joke, my tone lofty on purpose.

Landon laughs and sets the construction books on my desk. "Me and a few friends are going to Caruso's on Friday night. You're welcome to join us."

I purse my lips, trying not to show that I'm mildly taken aback by the invitation. "You and a few friends? Will this make me the odd woman out?"

Landon tucks one hand in the pocket of his jeans. "More like it makes me the odd man out. Both of my friends are married, and their wives will be there." Landon's eyes widen, stiff palm slamming into the air between us as if he can halt my train of thought. "I didn't mean to imply that it would be a triple date. That's not what I'm doing. I'm not asking you on a date." He sighs tersely and shuts his eyes. When he reopens them, he says, "Maybe I should stick to architecture and not speak ever again."

This makes me laugh. If it's not a date, then I'm game to meet some people. "Caruso's on Friday night sounds like a good idea."

Landon tells me what time, then he rolls up the blueprints and snaps a rubber band around them.

I walk him out of the trailer, pausing to look for Jake once we're outside. It's probably a good idea that they know each other, considering Jake is my second-in-command on this job. If this custom home goes well, it's likely they will work together on future custom homes.

"Do you have a couple minutes to meet my foreman?" I ask Landon.

He nods a yes, and we walk across the dirt to where the

cement mixer has backed up. I knew it had arrived, because I'd heard the loud beeping sound as it reversed.

Jake wears a hard hat, and those jeans that are too sexy for his own good. He holds a long handled trowel as he smooths cement back-and-forth.

"Jake," I shout as we get closer. The churning cement mixer roars. He doesn't hear me, so I have to get even closer. I touch his shoulder at the same time I say his name, and he must be lost in his own world because it startles him. He jolts, and I take a quick step back.

Right into Landon.

He grunts as my back slams into his chest. I whip around to apologize, but now my feet are tangled beneath me. Hands shoot out to steady me, two on my shoulders and two on my waist.

"Whoa," I say, faking a laugh to cover my embarrassment. "Good thing I had you both to help me. The plans for the day would've really changed if I face-planted the concrete."

Landon releases me. Jake's hands remain on my waist, and I swear I feel just the tiniest squeeze of my hips before he lets go.

I'm not sure if the heat on my cheeks is from Jake's touch, or my almost-fall, but I do my best to brush it off and act unruffled. Taking a step away from both men, this time without incidence, I say, "Whew. That was not the way I intended to introduce you." I make introductions, and despite the sweat and dirt likely covering Jake's hands, Landon extends his hand and they shake.

Reaching up, I place my hand on Jake's upper arm with the lightest of touches. Even so, I feel the hard muscle under his shirt, the way it dips and curves. Addressing Landon, I say, "Jake was telling me earlier how he wishes he could read blueprints. Any tips?" I look at Jake, thinking he'll be happy I've made this connection. He's not. His jaw tightens as he slides an irritated glance my way.

I'm confused. Didn't he say he wanted to get better at reading blueprints?

Landon bats the bound blueprints against his open palm. "It's mostly exposure. Is this your first time doing a custom home?"

Jake drags his thumb across the seam of his lips, and nods.

"More than anything," Landon says, "it's seeing what's on paper come together in real life. Blueprints make a lot more sense once you've seen that happen. Exposure, and experience, I suppose. The only other thing I'd say is to pay attention to the key."

Jake nods again. "Cool, man. Thanks." He seems antsy to get back to work.

"You bet," Landon says. "I'll be here a lot more in the next few weeks once the framers get started. I'd be happy to walk you through the blueprints as things are progressing." Landon's attention shifts to me without waiting for Jake to respond to his offer. "I'll see you on Friday night?" His eyebrows lift, and I nod my agreement. "I can pick you up," he offers.

"I'll meet you there." I prefer to drive myself, and if he picked me up it would feel more like a date.

Landon leaves, and now I feel Jake's stare heating up the right side of my face.

"What?" I ask, trying and failing to keep the irritation from my voice.

"You're going on a date with him?" He doesn't growl, exactly, but his voice deepens and he sounds incredulous.

I force my hands to stay at my sides, remaining casual.

It's a farce. Casual is the last thing I feel inside. "What business is it of yours?"

His lips form a hard line, and he grits out, "I thought you had a boyfriend."

"Why would you think that?" I'm almost positive I've never uttered the words *boyfriend* or *Brad* in his presence.

"Your dad mentioned it that day we were both in his hospital room. Brad?"

I shake my head. "No more Brad."

Jake suddenly looks horrified, like he thinks maybe he's made a colossal mistake. "Oh, God. He didn't die, did he?"

I press my lips together to keep from laughing at Jake's horror. "Figuratively, he did. To me, anyway."

Jake's eyebrows scrunch together as he tries to figure out what it is I'm really saying. I put him out of his misery and explain. "Brad decided it was a good idea to sleep with someone else while he and I were together."

Jake crosses his arms, eyebrows lifted. "He cheated?"

I love the way Jake says it. Like not only can he not believe it, but it infuriates him at the same time. "Yes."

"Hmph."

I shrug. "So, there you have it. I'm free as a bird."

Jake looks extremely unhappy. Maybe he was cheated on in a previous relationship, and now I've caused him to remember it.

He bends down to pick up the tool he dropped when he caught me from falling. "I'll see you there."

"Where?"

He straightens. "Caruso's. You're not the only one with a date on Friday night."

This news takes me by surprise, but it shouldn't. Jake is a catch. Of course he has a date. Ignoring that little green monster running amok inside me, I say, "Lovely." I smile, fully aware of how disingenuous it is. "Maybe we can have a round together."

Jake doesn't answer. He turns around and gets back to work. I'd love to jump in and help, but I'm not sure what it is they're doing. If this were a sidewalk or patio, I'd use my bent-edge trowel to go along the forms and create a nice, curved edge. This is foundation though, and it doesn't appear to require any finesse beyond making sure the pour is even.

I leave Jake alone, and walk to where Javi works his trowel.

As promised on my first day on the job, I ask Javi to teach me what he's doing. I do my very best to pay attention and learn, and for the most part, I'm successful.

In those moments when my attention strays from Javi, it makes its way across the square of wet concrete. Jake, working to evenly smooth the concrete against the forms, appears to be in his own world once again. It gives me the opportunity to surreptitiously watch him work.

He reaches out, body taut, muscles flexed as he steadies his lower half while his upper half does the work. He moves fluidly, in a rhythm that is as beautiful as any dance.

Whoever is going on a date with him tomorrow night is a very lucky lady.

Chapter 20

Jake

There's a knock on my front door, but I ignore it. My little sister won't wait for me to walk across the house. Her knock is more of a cursory announcement that she's arrived and letting herself in.

I'm pushing the chicken pot pie into the oven when Georgia breezes into the kitchen. She wears overalls, and a flimsy scrap of cloth that is far too small and tight.

"Nice excuse for a shirt," I say, but she pretends not to hear me.

"Whoa there, master chef." Georgia bends at the waist and inspects the food before I have the chance to close the oven door. She bumps me with her hip, but her legs are shorter than mine, so it's really my thigh she bumps. "Cooking from scratch just for me? I feel honored."

I close the oven. "Don't," I deadpan, wrapping one arm around her shoulders and giving her a quick side hug. "I bought it in the prepared food section of the grocery store."

She lifts a single finger in the air as she prepares to make a point. I swear my sister could argue with a brick wall. "But you could make it, right?"

I nod once, solemnly. Cooking from scratch saves a lot of money, and that has been important over the years. I also discovered that I actually like to cook. There's something relaxing about the process.

"Totally counts." Georgia saunters over to the fridge and opens it. She has my mother's diminutive stature and blonde hair, but our father's dark eyes. If given the opportunity, she'll complain at length about the unfairness of me getting our mom's green eyes.

Georgia comes away from the fridge with two beers. She twists off the tops, handing one to me. "Cheers," she says, lightly tapping the bottom of her bottle against mine.

"I don't think I want my babysitter drinking on the job." I raise my eyebrows at her and give her a look.

"Maybe if you paid her, she wouldn't drink on the job." Georgia takes a long, purposeful pull from her beer.

I frown. "I offered to pay you."

"Yes, I know. But if I accepted your offer, I wouldn't be able to drink this beer. Do you see the dilemma?"

I try not to smile at her, but it's damn near impossible. As much as she drives me crazy sometimes, Georgia is hands-down one of my favorite people.

She settles at the kitchen table, chin propped in her hands. "Where's Robbie?"

"His room. He said he has three more problems left on his math homework."

Georgia watches me remove two plates from a cabinet, along with forks and knives. "How did you end up with a studious kid?" she asks, teasing me.

I shrug. "Beats me."

"Must be Erin's genetics. God knows you weren't making sure homework due Monday was finished before the weekend began."

I stiffen at Georgia's casual mention of Erin. Normally a comment like that would roll off my back, but that was before Erin began making contact after all this time.

Georgia, oblivious to my discomfort, pulls a tube of Chapstick from her purse and asks, "Whatcha up to tonight?" She slathers on the Chapstick, wiping around the edges of her lips with a finger.

"Caruso's for a school function. Pretty much an excuse for a happy hour, and I'll be subjected to the school gossip."

Georgia nods knowingly. "Ooohh, the good stuff."

"Good stuff?"

"Which teachers are sleeping together, things like that."

I wrinkle my nose. "I'd rather not know those things. Especially because you're trying to get a job there."

Georgia rolls her eyes at me. "If they'll ever have another opening, you mean. Greer got the last one." She sighs. "Someone either has to quit, or die. Small towns can be really difficult when it comes to job openings and movement up the ladder."

If it wasn't for Emmett feeling bad for me after my dad died, I have no idea what I'd be doing for work. "I'll ask around tonight. Maybe one of the room moms will have some inside information."

One of Georgia's nostrils scrunches. "Are you going to be by yourself with the mom brigade?" She makes a mock horrified face.

I finish my beer and toss it in the recycling. "Rhodes will be there."

Georgia's mock horror turns real. She knows Rhodes well enough to know that isn't his scene. "Why will Rhodes be there? He doesn't have a kid."

"Nope. But he does have a date with one of the moms."

Georgia traces the label on her beer bottle with her finger, and if I didn't know any better I'd say she looks sad. Good thing I know better.

"What?" I ask.

She glances up at me. "Nothing." She says it like *how dare you ask me a stupid question.*

I point at the oven. "Forty-five more minutes, and then make sure you let it cool before you serve it. Whoever makes those at the supermarket doesn't score the top, so all the steam sits inside. You can score it yourself when you take it out."

She smirks. "I guess next time you should make it yourself."

"And rob you of the chance of searching the internet for what it means to score the top of pot pie? Never."

Robbie comes flying into the room, ready to tell his aunt about school and friends and whatever else is on his mind. I excuse myself to shower and change while they talk.

Fifteen minutes later I'm on the road. Colbie's car is already gone from her driveway, and I'm not willing to think too hard about why I noticed that detail.

My thumbs drum a beat on the steering wheel as I drive. What's this feeling in my stomach? Nerves? Nah. Can't be.

It's just some drinks with parents from Robbie's school. Nothing to be nervous about. I mean, yeah, Colbie said she'd be there with Landon. And she's going to put two and two together pretty quickly and realize I'm not actually on a date. Unless Kiersten has more than a few drinks, that is. She's been known to get handsy if she goes past three. I really hope that's not the case tonight, because I'm not interested in playing games. I won't use Kiersten to make Colbie jealous, even if it would be a satisfying stroke to my ego. Assuming Colbie reacted the way I want her to.

Wait...how do I want her to react?

I shake my head, annoyed at my thoughts. I'm being stupid.

I don't give a shit how she reacts.

I don't even care that she's going to be there.

She's my boss, and my mentor's daughter. End of story.

※※※

"What do you think, Jake?" Kiersten slings an arm over my shoulder. She's leaning sideways, her other arm resting on the large, high-top table we're occupying in the bar area of the restaurant.

There are ten people total, all women except for me and Rhodes. Kiersten's halfway through her second drink, her face only a few inches away from mine as she speaks.

None of the other moms are paying attention to her, so it seems it's up to me to keep her away from that third drink.

"What do I think about...?" Had we been in the middle of a conversation? I don't think so.

She rolls her eyes flirtatiously and shakes her head. "The bake sale. We need to raise money for teacher appreciation day."

I don't have the heart to remind her we covered this topic twenty-five minutes ago. "Are you hungry?" Kiersten needs to get some food in her, pronto.

"Food would probably be a good idea," she answers, hiccuping. She covers her mouth with her hand and blushes. "I haven't eaten since breakfast this morning."

"Why didn't you eat lunch?"

"I was just so busy running around." She shrugs, like it's not a big deal. "I forgot."

I cannot imagine a time when I forgot to eat. I'll get busy and put it off, but forgetting? I don't think that's ever happened to me.

The server stops at our table to see if we need more drinks, but I ask, "Can we order some food from you?"

She nods. "Shoot," she says, taking her order pad and pen from her waist apron.

I point my thumb at Kiersten, indicating for her to order.

"Do you have salad here?" Kiersten asks.

I know it's not my business what she eats, but...What. The. Fuck? Leafy greens and alcohol sounds like a recipe for disaster. "Kiersten, how about a burger? Or the chicken marsala? Do you like mushrooms?"

Kiersten misinterprets my concern for care. She leans her shoulder into me, and looks at me like she's touched. "It's so sweet that you want to order for me."

I take a new approach and make it about logic. "You can order whatever you want, but I think it's better to eat something substantial if you're drinking. You need food to soak up the alcohol, or you run the risk of feeling really bad later tonight."

"Good idea," she says, winking at me.

Oh, fuck. She thinks I meant something I most definitely did not mean.

I look to Rhodes, hoping I can get him to rope me into conversation so I can hit the ejector button on this interaction with Kiersten. No dice, though. He's been talking with Tessa since we arrived, but I can tell from his body language he's not into her. I wonder why he asked her on a date in the first place?

Beside me, I hear Kiersten ordering on her own, so I guess she took the hint. My gaze wanders, traveling over into the restaurant half of Caruso's. It's quieter over there, groups of twos and fours sitting at tables with proper stemware and silverware.

I've been trying not to look for Colbie, but I can't take it any longer. I want to see what she wore for her date. How she styled her hair. Did she spritz perfume in special places, leaving Landon a scented trail to follow later?

I spot her chestnut hair at the back of the restaurant. Landon is beside her, along with two other couples. So, not a real date then? A triple date?

She fibbed?

Just like you did.

I finish my beer and try to fend off Kiersten's advances. She's like an octopus. As soon as I shrug off one tentacle, there's another making its way around me. Kiersten's food arrives and I've never been so happy to see chicken marsala in my life. She's forced to use a knife and fork, which keeps her hands off me and her mouth busy chewing. Small miracles. I glance over my shoulder, checking on Colbie. It's probably the twelfth time I've done this, and I thought I was being sufficiently sneaky about it, but suddenly Rhodes is in my ear. "Just go over there and talk to her." He slides a second beer in front of me.

I thank him as he settles on the empty stool beside me. At the end of the table, Tessa is knee-deep in a lively conversation with someone else. "Go over and talk to who?" I ask, feigning confusion.

His expression says *nice try*. "Whoever it is sitting in the restaurant that you're keeping tabs on."

Kiersten shifts closer. She takes a bite, playing off like

she's eating, but I know better. She caught what Rhodes said, and now she's trying to get the tea.

I give Rhodes a warning look and shake my head covertly. Rhodes catches on. "My bad. I like that painting on the wall, too. I bet the owner would tell you where he got it."

"Thanks, I'll ask before we leave."

Kiersten returns to her normal position. Thank fuck. The last thing I need is a spin on the rumor mill. I spent more than enough time there when I came back to this small town as a single father. The reason why is one juicy nugget I'm sure plenty of people would love to get their hands on. People love hearing about the follies and foibles of others. It's like slowing down to look at a car accident; it reminds us we're doing ok in life because we're not the one in trouble at the moment.

"How's it going?" I ask Rhodes, trying to convey that I'm asking about the date without directly mentioning it.

He lifts a flattened palm an inch above the table, tipping it back-and-forth.

"Then why?" I ask.

He shrugs. "I'm about to head out to New York for a long job. It was something to do besides work."

I take a sip from my new beer. "Do me a favor and don't say that to anybody but me."

"Sounds awful?"

"Terrible."

He nods. "Who's with Robbie tonight?"

"Georgia."

He nods again, slower this time.

I can't help myself. I look out into the restaurant.

The *painting* is gone from the table.

"Here." I shove my beer to Rhodes. "You can have this."

164

He looks down at it. "I don't want that."

"Then don't have it." I stand. "I'll be right back. I have to take a leak."

I have no idea if Rhodes says anything else because I'm already hightailing it out of the bar area and toward the restrooms at the back of the restaurant. Conveniently located near Colbie's table.

I walk down the narrow hallway where the restrooms are located, but Colbie is nowhere to be found. Since I'm there, I slip into the restroom.

I finish up, and step out into the small hallway. At the same time, the door across the way opens. Colbie steps out.

Her eyes widen when she sees me. "Hey." Her voice is high-pitched, and her gaze flickers down the length of me before she meets my eyes. "I was wondering if I was going to run into you."

She wears a creamy white button down blouse tucked into a short suede skirt. Her toned legs go on for miles, and her shoes make her taller.

"I didn't see you out there." Colbie tips her head toward the rest of the place. "I thought you'd been stood up. Or you did the standing up."

My chin lifts slowly, eyes squinting. "So what you're saying is that you looked for me."

Her lips twitch like she wants to smile. The tip of her tongue darts out to wet her bottom lip. "I guess so."

Her admission feels like I've won a very big, hard-to-win prize. I have an urge to toss her over my shoulder and march her out of here. There's nothing for either of us here, so there's no reason to stay. The question is, what would we do if we left?

Colbie tips her head out to the restaurant. "I should probably get back."

Oh, right. Landon. Honestly, I forgot about the guy until now. "How's your triple date going?"

The corners of Colbie's lips turn down. "Why do you say it like that?"

"How did I say it?" A guy comes down the hallway, and I step away from the door to the men's bathroom so he can go in. This puts me a foot closer to Colbie. She's wearing more makeup than usual, and gold hoop earrings. Makeup or no makeup, she's beautiful. Even frowning at me, like she is right now, she's gorgeous.

Colbie's arms cross. It takes everything I have not to stare at the way it magnifies her cleavage. "You said it like it's not a thing," she grounds out, irritated. "Like the date's not real."

I can't help my smirk. "I think you're the only one who can say whether or not the date is real."

Now it's Colbie's turn to step aside for somebody coming out of the bathroom. She leans the back of her head up against the wall, but she keeps her gaze on me. "I thought it was supposed to be me going out with Landon and a few of his friends so I can get to know people. Once I said yes, he admitted it was two other couples. He says it's not a date, but it kind of feels like it."

My fingers stroke the scruff on my jaw. "Would you have said yes to him if he asked you on a date you were certain was a date?"

She looks at me like she's trying to figure me out. "Why do you ask? Why do you care?"

Somehow in the last twenty seconds, I've drifted closer to her. It would take very little effort for me to run my hands along her silk sleeve. "I don't care." The lie slips between my teeth.

"Jake?"

She says my name in this feminine way, soft and sweet.

"Hmm?" There's a freckle on the top of her right ear, and I have no idea why I like it this much.

Her hand comes up between us, a single fingertip poking at one of the buttons on the front of my shirt. "You look like you care."

Her voice has dropped, low and sultry, and it curls into my chest, making its way down to a part of me that would love nothing more than for me to steal her away.

All I can think about right now is putting my lips on hers. Colbie's eyes shimmer with lust, and she takes a deep breath. Her breasts strain her shirt with her inhale, causing it to fall open. Ivory. Lace. *Fuck me.* "Maybe I—"

"Jake?"

The voice is an arrow into our bubble, as disturbing as the drill at the dentist.

The spell is broken.

I rip my gaze from Colbie, who is already looking at the owner of the voice.

I cough, trying like hell to get control of myself. "Hey, Kiersten."

Colbie steps sideways, putting space between us. Eyes that only a few moments ago held desire now hold blazing anger. Each emotion for me. I can say quickly and with certainty which one I'd take over the other.

My mouth opens, ready to confess I was never on a date, but Colbie's already moving away. "See you Monday," she says as she goes, acknowledging Kiersten with a nod as she passes.

Colbie disappears back to her table. Kiersten makes her way toward me on unsteady feet. "Now I see why you don't like me," she says, her voice almost singsong, but there's hurt behind it. "You have a crush on Emmett Jones's daughter."

167

I stare at Kiersten. "How do you know who she is?"

"It's a small town," she says, like this should answer my question. "I bring donuts for the teachers every Monday morning, and I saw her at Honeybee when I was picking them up. She left, and I asked Jiminy who she was." Kiersten lifts her hands in the air and shakes them like she has done some kind of magic trick. Her eyes sparkle with pleasure at having a secret. "Emmett is your mentor, right?"

I don't say anything because the question doesn't need a response. She already knows the answer.

"I bet he's thrilled to know you have a thing for his daughter." Her smile has turned a little sour. I wonder if she knows how easy it is to read the insecurity on her face. I should feel anger at her over this thinly veiled threat of hers, but I don't. I feel bad for her.

"I don't have anything for her." My arms cross. "She's my boss, and we were discussing something that happened on the job this week."

Kiersten does a grumbly, disbelieving laugh in her throat. "Right."

As if I can see into the future, I watch the rumor mill starting to churn. Colbie and I will be a topic of conversation in no time. "Anyway," I point over at the bar. "I'm headed back that way. Are you coming?"

"I came over here for a reason," she responds with less warmth than is typical for her, and pushes into the restroom.

I pass Colbie's table. She makes it a point not to look at me, but damn do I feel the heat of her fury.

I'll need to explain about Kiersten and the real reason I was here tonight, but it'll have to wait. I hate the idea of her thinking something untrue about me, but there's nothing I can do for now. Sending her a text doesn't feel right, either.

I want to look her in the eyes and be certain she knows I wasn't flirting with her while I was on a date with someone else. The last thing Colbie needs is another reason not to trust someone.

I settle back on my seat beside Rhodes.

He gives me a long once-over. "You ok?"

"Fine," I mutter, glancing in Colbie's direction even though I know she's sitting with her back to me.

Rhodes pats my shoulder. "Too bad I'm headed to New York to work. This would've been fun to watch unfold."

"Shut up," I grumble, my eyes lingering on Colbie's dark hair.

She is beautiful, intelligent, capable, and kind.

Single.

And she should probably be off-limits.

It's the perfect recipe for destruction. Still, I can't help thinking about her beautiful face. And the way she bites the inside of her cheek when she's trying not to smirk at something I've said. Or how about yesterday, when Javi helped her finish concrete? Never thought a girl like her would waltz into my hamlet in the middle of Arizona, yet here she is. Though, I guess she's been here all along, in an odd way.

I shift in my seat, willing my erection to go away. There won't be a damn thing I can do with that until later.

Because I like pain, I opt for another peek over my shoulder at Colbie. She's laughing at something, her body twisted to face Landon beside her.

It's too loud in here for Rhodes to hear the growl in my throat, but he sees my scowl and laughs.

"Fuck off," I mutter.

It's official.

Colbie Jones just might be capable of reducing me to rubble.

Chapter 21

Colbie

Greer shows up at my house bright and early on Saturday morning with a box of assorted pastries. She'd texted during the week, as promised, and I told her whatever time she wanted to come over Saturday morning was fine. That was before I realized the week of accumulated early mornings would have me exhausted by the time the weekend hit.

"I really hope you have coffee," she says as I open the door. She's wearing gray leggings and a black tank top, bright orange sports bra beneath. I yawn my answer and step back. She sails past my pajama-clad self, the sweet scent of pastries floating by as she goes. "I always wondered who lives in the flamingo house."

I close the door and lead her into the kitchen. "The school crossing guard lives next door," I point east, to Alma and Arthur's house. "Why didn't you ask her?"

"That woman is like a miniature locomotive." Greer lowers her head and shoulders past me to show me what she means, knocking me out of the way as she goes by. "She walks everywhere like that. As if she's late. I haven't been brave enough to tap her on the shoulder and ask."

I give her a tired laugh and try to tame my rumpled hair. "Coffee before imitations. Come on." The coffee has just finished brewing, so I prepare two cups. Greer opens cupboards until she finds plates, then removes two. The smell of sugar overtakes the small kitchen when she opens up the box.

"Which one do you want?" She pushes the box my way.

I peer down. "Are any of them dairy-free?"

"What's your deal with dairy?" she asks. I know she's thinking about the pasta salad we ate last weekend, when I ate everything but the cheese. "I know you're not allergic to it."

"It upsets my stomach."

"Mine, too." She reaches into the purse she hung around the back of her chair, and hands something to me. "That's why I take these."

I take the bottle of pills she's holding out, my eyes widening and excitement growing in my chest. "Sweet Mother Mary you have digestive enzymes?" This opens up a whole new world for me. Here in Green Haven, at least.

"Yep. I take two of those, and then eat a slice of pizza. It's great."

I shake two into my hand. "I forgot mine at home."

She shakes her head. "Why didn't you go to the drug store and buy some?"

"I didn't know they were available everywhere. I get mine online."

"Ok, fancy pants." Greer reaches for a cruller.

I swallow the pills with a sip of coffee, then choose a pastry with a creamy center. "Here goes nothing!" My teeth sink into the sugary goodness and I try not to moan at the burst of flavor.

"How was last night?" Greer asks, sipping her coffee.

I'd called her last night on my way to Caruso's. I wanted to check on our dad, but also I'd been around men all week and I needed to chat with someone who spoke more than three-word sentences.

"It was fine. Landon is nice. So are his friends."

Her eyes lift as she leans in to take another bite. "Nice?"

"I told you it wasn't a date. It wasn't supposed to be."

"Right, but it was like an interview date. You know, where you see if there's enough chemistry to go on a real date."

"Hah." I swallow my bite. "Then I guess the purpose was served. There is no spark to speak of between us." Not to mention the fact that I don't want to conduct an interview date to see if there's chemistry. I want there to be undeniable attraction, that magnetism that causes limbs to stiffen while you rise up on the tips of your toes in anticipation. None of that happened last night. Not with Landon, anyhow...

"What else?" Greer presses. She looks like she knows something.

I shrug. "What do you mean?"

"I heard you had sparks with someone else."

My eyes narrow. "How could you have possibly heard such a thing?"

"You, Miss Big City Girl, need to remember that everybody knows everybody in this town. And if somebody doesn't know everybody, they know someone who does know everybody. Catch my drift?"

"Are you speaking in riddles?"

"Haha." Greer deadpans. "The parent happy hour in the bar last night were parents from my classroom. They have a group text that I'm in. It's supposed to be used for classroom and school-related conversation, but I think a few of the moms had too much to drink." She rolls her eyes. "I was getting notifications all night. I finally silenced them."

"Oh my God." My palm catches my drooping forehead. The surprise on that woman's face in the hallway comes barreling back to me. I have a feeling I was a topic of conversation in last night's messages.

"One of the texts said you and Jake were spotted in a dark corner with your hands all over each other." Greer's grinning as she takes her next bite, obviously enjoying every second of this.

I scoff. "Lies. He was on a date."

"No, he wasn't."

"Yes, he was," I insist. "I saw her."

"Colbie," Greer says my name sternly, like she's the big sister. "Jake was attending the parent happy hour. And he wasn't there with any of the moms. He was just...there."

I frown. Who the hell was the woman who showed up in the hallway and acted like she had a right to be shocked to see Jake standing so close to me?

I shake my head. "I'm confused. Jake wasn't on a date?"

"The messages from last night made it clear he was there on his own."

All the anger I've been directing Jake's way since last night begins to recede. "I was so mad at him." My fingertips press against my lower lip as I think about the way he towered over me in the hallway. He was this...this hulking man who was ready to eat me alive in the best possible way. I felt the desire coming off his skin, smelled the lust on his breath. My body had responded in a way I knew probably wasn't smart, but I didn't feel capable of stopping it. Nor did I want to. Until that woman appeared. "I thought he was cheating on his date. Or whatever you want to call it," I hurry to amend, since we didn't even kiss. "Screwing her over, disrespecting her, whatever."

Greer squints at me as she tries to understand. "How did he cheat or screw over his date? The one he wasn't on?"

I sigh and sit back, crossing my legs at the ankle and tucking them under her seat. Greer should be an investigator, with the way she's coaxing this answer from me. "We ran into each other. Yes, it was a hallway," I admit. Greer's eyes light up. "But we weren't in a dark corner, and his hands were not all over me." Just saying those words makes the tops of my thighs ache.

"Do you wish they were?" Her eyebrows waggle.

"Greer!"

"What?"

"You're my little sister. I can't talk to you about this stuff." I need Christina. I can say anything to her.

"Yes, I'm your sister, but I still live at home because it's cheaper and I'm saving up to buy a house. So, my sex life is abysmal." She takes a triumphant bite, like she's proved a point. "Besides, don't you think, at this point in our lives, we should aim for becoming friends, not just sisters?"

I take a sip of coffee. A bite of food. Anything to prolong my response. At some point, whether it's tomorrow or next month, we're going to have to get real about everything that happened. We're dancing around it now, not just because it's uncomfortable and unpleasant to talk about the hard stuff, but because we want to prolong the peace.

I cannot tell her everything that really happened. I know what it feels like to be told about your parents' misdeeds, and then be forced to see them, all while looking at them and knowing what they've done. How their mistakes have cost you. I will not dump my dad's past mistakes into Greer's present.

"Fine." I nod. "As friends, I can tell you that Jake and I had a conversation last night. It was flirtatious. He stood closer to me than necessary, and then a woman appeared and looked shocked and hurt, and I thought she was his date." I feel like a fool. The way I acted...Jake must think I'm a nutjob.

Greer shakes her head at me, like I'm clueless and pitiful. "His hands, Colbie. I asked if you wished his hands were on you."

Jake's work-roughened hands, sliding over my skin... skimming my nipples...drifting down between my thighs.

My breath is choppy when I answer. "Yes."

Greer celebrates with a fist in the air. "If you two got together, it would be the best thing. Jake deserves to be happy after everything he has been through."

"I've been wondering about that," I say, seizing on the chance to change the topic. "Where is Robbie's mom?"

Greer bites the side of her lip. "I'm not supposed to know, but when I was younger I had a habit of hiding in closets and jumping out to scare Dad. Honestly, I was probably too old to be doing it still, but it was a way that we connected, so I kept it going."

I try not to let this affect me, but it does. The pain is that of a nip, instead of a bite, and I push it away because I'm not interested in paying attention to it right now.

Greer continues, because she has no idea it hurts me to hear about something cute she did with our dad. "I was in his office closet when Jake stopped by. Robbie was a tiny baby, and Jake was asking Dad for help. I remember him asking for a loan because he needed to fight for full custody.

I didn't hear everything he said, but I specifically remember that Jake looked really sad."

Wow. Ok. Jake is a lot deeper than I initially thought. "Did he win full custody? I've only lived here for a week and a half, but he and Robbie are always together if you don't count work and school."

Greer's nodding before I finish my sentence. "He sure did. Again, I don't know the details because Jake has been tight-lipped about it all, but I heard Dad tell my mom that Jake had to fight tooth and nail to get Robbie."

That means somebody else fought for Robbie, too. His mother? And why did Jake end up with custody? What tipped the scale in his favor?

"Jake hasn't dated anybody since he came back to town, either." She gestures at me with her cup. "You'd be the first."

I lift a palm to stop her. "Hold up. Back to town? Where did he go?"

"He got a full-ride football scholarship to University of Arizona. He went to college, and three years later he returned with a baby."

I blink. "What?"

"Crazy, right?" She blows hair from her face. "I mean, obviously there's a lot more to the story. But those are the major plot points."

"Damn." I twirl the earring in my ear. "I think I owe Jake an apology."

"For?"

"I made sure he knew I was angry with him last night." I blow out a breath. "He didn't do anything wrong."

Greer opens her mouth to talk at the same time there's a knock on my front door. I stand, and Greer gets up with me.

"I don't know who that is," I tell her, gesturing at our food and drink, "but you don't have to go."

Greer looks at her watch. "I have to meet my run club in twenty minutes."

"Run club?" We make our way to the front door.

"A group of us get together and go for a long run every Saturday morning. You can come, if you want."

"Running isn't my thing. I get shin splints too easily."

"There aren't any barre studios here," Greer points out as I peek through the peephole to see who's there.

I whip around, back pressed to the door. "It's Jake," I whisper-hiss. My eyes are wide, my heart beats out a frenzied rhythm.

"You have to answer it," Greer whispers. "I need to leave."

"You can't sneak out the back?"

"No." She says the word with the kind of patience you'd use on an unreasonable child. "I'm not the other woman."

Her comment strikes a nerve. I push back my hair and swipe under my eyes for any remnants of last night's eyeliner. Then I answer the door.

"Good morning," I say, too high-pitched and perky even for my own ears.

His gaze switches from me to my sister, then back to me. "I'm sorry. I didn't mean to interrupt anything."

"I was just leaving," Greer says, squeezing past him. "See you later, Colbie. Bye, Jake."

We both say goodbye, and then there's nothing but silence as we listen to the sounds of Greer's car starting up and driving off.

"So," I say, when her car is gone.

"About last night," he says at the same time. He grins. "You go first."

177

Jennifer Millikin

I lean into the doorjamb. "I was going to apologize, but if you were planning to apologize also, you can go first."

He rocks back onto his heels and tucks his hands in his pockets. "I see what you did there." He runs a hand through his thick, dark hair. It's still messy from sleep, and I like that he didn't make sure it was done before he came over. "I'm sorry about last night. I let you think I was there on a date, and then..." he looks at me through his dark fringe of lashes. "You know. The hallway."

I nod. "My turn. I'm sorry I got so upset with you. My anger wasn't meant for you."

His head cocks sideways. "Who was it meant for?"

There's a small rock on the ground between us, and I push at it with my toe. "The last few guys I dated. Especially the most recent one."

I'm not really loving the vulnerability, but I know something private about him now, thanks to Greer. If I share something about myself with him, maybe we'll be on a level playing field.

"The last few guys you dated?" He sounds incredulous. "I know about Brad, but what did the other guys do to you?"

"What makes you so sure they did something to me?" My eyebrows lift, playful. "Maybe I did something to them."

Jake watches me. His green irises deepen, shifting from damp moss to a forest after a rain. He shakes his head. "People who do the hurting don't act like you."

His remark hits me in the center of the chest. Bullseye. "How do people who've been hurt behave?" I already know. I think, anyway.

His stare grips me, stealing the breath from my throat. "Like us," he murmurs.

Oh. Jake has been hurt. By Robbie's mother? Greer's comment comes back to me. He went to college, and three years later he returned with a baby.

I want to ask him about Robbie, but I don't want to pry about something monumental like the custody of a child. I focus on my part in his statement instead. "How do I act?"

"You put on a tough show, but you're here in Green Haven helping out your dad's business when you've been mostly estranged from him for years. You could've told him to find someone else, but you didn't. You could've quit that first day when you showed up on the jobsite and saw what was in store for you. You didn't. You bought books, boots, a tool belt and jeans—"

I'm horrified. "You know about the books?"

"I came into the trailer for water and saw them open on your desk."

I flush, and his hands reach into the space between us, shaking from side to side as if he means to brush away my embarrassment. "Most people are so afraid of failing that they don't attempt to learn. But you." His hands lift, almost like he's going to touch me the way he did last night. At the last moment he must think better of it, because his hands return to his sides. "You're not afraid to try. You've got it figured out. I'm in awe of you."

He says it softly, an admittance, and now I'm wishing he'd take those hands and put them all over me.

I swallow it all, the desire and the pleasure his compliment sets off in me. Both make me nervous. "I don't have anything figured out." How does he look at me and not see a mess? A woman who has a knack for showing men what they don't want? A woman who can barely accept affection from her father?

179

Jake's feet plant in a wide stance, as if he's settling in. "Don't do that." The timbre of his tone is gentle, yet firm.

The way he's standing releases a sense of ease inside me. "Do what?"

"Undercut your accomplishment. Your tenacity."

Who is this man on my front porch making these sensitive remarks? I'd thought he was a burly construction worker with a fantastic ass and a tendency to growl his words, and now here he is, peeling back a layer and showing me the deep thinker within.

"So, what is it?" I must have a confused look on my face, because Jake asks, "What did they do to you?"

"You know about Brad. The others didn't do what Brad did." I'm swept up in a wave of shame. I feel deficient, but I power on. "They essentially told me I'm emotionally unavailable. And they all went on to marry the next woman they dated. Making me the woman who helps men learn what they don't want."

"Isn't that what dating is? Figuring out what you don't want until you find someone who possesses most of what you do?"

"Yes, but it's hard to be the person before The One. Over and over and over."

Jake nods. "I can see that. Also, they're idiots."

"I appreciate that." A smile tugs on one corner of my mouth. It feels good to be honest and clear the air between us, so I decide to take it one step further. "I'm sorry if I've been short with you."

Jake pushes away my apology with a wave of his hands. "It's my fault. I was having a bad day when you called the trailer looking for your dad. I was rude to you, and I'm sorry."

I grin. "I accept your apology, Not Blake."

A laugh bursts from Jake, loud and full and happy. "If I hadn't been in such a bad mood that day, I would've laughed."

"This is nice." I gesture between us. "Not being so antagonistic."

Jake licks his lips, then clears his throat. "Yeah."

"About last night—"

"I'm sorry about that, too," Jake rushes to say. "Blame it on the beer."

"The beer?"

Jake nods once. I feel disappointed. I don't know what I'd been expecting, but I didn't think he'd blame those stolen moments last night on overindulgence.

I smile through my feelings. "Let's forget it happened." It's better this way, for many reasons. I'm his boss, he's probably one of my dad's top five favorite people in the world, I'm not staying in Green Haven, and I have the unique ability to send men running. I'm a walking red flag, and Jake has Robbie to think of.

Jake rocks back on his heels. "I have one more thought about those guys you dated."

"What's that?"

"They were lazy."

"Lazy?"

"They weren't willing to put in the work. I haven't known you very long, but I can say with complete certainty that you are worth the work, Buttercup."

Oh, my heart.

Jake grins. "Is buttercup better or worse than princess?"

"So much better." If butterflies in the stomach are how we describe nerves, how do I describe the fluttery feeling in my chest right now?

An old man and woman pass my house, out for a

morning walk. They peer over curiously, waving when they realize I've caught them peeping.

Jake looks at them over his shoulder, nodding a greeting. "I should probably get going," he says reluctantly when he turns back to me. He bites the inside of his lower lip and holds my gaze.

His mouth might be saying he should go, but his eyes are saying something else.

"Do you want to come inside?" I ask, thumbing behind myself. I'm not ready to stop this conversation. Not when I'm enjoying it this much. "I have coffee and pastries." I draw out the last word to make it sound alluring.

Jake's gaze flickers in the direction of his house. "I have Robbie."

Right. Single dad. Sole custody.

I open my mouth to invite Robbie over too, but Jake speaks first. "How about you grab the pastries, I'll grab the pot of coffee, and we'll walk one hundred feet to my house?" He smiles warmly, and I recognize the little kindled flame starting in my chest.

Jake Whittier.

My toes curl as I attempt to keep myself grounded.

This man is funny, and kind. Loyal, and steadfast.

He's nothing like the men I've chosen before.

Maybe that's a good thing.

Chapter 22

Colbie

After a quick change into a t-shirt and sweats that don't look nearly as good as Jake's, he and I walk to his house. I'm only a few feet into the home when he turns to me and says quietly, "Looks like Robbie's still sleeping." He takes my hand, leading me through the living room.

Our palm-to-palm contact has me dragging in a heavy breath.

The house is clean, and not overly furnished or decorated. The kitchen is tidy, and though I can't see evidence of cooking, a faint leftover aroma of a home-cooked meal clings to the air. We arrive at the back door. Shoes line the wall, placed side by side on a rubber shoe tray. Men's boots, a pair of slip-on Adidas sandals. Two sets of smaller sized sneakers, and a matching pair of slip-ons.

My heart tugs at the sight of the matching shoes. I have a newfound respect and admiration for Jake. He fought for custody, won, and became a single parent, all when he'd hardly been old enough to legally buy alcohol.

"Here we go." Jake holds open the door for me.

He's pointing at the four-person wooden dining set under the covered porch. I can hardly focus my attention where he's pointing, not when there's a garden to look at.

A real honest-to-goodness garden, with vines growing through trellises, and metal stakes giving stability to tall plants. Bright red tomatoes bunch together, and colorful bell peppers hang. Jalapeños dangle from a bush, some on their way to turning red.

"You're a gardener?"

He shrugs, taking the pastry box from me and setting it on the table. "I don't know if what I do can be called gardening. More like planting and praying."

"Is that your way of saying you don't have a green thumb?"

He balances a flattened palm in the air, tipping it back-and-forth. "Ehhh I'd say I have a green-ish thumb, that is also sometimes shades of brown."

"My gardening thumb is decidedly black." Looking at Jake's garden reminds me I have plants at my house in Phoenix that are likely thirsty. I'll have to ask Christina to water them. I certainly won't be calling my mom and asking her for a favor right now. "For example, I forgot about my houseplants when I said I'd stay here in Green Haven. Keeping things alive isn't one of my talents."

"You're intelligent," Jake remarks off-handedly, like it's obvious and doesn't require anything more than a simple statement. "All you have to do is set your mind to learning how to garden, and then you will." He lifts the top from the box of sweets, then squints at me. "You're like my mom in that way."

I tip my head playfully, quieting the thrill skipping through me. "Should I consider that a compliment?"

"If I've compared you to my mom, you should consider it a compliment."

There's something very attractive about a man who unabashedly thinks highly of his mother.

"Let me grab cups and plates," he says. "I'll be right back."

I settle into a seat at the table while he's gone, inching my sandaled toes into a square of sunlight and letting my eyes drift close. I don't open them again until I hear the sounds of the door opening.

Jake steps through holding two coffee mugs and two plates. He sets down the mugs and holds up the plates. "These were the best I could do. My sister babysat last night and even though she did the dishes, she didn't start the dishwasher." His smile is lopsided, and I can hear the love he has for his sister even through his complaint. "You get to choose. Which one strikes your fancy?"

"Hmm," I sit back, my gaze bouncing from plate to plate. "Spider-Man is pretty great," I say, tipping my head. "But Thor..." my head tips the opposite direction. "Well, he's Thor." I have to bite the side of my lip to keep from smiling too hard. There is no way I'm telling Jake that Christina referred to him as Thor.

"Thor it is," Jake announces, sliding the plate in front of me.

"I didn't choose him." I tap a finger on the blond head of the one-dimensional image of Thor.

"Yes, you did." Jake clears his throat. "Well, he's Thor," he mimics, his voice a higher register.

A laugh bursts from me. "First you compliment me, and now I'm detecting a hint of jealousy in your tone. Would it be too much to assume you've moved past disliking me?"

I'm trying to keep my tone light, but it's a struggle. All I can think about is last night. He didn't physically pin me up against the wall, and yet there I was, speared in place by something I cannot name.

Jake chooses a cranberry scone. "I've moved past disliking you, Colbie," he says, reluctantly. Reluctance at no longer disliking me? Or having to admit it? Or something else entirely?

"Why did you?" I ask, keeping my eyes off him and dragging out the selection of a glazed donut. "Dislike me, I mean."

Jake taps a knuckle on the table. I look up. He holds my gaze, and the longer I look into his eyes the more I memorize how the shades of green shift and coalesce. It's a warm, inviting place, this gaze of his. A place, perhaps, to get lost in.

He is thinking, considering, and suddenly I feel like his answer is going to be very different from what I'm expecting.

After a long moment, he speaks.

Chapter 23

Jake

"My dad was a good person. He taught me how to catch and throw a baseball, the same way I teach Robbie now."

Colbie watches me closely. She's not just listening to my words, she's reading my expressions, my hand gestures, everything I'm not saying.

Am I ready to tell her all this?

Yes, I think so. She has a right to know. Fair or not, it has been shaping my opinion of her since day one.

"My dad loved my mom. He loved me, and my sister, Georgia. He used to call us his 'reasons'. He'd walk in the door after work and say "Hello reasons one, two, and three." I loved it. I soaked it up." I smile through the pain of the memory. "To be somebody's reason for living is pretty great. It feels like an honor."

Colbie's hand creeps over the table, fingers sliding up and over mine. She doesn't say anything, just listens intently, so I keep going.

"He got hurt on the job one day, trying to move something that was too heavy for him. He threw his back out, and dislocated two discs. The doctor gave him a bottle of painkillers." I shake my head, not just in disapproval but also because it's been years since it happened and I still can hardly believe it. "He turned into an addict"—I snap the fingers on my free hand, the one she's not holding—"like that. It was downhill from there. Anything he could get his hands on. Then this guy, some asshole from Sierra Grande, came through town selling meth, and that was it. I'd been saving up my money since I was a kid, every birthday or Christmas or when I worked odd jobs that paid cash, I saved my money. He knew where it was in my room, and he stole it."

Colbie gasps, but tries to keep her composure. Her touch is warm on my hand, and it keeps me grounded and in the moment, holding me here so I don't stumble back into yesteryear.

"I was so terrified to leave my mom and sister with him, I almost didn't go to college. My mom forced me to go, said she would kick my ass if I didn't." I smile, not happily, at the memory. "I was walking out of Intro to Psychology when she called and told me he'd been found dead."

"Oh my God," Colbie breathes, her face showing the pain I work hard to mask. "Jake, I'm so sorry."

"Me too." It's been a long time, but I can still hear my mother's tone that day, the way she sobbed on the phone. "It gutted me and my sister, but it hurt my mom most of all. He was her high school sweetheart. Her everything. I tried to quit college and come home, but she wouldn't let me. I was angry at the world, and so damn hurt, and I dealt with it by drinking a lot. Getting so wasted I couldn't remember the night. It was like I had a goal to hurt myself the way I wanted to hurt him."

I drink my coffee, preparing for the worst of my story.

188

Colbie refills my cup. She keeps her left hand on mine, and I like its warmth and weight. I wish there was a way to bottle it, this comfort she provides. I've been without it far too long.

"I met a girl one night." I pause to see if Colbie's willing to hear this part. I think she's attracted to me, and I know I'm attracted to her, and I don't want to say more than she can handle hearing.

Colbie's expression is calm and open, gaze wide and waiting.

"We slept together, and if I hadn't woken up beside her, I don't know if I would've remembered her at all." Shame starts in my stomach, its heat creeping up to my neck. I hate this part. I hate that I don't remember Robbie's conception.

"Her name was Erin. Five weeks later she showed me a positive test, and even though it pissed her off, I insisted on a paternity test. When it came back affirmative, I couldn't believe it. How was I going to be a dad when my own had failed so miserably?"

"You play catch with Robbie," Colbie says. "You remembered the good parts of your dad."

"Right. That's what I had to do. Remember my old dad, the good one."

Colbie seems to have forgotten this whole conversation started because I'm supposed to be explaining why I didn't like her. In order to make her understand, I thought it was important to start at the beginning.

"Erin and I tried dating, but the truth is, we weren't compatible when there wasn't alcohol involved. I was better at faking it than she was, but looking back now I see how it would've been better to admit the reality of the situation. Instead, I tried to play house. It made her resent me, and Robbie, too." I see now what I missed back then. The storm

189

brewing in Erin's eyes, the way she'd turn away from the sight of me holding him.

"She left one day. She said she was done, and that was that." Ten years later and my jawbone still aches from the tension when I tell the story.

"And you ended up with sole custody?" Tears gather in Colbie's eyes.

"Erin's parents petitioned the court. I drove straight up here to your dad. He'd known me for years at that point. I told him everything. I knew nothing about the construction business, but he gave me a job. He taught me everything. He loaned me the money I needed to fight for Robbie. It went on for a long time, and ended up costing a lot of money. Erin's parents were well-off, and used to getting their way." I could say more, a lot more, but it still makes my blood boil. On this nice morning with this beautiful woman, I don't feel like experiencing that anger. "I had to hire a lawyer as good as theirs. I'm still paying your dad back. There's not much left on the debt anymore." Every pay day, an automatic payment goes from my account to his. It's ironic, considering he's the one paying me, but there's something about the ritual that makes me feel good. He could garnish my wages and I'd never see the money leave my bank account, but there's a pinch of accomplishment every two weeks when I see the transaction, a reminder that I fought for what I loved, that I'm gainfully employed and a man of my word. That's important to me.

Colbie nods, tucking a strand of hair behind her ear. "This is where I come in." Her voice is softened by trepidation. She didn't forget after all.

"I'd heard you on the phone with your dad, and you'd give him these reasons you couldn't visit him, or accept a visit from him. He'd do such a good job of playing it off

while he was on the phone with you, but when he got off—"
I look Colbie over, from her cute chin to her expressive eyes, making sure she can continue to listen to what I have to say. I'm not here to make her feel bad about her dad. When she nods me on, I continue. "He looked sad when he'd hang up with you. Sometimes, he'd cry."

At this, Colbie looks away. She bites her lower lip, maybe to keep herself from crying.

"For what it's worth, I don't think I ever disliked you. I think my anger was misplaced, and you were an easy target because I never had to see you in person, so it was safe to send it your way. Not only did I not have to face you, I didn't have to face *it*."

"But then I showed up."

"Right. You coming here threw me off. It forced me to see you differently. *You* forced me to see you differently. You're not who I thought you were. You never were. I was wrong from day one."

Colbie blinks back new tears. The sight of them makes me want to launch myself over this table and hold her. I refrain, because even though we have this attraction, I haven't determined if it's in both of our best interests to act on it.

"I did give my dad excuses," she admits. "They weren't even reasons, Jake. They were bullshit excuses because I wanted to punish him for leaving me and starting a new family. For not loving me enough to stick around like he did for Greer." Colbie's lips press together.

I don't know why Emmett left Colbie and her mom. He's never said, and I've never asked. I can't offer Colbie anything now but my ear and my understanding, the way she gave me hers. "I'm sorry that was your experience. I'm sorry you felt that way."

191

She nods. "Sounds as if we've both been hurt by people who probably didn't mean to hurt us."

I've never thought of it that way. Every time I think of my dad, I only think of how he let a drug take over his life until it killed him. I've never considered that he didn't mean to.

We're quiet, and when I look at Colbie I find her gaze already on mine. We stare across the table, indecision flickering over her features.

"What is it?" I ask.

"I think you might be trouble."

I breathe a smile. "Of the two of us, you're the one who is trouble."

Her pained expression recedes, replaced by heat and yearning. "I'm guessing you don't want any trouble?"

My heart beats faster in my chest. "Too late. You've been causing me trouble since the first time I saw you."

Colbie stands up. She walks slow and with purpose, rounding the table. I push my chair back, my heart beats going from fast to thunderous.

I want this. Her. I've shown her that which I carry, I've seen her own heavy load, and now I want to touch her, and taste her, and make her feel things that don't hurt.

Colbie settles onto my lap, legs pressed together and facing out toward the yard. My arms wind around her, gripping her hip. She lightly touches my cheeks with her heated palms, looks into my eyes, and swallows. Hard.

"My mom has always told me to design a life that has the least amount of awful." Colbie leans in, brushing her lips over mine in the most fleeting of kisses. "Jake, you feel like the least amount of awful."

I start to smile at this convoluted message that surprisingly makes sense, but Colbie's lips are on mine now, and there's nothing fleeting about it.

She kisses me once, twice, three times before I coax her mouth open with my tongue. I taste sweet sugar and bitter coffee, and then she moans and I taste that, too. Something else hides in the background, another flavor I can't name.

Her hands leave my face and climb into my hair, nails lightly raking my scalp. Our kiss grows hungrier, seeking, and she grinds against an erection I have no hope of hiding.

I rip my mouth from hers, dragging in a breath. I have just realized what that elusive flavor is. "Why do you taste like that?"

Ragged breathing shakes her chest, her eyes searching my face. "Like what?"

My head dips, forehead pressing to hers. The tip of her nose runs over mine, her lips close. If I moved an inch, I could capture them. "You taste forbidden," I grit out, my words tumbling over breathing that still hasn't evened out.

"I'm not forbidden," she whispers.

My boss.

Emmett's daughter.

A temporary Green Haven resident.

Maybe not forbidden, but almost definitely a dead-end road.

I drag my lips to the corner of her mouth, leaving a trail of heat in my wake. "Then why do you taste that way?"

Her head turns so her mouth is on mine again, and then—

"Da-ad?"

Colbie scrambles off my lap.

Robbie calls for me again, the sound closer this time.

I stand, adjusting my pants while Colbie presses her lips together and laughs silently.

I point at her. "Trouble."

Chapter 24

Colbie

That kiss was a lot of things.

And so were his confessions. Jake has been through far more than I could have imagined.

He's leading me into his house now, and I wonder how he's feeling. I'm not the one with a child to think about. Is he worried Robbie saw us?

We step into the kitchen at the same time Robbie comes from the living room. His feet shuffle over the hardwood floor like Jiminy walking around Honeybee.

Robbie stops and stares at me, confused. "What are you doing here?" His hair sticks up in the back. It's adorable how slow he is to wake up. Does he get that from his dad? For some reason I don't see Jake as being a person who hits the snooze button. He probably leaps out of bed every morning, ready to face the day.

I'm having a hard time focusing on Robbie's question because now I'm thinking about Jake.

Jake's hands...lips...other parts...especially the part I felt pushing against the front of his sweats like it was dying to get to me.

Forbidden. That's what he'd called me. I'm not, technically, but I understand what he means.

"Colbie brought over coffee and some sweet treats," Jake answers for me when it becomes clear I'm not capable of it. "They're outside."

I push my lips together to suppress a smile, and Jake smirks. He must know what I'm thinking. He turns his body away from Robbie, in my full line of sight, and adjusts himself again.

Even that one small movement is too much for me to handle, and my thighs are aching again, like they were outside when his lips were on mine and I ground my ass into his lap.

I need to go home. Immediately. I can't be having inappropriate thoughts about Jake while Robbie stands two feet away from me.

"Thanks, Colbie," Robbie says, rushing outside.

I get control of myself and say, "You bet, Robbie."

Jake chuckles as Robbie's dark hair and matching pajama-clad body disappears from view. I look up at him, and find his gaze is already burning into me.

"Damn," he says under his breath.

"Such is life when you're a single parent, huh?"

He lifts his shoulders once, dropping them right back down. "I suppose. I've never brought a woman here. I wasn't expecting...that."

"Me neither." I look down at myself. "Obviously. Look what I'm wearing." I grab the ends of my hair. "Look at my hair."

"I'm looking at everything about you, and I like it all. Makeup, no makeup. Hair messy, hair brushed. Clothes"—he grins—"no clothes."

I poke him in the chest, the way I did in the hallway at Caruso's. "You haven't seen me without clothes."

He closes his eyes and tips his face to the ceiling. "No, but a man can dream."

Jake insists on walking me out. I lean out the back door to say goodbye to Robbie first. He's happily chewing a donut, feet swinging back and forth under his chair.

"I'll see you later, Robbie." I wave.

Instead of a farewell, he asks, "Are you good at math?"

"Yes," I answer. Jake steps into the open door beside me, his chest brushing my shoulder.

Robbie raises his eyebrows at me. "Are you *very* good at math?"

I chuckle. "Yes."

"Would you mind helping me with my homework?"

Jake intervenes. "I can help you with your homework, buddy. Colbie probably has a million things she needs to do today."

Robbie frowns. "What do you have to do today, Colbie?"

I cough into a hand to cover up my laugh. "Well, I need to go to the grocery store and clean the house. And I have a few things to do for my other job." I need to get that new manager role posted on all the job websites. I can handle doing everything short-term, but I already see how this long-term arrangement won't be feasible. I underestimated how physically taxing it would be to work on the construction site during the day, then come home and cram seven or eight hours of work into five hours in the evening. Not to mention the early wake-ups during the week. I can already see the burnout looming, and I'd like to avoid it.

Robbie persists. "Can you come over later when those things are finished?"

"I will help you, Robbie." Jake's voice adopts a stern quality.

Robbie crosses his arms, digging in his heels. "You said you don't do math unless there's square footage and a calculator."

I turn my head to hide my grin, and find Jake scowling.

"Georgia was here last night," he says to Robbie, like he's making a point.

Georgia? Is this the little sister?

"She taught kindergarten, Dad." Robbie makes an exasperated face, like his dad is hopeless. "What does she know about fifth grade math?"

I'm in serious trouble of laughing out loud at this point. To stop that from happening, I say, "Robbie, I'd love to help you if it's ok with your dad." I raise my eyebrows at Jake, waiting.

He's still frowning. I don't think he appreciates losing.

"Fine," he concedes. "But it's customary to trade something for a service." He's looking at Robbie as he says this. "Either goods, or money."

Robbie scratches his head. "I don't have money."

Jake nods. "What kind of service can you provide?"

Robbie thinks about this for a minute. His eyes widen when he lands on something. "I can make Colbie dinner!"

An *oh shit that's not what I meant* look crosses Jake's face. He shakes his head slowly. "Robbie, I—"

Robbie's face is already falling.

"I'd love that," I say quickly.

The beaming smile on Robbie's face will be worth whatever it is I end up eating tonight. Even if it's a goldfish cracker peanut butter sandwich with sprinkles on top.

"See you later," I say to Robbie, and now that he's satisfied with the outcome, he lets me go.

Jake walks me out front. We stop just outside his front door. He pulls me over a little more, where there's a wooden post and we're somewhat off-display of the neighborhood. "You don't have to do it."

"Do you not want me to?" Fifteen minutes ago it felt like there were a lot of things Jake wanted me to do, but maybe not. Maybe it was the heat of the moment.

Jake runs his fingers slowly over my forearm. Tiny shivers race down my spine. "I don't want you to do anything you don't want to do."

I'd told Christina I was done with men for a while. I'd told my heart it could take a break, after the dating disasters in recent years. So what is it that I'm doing here, right now, with a man like Jake? A man with a son, and roots, and a whole town of people who love him, including my own father?

I palm the front of Jake's shirt. The thin fabric doesn't hide the ridges and valleys, the defined dips and bumps of muscle. "I'm not going to be in Green Haven forever."

"What does that mean?"

"It means, maybe we should enjoy whatever this is and not think too hard about it." I've never been casual with someone, but maybe that's what I need. I slip a single finger into the waistband of Jake's sweats, running it back and forth across the hardened muscle of his lower stomach.

A hiss of breath escapes between his teeth, and his muscle flexes under my finger. "Fuck," he moans quietly, his head dropping as his eyes flutter closed.

"Yes, that." I have to exercise control not to let my hand drift any lower, the way I want it to. "So much of that."

A screen door slams somewhere nearby. I take back my hand before we get caught. Drifting down the front walk, I say, "Text me what time I should be here."

Jake tucks his hands in his pockets. The lust in his eyes is gone, replaced by something gentler, more contemplative. Perhaps he, too, is trying to figure out what we're doing here. What our intentions are, and if it's a terrible idea to not think too hard about our mutual attraction.

Chapter 25

Jake

Robbie and I are on our way to the grocery store. It's abnormally cool for early fall in Arizona, and the windows on my truck are rolled down. Robbie sits in the back passenger seat, leaning over to feel the breeze on his face. The seat belt stops him from going very far, but his fine hair still blows wildly around his head.

"Colbie seems really nice, Dad," Robbie half-shouts.

Nice. Yeah. That's one word that could be used to describe her. There are plenty of others, and only about half of them are appropriate for me to say out loud to a child.

"I agree. She's a nice neighbor." That was lame. Did Robbie notice? I glance back at him. He's studying me, one of his nostrils scrunched. Yep, he noticed.

"You're acting sus."

"Sus?"

Robbie's eyes roll up to the ceiling. "It means suspicious."

"O-kay."

"What do you think we should make Colbie for dinner?"

I consider it for a moment. "This is going to be a tough one. She doesn't eat dairy, and dairy is in a lot of recipes."

Robbie's mouth hangs open. "She doesn't drink milk or eat cheese? I might have to rethink how nice she is." He grins to let me know he's kidding.

I laugh so hard I actually slap my thigh. "We're just going to have to get creative, buddy."

Robbie contemplates my sentence. "That's ok. I like being challenged."

I smile back at him. Damn, I love my son.

❧

Robbie and I stood in the aisles of Benson's Market for what felt like forever, consulting my phone for recipes and discussing whether or not they would be to Colbie's liking. Robbie veered toward fancy, and I had to rein him in a handful of times. Today is not the day I try to learn how to prepare a rack of lamb.

We decide to cook what we know: roast chicken, rice, and a salad. I'm also not sure how helpful Robbie is going to end up being in the kitchen. I tried to steer him in the direction of sandwiches and potato chips, but Robbie made it clear those foods were for lunch, not dinner. I had no idea my son had such rigid thoughts on what time of day certain foods are consumed.

Standing there in the aisles of the grocery store, I tried not to show my nerves to my son. But the truth is, I'm nervous as hell. I've never cooked for a woman I'm not related to. I've never had a woman in my house for any type of romance. Not that that's what this is. Right? She's coming to help Robbie with math homework. But earlier this morning...I could swear

I got drunk on her lips. Her kiss left me light-headed. And in desperate need to finish, which I did, two minutes after she left me standing on the front porch. I'd ducked inside to my bathroom, and pushed myself over the finish line in record time. Hopefully that means I'll be able to handle myself around her tonight, and not act like a horny teenager.

Robbie is helping me carry in the groceries when Alma, the old woman who lives between me and Colbie, walks out of her house. I wave at her, two grocery bags held aloft and dangling mid-air.

She starts toward me. I don't have a lot of time right now, not if I want to get the chicken prepped, but Alma is responsible for making sure my son, along with so many other children, gets safely across the street and into school. Therefore, she takes precedence over most things.

I meet her halfway. "Happy Saturday, Alma."

"Happy Saturday to you, Mr. Whittier."

No matter what I do or how many times I've said it, Alma insists on calling me Mr. Whittier. She looks like she wants to ask me something, so I get ahead of her and ask, "What can I do for you?"

"Arthur is having knee surgery in a few days, and he'll be in a wheelchair for a while." She makes a flippant gesture toward her house, and I get the impression she's frustrated. "And, well, I can't haul a wheelchair bound man up and down those three stairs."

"Say no more," I tell her, striding across her yard, the groceries still in my grip.

Setting them down, I walk the length of her house, looking over the stairs and the angle of her front porch. Robbie comes looking for me, and joins me in Alma's yard. "What are you doing, Dad?"

"Trying to figure out how I'm going to build a wheel-chair ramp for Arthur and Alma."

He nods. "I can help."

I smile down at him. I love his big heart, and his willing-ness to contribute. "I wasn't going to do it without you."

I tell Alma that I need to grab my tape measure. Robbie takes the groceries and carries them inside.

I'm jotting down measurements when Alma asks me if I've met the new girl living next door to her. My gaze flickers over to the flamingo yard.

"Yes," I answer, trying like hell not to be overwhelmed by the memory of Colbie's lips and scent and intelligence and smile.

And.

And.

And.

All the other good things about her.

"Seems nice," Alma shrugs. "I haven't met her yet."

"She's Emmett Jones's daughter."

Alma's brows furrow. I know what's coming.

"I thought he only had the one."

Poor Colbie. This is exactly what hurts her. Most people don't even seem to know Emmett had a daughter before he had Greer. It's not their fault. But if it's not their fault, who's fault is it?

The answer is one I don't like.

"She's from his first marriage," I explain.

Alma taps her cheek like she's trying to remember some-thing. "Emmett came to town a long time ago, but now that you're mentioning it I remember him having a little girl with him. Not all the time, but I feel like I can see her stand next to him at Sowed Oats. Of course, it wasn't called that back then. We knew it as the Ice Cream Shoppe." She waves a hand. "Anyway, listen to me, rambling on like the old woman I am."

"Don't worry about it. I'll stop by the lumber store this week, and by the time Arthur gets home from the hospital you'll have yourself a wheelchair ramp."

Alma looks at me gratefully. "Bless your heart, Jake. What would we do without you?"

I smile at her wrinkled face. "We feel the same. Where would we be without you making sure Robbie crosses the street safely every day for the past five years?"

Alma puts her hands on her hips and leans forward like she has a secret. "Robbie could cross that street just fine all by himself, but I can think of a few of the other boys who couldn't fight their way out of a paper bag."

Alma goes inside, and I go back into my house. I wash my hands, and take the chicken from where Robbie has placed it in the fridge. It's not where raw meat goes, but it's exactly at his eye level. The small detail tugs at my heart.

I call him to the kitchen, have him wash his hands, then teach him how to prepare a whole chicken.

Chapter 26

Colbie

"I t's not a date?"

"No."

"But you kissed him?" Christina's eyebrows lift.

I fidget with the cuff of my sleeve, trying not to show the thrill of excitement at the memory. "Yes."

"What kind of kiss?"

"The really good kind." I can almost feel it now, his body hard beneath me and his lips yielding to mine.

Christina eyes me meaningfully through the phone.

I release my sleeve and lean back on the couch. "The dinner is a thank you for helping his son with math. Think of it as a neighborly gesture."

"Was it a neighborly gesture when his tongue was down your throat?"

I laugh. I can't help it.

"Whose tongue was down her throat?" Daniel asks from somewhere off-screen.

I roll my eyes. "Hi, Daniel."

"Hi," he yells.

"Daniel was just on his way out," Christina says,

directing her meaningful look to her husband instead of me.

He laughs and calls, "Bye." The door closes.

Christina looks back at me. "Anyway," she grins. "Where were we?"

"Technically, we're supposed to be talking about the new position we're hiring for."

"Yes, but talking about your sexy neighbor—"

"And employee," I remind her.

"And your dad's mentee," she reminds me.

"Ughhh." I drop my head into my hands. "This is very stupid, isn't it?"

She shakes her head. "Nope. Get it."

"You are such a bad influence."

"I mean it, Colbie. Get it. Get whatever you want *it* to be. You want to fall in love with a small town single dad and make little small town babies? Get it. You want a hefty helping of the big D without an ounce of commitment? Get that, too."

"Oh. My. God." I gesture from the top of the screen to the bottom. "What is happening here?"

"I'm ovulating."

"So you're horny?"

"My body is telling me to mate."

"With Daniel, I'm assuming."

"Um, yes."

The importance of all this finally hits me. "Wait, are you trying again?"

Christina miscarried a year ago, and walked through a dark time in the months that followed. It's the reason she started therapy, though she swears she needed the help long before the miscarriage.

"We are," she smiles as she says the words. "I'm ready."

"Honey," I say, drawing out the word. Tears prick at my eyes. "I am so happy for you."

"Thank you. And now I want to stop talking about it, if you don't mind."

I know what she means. She's safeguarding her heart already. Trying to set up a framework so she feels the least amount of awful should the worst occur again.

"No more sex talk," I agree. "We need to hammer out the requirements of the managerial role so I can get the job posted."

For the next twenty minutes, we discuss job responsibilities and what we want in an ideal candidate. I take notes on my laptop while we talk, then tell Christina I need to go so I can type it up and get the role posted on the biggest job search websites.

"I'll mention the job opening when I'm teaching classes." Christina nods excitedly as she speaks. "Sometimes the best person comes from within."

"Lovely, thank you." Fingers crossed this position is filled sooner rather than later.

"Best of luck to you this evening," Christina says. "I want to hear all about it tomorrow."

"Best of luck to you this evening as well." I smile at her and flutter my fingers before ending the conversation.

❦

Jake texted a couple hours ago and told me what time to be over. I think I have just enough time to run to the closest store and grab a bottle of wine. Like going to my dad's for dinner last weekend, I can't show up empty-handed.

This isn't a date, but it's not a neighborhood get together. It's not one of the dozen or so meals I've eaten with Jake since starting construction more than a week ago, which have mostly consisted of sandwiches and burritos around a truck tailgate.

It seems I don't know what this is, I only know what this isn't.

I wish I had something nicer to wear tonight, but my clothing options are sparse. I need to drive down to Phoenix and get more of my stuff. Can I go to the valley and not see my mom?

I guess so, but she's going to find out. She knows I need to come get my things. I haven't heard from her since I told her I'm staying in Green Haven. She's sulking. And punishing me, too. When we talk again she'll inevitably ask me something about when I'm coming for my things, and then I'll tell her the truth because I don't like lying, and it'll be a whole thing.

Ugh. So there's that.

But for now?

There's tonight. And that, is what I'll focus on.

Chapter 27

Colbie

I'm on my way to Jake's, bottle of wine in hand, when Alma calls to me from her front porch. I hadn't seen her, so when she yells *hello there!* my hand flies to my chest.

"Hi," I answer, approaching her porch. "I'm Colbie. I'm staying next door."

Alma steps closer to the railing, garden shears in her grasp. Her hands tremble slightly, and she wears thick polyester blend pants with a collared blouse. "I know who you are." She grins mischievously and winks. "I've asked around about my new neighbor."

"Good idea." I smile back.

She nods at the wine. "Are you headed somewhere?"

"Oh, um, yeah. Next door"—I thumb left—"to Jake and Robbie's house."

"I see," she nods knowingly. "Well, don't let me hold you up. Just wanted to say hello since we're neighbors. Have yourself a good night."

She turns back to a pot of succulents, effectively

dismissing me. I cross her yard and over to Jake's, taking a deep breath before knocking on his door.

Jake answers. His hair is shiny, still wet from his shower probably, and he wears dark jeans with a maroon waffle-knit shirt. The fabric from his sleeves stacks on his forearm, tight around the muscle. He looks like a whole snack, and it's incredibly distracting.

"I brought wine," I blurt, holding up the bottle.

Jake stands in his open front door, a look on his face that's difficult for me to interpret.

Is he upset?

Worried?

"I hope that's ok," I say, lowering the bottle. "If you don't want alcohol in the house, just tell me and I'll run this back home and come right back." Jake stares at me, not saying a word, so my sentences pour out, like drawn butter on a burn. "I mean, I understand if you don't. It was presumptuous of me to bring it. I'm just going to take this back to my place. I'm sorry. I should've asked." I start to turn, but Jake finally thaws and reaches for me. He holds my forearm in a gentle grip.

One side of his mouth lifts in a shy but somehow still sexy grin. "You aren't the only one who's nervous about tonight." His fingertips brush my breasts as he takes the wine bottle I have clutched to my chest. "Not going to lie, I really like seeing you less than confident. Tells me you're human."

I smirk. "Aren't you fully aware how human I am?"

"Sometimes I wonder."

I laugh and brush past him into his home. "What are you cooking?" I stop and look back at him. "Is that chicken? It smells incredible."

"Thanks!" Robbie says brightly, coming in from the

living room. He's wearing a light blue polo, bare feet, and his hair is neatly combed. He looks like a mini-version of Jake, and it's adorable. "What's that?" He points at the bag in my hand.

"I brought you something." I reach into the bag and produce one of the many things inside. "Sparkling apple juice," I hand him the glass bottle. "And, in case you don't like that, I have six other options."

Robbie peers past me and smiles. "Colbie brought me drinks, Dad."

"I heard," Jake says, coming to stand beside me. There's an undertone of laughter in his voice, and some of my nerves fizzle away. I stood in front of the refrigerated cases at the liquor store, trying to figure out what to buy for a ten-year-old. I did my best to choose things that didn't have caffeine, or an ungodly amount of sugar, and hoped for the best.

"Take the bag from Colbie and put the drinks in the refrigerator, please."

I like how he speaks to Robbie, how his tone is kind and respectful. It's like he's always aware that Robbie is watching and learning from him.

Robbie follows the instruction, and Jake coaxes my purse strap off my shoulder. He deposits the purse on the side table in the living room and holds out the wine, reading the label.

"I bought you the same one," he says.

"Because of the label?"

He nods, fingertip tracing the crown printed on the paper label. "Seemed like it was fit for a princess."

I shake my head at him, but I'm also smiling.

Jake scrunches up one eye and tips his head. "Are you sure I can't call you that?"

"Yes," I groan. Jake takes my hand.

"Come on. Let's pour you a glass, your highness."

"Nice try."

He gives me a long look, and I feel it like an electric current, sizzling its way from the top of my head to the tips of my toes. He takes my hand, leading me away from the living room. "I like buttercup better anyhow. It suits you." He says it under his breath because now we're in the kitchen and Robbie can hear everything.

"I like it, too," I murmur, giving Jake a look that's fleeting but still heavy.

Robbie finishes putting the drinks in the fridge, and I sneak my hand out of Jake's grasp before Robbie can notice us.

Jake said he's never brought a woman here, and I don't want to step on any toes or create problems. "Do Robbie and I have time for math before dinner?"

"Have at it," Jake answers. "The chicken has twenty more minutes, and then it needs to rest for a bit when it comes out."

Robbie and I sit down at the dining room table, where his math book lies open. I peek over. "Dividing fractions?"

Robbie answers with a groan. I laugh at him. "It's not so bad. Show me how your teacher taught you to do it." I wink at him. "Math might have changed since I learned."

Jake breathes a quiet laugh as he sets my glass of wine in front of me. I murmur my thanks, and he walks back to the kitchen.

Robbie squints at me. "You kind of look like my teacher."

"Your teacher's hair is darker than mine."

The corners of his mouth dip down. "How do you know that?"

213

I poke him in his side and he wiggles away. "She's my sister."

"Dad, did you know that?" Robbie looks into the kitchen with an accusatory expression.

"Yes, I did." Jake has a kitchen towel slung over his shoulder. He stands in front of a wooden chopping board, knife poised over a rib of celery. The muscles in Jake's forearm flex with his grip on the knife as he dices.

The sight of him knocks me off-balance. The man can cook, wear a pair of jeans in such a way that it would give a nun a dirty thought, and kiss like sin. And he was broke and still fought tooth and nail for a tiny baby he knew he'd have to raise alone. There must be a catch somewhere, a fatal flaw lurking in the shadows.

As if he can read my thoughts, Jake pauses the cutting and glances over. He catches me staring, and stares back. My breath sticks in my throat. Is he thinking what I'm thinking? Can he see directly into my thoughts, just by looking into my eyes?

Robbie's voice interrupts the moment. "Ok, so Ms. Jones said..."

I tear my attention from Jake, but it's not without effort. There is something between us, a vibe, a connection, maybe even a live wire.

Robbie shows me where he's having trouble with dividing fractions, and I help him work through it. I've always been good at math, always enjoyed the way numbers made sense and fit together.

Jake turns on old country music while he's assembling the salad. A man sings about finding love, another laments their lover's departure. I wonder if Jake knows he sings along under his breath, as if the words are an afterthought.

Robbie and I finish his homework. Jake took the chicken

out to rest a few minutes ago, and the rice is finishing up on the stove.

"Does your dad always cook nice dinners like this for you?" I ask Robbie as he puts his binder in his backpack.

"He cooks a lot." Robbie answers, and then his expression turns guilty. "Do you know how to fish?"

I blink at the abrupt subject change. "I've never gone fishing."

"Dad said people exchange services for goods or money, and we both know my dad did most of the cooking tonight, so how about I teach you how to fish since you taught me math?"

"I think that sounds like a lot of fun, but maybe we should consult your dad first."

Robbie doesn't respond, but I'm sure he's heard me. He finishes packing up his backpack and says, "If you're my teacher's sister, then that would make you Mr. Emmett's daughter, right?"

"Correct."

Robbie nods thoughtfully. "Mr. Emmett told me about you once."

I flinch. Where is this going? "Is that right?"

"I told him I'm my dad's only kid, so all his love goes to me, just like all his love goes to Greer." Robbie pauses. "Er, Ms. Jones."

Robbie has no idea his words possess thorns, and they're digging into my skin as he speaks.

Is Jake catching any of this? I glance his way. He's frozen at the stove, holding a fork in mid-air. I don't need to see his face to know he is suspended in the moment, just like me.

"But," Robbie continues, "Mr. Emmett told me that half of his heart was missing. I didn't ask why." Robbie

215

looks at me thoughtfully. "I guess you're what was missing."

I swallow back the tears.

Jake clears his throat. He takes the top from the saucepan and begins to fluff the rice. "Dinner's ready," he says, his voice thick. "Robbie, please set the table."

I meet Jake's eyes. Even from across the room I see the shine of moisture in them, but also worry and fear. I'm not sure what that's about, and I'm not going to ask in front of Robbie.

I offer to help put the food on plates, and Jake hands me a plastic measuring cup from a drawer.

"What am I supposed to do with this?" I ask, confused.

He points at the rice.

"You want me to measure the rice?"

He breathes a laugh. "No, I want you to put the rice"—his pointer finger moves to the three plates lined up on the counter—"on the plates."

"With a measuring cup?"

"Yes. A measuring cup is an all-purpose tool."

I grab the handle of the pan. "Pretty sure it's meant for measuring."

Now Jake laughs. "It works best as a chili ladle."

I'm shaking my head and laughing as I scoop rice from the pan with the measuring cup.

Jake jostles my side with an elbow. "See? It works."

"Hardly," I retort.

False. It works just fine.

We eat dinner. It's simple, and delicious. The company is even better. Robbie tells knock-knock jokes to make us laugh, then Jake reminds him to eat his food while it's warm.

While Robbie eats, Jake asks, "What did the ocean say to the beach?"

Robbie gets a look on his face that says *oh boy*. "What?" he asks reluctantly.

Jake grins, preemptively proud of the punchline he's about to deliver. "Nothing, it just waved."

I laugh, then have to cover my mouth so I don't spit out the food I'm chewing.

Robbie looks back and forth between us and announces with an impish grin, "Dad jokes come with the territory."

"That's my line," Jake says, acting affronted. He ruffles Robbie's hair.

We finish eating. I offer to help with kitchen cleanup. Robbie and I are on dish duty, while Jake stores the leftovers.

When that's done, Robbie asks me to watch a nature program with him. I sit on one end of the couch, Jake on the other, and Robbie plops down between us.

We watch a show about birds, and when it comes to the part where the male birds show their bright colors and dance around to attract a female and mate, Robbie says, "That's what I'm going to do when I mate." Then he laughs at himself.

I look over his head at Jake. Jake's eyes widen and he shakes his head, clearly saying *we haven't had The Talk and it's not going to happen tonight*.

The show continues without any further commentary. When it's over, I get up and stretch my arms above my head. "I think it's my bedtime, Robbie. Thank you for having me over. I appreciate the dinner you cooked."

Robbie makes a face like he's remembering something. "Dad, I told Colbie I would teach her how to fish since you were the one who made most of the dinner. Is that ok?"

217

Jake peers down at Robbie. "Does Colbie want to learn how to fish?"

"I mean, yeah." I answer, smiling at Robbie and offering a fist bump. "It seems like an important life skill."

Robbie grins and nods. "It is."

I pick up my purse from the table where Jake set it earlier. Robbie accompanies Jake to the door, so there is nothing more than a second thank you and a wave on my way down the path through their yard.

Jake is unlike anyone I've dated, and that will remain a fact even if we never go on a date. If all I do is see him around the neighborhood and at the jobsite, he will still be a man I compare my future dates to.

But after tonight, I really, really hope that's not all that happens.

⁂

I left Jake and Robbie's house about an hour ago. I'm ready for bed with my face scrubbed free of makeup and my hair twisted into a bun on top of my head when there's a knock on the door. There aren't very many people I can think of who'd pay me a visit this late on a Saturday night, and there's already a smile on my face just thinking of the one person it's likely to be.

I cross the house, anticipation building with every step.

I stop long enough to check the peep hole, *because ax murderers*, and there he is.

I was right.

I unlock and open the door.

Jake has this habit of brushing two knuckles over his jawline, and he's doing it now, and it makes a spot below my belly button turn inside out.

I lean against the doorframe, just as I did this morning when he came over to apologize about last night. "Whatever you're selling, I'm not buying."

Laughter lights up his eyes. "The thing is," he drops his two-knuckle touch and takes a step into the doorway, filling up my personal space with that massive body of his. He grips the top of the doorframe with one arm, leaning a few inches closer so there is next to nothing separating us. "I'm not selling. I'm giving. Willingly."

I lick my lower lip and reach out, running my hand over his soft shirt. The heat is already building, a flame licking its way through my cells. I rise up on tiptoe, so I can be closer to him. His breath is warm on my cheek and he smells like heaven. "What are you giving?"

He moves quickly, lifting me. Jake's hands wrap around my waist, my legs tighten around his midsection. A muted squealing sound drifts from me as he walks into the house, closes the door with his foot, and spins me around.

My back is up against the door, and he holds me in place with his body. With a free hand he pushes my hair away, eyes searching my face. "Everything you're willing to take," he finally answers.

The talking stops, because now his lips are on mine. He kisses me like he is starving, reverent and demanding at the same time. I press into him, wanting to get closer.

He breaks off the kiss, but only so he can swipe his hot tongue across my lower lip.

I groan, and he responds with the same sound. "I wanted to kiss you good night."

"Is that all?" I taunt.

He pulls back so he can see me. The only source of light is a soft glow from the lamp across the room.

"Robbie is asleep. I can't leave him for too long." He

leans forward, nipping my lower lip. "I promise, the things I want to do to you, they're going to take all night."

His words make me whimper, and I press my hot center against his lower stomach where he's keeping me in place.

"Christ," he hisses, glancing up at the ceiling like he's searching for a way to steel his resolve.

I push one strap of my tank top off my shoulder. Jake looks down at me.

"I need to leave," he grinds out, his voice like gravel.

"So leave," I say, pushing off the other strap. His eyes follow the movement.

I'm too high up on his body for Jake to push himself against me, to find even an ounce of relief. His eyes are pained when he asks, "What are you doing to me, woman?"

"You can put me down," I half-whisper. "You can go."

"Can I?" The question is not, *is it physically possible for me to do that,* it's *am I willing to?*

Jake bites gently on my bare shoulder. "Pull down your shirt."

I grin into a tiny sense of triumph. "I thought you needed to leave."

"I do," he growls, the sound a vibration against my skin. "I need a visual to carry me through the night."

"You're going to stroke yourself to the thought of me?" Why do I love that so much?

His teeth graze my collarbone. "To the thought of you and that pink tool belt. And it won't be the first time today."

Well, damn. I'm so hot now, so ready, that I say, "You can turn me around and fuck me up against this door right now. I don't care."

"I care," he says, nipping at my neck. "Pull down your shirt."

I laugh. I can't help it. This whole situation is absurd and amazing and I like it.

I unwind one arm from around Jake's neck, and do as he's asked. I'm not wearing a bra, and his gaze flickers up to mine quickly, his excitement evident.

"Knew it," he grounds out, eyes locked on my chest.

"Knew what?"

"Knew they'd be this gorgeous." Appreciation and hunger trade places on his face. He hoists me higher, like I'm an elevator riding his body. "Give me one," he demands, and I'm surprised to find how much I like him telling me what to do. It's unlike me, but then again, so is everything I'm doing in my life right now.

I cup one breast and lift it to his mouth. He covers my flesh in suctioning kisses before focusing on the hardened peak.

I'm squirming, and incoherent, and Jake pauses with my nipple in his mouth to say, "Hold still."

I do my best, but it's hard when he's so good at what he's doing.

When Jake finally tears himself away from his task, his eyes are crazed. I'm about to remind him he's the one who showed up parched and is now refusing to drink, when he says, "They're calling for rain at the end of the week."

"Huh?" I frown in confusion, as does my lady boner.

"We won't be able to work. But Robbie will still have school."

Now I'm getting where he's going with that. "So, we'll put a pin in—" I look down at my bare chest breathing heavy against his own. "—all this?"

"I'd actually like to take you somewhere."

"Like a date?"

Jake nods.

221

"Is that a good idea?" I shift in Jake's arms so I can pull my shirt up.

His eyebrows furrow. He sets me down for the first time since I opened the door to him. "Is a date a good idea?" he repeats, confused. "I'd like to think so, considering we were just on one."

"Tonight was a date?"

Jake swallows and looks down. "Look, I don't just bring women into my house, even if it's my son's idea." He shifts his weight. "I'm sure you're used to fancy first dates. Flowers, nice restaurants, no ten-year-olds—"

The vulnerability in his tone tugs at my heart. "Whoa. Let me stop you right there." I place my hand under Jake's chin and draw his gaze to mine. "I didn't know tonight was a date, but now that I know, I can say with one hundred percent certainty it's the best date I've ever been on."

Jake frowns, unconvinced. "I wasn't able to give you a goodnight kiss."

His weak argument makes no difference to me. "Well, yeah, but if you'd been able to then you wouldn't have needed to sneak over here after Robbie went to sleep. This way, I got an epic goodnight kiss and some fringe benefits." I shimmy my shoulders, causing my breasts to bounce, and a smile blooms on his face.

He strokes my cheek with a thumb. "When I first met you, I didn't think you were going to be funny."

"In the spirit of honesty, when I first met you I didn't think you were going to be much of anything except a pretty face."

Loud laughter bursts from him. He shakes his head as he reaches for the door handle. I scoot out of the way, and he makes his way outside. He turns back. "I take Robbie fishing every Sunday morning. You're welcome to join us tomorrow."

"My dad asked me to have breakfast with him, but thank you." I also should probably drive down to Phoenix, but I don't want to get into that right now. This moment is too good. Instead, I pop up on tiptoe and Jake leans down. I feel his lips turn up in a smile when I brush a chaste kiss on his cheek.

"I'll see you at work on Monday." He backs away, disappearing into the darkness of the night.

I close the door, then lean against it like my back didn't get enough of the door already.

Jake thought tonight was a date. He wanted it to be. And he wants there to be another one.

And here I was thinking tomorrow's breakfast with my dad might be filled with awkward silences during lulls in conversation.

Looks like I just found quite the talking point.

Chapter 28

Jake

When Georgia called this morning at six, she asked if she could go fishing with Robbie and me. She has only done this one other time, and today I could sense how badly she needed me to say yes.

I did, but it was at personal cost to the enjoyment of the activity.

Growing up, my dad would take me and Georgia fishing, and Georgia developed a habit of detracting from everything that makes fishing enjoyable. To this day, she won't bait her own worms, she's never quiet, and the trip usually gets cut in half due to her complaints of heat, bugs, and whatever else she finds insufficient or intolerable.

But today, Georgia was not herself. She cast her line after I baited it, didn't complain, and didn't have much to say the entire time despite the uncommon call and request to join.

"You good?" I glance over to where she sits in the passenger seat. We're on our way to Honeybee for breakfast after a surprisingly successful morning. We are strictly catch and release kind of fishermen, so we don't have anything to show for our success except our stories.

Georgia nods and tries for a smile. "Yeah. I just needed to get out in nature, you know?"

I tap my thumb on the steering wheel and peer into the rearview. "Robbie and I know all about how good it feels to spend some time in nature, right?"

Robbie yawns. "You bet."

I chuckle and turn my attention back to the road. I had to wake Robbie up twice this morning, which is unusual for him when he knows that fishing is on the schedule. He'd slept in his fishing clothes, per usual.

Georgia says, "I texted Mom and asked her to meet us for breakfast."

"Good. Anything else you want to share?" I'm pushing Georgia, because I know something is up. Then it hits me that it might be related to a guy, so I add, "Kid-friendly, of course."

She's quiet. I peek over and find her looking at me. "What?"

"Nothing," she answers, after a long pause. "Nothing at all."

I'm not sure how much to press the issue, especially in front of Robbie, and it doesn't matter anyway because I just pulled into a parking spot at Honeybee.

·:·

I should have known she'd be here. There are a few other good breakfast places in town, but Emmett loves Honeybee. He jokes that he wants to be buried with a plate of their cinnamon swirl pancakes.

Robbie spots Colbie and Emmett the moment we step

inside. He takes off, forgetting his manners, and launches himself at Emmett. Colbie startles as Robbie comes up behind her, and Emmett barely gets his chair scooted back and arms open in time to catch Robbie.

"Whoa, snickerfritz," Emmett booms, holding Robbie close and giving him a shake. "I think maybe you missed me as much as I missed you."

Georgia excuses herself to the restroom to wash her hands, and my mom walks in at the same time I'm asking the hostess for a table. I wrap an arm around my mom's shoulders and give her a side hug.

"You're in luck," the young hostess says to us with a smile. I think she's one of Jiminy's grandkids. "This is our last open table."

She holds four menus to her chest and walks us to the only open table. Directly beside Colbie and Emmett.

I meet Colbie's eyes, and all I can think of is last night when I had her pressed to the door. The way she tugs at the collar of her shirt tells me she's thinking the same.

"Sorry about the interruption," I say, stepping up to the duo. Colbie's smile is instantaneous. I feel the tugging on my cheeks as my mouth mirrors hers. I have the strongest urge to kiss her right now, in front of everybody. I won't, of course, but I can't help thinking of how nice it would be.

My mother introduces herself to Colbie. "I'm Terri," she says. "Jake's mom."

Emmett answers before Colbie can speak. "Terri, this is my daughter Colbie." He gestures across the table, pride stretching over the planes of his face. "She's taken over Jones Construction for the time being."

My mom's surprised gaze finds mine for a fleeting second, then rearranges into a polite smile. "It's nice to meet you, Colbie."

Colbie smiles. "Nice to meet you as well. I guess you're the person responsible for raising such a hard worker."

My lips tug as I attempt to control my smile. Sure I'm a hard worker, but I also had her nipple in my mouth last night.

My mom laughs. "I get the feeling there are other adjectives you'd like to use to describe my son."

Colbie smirks. "I can think of a few."

Robbie disentangles himself from Emmett and looks at Colbie. "Hi," he says, then takes in the sight of the cheesy omelet in front of her. "I thought you couldn't eat dairy. That's what my dad said yesterday at the grocery store. I wanted to make you mac & cheese."

Colbie bursts out laughing. "Dairy makes my stomach feel yucky, but if I take it with some special vitamins it makes it ok."

Oh shit. I'd really given her a hard time about the dairy thing when she first came to town, assuming it was her being picky. Now I feel bad.

"Then I guess that means I need to make you mac & cheese." Robbie thinks about it for a second, then shakes his head. "Wait, no. If I'm making mac & cheese, then I can't teach you how to fish. I'd rather teach you how to fish."

I place my hands on Robbie's shoulders and begin to steer him away. "Pardon our interruption. We'll let you get back to your breakfast."

"Join us," Emmett says. He doesn't wait for a response, he's already pulling over the empty table where the hostess left our menus.

"You sure? You've already ordered."

"Of course I'm sure. Sit, sit," he pulls over a chair for Robbie. I retrieve a chair for my mother, then drag over the last two for myself and Georgia. The arrangement is such that there's an open seat beside Colbie, and I take it.

I'd like to whisper something in her ear, I'm not sure what because the last thing I am is suave, but I don't get the chance because Georgia walks up.

"Hi," she says, waving at Emmett. She places a hand on my shoulder as she pulls out her chair. "Sorry I took so long. I had to wash my hands four times to get the fish smell off them." She doesn't ask how we ended up joining Emmett, she just sinks into the seat beside mine and keeps talking. "Good to see you, Emmett. Please don't go scaring me like that again."

"Ahh," Emmett grumbles. He takes a bite of his pancakes.

Georgia leans over me to hold out a hand to Colbie. "Hi, I'm Georgia."

"Colbie," she answers, and they shake hands across me. Her eyes flash to mine, a question lingering in them. Colbie releases Georgia's hand, and asks in a polite, restrained tone, "How are you connected to Jake?"

Ohhhh. "Georgia is my sister," I blurt out, even though Georgia's mouth is poised to answer.

The relief on Colbie's face is plain, and even though I would love to tease her for it, I refrain. She's been hurt too many times, and now I'm understanding just how fragile her trust is. I'm not interested in making her question me, my actions, or my feelings.

The server, Patrice, comes and takes our order. When she leaves, Emmett asks Robbie, "What's this about mac & cheese and Colbie?"

Robbie answers. "Colbie came over for dinner last night. And she helped me with my math." He looks across the table at Colbie for confirmation, which she supplies with a head nod. "And I'm going to teach her to fish," he adds.

I look at Emmett. Will he be upset to know Colbie and I are spending time together? I wouldn't think so, not after all he and I have been through. He knows the kind of man I am. But I know what it's like when it comes to your kids. There is good, then there's *good enough for my daughter.*

"Interesting," Emmett says, finishing off his last bite of pancake. Colbie still has more than half her plate left. She eats much slower than Emmett, who has always mowed through his food.

Colbie's watching him too, trying to determine his response. He says nothing else, and I don't know if that's because he has nothing else to say or because Robbie is here and he doesn't want to talk in front of him.

Colbie side-eyes me, and we share a small shrug. My mother smirks.

Georgia starts talking to Colbie, asking her question after question, and finally I switch places with Georgia so I'm no longer in the middle of their conversation.

"I love barre class," I hear Georgia say. "I wish there was a studio here," she half-complains, one side of her nose scrunched. Then she asks question after question about how Colbie got into the business.

That leaves the four of us to talk, but Emmett isn't saying much. Is he angry? Emmett isn't a quiet guy. He can fill a silence. He can find common ground with just about anybody.

"How are you feeling?" I ask, mostly because it's an obvious question.

"Like I wish people would quit asking me how I'm feeling."

Wow. Ok. "Noted."

Thank God for Robbie. He saves the day by asking, "Will you come to grandparents day at my school?" He glances at my mom. "Mimi will be there, but I thought since I don't have a grandpa, you could come."

Everything about Emmett softens when he addresses Robbie. "I wouldn't miss it."

Emmett gazes at Colbie, sitting across from him and talking animatedly with my sister. He looks forlorn, and even though the bruises on his face have mostly healed, it looks to me like there might be bruises nobody can see. The kind that sit on your heart, and stay forever.

Emmett has been trying to see and get to know Colbie for years, but he probably didn't envision what all of that might entail. The flip side of the reunion coin might not be so shiny. It might hurt. There may even be emotions a person never considered they'd experience. It can't always be good, right?

Even more of a reason for me to ignore Erin. She called again this morning, just as Robbie had hollered "fish on!".

I'm not sure what to do about her. I wish I didn't have to think about it. It puts a fear deep down, the kind that bypasses layers and reaches the foundation. The fear makes me a little sick, so I shove my head in the proverbial sand instead.

Our orders arrive. Robbie digs in with gusto, taking fewer than six minutes to polish off the same size pancake as the one Emmett ate. He's showing off a little, just for Emmett. He loves when Emmett calls him a growing boy.

"You're a growing boy," Emmett says, nodding at Robbie with pride.

Robbie beams.

When Patrice drops our bill, Emmett is the first to grab

it. I reach around to my back pocket for my wallet, but he waves me off.

He reaches for his wallet too, but his eyebrows pull together. He uses the opposite hand to check his other pocket, and still he comes up empty.

"What the hell," he grumbles. He performs a second check.

"Here," I hold out my hand for the bill. "Let me get this one. You can get next time."

"No," he thunders. We all flinch. Robbie's lower lip trembles.

Immediately Emmett knows he's done something wrong. He's looking down at the ground and holding a hand over his forehead, pinching at his temples. "I'm sorry," he says, voice brimming with apology to us, and agitation at himself. "I don't know what came over me."

Colbie gently takes the check from her dad. "Don't worry about it, Dad."

Emmett's eyes flash to hers. Disbelief widens his eyes, and I think I see some gratefulness in there, too.

And I think I know why. Emmett once told me that she never calls him 'Dad'. She doesn't call him anything.

I remember the day Robbie stopped calling me Daddy. It felt a bit like a sucker punch, as painful as it was inevitable.

I'm sure Emmett is feeling a lot right now after hearing his daughter address him as Dad for the first time in years.

Colbie's chest is rising and falling with her quickened breathing. She knows what she did, and the impact it had. She takes cash from her wallet and places it on the check, then uses a salt shaker like a paperweight.

"I have to drive down to Phoenix and back today," she

announces, pushing away from the table. Her voice shakes when she asks, "Dad, are you ready to get going?"

Two times? Two times. Emmett's heart must be doing cartwheels.

He gets up. We have to stay because, like Colbie, Georgia is a slow eater.

Colbie waves at Robbie and my mom, gives Georgia's shoulder a friendly squeeze, but she saves the best for last. For me, she leans down and brushes a kiss on my cheek.

"Drive safe, Buttercup," I murmur.

She smiles as she pulls away, and even though I can tell she is feeling a lot of different emotions, she is genuinely happy when she looks at me.

Emmett, still embarrassed over his outburst, offers Robbie a high five and waves goodbye to the rest of us.

When they are out of earshot, Georgia turns to me. She looks so pleased as she says, "I like your girlfriend."

Chapter 29

Colbie

"I don't know what's wrong with me." My dad leans against his truck. He looks angry. Sad. Disappointed. Maybe even resentful of the way his brain is acting without his permission.

I take his hand. It is large, and callused, like a bear paw. I remember being little and comparing my hand to his. It dwarfed mine, and I loved that. I felt safe with him.

I look at his face. The week's worth of stubble is lighter in color than the hair on his head, and is already well on its way to being a beard. There's a scar on his forehead from a piece of concrete that hit him when he was jackhammering twenty years ago. These characteristics about him have always existed, and the fact they remain in place whether I'm around or not makes my stomach hurt. I'm not sure how much longer I'm supposed to guard my heart against a man who is easy to love. It takes a lot of energy and effort.

"You know what's going on with you," I say gently. "You have a brain injury. Cut yourself some slack."

On his face is an almost childlike uncertainty. He says, "What if this never goes away? I don't know how I'm going to live with it. I don't know how I'm going to expect everyone else to live with it." There is disgust on his face when he glances back at Honeybee. "You saw how I acted in there. I almost made Robbie cry."

"Jake can handle Robbie. He will help him understand. Robbie loves you no matter what."

It hits me then, this great big realization, and it feels like a slap in the face. Shocking, stinging, a reverberation through my limbs. "And so do I."

It's like my body takes a single, enormous exhale. A breath held far too long.

It's true. I love my dad, even when I don't want to. Or, even when I don't think I want to.

My dad's eyes fill with tears. He pulls me into his broad chest, his flannel so soft, smelling of basic soap and whatever it is that is quintessentially my dad. "I'm sorry," he whispers into my hair.

"For what?"

A tear that is not mine drips onto my cheek.

"Everything," he says.

<hr />

I drive to Phoenix and load up my car with clothing, various toiletries, and kitchen items Keli's parents don't own. And one specific kitchen tool Jake doesn't own.

Guilt, or perhaps propriety, wins out, and I call my mom to tell her I'm in town. She doesn't answer, so I leave her a message and tell her I'm free for an early dinner, but I can't hang around long waiting for her to respond.

I'm loading items into my car when her text message comes through.

I have a case going to trial tomorrow. I'm preparing for that tonight.

I know she's telling the truth. I also know she's still punishing me.

I could be nine years old again. I could be ten, eleven, twelve, on and on. She's testing me. Giving me the opportunity to beg, plead, cajole. She didn't tell me no outright, she only gave me her reason for why she couldn't.

I'm sick of playing games though, so I tuck my phone in my purse and hit the road.

Chapter 30

Colbie

It's Thursday. Today, the weather woman on the news has called for rain. Her exact words were, "Today is going to be a rainy one for those of you in the high country."

Green Haven isn't quite high country, but it's borderline.

My body is already used to waking up early, and even though I know we won't be able to work, today is no exception.

It's also the day Jake's taking me on a date.

It's not even six yet, and my limbs are awash with nervous energy. I change into shorts and a sports bra, then pull up the link for the in-class streaming service offered by the barre studio.

Christina isn't teaching today, but Aditi is. She warms us up, and then the class is underway. I don't have hand weights or props, but I make do with large water bottles and a small bouncy ball I found in the hallway closet.

Once that's done, I call the entire crew one by one and

make sure they know not to go to the jobsite. Common sense should keep them home, or at least away from work, but I would feel terrible if one of them showed up for nothing.

I shower and get dressed, pulling on a bathing suit, then jean shorts and a sweatshirt. I have no idea what the need is for a bathing suit, but Jake suggested I wear one when he texted last night.

We've seen each other every night this week, and it's Robbie's doing. He asks me for help with math, and last night he asked me to help him with his upcoming project for the school science fair. At first Jake tried to intervene, but I told him I'm happy to help. I think his protestations were mostly for show, because we both know me helping means we get to spend more time together.

Even if we don't have much alone time, we make the most of what we get. The second Robbie closes the bathroom door, Jake's lips find mine. Our hands stray, but not too far, until we hear the sound of the door opening. Then we jump apart, resuming our positions.

Seeing Jake at work and acting as if I don't want to kiss him is like a second job inside of the one I'm already working. Every time he walks in the trailer, I wonder if Blake can feel the shift in energy. Is it only me who senses how the air tightens with tension, how it grows taut every second Jake spends in close quarters with me?

At eight o'clock there's a knock on my door. It's Jake and Robbie, both holding onto their own umbrellas. Robbie wears a backpack. Jake wears a smile, and it's like there's a tiny sun hanging under the canopy keeping him dry. I can't believe I ever thought this guy was mean.

"Good morning, boys. Stopping by to say hello on your way to school?"

"Do you wanna walk with us?" Robbie asks, eyebrows lifted with hope.

"Sure. But," I look at the hooks on the wall next to the front door. They hold a few of Keli's parents jackets, and an extra set of house keys. "I have to search for an umbrella. Do you have time for that?"

"You can share my dad's umbrella." Robbie grins, and there's almost something mischievous about it. I already have my suspicions about Robbie asking me to help him with math, and this little smile adds to the case.

Jake lifts his umbrella a couple inches. "I think we can fit two under here."

I slide my feet into the closest shoes, which happen to be sandals. I don't care if my feet get wet. "Lead the way."

Jake's umbrella is large, so I don't really need to huddle against him, but I do. The opportunity is too good to pass up, and he smells divine so it's not as if being close to him is a hardship.

One block down, Alma marches us and a few others across the crosswalk with the stop sign raised in the air. She winks at me as we pass her.

Greer is out front, assisting with morning drop off. I watch her hold an umbrella over the head of a child climbing from the back seat of a car. Her hair is wet, but she wears a rain jacket, so at least her clothes will be dry.

I wave at her. She looks confused for a moment, but then she sees who I'm with and grins knowingly. I roll my eyes and shake my head, but I can't help a little smile on my face. Another car drives up, and Greer gets back to work.

Jake hands me the umbrella, then bends down to give Robbie a fist bump. "Love you, bud," he says.

"Love you too, Dad." Robbie turns for the building, his umbrella bobbing in a sea of other umbrellas.

"Ready to go?" I ask, rising on tiptoe to hold the umbrella over Jake. He takes it from me and shakes his head. "I like to wait and see if Robbie will wave one more time before he goes inside. He used to do it all the time, but" —he shrugs, and I swear there's sadness in the movement— "now he only does it sometimes."

"But you wait all the time?"

He nods. "I can't stand the idea of him turning back and me not being here."

My heart does this little flippy thing in my chest. "You are a very good dad."

Jake smiles down at me, but only briefly. He trains his attention back to the bobbing royal blue umbrella.

Just before he enters the school, Robbie turns around. Jake waves, and so do I. I guess today was a sometimes day.

Jake leans his hip into me. Thanks to our height difference, it's more like he's pushing into the side of my ribs. "You ready for our date?" he asks. Without Robbie around, and under the cover of relative concealment, his voice is deeper, huskier, his eyes burning a new kind of fire.

I lick my lips. "You wouldn't believe how—"

"Jake! Hi!"

It's the woman from the hallway at Caruso's. She has a serious knack for poor timing.

"Hi, Kiersten." The strain in Jake's tone is easy to detect.

Kiersten either refuses to acknowledge it, or is one of those people who miss subtle social cues.

She turns her smile on me, but I don't miss how it wavers at the corners. "Colbie, right?"

I should've known. It's a small town, and she seems the type to know everything about everybody. Or, think she does, anyway.

"That's the name they gave me at birth." Jiminy's line rolls out smoothly. Kiersten looks slightly confused, and irritated, that I didn't respond with the perfunctory answer she was expecting.

I hold out a hand. "And you are?"

"Kiersten." She shakes my hand. "My sweet Graham goes to school with Robbie. They've been good friends for years."

Jake makes a grunting sound. I'm getting the feeling Kiersten is exaggerating the two boys' friendship.

"Did you need something, Kiersten?" Jake asks. "Colbie and I need to get going."

Kiersten looks me up and down. I can practically see her wheels turning as she tries to figure out just how much of a threat I am to what she so clearly wants.

Jake.

I'm not interested in one upping her, or drama, or really anything immature that pits me against her. I don't love the idea of leaving Jake with a woman who so clearly wants him, but I refuse to allow Brad's choices to turn me into a paranoid woman. So, I say, "If you guys need a moment to chat in private, I can run along to my house."

Jake winds an arm around my waist, gripping my hip. "Stay."

Kiersten stares at Jake's hand on me, and turns on a fake smile. "It was nothing." She waves a hand. Her nails are painted a bright purple-pink. "We can talk later." Then she turns around and flounces away.

I look up at Jake. He shakes his head, eyebrows scrunched. "Let's get going."

We stop back at my place so I can grab my bag and finish getting ready. Jake stands in the doorway to the bathroom, watching me apply tinted moisturizer. "Why did you offer to leave me alone with Kiersten?" He looks genuinely perplexed.

I frown as I rinse my hands. "Did you want me to get my claws out? Stake my claim?" I turn to face him as I dry my hands with a washcloth.

"Kind of," he admits, looking sheepish. He comes closer. Reaches for my hip. Brushes the pad of his thumb along the bone.

I toss the washcloth on the counter. "Sounds to me like you want off the market."

His earnest gaze drops down to meet mine. "What if I do?"

My hands drag up his arms. "What happened to enjoying whatever this is, and not thinking too hard about it?"

"I didn't say that." He nuzzles the top of my head. "Those are your words."

"Jake." My tone is serious, and he pulls back to look down at me. "Green Haven is not my home, and you have Robbie to think of."

"I know." Jake's brows tug together, making him look like he's wrestling with his thoughts. "Robbie already likes you."

Honestly, I like him, too. A lot. And I like his dad. A lot. Which is why we need to understand what it is we're doing here. Clear-cut boundaries mitigate risks to the heart.

Jake grips my hips and lifts me, placing me on the counter. He steps between my legs and rests his hands on either side of me, caging me in. "I'm going to let you call this whatever it is you need to call this to justify it in your mind. But just so you know, I'm not interested in anybody else. If I'm kissing you, you'll be the only woman I'm kissing. If I'm taking you on a date, you'll be the only one. If what you need is casual, I can do casual. Just know I won't be doing casual with anybody else."

I'm not sure what to say, but only because I'm thinking one hundred different thoughts right now and they're running in all directions, bumping into each other inside my brain. I've never had a man look me in the eye and make such a declaration. Hell, I've never had a man make even half a declaration like that, with the ardent gaze and the confident tone.

Jake seems to understand this. He winds a hand around the nape of my neck and gently pulls me to his mouth. His kiss is soft, and filled with restraint.

"Come on," he says, stepping back and offering me a hand.

I take it, and hop down. "Where are we going?"

"It's a surprise. Put on some shoes you can hike in."

Chapter 31

Jake

I drove us ninety minutes out of town to my favorite hike, the Water Wheel Falls Trail. Luckily, it's in the opposite direction of the rain in Green Haven. Not so luckily, there's another weather system heading toward the area in a few hours, so we'll have to make the most of our time.

We talked most of the drive, ranging from what Colbie does on a typical day in Phoenix, to what made her and her best friend Christina decide to open a chain of barre studios.

Colbie mentioned she takes class a few times a week, and the longer we hike the flat, sandy trail, the more I notice she's in great shape. It's not a strenuous hike, but still. She hasn't broken a sweat, and as far as I can tell, her breathing is only slightly accelerated.

"Those barre classes must be a good workout," I say, hoping I don't sound like a creep.

"They're amazing," she responds. "Cardio, weights, even some light yoga. The whole package."

She walks in front of me during a narrow stretch, ass

and hips swaying, ponytail swishing over her back, and all I can think is *You're the whole package*.

I don't say that. Colbie doesn't respond well to compliments. We'll have to work on that, because I have a lot of nice things to say to her, and I'd rather not keep them inside.

"This is a lot rockier than I was expecting," Colbie comments as we leave the flat terrain behind and start on the rockier landscape. To the right, the East Verde River is full enough that it adds a peaceful soundtrack to the hike. "I can't believe I've never heard of this trail."

"Do you hike often in Phoenix?"

She's nodding. "Yep. Christina and I meet once a week and go. Not in the summer, obviously."

"Smart, considering it's a million degrees."

She snorts. "Exactly. But the rest of the year is fair game."

"Tell me about Christina."

"Christina is...amazing. She's blunt, but never in a mean way. Sometimes she says things I don't want to hear, but need to hear. They're trying for a baby right now."

"She's married?"

"To Daniel. Five years this December."

I hear the wistfulness in Colbie's tone. It strikes me that she probably misses her home in Phoenix, even if she is enjoying Green Haven.

The trail widens again, and now we're side by side. "Tell me about your mom."

Colbie sighs and her mouth twists. "She's mad at me right now."

"Why?"

Colbie sighs heavily. "Because I've chosen to stay and help my dad."

This topic of conversation is treacherous territory, and I need to tread lightly. My initial opinion of Colbie was rash and incorrect, but I have a strong feeling it's not the same when it comes to her mom. "Why does that upset her?" I ask carefully.

She answers my question with a question. "What have you been told about my mom?"

"Nothing." Emmett has never said a single word to me about Colbie's mother, negative or otherwise. That's not the kind of person he is. But I have overhead Victoria venting to Greer throughout the years, and from what I can tell Colbie's mother was not supportive in making sure Emmett and Colbie kept their relationship intact.

Colbie gives me a look that is part curiosity, part disbelief. "Seriously? All these years you've been spending a large amount of time around my dad, and he's never said anything about her?"

"No." I jostle her in the side as we walk. "He's never said anything bad about you either, just in case you were wondering."

She purses her lips and nods. "What did he say about me that wasn't bad?"

"It's not so much anything he said, but I'm pretty good at watching non-verbals."

"And?" Colbie presses. "What did his non-verbal say?"

"That he felt sad. He missed you." Her gaze goes to the ground as it moves beneath our feet. I jostle her again, and she looks at me. "That's not news to you." The reminder is delivered in my gentlest tone.

"No, that is most definitely not news." She clears her throat, straightening those shoulders in a way I've come to learn means she is mentally telling herself she's capable of handling something. "This is the longest I've gone without seeing my mom, and I'm trying to figure out why I don't miss her."

This feels like a confession, and I know it's best to keep my mouth shut and let Colbie continue.

"Growing up, my mom would tell everyone that I was her best friend. For a while I liked that, because it felt like a badge of honor, being seen as an adult and likable enough to be that for her. When my dad met Victoria and they had Greer, my mom would tell me not to worry because we have each other and that was all we needed. I agreed, because I was just a kid. What the hell did I know?" She shrugs once, quickly. "I was angry and resentful at him for starting a new family, and I thought my mom was right. My dad was preoccupied with his business, and he lived two hours away, and all I could think was that my mom was right about him." Colbie's head shakes slowly back and forth. "I'm starting to think she was feeding me lies. And now I have to grapple with the idea that both my parents failed me in very different ways."

I know how she feels, at least in part, and that's how I know there's nothing I can say that will make her feel better. In my experience, a parent's failure hurts twice: the first time it happens, and then a second time when you're an adult and you're finally sorting through the aftermath of the damage they caused.

I think I am, perhaps, not quite on the other side just yet. Like Colbie, I am still wading through the muck.

I take her hand, and give it a squeeze. She looks at me, her smile curving upwards, and there's an uncharacteristic softness to her. I like that she's showing that side of herself to me. It's a privilege, one I won't be taking for granted.

We reach the Water Wheel Falls, and Colbie pulls in an astonished breath. I've seen the waterfall at least a dozen times, but this time is different. It's better now, because I'm watching Colbie take it all in.

She stares up at the small gorge cut deep into the granite cliffs, then down into the pool of water below. "The water is...almost blue."

"It's one of my favorite places. I had to bring you here today ahead of the rain." The clouds have grown darker and heavier since we started the hike. We don't have a whole lot of time left, not if the rain starts when it's supposed to.

Colbie starts forward to the waters' edge. "What happens when it rains?"

"After it rains, the water becomes muddy and murky."

She scrunches her nose. I laugh. "Exactly."

Colbie glances up at the sky. "Do we have time for a swim? I'm guessing that's why you had me wear my swimsuit."

"We have time," I tell her, pulling off my shirt. "But not a lot. Let's get in."

I try not to stare at Colbie as she undresses, but there may as well be a fifteen-year-old boy living in my brain, because I can't look away. Colbie winds her hair in a knot on top of her head and secures it with a band from her wrist.

She's the first to step into the water, and she yelps. "It's cold." She steps in further.

I'm not going to make her go in the chilly water by herself, so I step in beside her and try not to react to the temperature of the water. She's right. It's pretty damn cold.

I reach for her and pull her into me. She wraps her arms around my back and buries her face in my chest. When my lower half has adjusted to the water temperature, I ask her if she wants to go in further. She doesn't say yes, but she nods her head. I lead her in, deeper and deeper, until it reaches her collarbone. She's shivering.

I hoist her onto me, and she wraps her legs around my waist. "Stay still," she whispers, reminding me of last weekend when I had her flesh in my mouth and gave her the same instruction. "I want to listen to the waterfall."

For the next five minutes, it's just me and her and the sounds of the water pouring over the rocks. Beneath the surface of the water, my hand begins to move. Not in a sexual way, just back-and-forth across her lower back. Her contented sigh heats up the section of my neck where her lips are pressed.

"Jake?"

"Hmm?"

"This place is beautiful, and I know it's one of your favorites, but I've had enough of it for now."

There is no mistaking the look she's giving me. I carry her out of the water, and she's laughing. From the small backpack I carried I produce an even smaller towel. She uses it first, then me. We pull our clothes and shoes on, then begin the short trek back to my truck.

I hold the passenger door open for her, watching her climb in. I lean in and kiss her, and she asks, "Do you ever wish you could fly?"

"Right now I do. The next hour and a half I have to spend driving home is going to be torture."

***

The storm in Green Haven has disappeared, leaving the sky a clear, cloudless blue.

In my truck cab, a tempest rages.

The closer we get to my house, the heavier the air in the

truck becomes. We've grown quiet these last few miles, but the anticipation crackles, speaking volumes.

I pull into my driveway and cut the engine. "Wait for me," I tell her. "I'm coming around to get you."

I hurry around the front of my truck. Colbie opens the door for me, and I don't waste a second. I pulled her into me just like I did when we were in the water, and she wraps her legs around my waist. I carry her like that into my house, not caring if we are spotted by any nosy neighbors.

Colbie hops down when we get inside, laughing and looking so damn happy. I cup her face in my hands, kissing her hard and long, until we need to breathe.

My nose presses to hers, and we share a breath and a stare and after that, it's on. A flurry of limbs leads to shucked clothing, and then her hands are in my boxer briefs, sliding them down my legs.

Colbie bites her lower lip, and wiggles her eyebrows, that playful gleam in her eyes. "Hmm," she teases, grabbing me and pumping her arm. "I think you're too big to fit." She sighs, releasing me. "It was nice knowing you."

"What?" I cry, looking down at the stiff flesh pointing at her.

"Just kidding," she murmurs, dropping to her knees and showing me that I do, in fact, fit in her mouth.

After thirty seconds, I'm hauling her back up. "This is going to be over before it gets started if you don't stop doing that."

She grins, running a fingertip around her mouth like she's fixing non-existent lipstick.

I pick her up again.

"I think you like carrying me places." She squeezes my sides with her thigh muscles.

"I think I do, too, Buttercup." I smack her once on the behind, hard enough to make her squeal.

Out of habit, I close and lock my bedroom door. I lower Colbie onto the bed, and she scoots over.

I lay next to her, and she stretches out, reaching over and running a hand through my hair. I start with a fingertip on the center of her lower lip, then run down her body, until I reach the apex of those thighs she's had wrapped around me so many times.

Her chin tips up to the ceiling and she gasps for air when my finger hits its mark. I kiss the space next to her mouth, trailing my lips over her cheek and down onto her neck. "Do you know how beautiful you are?"

Her vulnerable look is back. It's interesting how she can do this, go from playful to vulnerable in mere seconds. I like both facets of her personality, along with every other one I've encountered.

She doesn't respond, so I say it a different way. "You have the kind of beauty on the outside that makes me want to do this to you." Her back bows off the bed with the addition of a second finger. "And on the inside, you have the kind of beauty that makes me want to give you everything I'm able to give. It makes me want to kiss you"—I brush a kiss on the corner of her mouth—"and hold you, and watch you lose control." I add a thumb to that tight bundle of nerves, and soon she's shattering under my hand. I'm careful to make sure she's squeezed every drop from her orgasm before I roll over and reach into the nightstand for a condom.

Colbie lifts up on her elbows, watching me roll it on. She looks at me and nods, as if she knows I'm going to ask one more time if this is what she wants.

"Come here," she says, hands encircling the back of my

neck. She pulls me down, but I hover, balancing my weight on my forearms.

I tell her she smells divine, because she does. I tell her she is beautiful, because she is. I kiss her neck and her ears and her forehead all while my raging erection seeks her heat. "I don't have all night like I said it would take, but I have approximately one hour before I have to walk out of this room and be a dad."

I lower myself a little, letting a small amount of weight sink onto her. She grunts, and I lift back up.

"No," she says, wrapping her hands around my back and pressing me down onto her. "I like your weight. I want it."

I do as she asks, tipping to my left so I can balance my weight and reach between us. I grip myself, and even though it kills me just a little, I run myself through her heat, trying not to die at the anticipation.

I am right there on the edge, and I want to soak it all in.

The moment before everything.

I was going about my life, being a dad and a son and a coworker and a friend and a brother, and then...THEN...

Colbie.

Colbie and her quick wit, her jokes, and her smile.

Colbie and her willingness to learn, to join, to be a part of something.

I didn't know what I was missing, until what was missing stepped onto my path.

With my lips ghosting over hers, I ease inside of her, going slow until I fill her completely. A moan presses against the seam of her lips. Her eyes are on mine, hooded and hazy, as drunk on me as I am on her.

I set a pace, an unhurried, deliberate rhythm. Our noses

are tip to tip, and her breathing grows heavier. "You're so good at this," she manages to say.

"With you," I correct, my pace never faltering. "Good at doing this with you."

I see how much she likes those words, and her pleasure emboldens me. I feel her getting closer, so I pick up the pace and ask, "Still feeling casual about us?"

Her nails dig into my shoulders. "If I'm fucking you, you're the only one I'm fucking."

"That's right," I growl into her ear, sitting up and pulling one of her legs over my shoulder. I grip her hips and resume my pace, and I'm treated to the sight of her tipping her head back and loudly calling my name. It pushes me over the finish line, and then Colbie does the sweetest thing. She reaches up, placing a palm over my heart so I can feel her touch while I come. *Casual.* Right.

I roll over, spent, and Colbie follows. She drapes herself over me like she's unwilling to be apart. I get it. If I could sew us together, I think I would.

We're quiet for a few minutes. I'm curious to know what Colbie is thinking right now, so I ask her.

She traces a design on my chest with her fingertips. "I was thinking that I can't believe we're expected to get out of this bed and function like normal adults."

I smile and run a hand over her back. "There should be some kind of mandatory buffer time after sex like that. A transition period."

"That is exactly what I was thinking." She presses a kiss to my chest and climbs off the bed. I'd love to pull her back in, but I have responsibilities.

Colbie gets dressed, then steps into my bathroom. I use Robbie's, taking care not to throw the condom into his wastebasket. Thanks to his obsession with nature shows,

Robbie knows mating is a thing animals do. He doesn't know the details of the act, nor does he know that humans do it. The Big Talk isn't far off, but I'd like to postpone it to at least some other day in the not-too-distant future.

I find Colbie in the kitchen with a glass of water. She drinks half, then hands it to me and I finish it.

She leans against the countertop, elbows pointed back and fingers gripping the edge. She's smirking.

"What?"

"I just had sex with my employee." She makes a silly face like *oh shit.*

I smile proudly. "I just had sex with my boss." I refill the water.

Colbie bites the side of her lip. "Are we out of our minds, doing this?" She gestures from me to her.

"As good as we are at it?" I shake my head. "No way. We'd be doing a disservice to mankind if we didn't have sex."

Colbie laughs. "How do you figure?"

"Well," I set down the glass and grab her hand, intertwining our fingers. "We'd be walking around in bad moods all day if we denied ourselves. And then we'd be rude, or at least short-tempered, and it would affect how we treat others. That, in turn, would affect how those people treat other people. On and on that would go." I make my voice deep and melodramatic. "In conclusion, us denying our attraction would have ripple effects with unimaginable consequences."

Colbie's shaking her head, but her eyes are lit up. I like knowing I've entertained her, that I'm the man who put that glow on her face.

I catch sight of the time on the microwave. "I have to go get Robbie."

253

Colbie pulls her hand from my grasp. "Should I leave first, then you follow a few minutes later? Do I need to be in stealth mode?" She puts her hands on either side of her face and pretends to creep.

I kiss her forehead. "I don't consider you a secret."

She wraps her arms around my neck. "What do you consider me?"

I look down at her, she looks up at me, and I see something like a challenge in her gaze. She tells me she wants casual, but I get the feeling she wants me to fight for her, even if she doesn't realize it.

I tuck a strand of hair behind her ear, then cup her face with my palm. "My buttercup."

I'm rewarded with a smile, and a long, deep kiss that ends with me hurrying us out the door so I'm not late to get Robbie.

Colbie breaks away to go inside her house. I miss her as soon as she's gone.

Chapter 32

Colbie

I f what you need is casual, I can do casual. Just know that I won't be doing casual with anybody else.
    My naïveté deserves uproarious laughter.
I am so fucked.

Chapter 33

Jake

I am so fucked.

Chapter 34

Colbie

Saturday morning I'm woken by the screeching sound of a saw. I peek outside, and see Jake working in Alma's front yard.

I dress, make a pot of coffee, and bring him a cup.

He takes a break when he sees me walking through the swarm of flamingoes.

"Thank you," he says, taking the warm cup from my hands.

He gives me a look, and I feel it in the marrow of my bones. He's wearing glasses again, like he was the day Robbie fell off his bike in front of my house. I take a deep breath to steady myself.

"What are you doing?" I gesture at the sawhorse, the wood, and the tools.

He ignores me entirely. "I missed you last night." His voice is low, grumbly, and the tops of my thighs begin to heat.

"I missed you, too," I murmur. I really did. I gave him space in case he wanted it, but I didn't want to. I wanted to call or knock on his door. Robbie kept me from doing either.

I've never dated a man with a child. Is there a guideline somewhere, a list of acceptable behaviors?

Jake reaches out, running the tips of his fingers over the back of my hand. Bumps lift on my skin, a shiver rolling its way down my torso. "I thought about you a lot."

The way he grounds out those words, the way they contain more than just one meaning, sends my emotions spinning. I clear my throat. "Same."

"What did you think about?"

"What it is we're really doing." We keep using the word *casual*, though everything I think and feel is contrary to that word. I'm still grappling with how that can be.

"Why didn't you text, or call? Or come over?"

"Why didn't you?"

Steam curls over his skin as he sips from the mug of coffee. "I didn't want you to feel crowded."

I understand what he means. What I don't understand is my reaction. Suddenly, I want to feel very, very crowded. By him, and by Robbie.

"You don't have to worry about that." I drink my coffee and shift my weight, unsure of what to say next. Jake looks expectant, as if he's waiting for me to continue, and now there's a sinking feeling in my stomach. Is this what they all meant, my list of exes? Is this where my emotional well bottoms out?

I've already told Jake we are casual, I've set the parameters. He has agreed to them. Kind of, anyway, if you count him telling me he won't be casual with anybody else as agreeing to something.

He means it. Jake says what he means, and does what he says. He is a good person, solid and stable. Already I know enough to be certain he would be different from the other men I've dated.

Jake steps closer, and now our chests are only inches apart. "I don't have to worry about you feeling crowded?"

My head tips up to look at him. Relief and hope shimmers in those gorgeous green eyes. This is it. *Be brave.* "I'm starting to feel like maybe I want to be crowded by you. And by Robbie."

Jake pulls me flush against him. He smells like cotton, and sweat, and a scent that is simply his own. I don't know how to describe it, only that two days ago, as he rocked above me, I told myself to commit it to memory. What if I can do more than memorize it? What if I have it, every day? I won't have to make a deposit in my memory bank, because it will always be there.

What if I stop designing a life that doesn't hurt, and choose instead to live?

Jake hugs me hard. He kisses the side of my head, next to my ear. "You're worth the work. I told you that."

I raise up on tiptoe and smile against his neck. "You've been working on me?"

"No. I've been working on me. Making sure you see how great you are, so you can stop with this least amount of awful bullshit and fall in love with me already."

I resist the urge to stiffen, but I'm sure there's some part of Jake that was prepared for my reaction. "You want me to fall in love with you?"

"Eventually."

He turns his face so he can kiss my forehead. Against my skin, he says, "I can't let Robbie care for you even more than he does if you think that's never going to happen." His chest stops rising and falling, his breath held in his lungs as he waits for my response.

Two days ago we'd talked about being casual, but I think it was a way for us to justify what we wanted from one another. We'd said what we needed to say to get us to breach the boundary line, but now? Now we know how good we could be.

I look at Jake, the way his eyes track the expressions on my face as I work through my thoughts.

Old habits die hard.

But not when they're on their final breath.

I am sick of living with the shadow of my dad's choices hanging over me. With my mother's manipulations. I'm done letting trauma guide my decisions, attempting to keep myself from feeling hurt at the expense of not letting myself love someone.

"I—"

As if called, Robbie bounds from Jake's house. "Colbie!"

Jake and I break apart. Robbie bypasses his dad and wraps me in a hug. I hug him back, looking at Jake as I palm the back of Robbie's head. "It's safe to let him care for me."

Jake smiles softly, chin ducking once, his eyes bright with happiness. I like that he trusts me enough to know I would never say words I don't mean. A child's feelings aren't something to fool with.

Robbie looks up at me, one eye squinting from the sun. "My dad is building a wheelchair ramp for Alma's husband."

Oh, that's right. The tools. And the sawhorse. I'd been so wrapped up in Jake and our conversation that I forgot he'd been doing something.

"It doesn't surprise me a bit to hear that your dad is doing something nice for somebody."

Robbie grins at his dad. "Me either. He's done this for a few other people, so that's how he knows what he's doing. He said he'd teach me. Do you want to learn, too?"

I wink at Robbie. "I think I'd better."

Jake teaches us how to calculate slope, and explains the importance of working in sections so adjustments can be made as needed. He shows us how to measure the stairs, and work the saw. Robbie draws the measurements on the wood, and it's my job to operate the saw. Jake holds the nails in place, and Robbie hammers.

We carry the pieces over and fit them together like a puzzle, and Jake does the final hammering to make sure everything is properly aligned.

Robbie begs to test out the ramp with his bike, and Jake agrees. Robbie runs next-door for his bike and helmet, and when he returns, Jake says, "Robbie, what do you think about Colbie being my girlfriend?"

My eyes widen. This isn't at all what I expected when I came to Green Haven, but hearing the words *my girlfriend* makes me feel good inside, so I'll go with it.

Robbie looks from me to Jake, his bike trapped between his legs. "Isn't Colbie your boss?"

"Yes." Amusement warms Jake's tone.

"And she's Mr. Emmett's daughter."

"Correct."

Robbie squints one eye as he looks up at his dad. "And now she's your girlfriend?"

"As long as you don't object."

Robbie places his helmet on his head and looks at me as he snaps it into place under his chin. "You sure are a lot of things, Colbie." He pushes off with one foot and rides a circle around us. "You can be my dad's girlfriend, too."

He takes off for the ramp. Jake laughs and looks at me. "That was ok, right?"

"If I'm going to fall in love with you eventually, I better be your girlfriend first."

261

Jake laughs again. He looks so happy. I smile at him to make sure he knows I'm happy, too.

Happy and more carefree than I've felt in a long time. It's bizarre, considering my mom is angry with me, I'm working on repairing my relationship with my dad, and I'm doing a job that's still largely foreign to me. I'm not in my own home, I don't have my creature comforts, or my best friend. Yet, somehow, I'm fine.

Better than fine.

Chapter 35

Colbie

Christina's the first person I tell that Jake and I are seeing each other. She says she's happy if I'm happy, and then informs me she is going to steal my thunder. "I'm pregnant!" She screams the words, then adds, "I peed on a stick this morning, and there was a plus sign. A plus sign!"

I cry with her. She wants this so badly.

When we're done crying, she says, "This is kind of bad news for you, though."

"Why?"

"Because if all goes well, I want to stay home with the baby. For a little while, at least."

"Take as much maternity leave as you want. You're your own boss," I remind her.

"Right, but..." her voice falters. "What if I don't want to come back at all?"

"Umm..." my brain scrambles for the right answer. "Like, you'd want to sell your portion of the business?"

"Maybe?" She sighs. "I don't know. Am I talking crazy?"

"I guess not. These things take time, though, so it's good we're talking about this now."

"I just want you to know where my thoughts are."

I nod, though she can't see me. "Consider me warned."

"I did a phone interview with that person from the résumé you sent me. I really liked her, and asked her to come in tomorrow to meet in-person."

"You don't waste any time."

"I'm trying to keep you from burning out."

"I think we should be focusing on keeping you from stressing. Can you video call me tomorrow for the interview? Let me help out."

"Will do," she answers. "Enough with the tough conversation. You're dating the hot lumberjack!"

I laugh and let her pull me away from the topic of business.

When I tell my dad I'm dating Jake, he smiles and says, "You guys make perfect sense. He's a good man, and you're...well, you're you."

I call my mom to tell her I'm dating Jake, more out of habit than anything else. She's been my person for years, and being this far detached from her throws me off-kilter. It's been more than a week since I was in Phoenix grabbing my stuff, and we still haven't really spoken. I sent her a text on the day her trial started, wishing her good luck. Her response was a blunt 'thank you' and nothing else.

She answers, and the surprise I feel tells me I'd been expecting the call to go to voicemail. We get the niceties out of the way, and I say what it is I called to say. I want to be excited about Jake, I want to gush about how he's different from all the others, but I hold back. I deliver the news in such a way that I could be talking about buying cleaning supplies.

She breathes into the phone, long and loud, a stream of disappointment and annoyance I feel across the miles.

"I don't understand." Each word is spoken like it has its own period after it. Terse, tense.

Irritation gathers at the base of my spine. "There isn't a lot to understand."

"Did your father talk you into this?"

Like I'm so gullible, so devoid of internal direction, that I can't decide anything for myself. For that matter, she must think my dad is a magician, or hypnotist. "No, Mom. I have my own brain, and it came complete with decision-making capability."

She sucks in a surprised breath. I've never spoken to her like this. Nor have I challenged her. But the longer I'm apart from her, the more I'm seeing how I don't share her viewpoints on life, or love.

"Your new boyfriend's a single father, and a construction worker," she says sourly. The barbed criticism falls short of the mark. I don't see either of those as flaws.

"He's a man who stepped up when his child needed him."

"Is that what this is?"

"What are you talking about?"

"He stepped up for his child, and your father backed off from his. Now it makes sense." She sounds relieved.

My grip on the phone tightens. "That's not what this is."

She ignores me and says, "Are you going to become a stepmom? Is that what you want?"

It would be a lie to say I haven't thought that far ahead. How could I not, with a kid like Robbie? The images in my brain rival that of a Hallmark movie. Robbie's an easy kid, witty and intelligent. He's a deep thinker, and he has a big heart. And don't get me started about Jake. I could go on and on about him, the way I learn something new about him every time we're together, and the way I like each detail more than the last.

"I don't know what's going to happen in the future, but I can say for certain that whoever ends up that child's stepmom is a lucky woman."

My mom blows out a disbelieving breath. "Ok, sure. Stay in Green Haven, have your fling, repair your relationship with your father or whatever it is you're doing with him, and then come home. I miss you."

I swallow all the things I want to say to her. As if the lens I've been seeing her through is distance soluble, her manipulation of me has become clear. I don't know that she even means to do it. It doesn't make it ok, but in this moment, I don't have the energy to fight it. Instead, I say, "I miss you, too."

But I don't.

I really don't.

I've been beyond happy since Jake and I made things official. In every other relationship I've had, I've kept my guard up. This time, the guard is gone.

I tell her I have to go, then I hang up the phone.

❦

Jake and I are very careful at work, and so far I don't think anybody has caught on to us. It wouldn't be a problem if our relationship was out in the open, but I'm the only woman on the jobsite and I'm afraid the guys won't look at me as the boss anymore if they know.

Aside from my dad's accident and injury, the building process has gone smoothly. Today is the day we frame the house, and Landon is coming out with the safe room kit and to be a part of the framing. I'm not sure if he would be this hands on if it were my dad, or Jake, in charge, but I have to swallow my pride on this one. It's not as if I have experience, or know exactly what I'm doing. I've learned a lot in the past two months since I arrived, and a lot of what I read in my instructional books hasn't been put to use yet, but you don't find a lot of literature on panic rooms and false walls. Landon is necessary to the process.

Jake has just arrived on the site after dropping off Robbie at school when I tell him the news about Landon's appearance today.

"I actually forgot about him," Jake says, removing his ball cap and scratching his forehead with his thumb. He puts the hat on backwards and wiggles his eyebrows at me.

"You are going to make me regret telling you how much I like it when you wear your hat backwards."

"It feels worth it." He winks at me. "You didn't seem to mind it a couple nights ago."

My lips form a tight seam trying to fight my smile. Jake had waited until Robbie was fast asleep, then he snuck over. We had sloppy, fast sex against the front door, with Jake's hand over my mouth in case anybody was out for a late night stroll and passing by at precisely the wrong moment. Jake had worn his hat backwards that night, because earlier in the day I'd told him I like it.

"Anyway," I say pointedly, pulling him back from his dirty thoughts. "Landon wants to be there for the framing to make sure the safe room and false walls are done correctly."

Jake frowns with annoyance. "You can read blueprints."

"The Russells asked him to be there. He said they called him and asked him how the job was going, and he told them about my dad. He didn't outright say it, but I think they were concerned about me taking over."

"They only have to meet you once to know you're capable."

I glance around to make sure we're not in anybody's direct line of sight, then brush a kiss onto his cheek. "I love how you're in my corner."

"Always," he says, grabbing my hand and skimming his lips across my knuckles. "Did Landon ever call you again after your date?"

I give him a look. "I thought we established that it wasn't a date?"

Jake frowns. "Landon thought it was."

"I drove myself, and waved goodbye at the end. I'm positive he received the message. And no, he did not call me until it was time to start the framing."

"So I don't have anything to worry about? He's going to be hanging around the jobsite."

I roll my eyes in a huge, overdone way. Jake laughs. "Ok ok. I get it."

Reaching over, I poke his cheek and say, "You're cute when you're jealous."

He winks at me. "You're cute all the time."

I nod my head like he said something wise. "Very good response."

I move to walk away, but Jake stops me. "I'm just about ready to tell everybody we're together. It's killing me not to be able to kiss you when I want to."

I shake my head emphatically. "I'm afraid they'll look at me differently if they know."

Jake sighs. "Alright, boss. We'll do it your way."

An hour later, Landon arrives. Jake joins us in the trailer as we discuss the details of the blueprints. Landon knows false walls and a safe room is a first for everybody on this jobsite, so he's walking Jake and I through it, and then it's up to us to teach the crew.

Landon lays the blueprints on the architect's table in the corner. "You might remember from when I showed you last time, Colbie," Landon waves me over. "This is the false wall. The Russells want it at the back of the kitchen pantry."

I lean over to get a better look. Landon leans with me, his side almost pressing into mine. Jake stands a couple feet away, and given our earlier conversation, I can only imagine what he's thinking right now.

"Sounds good." I straighten. "I'm looking forward to the next few days. I think it will really start to become a home in my mind once we get the frame finished."

"Definitely. It's one-note now with just the concrete poured, but once it becomes 3-D, you'll start to see it in your mind's eye."

I look to Jake. His arms are crossed, his stance is wide, and I can tell he's trying to hide his annoyance. "You ready to get started?"

Jake and I are the last two people on the job for the day. Landon left midday, and Jake's mom is picking up Robbie from school and taking him to Sowed Oats for ice cream. I told Blake he could take off early and I'd finish the paperwork he'd been taking care of.

Jake steps into the trailer, his work jeans speckled with dirt and dust and whatever else he encountered on the jobsite.

He rakes his hand down his face and looks at the ceiling. "Fuck me, it's hot out there. What is with this late-season heat wave?"

I push back from the desk a few inches and lean back in my chair. "Please tell me you've been drinking water. If you pass out, there's no way I can carry you."

Jake holds up his water bottle. "I've been drinking water. And Gatorade."

I watch him walk over to the water bottle refilling station. He places his slate gray canteen underneath and hits the button.

"Are you hungry?" I ask, pulling my bag from underneath the desk. "I found the best peaches I've ever had at the farmers market in Sierra Grande. I have one left if you want it." I stand and offer him the fruit.

"Yes, I'm starving," he answers. "Thank you." He takes the fruit from me and bites down.

"Fuck that is delicious," he says, swiping the back of his hand over his mouth. I laugh.

"What?" he demands, taking another bite.

"You cursed again."

He breathes a laugh as he's chewing. "I cuss more when I'm hot. Where did you say you got these?"

"The farmers market in Sierra Grande. It's only held once a month, so you'll have to wait a few more weeks if you want more."

He takes another bite, and a drop of peach juice slithers down his chin.

I reach out with my thumb, cleaning the juice. His green eyes burn into mine, and heat ignites in my core. Instead of taking my thumb back, I let it trail along his jaw.

He chews, then swallows. Studying the fruit, he says, "When I was in eighth grade, I had a friend who had an older brother." He looks back at me, moving the fruit back and forth a few inches between us. "One day he told us that going down on a woman is the same as eating a ripe, juicy peach."

My thigh muscles clench, and I swallow. Hard. "Is that right?"

He takes another bite of the fruit. "Mm-hmm."

The vibration of the sound travels all the way down there, straight into that tight bundle of nerves. If I don't get a grip, I may be in danger of passing out. To cut through the tension, I grab for the only thing that has a prayer of keeping me upright. The boss card.

My eyebrows lift, a playful smile tugging up the corners of my mouth. "Do you think it's appropriate for you to speak this way around your boss?"

Jake leans in, his lips dancing over the shell of my ear. "Do you think it's appropriate that I put you on your hands and knees last weekend and fucked you from behind?"

The memory slams into me the same way he did.

He pulls back so he can see me, smirking when he gets a good look at my pink cheeks. "The muscles in your upper back clench when I'm inside you."

"You are so dirty," I whisper, but let's be real. I love every filthy second of it.

Jake leans down and swipes the tip of his tongue over my lower lip. "Let's get one thing straight. Nothing I do to you is dirty. Everything I do is meant to either make you happy, make you feel safe, make you feel wanted, or make you come."

My arms wrap around his neck. "Nobody has ever said anything like that to me." Nobody has ever made my needs a priority. I don't know if I've ever made my needs a priority.

271

"I mean it." His voice is low and deep, a baritone that pummels my chest.

"You...You can't say things like that to me. Or else..." my sentence falls away.

"Or else, what?"

This is it. This is the moment. Let down my guard and tell him that if he keeps treating me like a princess, the same princess he teased me about being, I'm in very real danger of losing my heart to him. "Falling in love with you *eventually* might happen sooner than I thought."

His eyes glimmer, and he looks both pleased and mischievous. "Let's see if I can hasten it a little more."

His fingers slip through my hair, and his tongue parts my lips. A low moan rises out of me, and he walks me backward, until the back of my thighs meet the edge of the desk. He eases me down onto it, pushing aside my papers and placing my laptop on my chair.

We're kissing again, needful and breathy, like each of us has something the other might die without. Jake pulls back, dragging in air, his gaze roaming the centerline of my body. His thumb grazes over my nipple, while his other hand exerts just enough pressure on my shoulder to communicate that he wants me to lie down.

I listen.

He grips the waistband of my jeans, eyes shimmering and hungry. I lift my behind an inch, and he slides the jeans down my legs.

"You're beautiful," he murmurs, eyes locked between my legs. His fingers travel over the silkiness of my underwear, locking on the sides of the fabric. He rids me of those, too, and trains his eyes on mine. I didn't realize he still had the peach in his hand, but he does, and now it's at his mouth and he's sucking juice from the fruit.

His name slips from my lips as I watch him swallow.

"Shhh," he says. He tosses the peach somewhere nearby. "I'm running a scientific experiment." His hands slide up the outsides of my thighs, where I've drawn my knees up and pressed them together. He grips my knees, applying pressure, and I widen. He moans, something primal and not at all resembling a word. Fingers digging into my hip creases, he hauls me to the edge of my desk.

We've had sex plenty of times by now, but this feels different. There's an air, an edge, almost as if Jake's staking a claim. Not that he needs to.

He positions himself between my thighs, finger dragging up my center. "So wet for me."

"Oh my God," I moan, throwing a forearm over my eyes, an uncommon shyness setting a blush on my cheeks. "Why are you making such a meal of it?"

His touch disappears. Panic makes me want to fly off this table, but I force myself not to move. Not to show him how much I actually love this.

"Colbie?" he says after an interminably long three seconds. "Look at me."

I remove my arm. He's not standing between my legs anymore.

"Lower, Colbie."

I prop myself on my elbows, and my gaze falls on him.

Kneeling. His face hovering an inch above me. "I'm making a meal of it," he says slowly, pressing the pad of his thumb against me and traveling a tiny circle, "because it's called eating."

He drops his face, and I don't think I'd call what he's doing now *eating*.

More like he showed up famished to a feast.

My breath goes shallow, my head tipping back and my

eyes closing. The feeling is exquisite, and I think it's possible I could break apart into tiny fragments at any second.

My fingers tangle into his hair, my nails scraping his scalp, when he murmurs against me, "For the record, you taste better than the peach."

Who knew words could deliver such pleasure? Jake resumes his task, until it becomes too much and I'm lifting off the table, hips rolling, incoherent and loud.

He stays planted, wringing every drop of pleasure from me, then straightens, fully clothed, a large smile on his handsome face. "I love listening to you."

I motion to the front of his dirty jeans. "Take yourself out of those jeans, and listen to me again."

He shakes his head. "I've been working all day. I need a shower." He grabs my underwear and jeans, threading my feet through my underwear first. "But once I'm clean, you'd better be ready, Buttercup."

"Is that a promise?" I lift my behind so he can slide my clothing up my body, feeling sated instead of anticipatory.

"Yes," he growls.

Jake follows through on that promise.

Twice.

Chapter 36

Colbie

"Well, hello there Colbie. Where have you been hiding yourself these last few weeks?" Jiminy raises a palm in the air as I cross the dining room at Honeybee. "Never mind, don't answer that. Your dad's been in for breakfast every day this week."

I smile at the old man running a cleaning cloth over the countertop. "Is he telling my secrets?"

"Just the juicy ones."

Jiminy's right. I've been MIA since Jake and I started dating. If I'm not at the construction site, I'm either at Jake's helping Robbie with math, or completing tasks for Burn Barre. Christina and I hired a woman for the managerial role a couple weeks ago, but it takes time to get them up and running in a way that allows me to hand off certain responsibilities.

Jake took Robbie camping about an hour ago, and they'll return sometime tomorrow. I thought it was the perfect time to visit Honeybee. I invited Greer, but she had her run club this morning. I don't mind eating alone, so it wasn't a big deal.

Jiminy pours me a cup of coffee once I get myself settled at the counter. I thank him and take the mug, but he instructs me to wait. "I got something for you on my trip to the bigger grocery store in the next town a while ago. I hope it's not expired."

He reaches into the refrigerator case, turns over a rectangular carton to read the use-by date on the bottom, then nods once in satisfaction. He plunks it on the counter in front of me and I gasp.

Almond milk.

"Jiminy." I press a hand to my heart. I want to climb over the counter and hug this sweet old man. "This is the nicest thing anybody has ever done for me."

He shrugs. "Well, I heard Jake say you couldn't have dairy, so I thought I'd pick it up when I saw it. It wasn't a big deal."

I pour a generous serving in my cup, just so he knows how appreciative I am. "It was a big deal, Jiminy."

He frowns at how happy he's made me. "Don't go telling anybody about it. Bob's been asking me to buy him peppered bacon for years, and I refuse." He grumbles and shakes his head. "You get what you get, and you don't throw a fit. But try telling Bob that." Jiminy adds an eye roll. I've never met Bob, but I can already see him in my mind's eye.

I take a big sip of my coffee. Jiminy watches. "Just right," I grin.

"Ok, Goldilocks. Do you want the omelet you seem to like so much?"

"Yes, please. With peppered bacon."

Jiminy playfully scowls. "You and Bob can keep wishing."

He walks away to put my order in. I'm on my second coffee refill when a woman seats herself four stools down from me. She's probably around my age, with long blonde hair that has a natural-looking wave. Her eyes are round, her cheeks pink, and she looks around nervously. She reminds me of a frightened deer, prepared to bolt at any second.

"Hi," I say, offering a smile. In Phoenix, I probably wouldn't have spoken to this woman. But here in Green Haven, I feel friendlier. Or maybe it's being deliriously in love that makes me so friendly.

Her head whips my direction. "Hello," she answers reluctantly.

"Are you new to Green Haven?"

She shakes her head back-and-forth in tiny, fast motions. "Just passing through."

Jiminy approaches her. She is all business when he takes her order. He gives me a look when he walks by me, as if to say *I dunno, your turn again.*

I decide to give it another shot, because we're the only people sitting up here, and the silence is almost painful. "Where are you coming from?"

"Phoenix," she says.

"That's where I'm from. I've only been in Green Haven for a couple months."

For some reason this seems to relax her. Maybe because I'm not a true local, so she feels we're on a more even playing field. "I'm Lindsay," she says.

"Nice to meet you, Lindsay. Colbie," I point at my chest. "Ever heard of Burn Barre?"

"Yes," she answers, nodding. Her shoulders relax, and she says, "I've been to a few classes. I couldn't walk afterward for, like, three days."

I laugh. "Sounds about right. My best friend and I co-own the studios."

277

"What?" Her face becomes animated. "What are you doing here?"

"My dad lives here." But he's not the only person keeping me here anymore. There's also Jake. And Robbie. And Greer, Jiminy, and weirdly, Victoria. "Where are you headed?"

"There's a once a month market in Sierra Grande I want to go to. I read about it in a magazine."

I nod knowingly. I know all about that market. And its peaches.

"I love that market." I squint at her, giving her a teasing look like I don't believe her. "Are you sure you're not trying to get a peek at Tenley Roberts?" I'd be lying if I said I haven't thought about day tripping to Sierra Grande to walk around the town in hopes of seeing the famous actress who fell in love with a cowboy and left the spotlight.

Lindsay smiles. "I wouldn't run the opposite direction if I saw her, but I really do want to go to the market."

Jiminy delivers my food, and before he walks away he says, "Your dad said Jake is having a birthday party for Robbie next weekend. Make sure you bring him in on his birthday, I always make him a banana split."

"Will do." I cut into my omelet. "You should come to the party. It's next Saturday at two. At my dad's house."

Jiminy grabs a rag and begins wiping down the empty end of the counter. "Tell Emmett I'll try and make it. No promises though, I'm usually here on Saturday's."

"I'm having dinner with him tonight, so I'll make sure to tell him."

Lindsay has pulled out her phone, so I don't interrupt her. I eat my omelet and pay Jiminy. Lindsay looks up as I'm standing up from my stool and winding my purse around my arm. "Enjoy the market," I tell her.

"Enjoy whatever it is you're doing here with your dad." She tucks a strand of hair behind her ear. "Maybe I'll see you at Burn Barre in Phoenix sometime."

I head out into the street, belly full and properly caffeinated. I'm on the hunt for the perfect birthday present for Robbie.

⁘

Victoria answers the door. Instead of saying hi, she says, "Thank God you're here." Frustration tugs her voice down to a lower register.

"What's wrong?" I step into the house.

"Your father is out back in his shed. He's driving me nuts." She sighs, deep and long, with an *ugh* sound to it. "I wish he could go back to the jobsite. He's like a toddler who needs to get energy out."

I chuckle at the comparison. "What is he doing in the shed?"

"He says he's making Robbie's birthday gift."

"Ok." I'm still not understanding what has Victoria upset. "Where's Greer?"

"She went into work, but she should be back soon. She wanted to redecorate her classroom and move desks around."

"I wish I'd known she was there. I would've walked down and helped."

Victoria glances out the window to the shed, then back to me. "Between us, I think Greer is seeing someone and keeping it a secret."

I feel a tiny flicker of something, maybe it's happiness, at her confiding in me. Drumming the pads of my fingers together, I murmur with a grin, "The plot thickens."

"Has she said anything to you?"

Shaking my head quickly, I say, "Not a thing."

"It's not like Greer to keep secrets from me," Victoria smiles like she finds something amusing. "That I know of, anyway."

Victoria's musings make me think of my mother, and how much easier it would've been to keep Jake, and Green Haven, and even the mending of my relationship with my dad, a secret from my mom. Unhealthy, but ten times more pleasant.

"Anyway," Victoria says, patting my arm. "You didn't come here to listen to me yammer on about Greer." She removes a plaid blazer from the back of a chair and shrugs it on. "I have a house to show. I'll see you later."

Victoria leaves, and I make my way to the shed. The freestanding structure is really more of a workshop than a shed, but for some reason that's what my dad has always called it.

I open the door and peek my head inside. My dad's standing over his worktable, safety goggles in place on his head. "Hi, Dad." The short jolt of discomfort I feel calling him 'dad' dissipates quickly. I need a little more time to get used to that, but I'm sure in the end it will likely disappear all together.

He looks up from his worktable, where different size pieces of wood are spread before him. "Hey, Sugar Bear."

I step in, letting the door close on its own behind me. "What are you working on?"

"A LEGO table for Robbie."

I walk closer to get a better look at what he's building. "That's perfect, because I found the coolest Lego set for his birthday. It's a fishing shack. The thing is a monster. I hope he needs help putting it together, because I want to build it, too."

My dad slides his carpenter pencil behind his ear and presses a kiss to my temple. "Things are going well for you and Jake, huh?"

"Yes," I nod. "Really well, actually."

"You sound surprised."

"I suppose I am. I came to Green Haven to visit you in the hospital." I hold my hands out next to me and turn in a half circle. "Now look at me." There isn't any real difference in my physical appearance, but the changes on the inside are numerous. Still, my dad grins affectionately at my display.

"How did your mother take the news?"

My hands drop. My dad never mentions my mother.

"She wasn't very happy about it."

"Hmm." Judgment lurks behind his tone.

"What?"

He shrugs and turns back to his worktable. "Nothing."

There's a stool in the corner, so I take a seat on it. I've been in Green Haven for two months, and I'm done dancing around touchy subjects. If I never came here I might've danced around them forever, but that's not the reality I'm living in right now. I chose to accept my dad's request, and I think I knew even then that this conversation was inevitable. We are alone out here, so it may as well happen now. "Are we ever going to talk about her? Are we ever going to talk about you, and what happened?"

The air in the shed grows taut, and even though there's a window propped open it feels like the airflow has slowed. My dad's gaze drops to the ground, like he's trying to gather his thoughts, and I'm glad he can't see me squirming on this stool, trying to figure out where to place my hands. Eventually I fold them and let them rest on the seam created by my thighs.

My dad turns a quarter circle away from me, pressing his palms to the top of his workbench and taking a noisy breath through his nose. "Where do you want to start?" His tone is a mix of dread and inevitability.

"How about the beginning?"

He nods slowly, only his back body visible to me. "I know you think I left you—"

"You did." The words are out before I can stop them, but I don't regret the lack of sugarcoating.

"There was a lot going on back then. A lot you don't know about."

"Tell me."

His head shakes slowly back-and-forth. "I can't."

"Why not?" My voice has an edge to it now. I don't understand.

"Your mother wouldn't appreciate me telling you everything that happened."

"What does that even mean?"

He finally turns around. He crosses his arms and leans his lower back against the lip of the table. "It means she likes to paint me as the bad guy, and I let that happen for a really long time because I couldn't bear for you to feel hurt by both of your parents."

His answer makes me think of my mom, and how she has never been afraid to cast him in unflattering light. "You're going to need to give me more to go on than that. I'm an adult. I can handle it."

My dad runs his fingers through his hair, tugging lightly and messing it up in places. "If I tell you this, it's going to give your mother a reason to finally drive up here. She'll be coming here to kill me though, which doesn't end well for me."

I don't crack a smile. He takes in my serious expression, and I think it's what turns the tide. Maybe he can see how badly I need this.

He adjusts his stance so his legs are wider than his hips, then he asks, "Do you remember Dustin?"

The name is vaguely familiar, but I can't figure out why. "Kind of?"

"He was a senior partner at the law firm where your mother worked when you were young."

He hasn't even said the words yet, and somehow I know exactly where this is going. My stomach is already turning.

"I found out your mother was having an affair with him. I was at a barbershop getting my hair cut, and he came in. He didn't recognize me from the office Christmas party months prior." My dad snorts derisively. I've never heard him make such a noise, but then again, I've never heard him talk like this either. "I recognized him though. Loudmouth guy, walking around with his chest puffed out. Very proud of himself, though for what I'm not sure." My dad stares at the bare wall, seeing something that happened decades ago. "He sat down and was going on and on about one of the junior attorneys he was"—he cuts off, and I know it's because he was close to saying *fucking*—"seeing. I told myself he wasn't talking about your mother, but then he said 'she has a kid and a loser husband who works construction. Good luck paying for the good life when you're a construction worker'." My dad drops his gaze from the wall to the floor. I wish he'd look at me, but I don't think he can right now. "His comment split me seven different ways. I felt humiliated, for many reasons. My wife was having an affair, and it felt like it was happening because of me, not in spite of me. Like my inability to provide had provoked her."

Nausea rises. My poor dad. And my mom...I'm not sure what to think. All this time she played the role of victim, and she played it well. "I'm so sorry, Dad."

Now he looks at me. "Don't feel sorry for me. No matter what she did, I made choices in reaction to her. Choices I'm not proud of." He sighs. "I heard Dustin's voice in my ear, so high and mighty, making it clear your mother had married below her. I wanted to prove him wrong, which seems stupid now because I've never seen the guy again. But"—he lifts his shoulders, dropping them once—"Dustin's opinion of me struck a nerve. It hit on my own opinion of me. I'd heard from guys who knew what they were talking about, saying all these small towns in central and northern Arizona were on the brink of major growth, so I followed their advice."

I'm still reeling from learning about my mom, but I seize the opportunity to set it aside for the moment. "You quit your job to form your own construction company?" It's a question, but I don't need an answer. Memories are flooding me now. "We took that plywood and used stencils to spray paint your name and number." I wipe a hand across my cheek and find that it's wet. "We made so many of them. We nailed them to stakes." More tears. "You let me use your hammer to drive the stake into the ground."

"I'm surprised you remember." My dad smiles in a sad way. "That was right after I moved up here. Seems like a rudimentary form of advertising, but those signs brought me more business than I ever thought they would."

His features curve upward in fond remembrance, but I pushed these memories down for a reason. They hurt.

It would be easy to let my dad off the hook right now. I

could thank him for telling me about my mom, and not ask him to explain what happened after he left, in the years that followed when the drift was slow but certain.

I am worth this. It's ok for him to be uncomfortable while I seek the truth. It's ok if it hurts him to talk about this.

Maybe that's why I've put distance between us for years. I knew I wanted answers, and it would hurt him to give them. I was, essentially, protecting him from me.

Not anymore. We'll never move forward if we don't spend some time in the past.

I straighten up and look him in the eye. He looks tired, and emotionally wrung out, but I press on. "I loved you. I was your sugar bear. What happened?"

A strangled cry escapes his throat. My first instinct is to soothe him, but I override it. I don't want to.

"I could tell you a lot of things about that time, but at the end of the day, none of them matter. All that matters is that I was weak, and I didn't try as hard as you needed me to. I didn't fight your mother when I should have. My short-comings got the best of me, and I will always be sorry. And I will always love you."

I press a hand to my mouth. I have to keep the sob inside, because I'm afraid if I let just one escape, they will all tumble out.

My eyes close, and just as I'm drawing in the air needed to steady me, my dad's arms wrap around me. There is no use trying to keep my sobs inside. They arrive, one on top of the other, great big heaving sounds. Years of anguish, of wondering, of feeling unworthy of the man who once was my hero.

He holds me until the tears subside. I desperately need a tissue.

My dad peels off the flannel he's wearing. Standing in jeans and a white undershirt, he hands the flannel my way and says, "Use this to blow your nose."

I hesitate. He says, "I changed a majority of your diapers. Your snot doesn't scare me."

My nose wrinkles. It's the perfect thing to say to lighten the heavy mood. Still, it's embarrassing. "I don't think grown women want to hear that."

He chuckles. "I suppose not."

I take his offered shirt and make use of it. He takes it back from me when I'm finished, balls up the part I used, and wipes his eyes with the opposite corner. "I have a confession to make."

I eye him warily. "What?"

"When I asked you to take over the job, it was a spur of the moment thing. I was planning to ask Jake."

"Oh." My heart sinks. I feel bad. Jake should be the one with this job, not me.

"I've been calling around and talking with the crew. Not to keep tabs on you, but just because I miss the work. They all say the same thing about you."

"That they're sick of my questions and having to teach me things?"

"They say you rarely stay in the trailer. That you're out with them, wearing knee pads and finishing concrete. You bought a tool belt—"

"Pink." I swallow the immediate thought of Jake's unabashed appreciation of the item.

He grins. "And you keep a basket of snacks stocked, and a purified water station." His lips press together, and he looks like he has something else he wants to say but he's not sure he should. "They say you remind them of me."

I grin. I hated the first time I heard that, but now I think

I might actually like it. "Jake told me that after the first day I was on the job."

Dad nods. "So, here I am, thinking hard about what's next for me. I do things sometimes that leave me scratching my head. Victoria asked me to make coffee yesterday, and I stood in the kitchen trying to remember where we keep the grounds." He tries to shrug it off, but I can see how much it bothers him. "I've had Blake turning away work for a while, but pretty soon Jones Construction is going to need to have its next job lined up. That crew counts on me to keep them working. They have families, and lives. With the way my brain has been acting, I can't schedule future work. It wouldn't be fair to anybody. If the crew is going to have to find a different place to work, they're going to need to know pretty soon. For some, it will include moving."

"What are you saying?"

"I wouldn't ask this of you if it seemed like you were unhappy here. But you're glowing Colbie, you really are. If you are interested, I would like for you to take over the company."

"Jake," I blurt out. "Jake is who should take over the company."

My dad nods. "I'll take care of Jake. He'll get a good bump in compensation, paid time off, and a new company truck."

"You've thought about this."

He nods. "I have a lot of time on my hands these days."

"I don't know, Dad." I haven't even told him Christina wants to pull back from Burn Barre. It's not hard to paint a happy picture of me, Jake, and Robbie. Fishing on Sunday mornings and eating breakfast at Jiminy's after. Walking Robbie to school and driving to work. Laughing and loving, like we already do, except this would be all the time. It wouldn't be perfect, but it would be good most of the time. I already know it.

"Take some time," my dad says. "Think about it."

"I will."

"Yoohoo," Victoria calls, opening the shed door. She peeks inside. "My appointment was a no-show. And Greer's home. She brought tacos, if anybody is hungry."

"Starved," my dad says.

We go in and eat. I can't stop thinking about my dad's offer.

Take over Jones Construction, permanently?

I can't.

Can I?

Chapter 37

Jake

Robbie doesn't want me to put up the tent.

He keeps saying he wants to sleep under the stars. I'm not sure if he got this from a book he's read recently, but sleeping under the stars sounds better in theory than in practice.

We spent the day hiking, so his core body temperature is higher than if we'd just been sitting around. Tonight will be chilly, and if anything more than a breeze starts up, it's going to go from chilly to cold really fast.

Robbie says he doesn't care if he's cold, but he says it in that way where I know he's just doubtful his dad knows anything. I can't remember if I did that to my dad. I'm sure I did.

I've been thinking about my dad a lot lately. Since Colbie came to Green Haven, and I began watching her take those tentative steps to patch up her relationship with Emmett. I'm happy for her, but it reminds me I'll never get the same chance. That hurts.

I have Robbie though, and that's kind of like a second

chance. I get to parent a son, instead of be the son. A second chance, but not the same thing.

Robbie walks around the area where we're setting up camp after our day of hiking. He's collecting sticks, rocks, pinecones, anything that strikes him as interesting. He returns to my side, arms loaded. We look through it together, and I let him think a rock he found could be an arrowhead.

It's not.

This morning, as I was finishing packing up the truck, I'd thrown two cots in with everything else. Just in case. It's a good thing I did, because it looks like we'll be needing them. If we're going to sleep in the open air, I'll at least have Robbie off the ground. It might make us feel the cold faster, but it'll make it harder for snakes and scorpions to reach him.

Robbie's eyes widen when I tell him this. "Scorpions don't live this high in elevation."

"Correct. But we're not that far from their natural habitat. We don't need any wanderers creeping in to snuggle." I tickle his midsection and he folds in half, laughing.

Robbie busies himself separating and organizing his collection. I finish setting up our cots, then top them with our thickest sleeping bags and an extra blanket tucked inside. Robbie helps me drag the generator to my truck tailgate, and I set up the electric heaters for nighttime use.

Robbie and I go for a short walk to get a better view of the sunset, and when we come back, he helps me get dinner started. The fire danger is at an extreme level right now, so we can't build our own fire. We'll have to use the propane stove tonight.

I've given Robbie the task of cutting potatoes into small

cubes while I handle the raw meat. "When I was a kid, my dad and I would go camping a lot. We'd build a fire, and my dad would wrap potatoes in tinfoil and place them so they were right on the edge of the flames." In my mind I see my dad walking around the campfire, nudging the foil-wrapped potatoes in closer to the flame with the toe of his boot.

This memory has been tucked back in my mind for a long time, and even though it hurts to talk about, there's something about it that also feels good. Like a quick push on the release valve of a pressure cooker.

Robbie pauses his task. "I'm sorry your dad died and you can't go camping with him anymore."

I close the plastic bag containing the steak and rub in the marinade from the outside of the bag. "Thanks, Robbie."

Robbie holds the knife just as I've taught him to, but instead of exerting pressure and slicing through the potato, he asks, "Where is my mom?"

My hand stills. My fingers shake. "I'm not sure." Guilt slams into me. I could be sure, if I wanted to. I could answer any of her text messages, or dial the number she calls from.

"Babies come from the female's stomach. Mammals have live birth, and we're mammals. So, I came from her stomach, and then she left?"

"It was kind of like that, yes." Tears burn at the backs of my eyes.

"Mammals have a high parental investment because their live young require care until they're independent. That's what my show said." Robbie's gaze meets mine, easily conveying his worry and confusion.

I get up and wash my hands using water from a five gallon jug I filled up before we left. Then I sit back down and place my hands on Robbie's shoulders. He looks up at me, eyes the same color as mine, but missing twenty years of hardship and heartache, joy and content.

He trusts me, completely, the same way I trusted my dad once upon a time. "Your mom couldn't be the mom you needed, so she asked me to be your only parent." This is mostly true. I'm struggling to explain something incomprehensible to a child.

Robbie stares down at the cutting board. That's when I see the tiny drops falling onto the food. Big tears from a little boy. This pain is one Robbie must experience, and I can't shield him from it. As much as I would like to protect him from every ugly thing in the world, I can't, I won't, and I shouldn't.

"Come here, buddy." I gather him in my arms. He cries, and I cry with him.

"Did she love me?" he asks, sipping air in the breaks between his sobs.

"Yes, she did." My lips are on his head, and I breathe in the familiar scent. "Nobody could know you, and not love you."

"Colbie loves me, right?" He's asking a question, but his tone has the strength of a statement.

I already know how I'm going to answer this question, but I don't know if my answer is the truth, because I haven't asked. I haven't thought to. "Of course she does. And so do I. And Mimi, and Aunt Georgia, and Rhodes, and Emmett. We all love you."

Robbie swipes his forearm under his nose. "Is Colbie going to be my mom?"

I swallow. It's one thing for me to tell him that Colbie loves him when I don't know for certain if that's the case. It's another for me to mismanage his expectations. "It's too soon for me to know that."

"It would be ok with me, if you wanted her to be my mom. She's really nice, and she's funny. She makes you smile a lot. And, um—" a sheepish look crawls over his face. "I don't really need help with math. I only needed help that first time, and you were so happy when she was at our house. And I was happy, too. Are you mad?"

I shake my head. "No, not at all."

Robbie looks at the potatoes. "I think we need to wash these."

We rinse his tears off the potatoes, and then we cook dinner. The shadows lengthen and the final stretches of sunlight disappear. Side-by-side on our cots, we take turns reading out loud from <u>My Side Of The Mountain</u>. I also brought <u>Where The Red Fern Grows</u>, but we've cried enough this evening. I'll save that one for another time.

I get Robbie tucked into a sleeping bag, nice and tight. He falls asleep first. I stare up at the stars, and listen to Robbie's soft snores.

I wonder what Colbie is doing now. Is she in bed? Is she reading one of those nonfiction books she likes to read at the end of the night?

Could she become Robbie's mother?

Reaching down into the sleeping bag, I ease my phone from my pocket. I pull up my photos, and flip through the last couple months of pictures. So many of Colbie. Me and her, her and Robbie. The three of us. I can't decide which is my favorite, but the one I took last weekend of Robbie teaching her how to hook a worm is up there in my top three. Colbie with her eyes scrunched closed, and her tongue stuck out in disgust. Robbie's head is thrown back as he howls with laughter. They are standing on the bank of the Verde River, the sun dappled water shining in the background.

My heart swells. I'm lying here, surrounded by dark-ness, listening to the thrum of crickets and other bugs, wearing a dopey smile.

I give up. I know what this is.

Love.

Chapter 38

Jake

R obbie and I returned from camping by noon so Colbie and my mom could take Robbie shopping for clothes.

Or was it school supplies?

Books, maybe?

I don't remember what cover story they used. All I know is that they offered, and I accepted. I needed time to build this junior workbench for Robbie's birthday gift, and when I mentioned to Colbie that Robbie was going to have to spend the afternoon with my mom, she asked if she could join and make it an outing.

"I want to get to know your mom better," she'd explained after Robbie and I finished unloading my truck when we got back, and then she kissed me. I sent Robbie for a shower, and then I hurried Colbie into my room. In seconds her clothes were on my bedroom floor, and my pants joined the pile, and I needed Colbie so desperately I think I would've agreed to walk backward naked in the snow at that point.

They've been gone a few hours, and I'm making good

progress on the build. I watched countless tutorials online before I started, and I ran through it in my head over and over, so I had a good idea of what I was doing before I got started.

I take a break to grab some food. There isn't much to eat in my fridge, which is something I'll have to remedy later this afternoon. I end up calling in an order for a club sandwich at Honeybee, then running down to grab it and eating it on the drive home.

I'm chewing through the final bite of my sandwich when my phone rings. I'm so lost in thought that the sound startles me and I drop my to-go cup of iced tea. The lid pops off and the light brown liquid immediately soaks into the seat.

"Fuck," I mutter, pressing the button on the phone without checking to see who the caller is. "Yeah?" I all but bark.

"Jake."

I freeze. Iced tea seeps into the upholstery. Her voice is soft, tentative, fearful. With only my name, she implores me not to hang up on her.

"Please, Jake. Don't hang up."

Automatically I glance in the back seat where Robbie normally sits. There's nothing to see except the toy car Robbie keeps back there. He plays with it while I drive, practicing moves for his favorite racing video game. This is the truck I drove him in when I came home for good. That is the back seat where he laid, passed out from exhaustion and dehydrated after a bad stomach virus, while I drove him to the emergency room for an IV. The last time I changed the brake lights, Robbie sat right here in the driver's seat and tapped the brakes when I asked him to.

I manage to ask, "What do you want?" That's all I can

get out right now. My whole body is on high-alert, my muscles clenched.

"I...I..." She takes a deep breath, the sound coming through the phone. "I want to see Robbie."

"No."

"Jake—"

"No. You put Robbie through enough."

"Jake—"

If she says anything after that, I don't hear it, because I've hung up.

My shaking hands grip the steering wheel, and my jaw screams with the pain of clenching my teeth together.

I want to see Robbie.

What the fuck? She can't waltz back into Robbie's life. She can't turn up and float onto the scene, as if she's stepping into an empty role. She didn't vacate the picture and leave us with an outline of herself. We colored her in with years of memories and traditions, with bike rides and books and Saturday morning pancakes.

Erin can't just reappear, like she's been waiting in the wings this whole time.

Can she?

I need time to think, and process. I need to spend time with Robbie, and try to figure out what he might want. And Colbie? What will she think?

It's a small miracle she's chosen a guy like me. I don't have a fancy job, and my baggage comes in human form.

My head drops into my hands, the earthy scent of spilled tea permeating the air. I feel petty, and bad, and terrified. My first instinct is to protect Robbie. That's what happens when you have a kid. You love them with a deep ferocity, in a way that never ends, it stretches out into

297

oblivion until you draw your final breath. Their pain becomes your pain, their joy your own.

My phone pings with a text, and I'm relieved to see Colbie's name.

> We're going to a couple more stores. How's it going there?

> Good.

I don't mean to lie, but I don't know what to say. It's not something to talk about through text, anyhow. Still, I feel bad, so I send an additional message.

> Looking forward to seeing you.

Colbie responds with two hearts, and I run my thumb over them on the screen. She's come a long way since that night in the hallway at Caruso's. So have I, for that matter.

I leave my truck, going around to my backyard. I continue building the workbench for Robbie. I do everything I can to push Erin from my mind.

Chapter 39

Colbie

J ake's mom volunteered to take Robbie for the night.

I felt flustered when she'd asked, because I know that she knows what that entails. If there were any doubt, it disappeared when she'd whispered, "I know how hard it can be to get alone time when there are children running around."

I tried not to blush, but I failed.

Jake texted earlier and said he grabbed a few things from the grocery store and is making dinner for us. I haven't told him not to expect Robbie, and my heart beats faster at the anticipation of the look on his face when he realizes it's just the two of us tonight.

And when he sees what I'm planning to wear, I think he'll combust. How many times has he mentioned that he likes my pink tool belt? After tonight, I think he'll like it even more.

I stop at my house and take a quick shower. Jake likes when I go without makeup, but I throw a little bit on, just for me.

I look...good.

Confident. Sexy.

And really happy. My dad was right. I am glowing. But it's best not to think of my dad right now.

I pull on my prettiest matching bra and underwear set, clip on the tool belt, then wrap myself in the knee-length coat I bought for the cold mornings. Slipping on stilettos, I teeter out of my front door, praying I can make it two houses down without being spotted.

I almost do.

I'm striding up Jake's driveway, certain I've made it because I'm in the homestretch, when I hear, "Colbie!". Alma waves from the top of the wheelchair ramp.

"Shit," I mutter. I plaster a smile on my face and pivot, walking closer to Alma. I cross my arms in front of myself as I go, even though the coat is belted and cinched.

"Hi, Alma."

"I just wanted to give this to you," she thrusts a loaf pan at me. "It's chocolate chip banana bread. I baked it for Jake this morning. Would you mind giving it to him?"

"No problem." I take the food from her outstretched arm, remembering Keli's warning about Alma's cooking. Does that extend to baking?

Alma looks me up and down and grins like she's in on a secret. "Bet I know what you have on under there." She keeps smiling and nodding her head.

I highly doubt she'd guess I have on a tool belt, but her thoughts point in the correct direction.

"I don't know what you're talking about," I say coyly.

"Yeah, yeah. I remember those days." She winks, and shimmies one shoulder. "I was a stunner, too. Played all kinds of games with men." She points back at the house. "Not with Arthur. He's my third husband. We were old when we got married."

I laugh. "I think we need to have a cocktail sometime so I can hear more about that."

Alma retreats to her front door. "You have yourself a nice night, honey."

I return to Jake's driveway, but now I'm holding this loaf of banana bread and it really doesn't go with my outfit. I don't knock on the front door anymore, so I let myself in and quickly deposit the banana bread on the side table in the living room.

Jake walks in from the kitchen. The man is wearing blue jeans, a navy blue t-shirt, and an apron. It's as if someone has taken the word 'sexy', and sculpted it into human form. I'm already dying to get my hands on him.

Jake's eyebrows tug together in the center. "Where's Robbie?"

My tongue runs the length of my upper lip and I take a slow step forward. "Robbie is staying with your mom tonight."

A lazy smile lifts one side of Jake's mouth. "Oh yeah?"

Two more steps forward. "Mm-hmm."

He leans one shoulder on the wall, and looks me up and down. So. Slowly. "What do you have on underneath that coat?" His voice is low, rumbly, like the growly purr of an old car engine.

My fingers toy with the tied belt at my waist. "That depends. What do you have going on in the kitchen?"

"Nothing I can't step away from."

"Well, then," I stand just outside of Jake's reach, untying the belt and gripping the coat's soft fabric. I open the coat slowly, and an appreciative moan rumbles from Jake.

"Fucking hell," he murmurs, closing the distance with a single stride. His hands are under the coat, sliding up my

301

chest, slipping the coat from my shoulders. It slides down my arms, falling with a soft thud at my feet.

Jake steps back to look at me. He holds one of my hands aloft as his eyes rake the length of my body, pausing on the tool belt. An appreciative smile tugs at his mouth. "That goddamn tool belt."

I jut one hip out and make a playful pouty face. "You like it?"

He nods. "I like it." His eyes lock onto mine, his expression determined and purposeful. "But I love the person wearing it."

My eyes widen, but Jake doesn't give me a chance to respond. He closes the space between us, his hands threading through my hair and his lips pressed to mine. The kisses are soft at first, sweet, and then urgent.

My hands drop to Jake's belt buckle and he steps back to give me room to work. He does away with his shirt, and I want time to admire the piece of work that is his body. His expansive chest, his broad shoulders, the way his waist tapers down, the line of hair that disappears into the band of his jeans. I trail my hands over his shoulders, stopping briefly at the place above his heart. I am beyond appreciative of the organ in his chest, providing him with life and me with everything he's willing to give.

My fingers drop lower, traversing his happy trail and moving onto the button at the top of his jeans. Jake leans down, kissing my forehead while I flick open the button. The sound of the lowering zipper prompts a hot stream of air from Jake. I work his jeans over his hips, and he helps me get them down his legs.

Jake takes me by surprise by spinning me around and holding me against his body. I feel him working his boxer briefs down his legs, and then he's pressed against me, his hot erection against the skin left bare by my light pink lace thong.

"You're in for it," he whispers in my ear, starting us toward his bedroom. "Coming into my house wearing that? Do you know what I'm going to do to you?"

I press back against his length. "A girl can dream."

He growls into my ear, a sound that harkens back to the very first time we spoke on the phone. My heart does a jumpy twisty turny maneuver at the memory.

We reach his bed and he bends me over, so I'm L-shaped against his flannel sheets. He starts at the top of my back, running his scruffy face against my skin until I'm covered in goose bumps. He reaches a hand between my legs, knocking them apart. He cups my center, kneading the heel of his palm against the fabric still covering me. I whimper into the soft sheets.

"You smell incredible," he says, his mouth at my ear. "And this thing?" The tool belt around my waist moves back and forth. His fingers slide under the belt, and my body is lifted, airborne until my knees hit the mattress.

He rolls me over, and now I'm flat on my back. The rough fabric of the tool belt scratches my skin, but it doesn't hurt.

"Mmm," he grounds out, eyes tracing my midsection, dipping lower to the tops of my thighs. "I'll never be able to look at you at work again."

"As your boss, I think that might be a problem."

"Oh yeah?" Jake's hand slips down, feathering over the underwear I'm still wearing.

"Yeah," I manage to say, but my tremble breaks up the simple word.

"How about as my girlfriend?" He pushes aside the fabric, dipping a finger into me. "Now what do you think?"

I squirm. He grins.

What is it about this man that makes me come undone? It's a wonder to me, but not a mystery. I think I know everything about him that's making me feel this way.

Jake works the thong down my leg, tossing it to the ground. He hovers above me, keeping his weight off me, and devours my mouth. My hands roam his body, careening over his shoulder blades and sliding down his lower back, until his ass is in both my palms. I arch into him, trying to bring us closer, but he only chuckles. I nibble at his lower lip, and let my hands wind around the front of his body. I hold him in one hand, working him, and he tries to laugh again but it's strangled. "You drive me the right kind of crazy."

The right kind of crazy...

The least amount of awful...

What if it's really the most amount of awful? Is that where the magic happens? A place where someone can do catastrophic damage is also the place where the most love can occur?

I let go of Jake, reaching up and touching his face.

I'm filled with an urgency I've never felt before. I need him. I need him now. I need him to fill me, I want his weight and his heat. I want him in me, and all around me.

"Jake?"

Is it the seriousness of my tone that has him frozen in place, mouth parted, eyes a mixture of desire and high hopes?

I open my mouth, and I say something I've never said to another man. Not because I was emotionally unavailable, but because I didn't feel it. "I love the person wearing"—I skim his body quickly—"nothing, right now."

Jake tucks a hand against my cheek and captures my mouth. Against my lips, he murmurs, "I love you, Colbie."

These words are sweet, and new, and I love them, too.

Jake reaches down, situates himself between my legs, and eases inside me.

Fireworks.

He kisses me tenderly, pulling back and then sliding in again, filling me. I cling to him. He pushes deeper, harder, faster, with a sense of purpose. The fire in my core builds, burning hotter and brighter, and I know what's coming. It happens every time with Jake.

My head tips back. Jake kisses my exposed throat while I fly high, then crash back to earth. I haven't yet caught my breath when he sits back on his knees, and I feel him leave me. He leans forward, gripping himself. Eyes scrunched, he shudders and finishes on my stomach.

On my tool belt.

He collapses beside me, peering over with only one eye open.

I lift my head and gaze at my navel. "Did you—"

"Yep."

I laugh and shake my head. "Did you plan that?"

"Only from the second you opened your coat."

I laugh again, and he rolls over, pulling me in with an arm around my chest. My nails lightly scratch over his arm.

He looks at me with soulful, sated eyes. "I told you I'd make you fall in love with me eventually." He moves his head closer, placing a soft kiss on the outside swell of my breast. "What did it?"

I train my eyes on the top of his head, studying the slant of his nose from an angle I don't find myself in often. "I was thinking about you, and how you're the most amount of awful."

Confusion drifts across his face as he tries to put that together.

Running a hand through his hair, I say, "What I figured out, is that if I keep on going with this least amount of awful nonsense, I'm never going to get the good stuff, either. You said I was worth the work. I say you're worth the risk."

Jake places a kiss directly above my heart. "I like the way you think." He rolls off me reluctantly, turning back and reaching out a hand for me. "We're both at risk of starving to death if we don't get out of this bed." His eyes drop to my stomach. "And we should get cleaned up. How about I feed you, and then we spend the rest of the night in here, and I'll show you how awful I can be?"

I grin. "Awful is a two-way street, baby."

Jake lifts his eyes to the ceiling. "Dear God, I hope so."

Chapter 40

Jake

My mom describes moments full of happiness as bursting. When I was younger and she said that, I'd picture bubbles, translucent but shimmery with color, growing larger and larger. In this vision, the bubbles never popped.

Bursting is how I feel about Colbie. She's stepped into my grayscale world and imbued it with color. Recently I noticed this thing she does when she's happy and sitting in a chair at the same time, she leans forward in her seat and grips the edge, like she's keeping herself from coming out of her seat.

Because she, too, is bursting.

With Colbie, it's like the happiness doesn't stop. I know she's not perfect, but she's damn near close.

Colbie and I are on our way home from the jobsite now. We haven't been driving together as often because she's needed to stay later than me. It's struck me on more than one occasion that being home in time for Robbie to get off school and being the boss who stays late on the job wouldn't

307

have worked out. In the end, it's good Emmett gave Colbie the position.

The crew knows about us now. It was too hard to keep it a secret for long, not with the small town gossip mill running. Colbie got ahead of it during one of her morning meetings, confirming she and I are dating but promising nothing on the job will change. She also threatened to take away the snacks if anybody gave her shit, and I think the guys are partial to her snacks.

I'm partial to her snacks, too. And everything else about her. The way she talks excitedly about Robbie's birthday tomorrow has my heart twisting in ways I didn't think possible. Last night she spent three hours making a birthday banner that has pictures of him in the shape of the letters in Happy Birthday.

I'm holding Colbie's hand across the center console when my phone starts ringing. The sound and lit up screen grabs Colbie's attention, but I keep my eyes on the road. "Who is it?"

"I don't know. It's not in your contacts, but the area code is local." Colbie points at the phone. "Do you want me to answer it?"

My stomach sinks. I glance down at the screen, and my stomach descends further. "No."

Colbie doesn't say anything. The phone rings two more times, then there's nothing but silence in the truck cab mixed with the engine and rushing road noise.

The phone dings, notifying me of a voicemail. I don't want to listen to Erin's voice. Erin's pleading. Erin reminding me she has a right to see Robbie. Whether she's correct or not doesn't matter to me in this moment, because I just don't want to hear it.

Colbie pulls her hand from my grasp. She presses it against her other hand and tucks them between her knees.

I look over at her. Her lips are smushed together. Her whole body is rigid.

"Everything ok over there?" Stress pulls at my tone.

"Who was that on the phone?"

I drag the hand she abandoned down my face, tugging at my lower lip. I don't want to tell Colbie about Erin's calls. I'm so in love with Colbie, and she loves me and my kid. I don't want to introduce Robbie's mother into the picture. I don't want it to be difficult for Colbie to love me, and I'm afraid that's what will happen if Erin steps into our lives.

"Fucking tell me if there's another woman, Jake. I can't be the fool again." She pushes the last word through gritted teeth.

Is that what this is about? She thinks I'm cheating on her?

I look over my shoulder, then make the quick decision to pull over onto the side of the road.

Colbie exhales sharply, crossing her arms in front of her chest. It looks like she's preparing herself for bad news, for awful news, and that makes me sad. This is a woman who knows what it's like to feel like she's not enough, to be told she's not enough.

It makes me want to hunt down every man who has hurt her and teach them lessons they won't forget.

"There is nobody else, Colbie." I curl a finger under her chin and pull gently until she finally relents and allows me to guide her gaze to mine. "You're the only woman I want."

She stares at me for a full five seconds before she says, "That's what I thought, but...Who was on the phone?"

Deep breath. And a second for good measure. "That was Erin. Robbie's mom."

Colbie inhales sharply. "Robbie's mom? I know she called you that one time…"

"She's called or texted a handful of times. I've ignored her, but I accidentally answered that day I built the workbench. She wants to see Robbie."

Colbie nods, her eyes roving my face. "You look like you don't want her to."

"I don't."

"Why?"

I drop my finger from her chin. "She left him."

"A long time ago. When she was barely an adult."

"I was barely an adult, too. I stayed."

Colbie chews the inside of her lower lip. I wish I knew everything she was thinking. I wish her brain printed headlines so I could respond to her thoughts. I feel like she's choosing her words carefully right now, and I wish she wouldn't. I want her to throw them at me, so I can defend my unwillingness to allow Erin to see Robbie. I want to sit here in the driver's seat and feel justified in my choice.

"Jake," Colbie says my name, then hesitates. She pushes at a speck of dirt on the thigh of her jeans.

"Just say it."

She levels her serious gaze on mine. "I don't want to give too much opinion on this, because I don't know what it's like to be in your position. But I will say that you should consider future Robbie. Adult Robbie. What will you say to him when one day he finds out you kept his mother from him when she tried to return?"

The muscles in my neck tense, and my molars grind together. "Maybe he'll thank me for protecting him."

She shrugs. "Maybe. But maybe not. You don't know what it feels like to grow up without a parent providing a constant presence. You don't know what it feels like to wonder what life would be like if they were there."

My eyebrows lift, and I feel the indignation rising, too. "You don't know what it feels like to have a parent whose presence hurts more than it helps."

Colbie holds up her palms, calling a truce. "I don't want to argue with you about this. It's not my place. But I think you should remember who this is really about at the end of the day. It's not about you, and it's not about Erin, and it's not about choices she made a long time ago."

I sigh. "It's about Robbie."

It all comes back to him. I only get one shot to make the right choice.

What if I make the wrong one?

••.

"Thank you for letting us have the party here."

Victoria glances over from the vegetable tray she's arranging. I don't have the heart to tell her none of the children will eat anything from that tray. Not when there's hot dogs, hamburgers, and fruit snacks.

"Of course. You know how much we love Robbie. Emmett thinks of him almost like a grandson."

That makes me happy. It's important Robbie have people in his life who care for him, aside from me.

Erin?

The name slams through me, a jolt I don't want or need. It's Robbie's birthday today.

Imagine what that feels like for Erin.

No. This is Colbie, rubbing off on me. Colbie's empathy, seeping through her skin and into mine when I hold her in my arms at night.

It's been a full twenty-four hours since Colbie and I disagreed, and I'm starting to see it the way she sees it.

A little, anyway.

Maybe, if I let Erin into Robbie's life, there won't be problems. Maybe there will just be more love. This is a hard one, and luckily I don't have to spend too much emotional energy on it today. Today is about celebrating Robbie, and that's what I'm going to do. All these big, heavy thoughts can wait until tomorrow.

Colbie and Greer are in the backyard decorating. Greer's holding up one side of the banner while Colbie affixes her end to the wall. Emmett bought two extra tanks of propane to heat the pool, and enough food to feed an army. Robbie hasn't had any sugar yet and he's already bouncing off the walls, his body full of excitement. Victoria puts him to work arranging a fruit tray, and I finish helping Emmett clean the grill.

Georgia and my mom show up and start pitching in. We're finished with everything ten minutes before the party is supposed to start, and Georgia comes to stand beside me.

She leans into my side with a gentle push of her shoulder. "You and Colbie seem to be doing well."

"We are. She's great."

"She is." Georgia looks out at the backyard scene. "Will Rhodes be here today? I haven't seen him around recently."

"He went to New York, and then found another job in Texas."

Georgia frowns, a worried 'v' forming between her eyebrows.

"What?"

She shakes her head. "Nothing. It just seems like he's been taking a lot of out-of-state jobs lately."

Georgia has always liked Rhodes. I think she sees him as

another big brother, especially after I left for college and he was around during my dad's final years. "Don't worry about him." I wrap an arm around her shoulder and give her a squeeze. "He's always been pretty good at taking care of himself."

"Right," she nods. "He's very good at that."

Guests begin arriving, and soon Robbie is surrounded by his classmates. They're like a swarm of bees, buzzing animatedly around each other. Eventually they realize they are at their teacher's house, and they all start talking about that like it's the coolest thing that Robbie's birthday party is here. Robbie's shoulders lift and his chest puffs out with pride. He feels special, and important, and I watch it all from the sidelines.

Colbie stands beside me, an arm threaded through mine. My mom and Georgia are acting as lifeguards, each of them positioned at opposite ends of the pool.

Robbie cannonballs into the water. "Look how happy he is right now," Colbie says, in this motherly way, as if his happiness brings her real joy.

I turn my face, nuzzling into Colbie's hair. "When I took him camping a couple weeks ago he asked me if you are going to be his mom."

Colbie looks up at me. "What did you say to him?" Her voice is soft, and it matches the vulnerable look in her eyes.

"I told him it was too soon for me to know that."

She nods.

"Does that scare you?"

It would be normal, if it did. Robbie and I are a package deal, and Colbie knows that.

"It doesn't scare me so much as it doesn't feel like my place." Colbie sighs. "Robbie has a mom who is trying to

313

reach out to him. I can't slot myself into a spot she wants to occupy. That's not fair to Robbie. Or her."

I'm trying not to frown, but I feel that steely resolve inside me gaining ground. Why does Colbie need to consider Erin in any of this? This is about me and Colbie, and Robbie, too. I want to create a happy family with Colbie. The three of us. We're already well on our way to being there.

"Hey, Jake?" Greer sticks her head out the sliding glass door at the back of the house. "There's someone at the front door for you." She glances at Colbie, a twinge of worry in her eyes. "It's a woman?"

My stomach rolls. A sour, acidic taste creeps into my throat.

It's Erin. Somehow, she has found us here. It probably wasn't all that difficult.

I look at Colbie.

Her expression tells me she knows. Like me, she can somehow see without being shown. "Would you like me to go with you?"

Instead of answering, I take her by the hand. We pass Greer, who doesn't say a word, and wind our way through the house to the front door.

Stomach knotted, I reach for the door handle. Colbie's standing on my right, so she has a split-second lead on seeing Erin first.

"Lindsay?" Colbie says, her head rearing back a few inches in surprise.

I look from the woman on the threshold who is most definitely Erin, then back to Colbie, confused.

"Hi," Erin says before I can say anything. She attempts a smile, but it falls quickly, replaced by a look of fear and worry. "Jake." She nods at me, then looks at Colbie. "I lied to you that day in Honeybee, I'm sorry. I was afraid if I told you my name you'd know who I am."

Colbie and Erin know each other? At this point I don't know what to be more shocked by.

I hear Colbie say, "It's ok," but I'm not looking at her. I'm staring at the woman who wants to show up after all this time and threaten my way of life. Those kinder feelings I was experiencing are gone now. I feel so...so...angry. "What are you doing here?"

Erin flinches at my tone. "You won't let me see Robbie. I don't know what else to do." Her eyes plead with me, upturned palms shaking in the doorway.

"You left. You don't have custody. I do. And I get to choose who sees him."

Her lower lip quakes. She bites it like she trying to make it stop. "I understand that. And I'm very sorry for everything that happened. I'm here now, and I don't know where else to start."

I tear my gaze from hers, because it's too much for me to take right now. I stare down at my shoes, trying to get my bearings.

I don't realize I'm shaking my head until she says, "I don't want to take legal action, but I can't hold off my parents much longer."

My head whips up. "What the fuck did you just say?"

Colbie places her hand on my arm, a warning to calm down.

Erin gulps. "My parents—"

"I don't want to hear about your parents ever again. They're assholes who didn't even fucking see Robbie as a person." My fingers flex and curl, as if I can release even a small portion of this fury through my fingertips. "They saw him as something to win. They didn't want to be embarrassed their daughter had given up custody, so they tried to get it for themselves because that was better than nothing. Fuck your parents."

"Jake, if we could please just talk about—"

"No." I look away, staring at a pot of flowers beside the door without really seeing them. I start taking deep breaths to calm myself down.

I hear Erin say to Colbie, "Again, I'm sorry I told you my name was Lindsay."

In my peripheral vision I see Colbie tuck her hands in the pockets of her black jeans. "No worries. Did you enjoy the market in Sierra Grande?"

"It was amazing." Erin's tone is lighter now, and I find myself looking at her.

I didn't realize it, but I'd been picturing her as strung out from years of partying and poor choices. That's not at all how she looks. She appears healthy, her blonde hair long and shiny, her eyes clear and bright. My subconscious formed an image of her, and it couldn't be further from the truth. Similar to the way I did with Colbie.

Erin glances at me with concern, but she keeps talking to Colbie. "There were fresh baked cookies, local honey, wine tastings, and I bought the best goat cheese I've ever had."

Is this really Erin in front of me, talking to my girlfriend about goat cheese? Maybe this is a dream, and I'll wake up and roll over and tell Colbie and she'll tell me it's a sign that I should call Erin back.

Colbie shifts, her arm rubbing against mine, and asks, "Did you get to see Tenley Roberts?"

Nope, not a dream. Colbie is having a conversation with Erin, like they're friends. She's in the middle of the most awkward, uncomfortable situation in the history of the world, and somehow she's making it work. God, I love this woman.

"No, but the goat cheese had a sticker on it that said Hayden Cattle Company. Hayden is the last name of the man Tenley left LA for."

Colbie draws in a shocked breath. "Stop. Guess I'm adding goat cheese to my farmers market list."

The conversation between them falls quiet. Erin looks tentatively at me.

"Erin—" I say, but she speaks at the same time.

"Jake, please listen to me."

I motion for her to continue.

"I have a daughter. She's seven months old." Erin watches me digest this information, and I wonder if my exterior reflects how I'm feeling on the inside, which is floored.

Her bombshell sits in my throat, making it hard for me to breathe. "Robbie has a sister?" It makes me think of what Colbie said when she first arrived in Green Haven, about how her father had a daughter he stuck around for. Then it strikes me Robbie will likely feel the same way. His mother had a child she didn't abandon. Inevitably this will lead to question of *Why?*

Why one, but not the other?

Erin's crying now. "My fiancé died in a snowboarding accident, and two weeks later I found out I was expecting." She sniffs. "Jake, I'm sorry. About everything. I learned some lessons the hard way, and I'll always regret leaving you guys. I want to own up to my mistakes. I want to know Robbie. I've always understood what I left behind, but now I see my daughter, and every day with her is like a tiny stab to my heart. Her first smile, the first time she rolled over and sat up, all of it, I was happy but I was crying on the inside because I didn't know when that happened for Robbie." She swallows. "I don't know his first word."

I don't know if it's Colbie's influence, or the thawing of my heart toward Erin, but I feel bad for her. "Dada."

Erin's eyes light up. "That was his first word?"

I nod. "I think it's most kids' first word because the sound is easier to make, but yeah."

"I know this is terrible timing, with today being Robbie's birthday and all, but when I was at that café and overheard Colbie say he'd be here..." She wrings her hands and rocks back on her heels. "I figured it was my only shot. You don't respond to me when I call and text, and I thought maybe if you'd just see me in person, you'd change your mind." Erin's gaze goes to Colbie. "I swear I'm not a cyberstalker. You were talking to that nice old man and you said Robbie and Jake's name, and I couldn't believe it. It felt like fate. Then he said the name Emmett, and when I added the name of the town in the internet search, it was right there. It was so easy, it seemed meant to be." Erin looks back to me, eyes pleading. "It doesn't have to be today, Jake, but please. Please let me see Robbie."

It is only now I realize I'm clutching Colbie's hand, squeezing so hard she is beginning to wince. I release her, but she responds by recapturing my hand and keeping it there. I look her in the eyes, those beautiful eyes I'm desperately in love with, and she nods ever so slightly. Giving me the nudge I need.

I can't believe I'm about to say this, but here it goes. "Can you come back in two hours? The party will be over by then." I don't want to drop this bomb on Robbie while he's in the middle of his birthday party, and this way I'll have time to prepare him. How I'm going to go about doing that, I have no idea.

"Yes," Erin says quickly. "Oh. Oh my gosh." She palms her chest, blinking in quick succession. "I'm going to see Robbie." Her gaze flickers between me and Colbie, her breath shallow and her breathing rapid. "I need to get a gift. What does he like? Are there any stores around here?"

Colbie puts forth a single finger. "Hold that thought."

She dashes inside, leaving me alone with Erin. We look at each other. She's a stranger to me now, but once upon a time I liked her.

She tucks her hands into her jacket pockets and rocks back onto her heels. "Thank you for giving me a chance. I'm sure this isn't easy for you."

I'd like to tell her to be careful with him. I want to tell her that he doesn't know much about her, so please don't begin by trying to explain where she's been. Start surface level, because the deep shit is painful and unnecessary right now. I want her to know not to expect too much, he's a ten-year-old boy. Don't pressure him. Don't show disappointment if he doesn't respond the way she hopes he will.

But all I say is, "Sure." I am so damn overwhelmed that I can't get the words to move from my mind.

Colbie reappears carrying a large rectangular wrapped gift. "Give him this," she says, holding it out to Erin.

Erin shakes her head. "But—"

Colbie persists, pushing the box into Erin's hands. "No buts."

"I don't know what to say. I...I..." Gratitude pulls her cheeks into an emotional smile. "Thank you."

"You're welcome," Colbie says warmly.

Erin glances from Colbie to me. "I'll be back in two hours."

We both say goodbye and she walks away, to a car parked down the block.

319

"Fuck," I mutter, releasing just a smidgen of the pent-up emotions swimming through my head. Colbie's arms wrap around me.

"You did the right thing," she says, her voice solid and sure.

We share a kiss, something chaste and kind and full of love. I thumb the space beside her ear and murmur, "You're like a hug for my heart."

"That's the cheesiest thing I've ever heard, but it makes so much sense."

Colbie's response makes me laugh, and I need it.

Not shockingly, this woman is once again everything I need. Everything I want.

If I didn't have her by my side, I don't know how I'd get through this day.

Chapter 41

Colbie

I didn't do it for Erin.

Robbie will feel like his mother came prepared. Yes, she left him once upon a time, but she doesn't always do things incorrectly.

I smiled when I handed the gift to her, but on the inside, I cried.

Why does doing the right thing feel...well, awful?

Chapter 42

Colbie

J ake has been antsy since Erin left. I know he's trying, but he's distracted. His fingers shook when he lit the candles on Robbie's birthday cake. The parents who dropped kids off have all arrived on time for pick-up.

When the last parent leaves, Jake ushers his mom and Georgia into Emmett's office to tell them about Erin. I help Victoria carry in the food from a table that was set up in the backyard, and she asks me what's going on. I explain, but even as I'm saying the words they hardly feel real.

"It's good Jake is allowing Erin to see Robbie." Victoria slides the trays of leftover hotdogs and hamburgers onto the kitchen island. "People can't go around keeping a parent from their child, as you know." She removes two large glass containers from a cabinet and hands them to me for the leftovers.

I take them, catching her gaze and shaking my head to show her I don't understand. "As I know?"

She stops what she's doing to look at me, a look of pity mixed with something else I can't decipher. "Your dad told me he talked to you about everything that happened when you were little."

"About my mom and the cheating?"

"Right." She opens a drawer, pushing aside its contents as she searches for something. "And keeping you away from him and everything. I just think it's wonderful that Jake isn't doing that with Robbie and Erin." She finds what she's looking for and closes the drawer. "And who better to be with Jake while this is happening than you?"

"Right. Because I was kept from my dad," I end the sentence slowly, the words and their meaning sinking in.

Instead of one solid punch, this feels like one thousand tiny blows.

"Although, I guess in your case it wasn't really that you were kept from your father. More like you were discouraged from him."

"Uh-huh." I grab a pair of tongs and lift the hotdogs into the container, lining them up in a neat row. "I was pretty young when all that went down, I don't remember much of it. How, specifically, did my dad feel discouraged from seeing me?"

Victoria senses something is off about my question. She stops what she's doing, and stares at me. "Your father said he told you everything."

"He told me about my mom cheating on him. When I asked him what happened through the years, he was vague and said none of it really matters anymore and that he is sorry it happened."

Victoria covers her mouth with a hand. "Oh, Colbie. I'm so sorry. I thought you knew."

"Now I do. Kind of." I place the top on the container and click it into place. It's amazing I can still function given the way I feel inside. I want to pull my hair out. I want to pull my mom's hair out, too. "Can you please fill me in?"

"It was a long time ago." Victoria touches the top of my hand. "I'm sure your mom is not the person she was back then. I'm not the person I was back then either. I should have had more patience with the whole situation."

I sigh. "She is the exact same person. So, come on," I coax. "This isn't fair to me."

Victoria's head tips back-and-forth ever so slightly, as if she is not certain she's going to divulge. I'm not sure what it is that makes her decide to go for it, but she starts speaking.

"She would tell you things that weren't true, like that I didn't like you, or that you weren't a part of our family once Greer came along. Those were outright lies, by the way. I loved you, not only because you were a part of your father, but because you were spunky and smart. You read nonstop and then you'd say these huge words and shock adults. I think your mom saw that you liked me, and it made her jealous."

I hate how easy it is for me to go back in my mind and see the moments Victoria is referring to.

"I'm sorry I'm the one telling you all this. Your dad..." she trails off, rubbing at one forearm like she's cold. "He says things, and does things, that are worrisome. I keep waiting to get my old Emmett back, but I don't know if that's going to happen." She shrugs resolutely. "For better or worse, right?"

"Right," I echo.

"There you are," Jake says, striding into the room. "Have you seen Robbie?"

I shake my head. I'm dying to tell him everything I just learned about my mom, but Jake is in the middle of his own crisis. It's arguably far larger than mine.

Victoria answers. "Emmett was giving him the Lego organizer he built for him. Garage, I think."

Jake presses a swift kiss to my temple before moving on to the garage.

"You guys are good together," Victoria says, taking the now empty trays and placing them in a sink of hot, soapy water. "I've known Jake since he was about Robbie's age. He's always been a nice person, but you bring something out in him. Don't ask me to tell you what it is, because I don't know. I think it's something that happens when people are right for each other. The same way people who are not right for each other can bring out bad sides."

Greer walks in with her arms loaded down with the same decorations we put up a few hours ago. The topic of conversation changes to some drama at the elementary school, and I'm happy for it. I have enough of my own drama at the present moment. I need the mindlessness of hearing about somebody else's.

Chapter 43

Jake

If moments filled to the brim with happiness are bursting, what do we call the moments just before something life-altering happens, when we see the event on the horizon? Maybe it depends on the outcome.

Looking at Robbie now, surrounded by birthday presents, his head bent over as he compares a smashable geode kit with a rock tumbler, I feel an eerie sense of foreboding calm.

A steel moment. That's what this is. Moments that are filled with calm preparation, a bracing for the chaos.

I only wish there was some way for me to warn Robbie of what I'm about to tell him. There isn't, of course, and the time is only drawing nearer.

I bend down to where Robbie sits, knees pressing out, and balance my elbows on my knees. "Hey, bud. Quite a birthday haul you have there."

"Yeah," he says quietly, and I hear a twinge of disappointment in his tone.

"What's wrong?"

He shakes his head.

I nudge him gently with my elbow. "I can't help you if I don't know what the problem is."

Robbie sniffs. "Colbie didn't get me a birthday present." He wipes a hand under his nose. "I don't mean to sound ungrateful. All of this stuff is nice." He taps the geode box. "And Mr. Emmett made me the coolest Lego organizer, he built it himself." Robbie shrugs. "I guess I really wanted something from Colbie."

My heart drops. Poor Colbie. I'll have to run out the first chance I get and buy something to replace the gift she let Erin use.

"Your birthday isn't over. I bet Colbie has something for you."

His little head moves up and down. "You're probably right. She wouldn't forget me."

"Never," I assure him. I sigh internally, knowing I need to get to it and tell him about his mom. I sit back, my legs stretching out beside Robbie. "Can you sit up and look at me, please?"

Robbie does as I ask. There must be something about my tone of voice because his eyes look worried. "What's wrong?"

"There's nothing wrong. But I do need to tell you something." I lick my lips, sifting through my thoughts and trying to find the best words to use for my son. "Your mom called me. She'd like to see you."

Robbie's eyebrows tug. He doesn't look upset, or excited, or any emotion at all. More like he's pondering these words, and their meaning. After a few quiet seconds, he asks, "She can be a mom now?"

His answer confuses me. "Um, I think so."

Robbie picks up on my confusion, and explains. "When

we went camping you said she couldn't be a mom, so she asked you to be my only parent. That changed?"

Oh, right. I didn't forget I said that, but I pushed it to the back of my mind. "That has changed. She wants to see you. How do you feel about that?"

Robbie's lips twist. As does my heart. This situation would be a lot for an adult to handle, and here it is, being handed to an eleven-year-old boy. When Robbie is an adult, this will be a time he looks back on. This experience will be formative for him, and I hope he remembers it in a good way. I want him to see me as a man who made a good choice for his child, who taught him how to accept apologies and offer second chances to the deserving.

Is Erin deserving?

I think so.

But only time will tell.

"Robbie, listen." I take my son's hand, remembering exactly what it felt like to watch all five of his tiny fingers grip one of mine. "You can say no. Or you can say yes. You can change your mind at any time."

"How does it work? She's just my mom? She's around?" He makes a face like he's horrified. "Is she going to live with us?"

"No, no. She lives in Phoenix." At least, I think she does. We haven't discussed any of these details, but it seems likely.

Robbie sighs heavily, and I feel terrible. It's my fault he's feeling this way, because I've brought this to him. Should I have denied Erin? Should I have waited to see if she would take legal action? Maybe what Robbie really needs is—

"I want to see her." His voice is small, but certain. "I want to know my mom."

I bite back emotion. My boy. My brave, sweet boy. "Are you sure?"

He nods. Then he squares his shoulders, and I hide my automatic smile. The squaring of the shoulders is a Colbie move, through and through. He didn't do that until he met her.

"When will I meet her?"

"She's in Green Haven right now."

"On my birthday?"

I nod, watching for his reaction.

He shrugs, his face stoic. "Oh. Ok."

"Would you be ok with seeing her today?"

"I guess so."

"You can say no," I remind him. He rolls his eyes, and the normalcy it brings makes me happy.

"No rolling eyes at your father," I say, more for continuity than anything else. Right now I don't care if he rolls his eyes.

Colbie steps tentatively into the living room. Her eyes ask me if she can approach, and I nod.

She's halfway across the room when the doorbell rings.

Chapter 44

Colbie

Erin must have set a two-hour timer. The doorbell rings at the precise minute she's due. I wonder if she sat in her car out front and waited.

Robbie scrambles up off the ground. He stuffs his hands in his pockets and swallows hard. Jake grips Robbie by one shoulder and looks him in the eyes. "Whatever you feel is ok. You're the leader of this. When you're done, just say so."

Robbie nods.

Jake's not finished. "You're brave, and strong, but you don't have to be. Not all the time."

"Ok, Dad."

Jake goes to the door. I stride over to Robbie and nudge him gently. He looks up at me, and it's like looking into Jake's eyes. I wink, and nod at him. The corners of his mouth turn up, but it's not really a smile.

Jake opens the door, and there's Erin, my present in her arms. She nods hello at Jake, and waits for him to invite her inside. He steps back, and opens one arm wide.

Erin walks into the house, eyes searching. The living

room is not far off the entrance, and because it's an open floor plan a person can see directly in as soon as they walk in the door.

Erin's eyes fall on Robbie. Even from across the room I see her hands shaking, the iridescent ribbon wrapped around the gift catching the overhead light.

Jake leads her over, gaze flickering to me before locking in on Robbie.

He stops a couple feet in front of Robbie, Erin on his right and a few inches behind him.

"Robbie, this is your mom, Erin." Am I the only person who hears how Jake's voice breaks when he says 'mom'?

Erin stays where she is, but waves. She's trying to smile, but it's not a normal smile. There's too much emotion, and her lower lip quivers. "Hi, Robbie. It's nice to see you."

Robbie nods. "You too."

"Happy birthday," she says. She holds out the box. "Here's a gift."

I notice how she doesn't say *I bought you a gift* because that would be untrue. I like that she's careful with her wording.

"Thank you." Robbie accepts the extended gift. He looks at Jake. "I don't know what to say now."

Erin smiles, and this time it looks a little more normal. "I don't know what to say either, Robbie. It's ok."

Jake points at the package in Robbie's arms. "You can open your present."

Robbie sits down on the couch. Erin selects a seat in an armchair opposite him. Jake sits beside Robbie, but I skip over the open spot on the other side of Robbie and go to the chair next to Erin. I don't want her to feel like it's three on one, or that I am sending a message to her by choosing to sit beside her son.

331

Robbie tears off the paper. "Wow," he nearly shouts. "This is so cool. Dad, look! It's the Old Fishing Shack LEGO." Robbie looks at Erin with confused exhilaration. "How did you know I like Legos and fishing?"

Erin glances at me, and I think she's getting ready to tell him the truth.

"Must have been a lucky guess," I answer with forced cheerfulness before she can spill.

Erin nods her gratitude at me, then asks, "What else do you like to do, Robbie?"

Robbie tells her he likes nature shows, and when his dad teaches him how to cook and build things. "How about you?" he asks.

"I like to paint, but I'm not very good. I read a lot, and I hike. Or I used to, anyway. I don't have a lot of time for those things right now."

"Why not?"

Erin glances at Jake. His face is blank, though I'd bet all the money in my wallet he's feeling a torrent of various emotions right now. Erin says, "I have a daughter. She's still a baby, and babies are a lot of work."

"You have a daughter?" Robbie looks at his dad. "Does that mean I have a sister?"

Robbie doesn't sound happy. He sounds befuddled. And I think I know why.

"That is what that means," Jake confirms, his voice almost apologetic.

As if a switch has been flipped, the light in Robbie's eyes extinguishes. He falls silent.

Moisture pools in Erin's eyes. She tries again. "Her name is—"

Robbie explodes. "I don't care what her name is. My

dad said you couldn't be my mom, and you had to leave. But you're someone else's mom?"

Jake says Robbie's name in a low tone. It's not a warning, but more of an interjection.

Tears stream down Robbie's face. "I'm sorry," he whispers, his voice tiny and more childlike than I've ever heard it.

Erin cries, too. She stays planted in her seat, and I'm glad. Robbie doesn't seem like he wants to be physically soothed right now, and definitely not by his mother.

"I'm really sorry I couldn't be a mom to you, Robbie. I remember the first time I looked into your eyes, and I replay that in my mind every single day. You were never the reason why I wasn't there for you. I was the reason. It's all my fault."

Robbie's head is bowed, and his shoulders shake. Jake wraps his arms around his son and pulls him against his chest. Robbie is trying to pull it together, but I can't imagine how hard it must be for him. I'm thirty years old, and I'm just now learning how to let myself love my dad. This afternoon, the rug was pulled out from under me when I learned the truth about my mom. Here I am, an adult trying to navigate complicated emotions. How is a young boy supposed to do it?

It hits me that I'm in a unique position to help him. "Hey, Robbie?"

He turns his head so he can see me from his place against his dad's chest. "You love Emmett, right? You love my dad?"

Robbie nods.

"Did you know I didn't grow up with him? I lived in Phoenix, and he lived here with Victoria and Greer. I know what it feels like to wonder why your parent stuck around for one child, but not you. It really sucks, doesn't it?"

Robbie sits up. "Yes."

"I don't know about you, but it made me feel like I wasn't good enough for my dad. Like he tried a second time, and got the daughter he really wanted."

"That's kind of how I feel. But also I feel really mad and sad and confused."

I lean forward, maintaining eye contact. "Those emotions make sense. But you need to know that your mom wanted you. She didn't have your sister because you weren't good enough. My dad didn't have Greer because I wasn't good enough." Funny how you can say something, and still not totally believe it. I want to believe it though, because I know it's the truth, and that will have to work for now. "You are loved, and wanted, and important, and special. There is nobody else on this planet like you."

Jake mouths thank you over Robbie's head. I acknowledge him with a tiny dip of my chin.

Robbie glances at the LEGO box on the ground. "It's my birthday, so this all seems really unfair."

"That makes sense." I nudge at the LEGO with my toe. "Pretty cool gift."

Robbie lifts his eyes to Erin. "Thank you."

"You're welcome." Erin hits her thighs with her palms and starts to stand. "I'll get out of your hair. Your dad has my phone number, Robbie. We can talk as much, or as little as you want. You call the shots, ok?"

Erin is halfway to the door when Robbie shouts, "There's cake."

Erin turns around. Her gaze sweeps the room, then lands on Robbie. "I like cake."

Robbie sniffs. "It's strawberry cake with vanilla frosting."

"Strawberry is my favorite flavor."

"Mine too."

Robbie gets off the couch and walks to Erin. He looks so much like his father, both nurture and nature at play, but he has her nose.

"Come with me to the kitchen," he says to her.

They leave the room, and Jake relaxes for the first time since Erin knocked on the door during the party. "Fucking hell," he breathes, raking two hands down his face.

I go to him, sitting down beside him and pressing my face to his neck. "That was hard."

"I think I'm glad I did it. I'm not sure yet."

I pull back. "Only time will tell. But it might work out ok."

"Did you mean all that stuff you said about your dad and Greer?"

"Yeah."

"He heard you talking."

"No he didn't." I frown. "He wasn't in the room."

"I saw him in the reflection of the glass door on the TV stand."

"Shit," I mutter, sitting back in Robbie's spot. "I'm not sure I wanted him to know that." In a way, it feels embarrassing. I want to appear strong, a woman who would never think such a thing. In another way, it's a relief. I've been sitting alone in these thoughts for a long time, and they've become exhausting.

"He should know how you feel, Colbie." Jake shifts to face me, his palm cupping my cheek. "If I had the chance to look into my dad's eyes and tell him he broke my heart, I would do it."

"What does it even matter anymore? What good will it do? I'm an adult. He's old. What's the point?"

He shrugs. "All I know is that the hurt gets heavier the longer we carry it."

I tip my face closer. The stress of the day has brought out a small fan of fine lines around his eyes. "You sound wise."

"I'm learning. Just like you."

"I'm happy I have you to learn with." I kiss him, a simple peck.

Sounds come from the kitchen. More voices than just Robbie and Erin. I stand, and pull Jake up with me.

We go into the kitchen. Everybody is in there: Robbie, Erin, my dad, Victoria, Greer, Jake's mom, and Georgia. Robbie has taken care of introductions, but Terri and Georgia remember Erin. Of course.

The conversation dips in points, growing quiet or awkward, but it's my dad who keeps the wheels turning.

What do you do for work, Erin?

So, Erin, what do you do for fun?

Erin, have you ever been to Mexico?

Before our eyes, Erin transforms into a real person. Her leaving stops being the only thing we know her for. She has hopes and dreams, a cat named Stinker Belle, and a dimple in her chin when she laughs. She becomes a living thing, not a sad tale.

She becomes Robbie's mom.

And my heart breaks, right in the middle. Not in half, but it's like when a rock hits a windshield and leaves a starburst. It might not be all the way broken, but it's not the same anymore.

I haven't only fallen in love with Jake. I've fallen in love with Robbie, too.

Robbie yawns, and it's a cue that it's time to end the night.

Erin is the first to go. I think she'd probably stay all night, surreptitiously watching Robbie in wonder. She knows she's the guest, the interloper, and emotions are running high from her presence. Terri and Georgia leave too, and then my dad helps me carry Robbie's birthday gifts to Jake's truck while Jake assists Robbie in locating his shoes.

The old fishing shack box is on the top of the pile I'm holding. My dad eyes it knowingly, but says nothing.

"She needed something to give to him," I explain. "Can you imagine the position she was in today, and then to be without a gift on top of it all? She needed to make a good first impression."

The backs of my eyes sting, but I push aside the emotion. It was just a present. No big deal.

"It was kind of you."

"Thanks."

"Colbie," my dad's voice turns to gravel as emotion tumbles through. "I heard what you said. I need you to know you were never runner-up. Or second best, or a failed attempt." His voice breaks. "I can't believe you thought that. I can't believe you felt that." He shakes his head. We reach Jake's truck. I balance the boxes in one hand and open the back passenger door with the other. "But I see how you could come to that conclusion." I deposit my boxes, and take the gifts from his arms and set them inside. He pulls two gift bags off his wrists and hands them to me. I get everything situated and close the door.

Deep breath. I can do this. I can hear this. It's ok.

My dad sets his hands on my shoulders. In the glow of the nearest streetlamp, I can't help but think my dad looks old. Not decrepit, just exhausted. It's been a long, emotional day. I probably look like I've aged ten years since this morning, too. "You're the only person in this world who made me a father. I don't know what to say to make this better. You've been living with these thoughts for a really long time, and maybe it'll take that long to erase them." He hugs me. A real hug. The way a dad hugs his little girl, like she is the most precious thing, an angel sent straight from God.

The burning sensation behind my eyes returns, and my whole body is awash with a sense of freedom. With permission. I don't have to be shackled to these emotions anymore.

I nod my acceptance of his words, hoping he knows what they mean to me.

Jake approaches with a drooping Robbie in tow. "We have a tired one."

Dad releases me. I go around to the other side of the truck and open the door, helping Robbie in. He slumps over, his head resting on a small pile of gifts.

Jake shakes my dad's hand. "Thank you for everything today. And for letting Erin into your home."

My dad nods. "People make mistakes of all shapes and sizes. The opportunity to apologize and move on is a gift, because there are some mistakes you have to live with for the rest of your life no matter how sorry you are."

He steps back from the truck and opens my door. I climb in, turning so I can look at the two men I love. One I've loved since I was born, and the other stole my heart like the best kind of thief.

My dad closes my door and winks at me through the window.

Jake drives us to his house. Robbie passes out on the drive, and we listen to his soft snores. Despite repeated attempts to wake him when we arrive, he refuses to rouse.

Jake ends up carrying the sleeping birthday boy inside, and I carry his shoes.

I'm thinking about going to my house to sleep. It's been a long, hard day and maybe Jake needs room to think about everything. A lot has happened.

I turn for the door after I've placed Robbie's sneakers on the shoe tray by the back door, but Jake catches my hand.

The look in his eyes tells me he knows what I'm thinking. "Stay," he murmurs. He turns my trapped hand over and traces the lines in my palm. "I need you." He keeps ahold of my hand, as if he fears I might slip away if he lets go.

We walk to his room, and undress. We slide between his sheets, and minutes later, his body sinks into mine. It's the kind of lovemaking that speaks in nonverbal. It's slow, and sweet, the languid roll of hips, the clasped hands and shared breath. It's everything my heart needs.

I stay.

Chapter 45

Jake

Robbie and Erin have spoken on the phone three times in the month following his birthday. She makes him laugh. He recommended a nature show to her, and she watched it so they could talk about it. Then he recommended another, and she watched that, too.

She called me last week to ask about when she can come up and bring her daughter to meet Robbie. I guess I'd been expecting this question, but it still managed to startle me. I'd known Erin was serious about being in Robbie's life, but introducing a facet of her life to him makes it more permanent. The more they intertwine, the less likely it becomes she could disappear again. Not that I think she will, or that I want her to, it's just a realization to go along with all the others piling up these days.

I'd told Erin she could visit next weekend, but then the week passed and suddenly next weekend is today.

She'll be here in an hour. Robbie asked if she could come to our house, so he can show her his room. Despite how awkward it is to think of Erin in our home, I agreed.

Erin, to her credit, suggested I take Colbie out for a few hours and get a date out of it.

Colbie has been far more understanding in this situation than I think I could ever be. She wants the best for Robbie, even when it means sharing him. Should it even surprise me that she is the one showing me how to lead with empathy and kindness? I tell her how grateful I am, but today I'm finally going to get the chance to do something nice for her.

Colbie stayed over last night, like she does most nights, but went home a couple hours ago. She had work to do for Burn Barre, but I also think she didn't want to be here when Erin showed up. I don't blame her.

I peek my head in Robbie's room to check on him. He's been cleaning and organizing his room all morning, and now he's lying on his bed reading the latest issue of Bass-Master magazine. It arrived yesterday, along with a fishing tackle subscription box I told him was his birthday present from Colbie. He liked it, and thanked her when she came over last night. She smiled and hugged him, then met my eyes over his head. Her eyes looked sad, and I understand why. The LEGO she got for him would have been something they'd have done together.

"All set for your mom?" I ask, even though I can answer my own question by looking around his room.

He sets his magazine on his lap and looks at me. "And Bella."

Bella, who is eight months old today, according to Robbie. Yesterday, he was worried we don't have toys for Bella to play with while she's here, but I assured him Erin would probably have things for her.

There's a knock on the door, and Robbie leaps from his

bed. "They're early," he comments on his way past me. "Come on."

Robbie yanks open the door, and it's like stepping into the past. We've aged, and the baby is a handful of months older than Robbie was, but we could be twenty-one again.

Erin swallows hard and blinks. Are her thoughts similar to mine?

"Hi, guys." She forces a smile. "Robbie, this is Bella." Erin shifts to show a sleeping Bella's face. "She'll wake up soon. She always sleeps on long car drives. I think the engine soothes her."

Robbie backs away from the door and asks Erin to come in. He shows her to the living room, which is sweet because it's only a few feet away. I watch him take her diaper bag and place it on the coffee table. I listen to him ask if he can get her a drink. When he goes to get her a glass of water, she gazes over her daughter's head at me and says, "You've done a very good job with him."

I nod my thanks. When Robbie returns, I tell them I'll be back in a few hours. Suddenly I can't wait to get my hands on Colbie, to put this idea I've had for a while into action.

⁂

"What do you have planned for me?" Colbie's eyebrows lift as she glances into the back seat of my truck. She eyes the paper bag filled with our lunch from Honeybee, her gaze curious.

"Not telling," I respond.

"Hmph," Colbie says, pretending to pout.

I reach over, chucking her on the chin. "I promise you'll like it."

When we arrive at our destination, Colbie's curiosity deepens. I cut the engine and she turns in her seat, staring at me. "Why are we here?"

I peer out the windshield at the small home. There have been two owners since Emmett, but the house has remained mostly unchanged. That includes the most important part of it.

Colbie's handprint.

"Come on," I say, purposely not answering Colbie's question. I hop out, then round the front of the truck and open her door. She gives me a shrewd look as she tries to understand what's happening.

She follows me to the truck bed, where I reach in and pull out my circular saw. I stopped at the store yesterday for a new diamond blade, and safety goggles for us both to wear.

Colbie watches me, cataloging what I'm holding, and then I watch her expression shift as it makes sense.

"Oh," she breathes, her hands at her mouth. "Jake."

I lean in and kiss her, but my hands are full so I can't touch her. When I pull back, her eyes are shiny. I nod toward the side-gate off the driveway. "Let's go."

"Are we allowed?" Colbie asks, glancing at the home while her eyebrows draw together with worry.

"This place is about to go on the market again. Victoria is the realtor, and she asked the seller if it was ok."

"But you're going to bust up a perfectly good slab," Colbie protests.

I smile at her verbiage. "You're talking like a construction worker."

She taps the button on my shirt. "I am one."

"Follow me," I say, striding toward the gate. "In

343

exchange for cutting out your handprint, we're pouring a new patio."

"We?"

"Your dad. I tried to tell him I would do it, but he jumped at the chance. I think he's dying for something to do."

Colbie laughs. When we get to the gate, she reaches her arm over and lifts the latch. "Where's the homeowner?"

"He's already moved. The place is empty." I hold open the gate with my back, and Colbie steps through. I watch her walk across the small path to the back of the house. The handprint is on the side closest to us, and she reaches it in seconds.

She bends down and traces the lines in the concrete with a fingertip. "Look how small I was."

I set my saw on the ground and walk closer. The impression of her fingers seems tiny, smaller than half the size of mine, the palm of her hand no bigger than a plum. Beneath the handprint are the words *Sugar Bear*. "Little Colbie," I murmur. I bet she was adorable. Full of sass and unrelenting questions.

She overlays her adult hand on her child imprint. "I remember the day we did this. My dad fed me a bowl of mint chip ice cream for breakfast, and I helped him smooth the concrete after he poured it."

She's not looking at me, but I can hear the smile in her voice. She likes this memory. Treasures it.

"My dad was in on this?" She looks at me over her shoulder, chin lifted.

"Yeah."

"But it was your idea?"

The tone of her voice is even, and suddenly I'm

344

worried. Did I overstep? Does she wish her dad would've had this idea, instead of me?

But then a smile curves up both corners of her mouth, and even though it's not the kind of smile that betrays an outward joy, it's the kind of smile that shows an inner happiness. A swath of warm gratitude.

She stands up, wrapping her arms around me and pushing herself up on tiptoe. "Thank you," she murmurs, her lips on my ear.

I kiss her once, lightly, because as much as I love to ravish this woman, I also love her soft, short kisses.

"How does this all work?" Colbie gestures at the saw on the ground a few feet away.

"You wear these." I hand her a pair of goggles. "And stand back."

Colbie frowns. "I want to help."

"I bet the eight-year-old version of you said the same."

Colbie laughs and nods.

Sinking to my knees, I pull the saw over. "This thing can have a little kickback, and that can be dangerous even for someone who knows what they're doing. So, please, just listen when I say to stand back. And cover your ears, it's going to be loud."

Colbie pretends to huff, but her hands are gripped together, a sure sign she's excited. "Fine."

The project takes fewer than ten minutes. The diamond tip is very sharp because it's new, and there isn't much to cut. I pry the square of concrete away from the ground, swiping away the dust and sitting back. Blowing on it lightly, the remaining dust falls away.

"Here." I pull off my goggles and get to my feet, holding it out.

Colbie removes her goggles, too, and takes the handprint from me. She sighs deeply as she looks down at it. A lone tear falls over her cheek, and she shoulders it away. "I don't know why I'm crying."

"I do."

She gazes at me for a few seconds, then says, "Yeah, I guess I do know why."

My arm slips around her shoulders. "It's crazy to think the people who are supposed to keep the most tender versions of us safe, are sometimes the ones who hurt us."

Colbie leans the side of her head on me. "Crazy is one way to describe it." She turns the concrete a few degrees to the left, examining it. "I can't thank you enough for this."

"It's my way of thanking you, for everything you've done for me and Robbie. Had you been against Erin getting to know Robbie, it would've influenced my decision. But you were so nice about it, and I appreciate that more than you'll ever know."

Colbie shifts so she's facing me. I press a hand to her cheek, my thumb stroking over her soft skin. "I love you, in this way that feels foreign but also comforting. You're the first thought I have when I wake up, and my last thought before I fall asleep." Colbie nuzzles her head into my hand. "You're the most awful thing that's ever happened to me."

Colbie smiles, her shoulders shaking with her laughter. "You're the most awful thing that has ever happened to me, too. And I love you. I love you so much."

I remember the picnic I have for us in my truck, so I tell Colbie we should get going. She carries the goggles while I take care of the saw. I find a little spot north of town, on the banks of the Verde River, away from where we go to fish, and we have lunch.

I'd really like to get Colbie alone right now, but there

isn't enough time or privacy, and Robbie is waiting for us. It'll have to wait until later.

Colbie comes back to my house with me, and plays with Bella. She and Erin make conversation, and after a while Erin leaves. It feels like something that could become normal one day. Could it really be that this will work out after all?

Robbie asks me if we can do our Sunday morning fishing, and even though all I want to do is sleep in with my arms wrapped around Colbie's warm body, I tell him yes. Colbie says she's going to sit this one out, but promises to use the time to get the supplies they're going to need for his science project that's due at the end of the week. I manage to get Robbie in bed early using the excuse that we have an early wake-up.

At long last, I get Colbie alone.

Truth be told, I'd wait forever.

Chapter 46

Colbie

I t's a Sunday morning, so Jake and Robbie are going fishing. It's still dark outside, but Robbie likes to be at the lake by first light. I woke up early to make them breakfast. I don't think Robbie has realized I'm in the kitchen, or he probably wouldn't be saying what he's saying right now.

"If Colbie wasn't your girlfriend, do you think you would be with my mom?" He rubs his bleary eyes with fisted hands. He's facing away from me, slumped in his chair because he's still half-asleep.

Usually Robbie refers to Erin by her name. This is the first time he's called her his mom.

Jake meets my eyes. He looks apologetic.

I feel like an intruder. On their conversation, and, perhaps, in their lives. I know Jake loves me. I don't have any doubts about that. But am I doing the right thing?

I stir the scrambled eggs in the pan, and try not to cry. I think I've cried more in Green Haven than I have in my entire life.

"No, Robbie." Jake's tone is gentle, but firm.

"Why not?"

"Your mom is a very nice person, but she is not who I love."

"You loved her enough to mate with her."

If there weren't more rocks making more starbursts on my heart, I might laugh. Instead, I use the spatula like a spoon and push the finished eggs into the waiting tortillas.

"Most animals don't mate for life," Jake reminds him, continuing the animal analogy.

"Alpha wolves." Robbie perks up now that his favorite subject is being discussed. "Eurasian beavers. Quail. They all mate for life. That's what I'm going to do, too."

"What? Become a Eurasian beaver?"

"Dad," Robbie groans. He has shed a majority of his sleepiness by now.

Robbie's questions and musings are that of a child, his naïveté and innocence endearing. With limited knowledge and experience, Robbie is trying to understand the complex inner workings of adult relationships.

"I hope you are able to mate for life, buddy. Now go put your shoes on and let's get going. Start thinking about what lure you want to use."

Robbie pushes back from the table. "I have to start thinking about my science project, too. It's due soon." He lopes down the hallway. He still doesn't know I was here.

Jake wastes no time coming to my side. "He doesn't know what he was saying."

"I know. But he seems to be able to articulate how he is feeling." I fold the second burrito and wrap it in foil, placing it beside the first one on the counter.

"He's a kid. He's never believed in the Easter Bunny, but he definitely believes in Santa."

As if that lopsided logic explains everything. "There's far more to be gained from believing in Santa."

Jake ignores my attempt at alleviation. He lifts my chin with a curled finger and a thumb, encouraging me to meet his reverent gaze. "Don't hear his words and magnify them. Please. I know this situation isn't ideal, but I love you."

I look at him, and I think about the first time I saw him walking into the gas station. The way he had to adjust himself to get through the door, the way I felt called to him, the way his personality came at mine like it was issuing a challenge.

I know why it didn't work with Brad, or my prior relationships.

Maybe they were lazy, like Jake claims.

Maybe I was emotionally unavailable, like they claimed.

Here's what I have to say: it didn't work, because they weren't Jake.

End of story.

I don't want anybody else.

"I love you, too."

Chapter 47

Jake

I've sensed Colbie's hesitance, the way she second-guesses herself, since Erin showed up.

I don't blame her.

How would I behave, if the tables were turned?

I probably wouldn't have handed over a thoughtfully chosen gift the way she did. I like to think I would be magnanimous enough to encourage a relationship the way she has, but I can't say for sure.

Colbie is by far the best person I've ever met. She has never acted like Robbie is in the way. She doesn't become frustrated when he keeps us from spending time alone. When we sit on the couch to watch Robbie's favorite shows, she makes sure he's between us. She has never, ever made me feel like the smallest and most important person in my life is an inconvenience to her.

She puts Robbie first, the same way I do. This is how I know she would bow out to make space for Erin if she thought it was best for Robbie.

It wouldn't be best for Robbie, because it wouldn't be

best for me. As smart as Robbie is, he is still a child who views the world through a child's eyes.

Colbie has come a long way since she arrived in town. So have I. Her heart was closed, and I was patient with it. My reward was her opening up to me, giving to me what she did not give to anybody else. Her vulnerability. I showed her that if she gave me her heart, I wouldn't break it.

I won't, either. Now, or ever.

But I fear she'd be willing to break her own heart.

And Robbie may have just handed her the reason.

Chapter 48

Colbie

"I don't know what to do. Please tell me. Give me a map, or something." I rest my chin in my hands and wipe at my eyes. I'm not crying, but I'm frustrated.

After Robbie and Jake left to go fishing, I came home and waited until it was a decent hour, then I called Christina. She made me wait for her while she brewed her coffee, then she sat down and asked me to repeat everything I overheard in Jake's kitchen this morning.

Christina sips her decaf coffee, lips twisting as she thinks. "What are you going to do?"

"That's why I called you."

She gives me an exasperated look. "I know you count on me to tell you the truth, and the truth is I don't know what you should do. The water is too muddy."

"Muddy?"

"Yeah. Like, you have a kid's feelings to think about. Murky territory."

"Murky, and muddy. How delightful."

"You're the one who fell in love with a single dad."

There wasn't a chance in hell for me. I see that now. It

was over from the start. Falling in love with Jake was easy, effortless. He made it so.

"Would it be kinder to step back, give Jake and Robbie space to figure all this out? Erin just smashed into their lives like an asteroid hitting earth. All the good intentions in the world didn't decrease the aftereffects of her." I grab a napkin and blow my nose, because now I really am crying. "I feel like I'm in the way. I felt stupid, standing there in the kitchen this morning, cooking breakfast. I felt..." Oh. That's why this hurts so much, this knife-twisting pain in my chest. "Unwanted. I felt unwanted."

Christina's lips turn down. "Honey. I'm sorry you felt that way. It's definitely not true, but that's still a lousy way to feel."

"I don't know what to do."

"What does Jake say?"

"That he loves me."

"Go with that."

"Is it that easy?"

"Sometimes, simple is best."

"How can a simple answer solve a very messy situation?"

"Probably better than a messy answer."

Her response makes me smile. She's not wrong.

We spend a few more minutes talking about her most recent doctor's appointment, and covering a few things we've been needing to discuss for Burn Barre. We've been tossing around different ideas for the future of our business, and what we've settled on necessitates that I eventually return to Phoenix to get things figured out.

I still haven't confronted my mom about everything, but I know I need to. We've exchanged surface-level text messages for the past month, basic *hello's* and *what's new with you* types of conversation. She must know that I know. She's probably waiting for me to start the conversation. It would be nice if she could be the one to speak up about everything, but it's not her style. The lawyer in her stops her from incriminating herself by being the first to talk.

I hang up with Christina. I take a shower, then head out to pick up the supplies Robbie needs for his science project.

⁂

Dumping my armload of supplies on Jake's kitchen table, I fan out the various materials and line them up neatly. Retrieving the list from my purse, I do a double check that I got everything. I like looking at the list because it was written by my sister.

Once I confirm I'm good to go, I grab a drink of water and wind my purse over my shoulder. I have a lot to take care of today, including a visit to my dad's house. I've been seeing him for lunch or dinner every Sunday, and it's become something I look forward to all week. Usually Jake and Robbie join us, unless fishing runs long.

I'm fitting my spare key into the lock on the front door when I hear a car pulling in behind me. At first I think it's someone who needs to turn around and is using Jake's driveway, but the engine cuts off and a man and woman get out.

"Hi," I call, coming closer. "Can I help you?"

The man, wearing a camel-colored peacoat that I find obnoxious because nobody in Green Haven wears a peacoat, says, "I'm looking for Jake Whittier."

I root myself where I've stopped a few feet from the silver BMW. "Jake's not available right now. Who should I tell him stopped by?"

The man eyes me. His gaze runs over me, his expression

355

shifting in a way that makes it obvious he finds me lacking. "Are you his girlfriend?" One side of his upper lip curls a fraction, but it's enough to tell me how I should answer this question.

"No."

"Who are you?" The woman, standing in the open passenger door, finally speaks.

"Who are you?" I ask, squinting at her.

She huffs. "We're Mr. and Mrs. Brinkman."

I try not to show the surprise I'm feeling. "I'm the tutor."

Neither asks me for my name, unsurprisingly. They probably see me as the help.

The older man asks, "Do you know when Jake's going to be home?"

"No. I need to get going though, so best of luck to you." I wave and walk away, but I feel their eyes on me the entire short walk home. As soon as I'm safely inside, I send Jake a message warning him about the Brinkmans.

Chapter 49

Jake

I arrive home from fishing to find the silver BMW parked in my driveway. Thanks to Colbie, I had a heads up about Erin's parents. I just didn't think they'd still be here an hour later.

"Who is that?" Robbie asks, gripping the side of the passenger seat and pulling himself forward to get a closer look.

I don't answer. Instead, I pull in on the driver's side of the shiny sedan. I'm irritated they've parked in my driveway, so I park so close to the BMW that the driver will be forced to get in on the other side of the car and climb over.

"Stay in the truck," I say, quickly cracking all four windows even though it's not hot out. Robbie obeys. He can tell by my tone that this is not the time to argue with me.

I get out and stride forward, meeting them in the yard. "Mr. and Mrs. Brinkman."

I don't say *it's nice to see you again* because it is not.

These people wanted to take Robbie. They did not want shared custody. They wanted full. They tried to paint me as a careless twenty-one-year-old who wasn't responsible

357

enough to use a condom. Their lawyer brought my father's drug use into it, and tried to say the home I'd be providing was unsafe for a child. But my lawyer was good, and he proved the home Georgia and I grew up in was loving and stable, and my father's choices had no bearing on my ability to care for a child. In this instance, the fact that he was dead worked in my favor.

I don't just dislike Erin's parents. I despise them.

Mr. Brinkman straightens up to his full height. He is still a good four inches shorter than me. He is an unimpressive man, and all the money and luxury cars in the world can't change that.

"Is my grandson in that truck?"

I cross my arms, widening my stance. "My son is in that truck."

Mrs. Brinkman stands just behind her husband, as if deferring to him. She is skinny as a rail. I remember the first time I had dinner at their house, and the way she picked at her food.

When Erin got pregnant, they said it was my fault. Erin was very much a participant in the act, and I told them so. They didn't like that. I think they thought I was going to sit in their uncomfortable leather armchair and take their verbal assault. I was raised to be respectful, not a punching bag. I stood up for myself.

The Brinkmans never liked me in the first place. To them, I was a hick from a small town, the son of a blue collar worker. Finding out their precious only child was carrying my child was a blow to them.

The Brinkmans were used to people doing what they said, and I wasn't going to be one of those people. When they fought for custody, they truly thought they were going to win. They didn't expect me to have the resources I did, and had it not been for Emmett, they would've been right.

I didn't capitulate back then, and I won't be doing so today. "What do you want?"

"My daughter deserves to be with her son."

"I haven't said any different."

"I came here to tell you in-person that we're going to sue for custody. Erin thinks you're going to continue to be kind and let her see Robbie without any fuss, but I know how this will go. Erin's parental rights need to be reinstated legally."

A fire starts up in my limbs. I know better than to say what I want to say. From this point on, I must be a bastion of restraint, calm and cool, never ruffled and never giving in to the desire to shove this fool from my face.

Colbie's car rolls down the street. Dread fills me. I don't want the Brinkmans to know about Colbie. There's nothing wrong with me having a girlfriend, but who knows what they will turn it into. Will they drag Colbie through the mud, too?

I turn toward my house, just a few degrees, enough that my shoulder and part of my upper back faces the road. In my peripheral vision I see her pass, but I do not look at her.

I'm sorry.

Mr. Brinkman looks over my shoulder, probably at Colbie, as she gets out of her car and goes inside. He gives me a cool look. "We met your girlfriend this morning."

"I don't have a girlfriend."

His eyebrows lift. "Your neighbor has a key to your house?"

I don't want to discuss Colbie. I don't want them to spend even one more second considering her. "Mr. Brinkman, I will work with a lawyer to establish visitation rights for Erin." I'd already been considering this, so it's not a concession on my part.

"I said custody, Jake."

"Do you think a judge is going to go from nothing for the last ten years, to custody? Really?" I stay calm. So, so calm. Save the outburst for later. "Robbie is more than a thing to own."

It hasn't escaped my attention that they haven't asked for me to open the truck. If they wanted to see him so badly, if it was Robbie who they truly cared about, wouldn't they be asking that of me?

"It's time for you to go." I step aside and gesture to their vehicle.

Mrs. Brinkman huffs and walks to the car. Which also means she's walking next to my truck, and Robbie. I keep an eye on her. At this point, I'm not sure what the Brinkmans are capable of, in the name of getting their way.

"I hope you're ready for this, Jake." Mr. Brinkman walks closer to me, his pointer finger nearly touching my chest. "My daughter is a good mother. Her choice is what kept me from leveling you ten years ago, but now"—he glances at Colbie's house, the threat implicit— "there's nothing holding me back."

He stomps around the back end of my truck. Not even the front, where he could peer in and get a look at Robbie. I wait for them to leave. I'm sure Erin's old man is enjoying climbing over his fancy gearshift.

Robbie's door opens as soon as they're down the street. "Those were my mom's parents, weren't they?"

"Yes."

"They don't seem very nice." Robbie sounds sad.

I palm the top of his head. "They aren't."

"Why is my mom nice if those are her parents?"

"Not everybody takes after their parents. Some people see how their parents behave, and choose to go in the opposite direction."

Robbie hugs me around the waist, pressing his face into the bottom of my rib cage. "I want to be just like you, Dad."

Have sweeter words ever been spoken?

The only ones I can think of are Colbie's *I love you's*.

Colbie.

I need to see her, explain what that was all about.

But first, I need to make sure Robbie is feeling ok. I can't take him inside, then go running off to make sure my girlfriend isn't upset.

We go in the house and get cleaned up. Robbie assures me he's fine, but he spends the rest of the day attached at my hip.

He's not fine.

I don't end up with a moment to myself, so I can't call Colbie and talk to her about what happened. I want to know what the Brinkmans said to her.

A knot of fear rolls around my stomach. Between what Robbie said this morning, and her run-in with Erin's parents, how much more can she be expected to withstand?

❀❀❀

I'm sitting on the darkened porch drinking a cold beer when I notice her walking across my yard. Her hands are shoved in her jacket pockets, and her head is down. She doesn't see me, so I clear my throat so I don't end up scaring her.

She looks at me, squinting in the darkness. "Why are you out here?"

"Thinking." I shift, placing one ankle over the opposite knee. "I was hoping you'd come over."

She takes the seat beside me, lightly knocking her knee into mine. "Why didn't you ask me to come over?"

"Worried, I guess."

Colbie nods. "About Erin's parents?"

"Yeah. They told me they're going to sue for custody. "

Colbie gasps. "Can they do that?"

"I guess so. But they can't win. It'll just be a waste of everyone's time and money." The thought depresses me. I've worked hard to save a little of every paycheck, and I had big plans to one day take Robbie on some epic wilderness adventure. Spending it on a lawyer will be worth it because of what it will mean for me and Robbie, but it's low on the list of ways I'd like to spend my savings.

"They came all this way to tell you that?"

"They like to intimidate. They should know better when it comes to me, though. I'll always do what's right when it comes to my kid." I take a pull from my beer. "And if it were right to let Robbie have a relationship with them, I would do that. But it's not. They didn't even ask to see him today."

"Their loss."

I nod. "Abso-fucking-lutely."

"I told them I was the tutor."

I breathe a laugh. "I don't think they believed you."

Colbie bites the side of her lower lip. "I hope I didn't make anything more difficult for you."

"What do you mean?"

Colbie steeples her hands and presses them between her knees. "My mom practices family law. Have I ever told you that?"

I shake my head. *No.* Anxiety gnaws at my stomach. I

don't like where this is headed, and she's barely begun speaking.

"She's one of the best in the state. Shocking, I know, considering her personal life has been a dumpster fire for a long time. Anyway, I grew up listening to her talk about cases. She'd fight tooth and nail to help her clients, and she'd always use the word 'optics'. I remember this one client she had, a woman who was asking for full custody of her daughter. The woman had a boyfriend, some guy who drove a Harley and was covered in tattoos." Colbie glances at me. "You're probably thinking, *who cares*, and you're right, obviously tattoos don't define or announce your character. But, optics. How does it look from the outside? My mom told her, *You can sing sweet melodies all day long about how loving and healthy your relationship is, but at the end of the day, the judge has to make determinations based on what he sees.*"

"What happened?" I'm afraid to know, but I'm curious.

"The woman didn't listen. She was awarded partial custody."

"Because of the boyfriend?"

"Because of optics."

"Because of a judgmental judge."

Colbie's lips quirk.

"I heard it." My lips turn up in a smile, but I don't feel happy. "So, what does all this have to do with us?"

"If the Brinkmans follow through, I hope my being in your life doesn't pose an issue."

"How is me having a girlfriend a bad thing?" Even as I ask the question, I know the answer. Look what they did with my dad's memory, dragging it through the mud the way they did. They'll pull Colbie into this without hesitation.

"It's not bad on the surface. But look below. We've only been dating a few months."

"So?"

"Your attention is divided. You're neglecting Robbie."

I frown. "What are you talking about?"

"That's what they might say. You have to think about everything from their point of view. Look through their lens and find the light they'll cast you in."

"Fuck," I lean forward so I can rest my hands on my knees. "You're my boss."

Colbie pulls her knees into her chest, her feet on the seat of the chair. "I forgot about that one."

We're quiet. Crickets chirp, and the wind pushes through the trees that line the west side of my yard. "This is all bullshit, Colbie. They're not going to go through with it. I'll talk to Erin. Her parents are the definition of blowhards. Her dad probably lost a golf game and felt pissy." I draw Colbie's gaze, then take her hand. "Everything is going to be fine. You'll see."

Colbie leans her head on the back of her chair. "Famous last words."

Chapter 50

Jake

I was right. It's been a month, and not a peep from a lawyer. I talked to Erin, and she assured me she'd calmed her dad down. He told her he wasn't suing for custody. When he pressed her about the woman coming out of my house, she'd lied and said she didn't know who it was.

I think we're in the clear.

· · ·

I'm just stepping from the shower when there's a knock on my front door. Colbie drove home from work with me today, but as usual went to her house to shower and change. She'll be back over for dinner soon.

Robbie is on a video call with Erin in his room, so it's on me to answer the door.

I pull my shirt over my wet hair and yell, "Coming," when the person knocks a second time.

Opening the door, I find a man with a very ugly brown plaid shirt tucked into khakis with cargo pockets.

He thrusts something at me. On instinct, I reach for it.

"You've been served," he says without an ounce of emotion, then takes off.

I stare down at the papers in my hands. By the time I look up, he's long gone.

I go in the house and find Robbie lying on his bed, his iPad propped up by a stuffed animal. "Robbie, can you please give me a minute to talk to your mom?"

"O-kay," Robbie says, looking at me side-eyed. "You're being sus."

I motion out of the room. "Just go, please."

Erin is quiet. I wait until I hear Robbie's bedroom door close.

"Papers?" I hold them up.

Guilt rides across Erin's face. "I wasn't planning on being on with Robbie when this happened, I promise. He called me, and I couldn't avoid his call."

"You could have."

"I won't," she corrects, and I understand what she means.

"I haven't opened this yet." I smack the envelope against my palm. "What am I going to find when I do?"

"Jake—"

"What is it, Erin?" My voice is hard.

"Custody papers."

Heat builds in my arms. "From your parents?"

She looks me square in the eyes. "From me."

Through clenched teeth comes a sound, something unintelligible. "What are you seeking?"

"Joint."

My eyes close. My chin drops to my chest. Fifty percent of Robbie? My entire world, my sun, my moon, my stars.

She wants half of it.

Is she entitled to it?

No. Yes.

Fuck. I don't know. I don't know what's right. I only know what I want, and that's Colbie and Robbie.

"My parents wanted me to go for full, but I argued."

Is that supposed to make this hurt less? "Why? Why argue? Why not let your piece of shit parents have their way like they're used to?"

"I said it wasn't fair to you. To make you go through that again. Plus, we all know I wouldn't win." Erin takes a deep breath. "I don't want to take Robbie from you. But I want to have him, too."

"There isn't more of Robbie," I hiss, trying to keep my voice down. I don't want Robbie to know what's happening. "You cannot have some of him, without taking him from me."

"You sound like my parents."

I flinch. I feel like I've been slapped in the face. She's right. I'm talking about him like he's an object, an amount.

Sure, I'd have to give up some of Robbie's time, and I don't know what the ramifications of that could be, but there isn't a finite amount of Robbie's love. He has the capacity to hold as much as he needs. He can love me the same way he does now, and make room for his mother.

I'm willing to bend, but not all the way. Joint custody is too much for me.

"I have to go."

Erin says something, but I'm already walking away. I'd rather hurl the iPad against the wall and listen to it crack, but I don't. I tell Robbie he can come back and talk to his mom. Then I go in my room, and call someone I haven't talked to in years.

My lawyer.

Chapter 51

Colbie

The awful has arrived.

I listened while Jake raged.

I soothed while he cried tears of frustration, and fear.

I'd hoped with all my might that it wouldn't come to this, but I had an idea in place in case it did. Now I only have to execute on it.

And in doing so, break my own heart.

※

The thing about small towns is that they operate differently than cities.

In Phoenix, you leave a message with your lawyer's administrative assistant, and hope they will get back to you within a few business days.

In Green Haven, you locate the town's one and only attorney eating steak and eggs for breakfast at Honeybee. You tell him what you want to do, he says he'd like to finish his coffee first, and then he deliberately drinks every last drop. You pay his tab, because you feel bad for interrupting his breakfast, and then he walks you three streets over to his office.

My dad is already sitting at the shiny oak table in the conference room when we enter. I settle into my seat, and he leans forward, hands folded and resting on the table, and asks me, "Are you sure about this?" For once in his life, my dad is dead serious.

Bill Folsom, attorney-at-law, sits down at the head of the table in the conference room of his eponymous office.

I nod at my dad. "I am one hundred percent certain this is the best course of action for Jones Construction." And also for Jake, but I don't say that.

My dad studies me. "And you? Is this the best course of action for you?"

"Yes." *No.*

He nods at Bill, consenting.

Bill taps the table twice with an open palm. "Let's get started then."

⁂

I feel bad ignoring Jake's call, but I'm in the middle of signing a mountain of documents. An hour ago I sent him a text telling him I wasn't going to be at the jobsite today, and asked if he could fill in for me. He'd agreed, and asked if something was wrong. I wasn't able to answer, which explains why he's following up his message with a call.

I ask Bill to hold on for a moment. He gives me a reproachful look, but I ignore it and type out a message to Jake. It doesn't go through.

I lift my eyes to find Bill looking at me with a little too

369

much enjoyment. "Cell service is terrible in the conference room."

We keep going with the signing.

By the time we are done, my stomach is growling. My dad asks me if I'd like to get brunch. I hesitate, knowing I need to talk to Jake, and Robbie is at school. This is one of the rare times where Jake and I can have privacy to speak freely.

"The inspector is probably still there, Colbie," my dad reminds me gently.

"Oh, right." I forgot the pre-drywall inspection was this morning. We step outside, and I resend the text that wouldn't go through.

> Everything is fine, just had something to take care of. Love you!

Dad and I walk the three streets back over to Honeybee. We step inside, and the hostess says, "They're waiting for you in the last booth at the back."

I hear 'they' and my mind immediately goes to Jake and Robbie. That's impossible, of course, given that I know where Jake and Robbie are right now.

Dad and I round the only corner in Honeybee and I see Victoria and Georgia in the booth.

"I text Victoria to meet us," my dad explains before I can ask. "She said she was already meeting Georgia here. How's that for good timing?"

"Impeccable," I respond, trying like hell to sound upbeat. It's nearly impossible to feel happy right now. Not when I know what's coming.

Victoria stands up and hugs me, then kisses my dad. Georgia hugs me, too, and I get an overwhelming feeling like I want to hold her just a moment longer.

We settle back down in the booth, and after we order Victoria explains she was meeting with Georgia to brainstorm career moves.

"Career," Georgia repeats, adding an eye roll. "What career?"

"Stop," Victoria says firmly. "That's what we're going to figure out."

"Speaking of career," my dad interjects. "Colbie has some news."

I don't want to tell them the plan he and I settled on without first telling Jake, since it affects him the most. But, there's other news I can offer. "I have to go back to Phoenix for a while. My business partner and I are turning Burn Barre into a franchise, and I need to attend to that."

Victoria claps. "Congratulations." She looks at Georgia. "I think a new career opportunity just fell into your lap."

Georgia's shaking her head. "I'm a kindergarten teacher. I have a degree in early childhood education."

Victoria lifts two palms in the air, moving them up and down like she's weighing something. "Po-tay-to, po-tah-to."

My dad laughs, leaning in and kissing Victoria's hairline.

"Colbie," Georgia turns beside me in the booth so she can put her full attention on me. "You're coming back, right?" Her forehead scrunches, and I see what she's really asking. *Are you breaking my brother's heart?*

This is tricky territory, because as far as I know Jake hasn't told anybody else about Erin going for custody. That situation is his to tell, not mine, so I steer clear of the whole subject by saying, "Of course. A majority of the people I love are here."

Georgia's forehead evens out. My dad and Victoria smile in that wistful, parental way.

I excuse myself to the restroom, and when I return the server is delivering our food. The plate that has been set in my place isn't what I ordered, and from my spot behind the server I hear Victoria say, "Sorry to be a pain, but my daughter ordered the omelet."

The server steps away with the mistaken order, but I'm frozen. Victoria meets my gaze. Her eyes squint in apology, and she says, "Was that ok to say? I'm sorry if it wasn't."

I thaw, and slip into my seat. Her hand is on the table, and I slide my own over the top of hers. "It was more than ok."

She smiles, and I think my dad might be about to cry. Hearing Victoria refer to me as her daughter gives me a sense of belonging I hadn't realized I'd desperately needed. It's odd, this feeling, but ultimately it's the reason I came to Green Haven.

To heal.

It doesn't escape me that I'm trading one wound for another.

·:·

I call Jake when I get home, and he answers on the second ring. "I was starting to feel worried." The sounds of the jobsite make their way through his phone.

"I'm sorry about that." I don't mean to sound elusive, but I'd rather have this talk in person. "Can you take off early? We need to talk."

A steady stream of air crackles into the phone, as if he has sighed directly into the mouthpiece. "I think I know what this is about."

"Um, I don't think you do."

"Oh," Jake sounds confused. "Then what do you need to talk about?"

"Is the inspector gone?"

"Yes."

"Maybe you could send the guys home early and come to my place?"

Jake is silent for what feels like an eternity. "I don't like the sound of this."

I don't particularly care for any of this.

But sometimes you can't help who you fall in love with. And sometimes, you have to carry their baggage, not because you should, but because you choose to.

"I'll be over soon," he says, and hangs up.

I sit back in the chair and look at the kitchen. I don't know when I went from seeing this place as Keli's parents house, to my home, but I'm looking at it now and seeing it as Keli's parents house again.

Jake knocks on the door, and the sound reverberates through my heart.

I answer the door, and right away I wonder if I'm making the right choice. The look on his face tells me his heart may already be broken.

He stomps past me, frustration wafting off him. He's not just heartbroken in advance, he is stirring for a fight.

I close the door, and he whirls around. He's dressed in his jobsite uniform, dirty jeans and an equally dirty t-shirt. "Spit it out," he says. "Just get it over with."

"Jake, I—"

"You know what? No." His hands run through his hair. I've never seen him like this. It's like he's coming out of his skin, but only just barely controlling it. "I'm not letting you do this. I've been paying attention. I've been watching. Looking for signs that you were going to spook. I didn't just want to keep Erin away because of Robbie, it was because of you, too."

That right there, is exactly why I'm doing this.

"Would that have been the right thing to do? Keep your son's mother from his life because you're afraid I won't like having her around?"

"It doesn't matter if that was the right or wrong thing to do. I already did it, because you supported it. Now look." He gestures at me. "Your foot is out the door. You might as well be halfway to Phoenix by now."

"I'm not. I'm here."

"Not for much longer. Why didn't you come to work today? Where did you go?"

"I was at Bill Folsom's office with my dad."

That stops him in his tracks. "Why?"

"Because my dad wanted to give me half of the company."

"That's what you were doing? You were taking over the company?"

"No. I was accepting my share of the company. The deal isn't done yet, though. We need a third owner's signature."

"Three owners? Your dad, you, and...?"

"You."

His head rears back as if the shock is physical. "Me?"

"My dad put twenty-five percent of the company in your name."

Jake cups a hand over his mouth and blinks rapidly. "I don't understand."

"He owns fifty percent, and you and I share the other fifty percent equally."

His head shakes slowly back and forth as he tries to absorb this information. "Why?"

"You deserve it, that's why. But, it's more than that." I walk to the living room and sink down onto the couch. The weight of this next part is too much for me.

Jake takes my cue, and comes to sit beside me. He has that masculine scent, sweat and pheromones whatever else it is that makes him *him*. I think I could bury my nose in his neck and die happy.

Or heartbroken. We'll see.

"It's not just that you deserve the company, which you really do. It's also that it will look good for you in terms of custody."

He leans forward, hands clasped between his drawn apart knees. "Optics," he says, a twinge of disgust in his tone. "I can't believe you arranged all this."

I shrug, but the motion is the opposite of the way I feel. Shrugging makes it seem like none of this is a big deal, but it is. It is the biggest, messiest, most painful deal.

Jake stares at his hands. I want to touch him, run my fingers through his hair, trail my hand over the cotton shirt he wears. I want this man more than anything, but I can no longer have him. What I'm about to do is a risk, but I'll never forgive myself for not taking it. There have to be things we do in this life that are bigger than us.

I adjust how I'm sitting so that one of my legs is bent on the couch and I'm facing him. "Jake, let's be real, I don't deserve to take over Jones Construction. I'm good at learning and reading and understanding, but the sweat equity is yours."

Jake eyes me. "So is this it for big news? Because I have

to tell you, the look on your face right now tells me you're holding another shoe, and it's about to drop."

I'm not sure where to look. I don't want to look at him. I don't want to see his face when he hears the second part. "I think we should take a step back from our relationship while you're going through the custody situation. That way it looks like your whole life is about Robbie."

"My whole life *is* about Robbie." With those words, Jake draws my gaze to his. "Or it was, anyway," he admits.

"I know this isn't what either of us wants to hear, but if we—"

"You don't seem upset."

It takes some time for me to find my words, and when I do, all I can manage is, "Excuse me?"

"You don't seem upset," Jake repeats. "You're talking with this even voice, like this relationship is *meh*."

My entire body feels like it's crying, and Jake says I'm 'meh'?

This is what Brad meant when he said I don't have emotions. I let Brad say and think that because, at the end of the day, I didn't care as much as I thought I should.

This is different. I don't just care about Jake. I love him. I love him in this way that feels heavy and light at the same time, like I'm tethered to the world but capable of floating away. Sometimes I look at his face and it feels like my heart can't fit in my chest anymore because it's too big.

But apparently none of that shows on my face. And really, that just pisses me off, because what about all my actions over the past few months?

"You're wrong. I'm not *meh*. This relationship isn't a white cake with vanilla frosting." I get louder. More vehement. "I've never been in love like this, but I am. With you, and your son, too, and it's looking like it would be better for

376

you if I weren't. I'm not meh, Jake, I'm devastated." I palm the space above my heart. "In my chest right now are scattered pieces of my heart. I don't know what to do, I only know what not to do."

Jake's chest heaves. His lower teeth bite into his upper lip like he's trying not to cry.

"I shouldn't be your girlfriend anymore." I say it quietly, my fire dying.

Jake's voice is strangled. "You don't mean that."

I feel tears in my eyes, and I hate them. I don't want to cry them. I want them to disappear, along with everything else causing them.

"I have been over and over this in my head, and I keep coming back to the same conclusion. What happens if we stay together, and you don't get the outcome you want? What then? Do you blame me?"

"Never." He speaks with such certainty, but he cannot be one hundred percent certain. We haven't been tested in that way.

I purse my lips and wait.

Jake growls. I can't believe how quickly I've gone from disliking that sound the first time I heard it, to loving it. "This is unbelievable." He's up off the couch now, pacing. "I didn't ask for this. You didn't ask for this."

"Nobody asked for any of this, including Robbie. And since Robbie isn't capable of making decisions for himself, it's up to the adults in his life to do that for him."

Jake stops suddenly. He looks at me. There's an understanding in his eyes that I dislike, even though I know it has to happen. "We can't be together." He sounds broken, like someone has reached into his chest and severed his heart.

"No." I'm crying. Doing something painful for the right

reasons doesn't make it any less painful. There's no salve in the altruistic, at least not right now.

"Come here," Jake says, even though he's the one coming to me. He sits down beside me and pulls me on top of him. I kiss him. I kiss him like this might be it. Because what if it is?

We don't waste time. We are not slow.

Jake doesn't know it yet, but I won't be here much longer. Christina needs my help working through the transition of the stores, and there's no point in drawing out my return to Phoenix. Rip off the bandage.

But we have right now. We have these kisses, and these touches, these hands and hearts. Jake helps me ease his work jeans down his hips. I'm wearing a dress.

I lift up, position him against me, and sink down. Impaled. By Jake. One of my favorite places to be.

"I love you," he whispers, teeth grazing my shoulder. He pulls down the front of my dress, folding down the cups of my bra and attaching himself to one nipple.

With one hand gripping the back of his neck and the other firmly planted in his hair, I use him for leverage as I work myself up and down. His breath is hot against my skin. One of his hands disappears between my legs, working, and between the two of us it doesn't take long before my head tips back, his name on my lips.

Jake follows immediately, suctioning my breast so that I feel the vibration of his groan against my rib cage. He releases me from his mouth, and places a kiss on the top of my chest.

"I want to stay like this forever." It's him speaking, but he may as well be speaking for me. I feel the same way.

I kiss his forehead. "It doesn't have to be a real goodbye.

Let's call it a 'so long'. Until you get everything figured out."

"So long," Jake echoes. "I like that better than goodbye."

I kiss the corner of his mouth, then keep going, placing tiny pecks on the outline of his lips.

Jake sighs. "Colbie, I'm so in love with you."

"Same. I am so in love with you."

We are nose to nose, forehead to forehead.

"You're going to leave soon, aren't you?"

I nod. "I would have to go to Phoenix regardless. There's a lot to do for Burn Barre." I lift up, and feel him slip out of me. "I guess you get to be the boss now."

"I was happy as your employee."

We get dressed, and take turns in the bathroom.

"I have to get Robbie," he says, when he walks out. I nod through the lump in my throat.

Jake extends a hand. "One more time?"

Walking with him to get Robbie will only break my heart more, but what's another blow when it's already shattered?

Chapter 52

Jake

After watching my dad give his life away little by little, I thought I knew pain.

But this? This is a unique brand of it.

Colbie walks ahead of me on the sidewalk with Robbie. His backpack bounces with his steps. Colbie's doing her best to stay upbeat, but I see the anguish in the slope of her shoulders.

Alma holds up her stop sign, grinning at me when we pass her in the middle of the crosswalk. She loves that Colbie and I got together.

I let Colbie and Robbie do the talking on the short walk home. Robbie tells Colbie about the garden next to the science teacher's classroom. He calls the potatoes 'monstrous'. He tells her Greer taught distributive properties in math, but it was a difficult concept for a lot of his classmates to understand.

"What about you?"

Robbie looks over his shoulder at me, then back to Colbie. "I think I understood it, but I might need your help."

We're almost to Colbie's house. I don't think of it as Keli's parents house anymore, even with the flamingoes. I'll never look at it and not see Colbie.

"I have to go back to Phoenix," Colbie keeps her tone cheery, "but you can FaceTime me if you need help."

"How long are you going to be gone?"

"I'm not sure. You know I have another business down there, right?"

Robbie nods.

"My business partner is pregnant, and she doesn't want to work for a while after her baby is born. We have a lot to figure out, and I need to be there to do it."

"And then you'll come back."

Like an arrow, Robbie has found his target.

Colbie slows to a stop at the edge of her yard. "I'll definitely be back."

Of course she will. Her dad is here. Greer and Victoria.

Me and Robbie?

So long.

"I'll miss you." Robbie throws his arms around her. She hugs him back, cradling his head in her hands.

He pulls away. "Why are you crying?"

Colbie forces a smile and wipes her tears. "I'm thinking about how much I'm going to miss you, that's all."

Robbie smiles. He likes the idea that someone could miss him enough it brings them to tears. "I'm going to start my homework." He lopes off toward the house, leaving me with Colbie.

I look at her.

She looks at me.

The corner of her mouth tugs, not a smile but more of a *I don't know how to do this, do you?*

"So."

"So." I clear my throat. "Good luck with Burn Barre."

"Good luck with Jones Construction."

Her eyes search my face.

"Are you memorizing me?" My attempt at levity falls flat. There's no helping this situation.

She shakes her head. "I did that months ago."

I shift my stance, restraining myself from lunging forward and wrapping my arms around her. "I want to hug you, but I can't. I'm afraid of the scene I'll cause."

"Same."

I step past her on the way to my house. I brush the back of her hand with my fingertips. "I love you."

I hear her sharp intake of breath, but I don't turn back for it. I can't.

"I love you." She could've whispered it, but she didn't. She said it loudly, straight and sure.

I'm halfway past Alma's house when Colbie calls my name. I turn around. She's on the bottom step of her stairs. Her hair hangs past her shoulders, her dress floats around her ankles, and all I want to do is pick her up and take her and Robbie to a place where none of this is happening.

She waves. "So long."

I say it back. She goes into her house.

I go through the motions with Robbie, but it's hard to be fully present when it feels like your heart has been scooped out of your chest.

The next day, Colbie's car isn't parked in the driveway when I get home from work, and I tell myself it could be because she ran an errand.

It's not there in the morning the next day. Or the afternoon, when I go to get Robbie from school.

Three days of this, and I know.

Colbie is gone.

Chapter 53

Jake

I'm not sure where else to go but Emmett's.

He steps back from the door when he answers, ushering me and Robbie inside.

"I was wondering if you'd be along." He tickles Robbie, then sends him into the kitchen to make brownies with Victoria and Greer. "Don't let them put walnuts in the batter," he calls after Robbie, sticking his tongue out and making Robbie laugh.

"My office," he says to me, reminding me of a little over a decade ago when I showed up here with Robbie in his infant carrier.

We settle in his office, and Emmett pulls two beers from the mini-fridge he keeps in the corner.

"So," he says, handing me a bottle and leaning against the front side of his desk. "She's gone."

Emmett looks just a little heartbroken himself.

I take a drink, frowning after I swallow. "Why'd you let her leave? Why'd you agree to give me part of the company?" My questions are more like complaints, and rhetorical.

Emmett grunts. "You already know the answer to the

second one. As for the first, there's no holding Colbie back when she has her mind set."

"Do you think she knows what she's talking about? That all this sacrifice will be worth it?"

Emmett crosses one ankle over the other. "Colbie's right about how things look to a judge. Her mom talked about that a lot, when she wasn't telling me I was a disappointment as a husband." He grins wryly. "Look, I don't know if what you two are doing will make a damn bit of difference, but if for some reason things don't go your way, you'll wish you'd pulled out all the stops. This isn't something to gamble with." He nudges my foot with his own. "Besides, this is temporary, right?"

"Yeah," I nod, dragging a palm across my overgrown stubble. I haven't had a reason to shave in a few days. "As long as she doesn't meet someone in Phoenix."

She could meet a man who isn't carrying around suit-cases of baggage. Someone who isn't a single father facing down a custody hearing with his ex that popped up from out of nowhere.

"Knock that shit off," Emmett says, nudging my foot a hell of a lot harder this time. "Have some confidence. Colbie loves you, and that should mean something because my little girl does not love easily." He sighs when he realizes what he's said. "I guess that's an attribute caused by yours truly."

I drink my beer to avoid answering.

"I'll see her in a few days. For Sunday lunch. We're keeping up the ritual."

"She's coming here?" The excitement I feel trickles into my voice.

Emmett shakes his head. "We're meeting at that cafe in

Black Canyon City, off the I-17. Halfway between here and Phoenix."

"Right." I take a pull of my beer. "The place with all the pies."

Emmett nods. "Is there anything you want me to tell her?"

There are a hundred things I want to say to her. *I miss your smile. I want to put my hand on the small of your back, and run my fingertips in that crease of space behind your knee. I want to watch you squint at the morning sun, and point your toes when you stretch out on my bed. I want to love you, with my heart and my hands and my lips.* Of course, none of these are messages that can be passed through her father. "No, but thanks."

Robbie calls through the office door, "Victoria says if you don't want walnuts in your brownies you're going to have to stop her yourself because they're her favorite."

Emmett pushes off the desk, beer in hand. I follow him out, but before we walk through the door he looks back at me. "Hang tight, son. Have faith."

I clap him on the back. Those were his words to me more than ten years ago in this very room.

We go to the kitchen, and I spend the rest of the night pretending like my heart hasn't been mowed through with a circular saw.

Chapter 54

Colbie

Two Months Later

"Eating for two is glorious." Christina reaches for another piece of maple-glazed bacon. "I highly recommend it."

Christina can barely fit in the booth she requested. Her hair is thick and shiny, her skin luminous. I watch her crunch through her bacon, and say, "You are impressive."

She lifts her face and drops a bite in her mouth. "Thank you."

My phone screen flashes with an incoming call. Every time it does that, my heart lurches, wanting to see Jake's name. Today is no exception.

"Who is it?" Christina attempts to peer over the table to my phone, but her stomach stops her.

"My dad." I silence the call.

"You can answer if you want. Tell him we're celebrating with bacon."

"I'll call him later." I love how casual I sound. A phone call from my dad no longer incites panic. "He'll be excited for us."

The decision to turn Burn Barre into a franchise was one of the best we've ever had. Christina and I will stay on as the franchisor, growing the brand and finding franchisees. The stores will be run by the franchisees and whomever they hire, meaning Christina will have more time to focus on the day-to-day with her little one. And me?

I'm waiting.

My mother hates that I've placed myself in a holding pattern while Jake deals with his situation. On the day I returned from Green Haven, she came to my house and helped me unpack. I told her everything I learned about her and my dad, and she, with her spine ramrod straight, said she has zero regrets. She said she did what she thought was necessary to keep me from learning the hard way about men like my father. I didn't ask what she meant by 'men like my father', because I don't care. She feels justified in her choice, and nothing I say will change that. I'd planned on telling her I knew about her cheating on my dad, but in the end I chose not to. Not because I wanted to show her mercy, but because I wanted to be merciful to myself. I'm choosing not to care, and I have to say, not caring is a great place to be. I pointed out that all she managed to do was cause chaos and delay the inevitable. She said, "Causing you pain wasn't my intention." It's the only partial apology I'm going to get from her, and it no longer matters, anyway. I can't waste time on it anymore. If she can't see when shown, that's her problem. And that's ok.

Jake and I have maintained a steady stream of text messages. We talk about everyday things, like how Robbie was awarded second place in the science fair, and how close the job is to being finished, and how the crew was mad at me for leaving and made Jake promise to keep up a steady supply of snacks. Every morning, I wake up to a text with three simple words. *I miss you*. Every night, he writes *I love you*.

My heart, my mind, my entire body aches for him. Waiting isn't a problem when the reward is the rest of my life.

Christina stares across the table at me with concern. "Are you nervous for tomorrow?"

As thrilled as I am about this next phase of my business, I can't stop thinking about the custody hearing scheduled here in Phoenix for tomorrow morning. "Yeah." I fiddle with the cloth napkin on my lap, rearranging and smoothing it out. "Thank God Erin's parents didn't talk her into going after full custody." I shake my head. "My mom is no picnic, but can you imagine having Erin's parents?"

"No, I cannot." Christina finishes the strip of bacon. "You're going to see Jake after the hearing, right?"

"I'm dying to see him, and if I were stranded in the desert and had to choose between water and Jake, I'd choose the man."

Christina laughs. "Did you make a plan?"

"He said he'd call after the hearing."

"Are you pressing your hands together on your lap?"

I glance down at my clasped hands. "Yes."

"That means you're excited, but you're trying to contain it."

"Correct." I'm trying not to smile.

"I'm sure he's excited, too. There's a lot riding on tomorrow, but you'll be there once it's over. No matter what, this separation has an end point. You know—" Her eyes widen. "Your phone," she points at the table in front of me. "Correct me if I'm wrong, but that name is easy to read upside down."

I look at my phone, and my pulse thrums instantly, a boiling in my veins. *Jake.* I stare down.

"Colbie, answer it."

I snatch my phone from the table. I haven't heard his voice since I left. I've wanted to call a million times, but I was afraid my resolve would shatter if I heard the voice that snuck its way into my soul. I'm breathless when I say, "Hello?"

"Buttercup." Smooth. Strong. A smile hides in the syllables.

I melt. Into the booth, I become a puddle. "Jake," I breathe his name.

"I won."

"You won?"

"Erin gets visitation. She can try for joint custody at a later date, but for now, the judge said visitation is a sensible next step after all these years."

I'm smiling so hard my cheeks hurt. "Congratulations."

Christina's motioning rapidly across the table, trying to understand. "What is happening?" she whisper-hisses.

Ignoring her, I ask, "So the hearing was today?"

"Yes. It was moved up. I wanted to surprise you."

"You're here? In Phoenix?"

"I'm at your house right now."

"What?" I screech.

"For the love of God, tell me what's happening," Christina pleads.

"How do you know where I live?" I'm already grabbing my purse and digging through my wallet. I throw a hundred dollars down on the table, far more than the cost of our food, and stand up. "Come on," I say to Christina, grabbing her elbow and urging her to stand.

"There was a return address on the delivery slip from

the baskets you sent the crew. I took a picture of it." The week after I left Green Haven, I sent baskets with goodies to Blake, and he handed them out to everyone. It was an apology, and a farewell.

"My bacon," Christina moans, threading her arm through her purse straps.

I grab the plate of bacon off the table and march Christina through the restaurant. Into the phone, I say, "We will be there in ten minutes."

"I'll be waiting."

I hang up, smiling so wide the corners of my mouth could meet at the back of my head.

"We'll be where in ten minutes?" Christina asks.

"Jake's at my house."

I explain what I know on the drive. As much as I'd love to race home, I have two extra lives in my car, so I take my time.

I pull up, and Jake's leaning against his truck, one ankle crossed over the other. I throw my car in park, and jump out. He's already striding across my front yard, those long legs carrying that tall frame my way.

He'll have to run if he wants to beat Robbie.

A flash of dark hair tears past Jake.

"Colbie!"

Robbie leaps into my open arms. I spin him around, breathing in his little boy smell. "I missed you so much," he says.

"Not as much as I missed you."

I'm crying. I didn't realize just how much I'd been holding in everything I've been feeling since I left Green Haven.

I set Robbie on his feet.

Jake stands a few feet away, watching us. The love on

his face is palpable.

"You," I say, stepping closer.

Jake closes the space in one step. He grabs me, lifting me into his body, supporting my backside with one forearm and digging through my hair with the other hand. He kisses me, his lips speaking all the words.

I missed you.

I love you.

It was worth it.

He pulls back. My heart hammers in my chest. I feel like I could fly.

"Marry me," he whispers.

I blink. Stare. Drag air into my lungs. "What?"

"Marry. Me." His gaze searches my face, flitting from my cheeks to my mouth, back to my eyes. "Why wait? We've waited enough."

A smile splits my face. "Yes." I kiss his mouth. "Oh my God, yes." My face tips to the cloudless sky. "Yes," I yell. Jake's laughter jostles my body. He spins me around.

Robbie bounces in place, and Jake sets me down. "Group hug," he says, pulling Robbie into us.

My car door opens and closes. Christina ambles over. She's holding the plate of bacon.

"Christina, this is Robbie and Jake."

Instead of saying hello, Christina looks at Jake and says, "What did you ask that made Colbie yell the word 'yes' to the sky?"

Robbie resumes his bouncing. "My dad asked Colbie to marry him!"

Christina smiles like she's never heard better news. "That's what I thought." She gives me a wink, then offers what's left of the bacon to Robbie, who grabs a slice. To Jake, she says, "Nice to meet you in person. It's only right that you know your fiancée stole a plate today. I want to make sure you know what you're getting into."

Jake looks at me. "I'm not surprised. She's stolen all kinds of stuff from me." He begins ticking off on his fingers. "My common sense, my heart, my use of the word princess, the measuring cup I used as a ladle. I could go on and on."

Christina grins. Jake passed her first test. Good sense of humor.

Jake reaches for my hand, fingers weaving through mine. "What now?"

"We ride off into the sunset, obviously."

Robbie looks at the sky. "The sun won't set for, like, seven more hours."

"I have a crib that need to be assembled," Christina says to Robbie. "Do you want to help me?"

Robbie looks at Jake. "We can do that," Jake says.

"Oh no," Christina shakes her head. "That's really a job for two people. Just me and Robbie."

Jake catches on. He drives Christina home, Robbie in tow, and makes his way back to my place.

I leave the front door unlocked, and he walks in.

I'd like to say we took it slow. That we savored.

We did not, in fact, savor.

We were ravenous, and it showed. Clothes were torn. I left marks on his back. He bit me, in a good way.

Now I'm draped over him. His fingertips turn circles on my back.

"Thank you," he says quietly.

"For?"

"Giving me space to do what I needed to do for Robbie. For putting his best interest before your own."

"He deserved it. So did you. So did we."

Jake guides me onto my back. He leans on one arm,

looming over me. When he strokes my face, my heart fills with this wonderful, sated feeling. Like walking into a cozy home after a long day at work, putting on your fluffiest socks, or reading the satisfying ending to a good book.

Jake's gaze roams my face. "I'm happy Brad cheated on you."

I know exactly what he means. "Me, too."

"You're worth the work it took to get you to fall in love with me."

"You're worth the work it took to let myself fall in love with you."

Jake kisses me.

Now, we savor.

Chapter 55

Colbie

I've given a lot of thought to this concept of love and intimacy, and here's what I think.

Intimacy isn't only about being vulnerable enough to let someone else know you. It's about letting someone else discover you.

We can't always see ourselves clearly. Partners don't see us with perfect clarity, either, but they take our flaws and spend time understanding them. The investment in loving us through our faults, that is intimacy.

Epilogue

Jake

Colbie and I married three months ago. It was a tiny affair, in the backyard at her dad's house.

Colbie's mom attended, and even though I'd already met her a handful of times, it was awkward having her around Emmett. I don't think she's a terrible person, but she's bitter, and it's obvious she's believed in that least amount of awful nonsense for too long. Also, Colbie filled me in on her dad's half of the story, and, true to form, I'm defensive of him.

Erin came to the wedding, and brought Bella. Robbie is getting a lot of practice having a little sister. That's a good thing, because Colbie and I ended up making a honeymoon baby. Colbie swears it's a girl, but we'll find out for sure at our next appointment.

Colbie moved into my house while we build a new place further out of town, near Emmett. It's a hands-on build, especially since we both know what we're doing. She'll have to slow down the further she gets in her pregnancy, and I dread the day I have to point that out to her. My wife is determined, and stubborn.

395

Rhodes came back for the wedding, and he's been working in town ever since. It's nice having my best friend back, but he's been distracted. Something is going on with him, but between work, Robbie, getting married, and building a house for my growing family, I haven't been able to get him alone and talk.

That should change tonight, because Colbie invited Rhodes and Georgia over for dinner. They arrived separately a half hour ago. I handed them each a beer and sent them out back while I prepped the meat.

With a tray loaded down with steak and chicken, I make my way to the back door toward the outside grill. I'm just about to step outside, when I see something that freezes me in place.

Rhodes and Georgia, standing beside my neglected garden. Georgia looks like she wants to tear Rhodes' face off. Rhodes looks like he's just about had it.

My eyes must be deceiving me. What do Rhodes and Georgia have to be angry about?

Georgia spots me, and takes a step away. Rhodes looks at me, and strides forward. He opens the back door and takes the tray. "Got the grill going for you," he says. "Should be hot by now."

"Thanks." I look from my little sister to my best friend. "You two good?"

Georgia glances at Rhodes. "He was telling me about something that happened on one of his jobs."

Rhodes waves a hand. "It's not worth telling again."

I open the grill, the meat sizzling when I place it on the heat. Georgia stands on my right, Rhodes on my left. Just like when we were young.

"You're sure everything is fine?" I ask again. I can't shake the feeling that something is off, but I don't have the energy to look hard. My life has been full of enough chaos and drama. If I have to put my head in the sand for a few more months of peace, I'll do it.

Georgia and Rhodes share a look.

"Absolutely," Rhodes says.

"Totally." Georgia announces.

Colbie and Robbie step out the back door. Colbie wears a dress tight enough to show the beginning of a bump.

Rhodes takes over at the grill so I can greet Colbie. Whatever is going on with him and Georgia, I leave it behind me.

I need to hug my son, and get my hands on my wife.

***

It's impossible to erase your brother's best friend from your life. Especially when you love him. But nobody knows that little secret, just like nobody knows about what happened before. Because Georgia and Rhodes? They were never supposed to be.

Read about Georgia and Rhodes' second chance, brother's best friend romance in <u>*Better Than Most.*</u>

Also by Jennifer Millikin

Acknowledgments

Dad. Thank you for answering my calls when I had questions about concrete. Thanks for giving me mint chip ice cream for breakfast when you poured our patio, and letting me stick my hands in the concrete.

Readers. I have an infinite amount of gratitude for you. I don't think I'll ever get used to the way you make space in your hearts for my stories.

Kristan, Crystal, Julia, Sheryl, Jan, Ventura, Melissa, Erica, and Autumn. THANK YOU for working with me to make this story the best it can be. Your contributions are invaluable.

Jen's Jewels, I love you! Thank you for being a place where I can pop in and say random things, and for spending time in our little corner of the internet.

About the Author

Jennifer Millikin is a bestselling author of contemporary romance and women's fiction. She is the two-time recipient of the Readers Favorite Gold Star Award, and readers have called her work "emotionally riveting" and "unputdownable". Following a viral TikTok video with over fourteen million views, Jennifer's third novel,  *Our Finest Hour,* has been optioned for TV/Film. She lives in the Arizona desert with her husband, children, and Liberty, her Labrador retriever. With fourteen novels published so far, she plans to continue her passion for story-telling.

Made in the USA
Middletown, DE
31 August 2024